The Heresy W

Rob J. Hayes

Copyright ©2012 by Rob J. Hayes
(http://www.robjhayes.co.uk)

Cover image ©2013 by Sigbjorn Pedersen
Cover design by Shawn King

All rights reserved.

The Heresy Within
(Book 1 of The Ties that Bind)
By
Rob J. Hayes

Rob J. Hayes

**For my father who supported me
even when he shouldn't
and
For my mother who believed in me
even when I didn't**

Part 1 – Friends and Enemies

The Arbiter

"Burn them all!"

Thanquil tried to suppress the sigh that snuck up on him. He failed.

"Something to say, Arbiter Darkheart?"

"No, Arbiter Prin," Thanquil said with a smile. The lanky Arbiter Prin glared back at him with hollow eyes. He was a dangerous man to be on the wrong side of and Thanquil had no intentions of making yet another enemy within the Inquisition. "Only, I'm not sure it's really necessary to burn them." The words spilled from Thanquil's mouth before he had a chance to stop them.

Prin's face contorted with rage, a nasty snarl forming on his thin lips and beads of sweat standing out on his forehead. He took a couple of steps forward and Thanquil found himself far too close to Prin for comfort. The man was even uglier up close.

"Are you in charge here, Arbiter Darkheart?" Hot, sour breath blasted Thanquil in the face with each word and wide, angry eyes bore into his own.

"No, Arbiter Prin," Thanquil replied, looking down, looking to the side, looking anywhere but at the ageing Arbiter now invading his personal space.

"Why are you here?" Prin's voice was deep, too deep for such a skinny man.

"Just passing through on my way to Sarth." Thanquil's own voice sounded shaky next to Prin's. "Thought I'd help out seeing as how..."

"Do I look like I need help, Arbiter Darkheart?" Hot, sour breath again with a strange hint of vanilla.

Thanquil looked at the gathered crowd; scared faces glanced back and then dropped their eyes to the ground, not wanting to catch an Arbiter's attention. Soldiers, some with swords, others with pikes but all wearing the blue-black of Sarth on their uniforms. Then there was the family tied to stakes in the centre of the town square. A mother and father, both plain-looking. The mother cried, the father looked both angry and scared but no tears there. A daughter, just reaching her womanhood, was shrieking apologies for something or other and crying out a name over and over; could have been Arcus but Thanquil couldn't tell and didn't care. The fourth member of the family was a small lad, no more than five years old. The boy looked more confused than scared.

Prin followed Thanquil's gaze and snorted. "What's the matter, Darkheart? Brings back memories?"

Thanquil put on his very best menacing face and stared a hole through the man in front of him. "Yes, Arbiter Prin, you do look like you need help. But not any of the sort I can give." He tapped his head with a single finger to drive the insult home. It was a petty and a foolish thing to say, Thanquil knew, but it felt damned good saying it.

Arbiter Prin snorted again then turned around and stalked towards the bound family. Thanquil felt like sighing with relief but he held it in this time. No use arguing any further, despite the fact that burning the family alive was more than extreme. A simple beheading would have served the purpose just as well and wouldn't have involved the stench of burning flesh which, Thanquil knew first hand, was damned hard to wash out of clothing.

Thanquil dug his hands into the pockets of his dirty, brown coat and resigned himself to watching a burning. He wasn't going to give Prin the satisfaction of seeing him leave before it was done.

There was something in his right pocket. Something metal, smaller than a coin but thicker and with stub coming out of the flat side. Thanquil had no idea where it had come from, no idea who he'd stolen it from or when or even where. He had a habit of finding small objects in his pockets. This one seemed to have some sort of engraving on it. He ran a calloused finger across it and recognised the design: a sword in the middle with a sun above it and a single ray of light shining down. It was a button from an Arbiter's coat. Thanquil looked down at his own brown coat with all of its buckles, buttons, and pockets. All eight buttons were still attached. He looked over towards Arbiter Prin, the exact same coat though muddied and a little longer. Two buttons missing. Thanquil grinned, he wasn't about to give the button back. Small victories,

Inquisitor Heron had once told him, can defeat even the largest of men, and Arbiter Prin wasn't that large.

Thanquil removed his hands from his pockets, and then ran them through his mess of greasy hair. It was getting long again, almost down past his ears, and starting to curl. Then he rubbed at the stubble on his chin which was beginning to verge on being a beard. He'd need to shave soon. Then he started cracking his knuckles one by one. If Prin was going to burn them the least he could do was get on with it.

"Bloody witch hunters!" someone screamed from the crowd.

Prin's head snapped around looking for the source of the voice, his hollow eyes bulging from dark sockets, his lips curling up into a horrific sneer.

"Damn," Thanquil sighed out then held up a placating hand towards Prin. "You just get on with your burning. I'll deal with the disgruntled masses."

Arbiter Prin turned away and Thanquil walked towards the crowd, the soldiers with their pikes and dirty uniforms stood aside to let him pass.

"Which one of you was it?" Thanquil asked to the crowd.

"Me," said an older man. Grey hair dropped in clumps around his weather-beaten face. He looked surprised that he had owned up to it. There were tears in his eyes.

"You know them?" Thanquil asked again. He didn't like asking questions.

"That's my boy an' his family. They done nothing wrong."

"Yes they have," Thanquil stated in a firm voice. "They wouldn't be up there if they were innocent. Heresy comes in all shapes and sizes. They have been questioned and they have been found guilty and they will suffer the consequences for their evil."

"You're all the same you witch hunters. You don't care..."

Thanquil's hand shot out and grabbed the man by his tunic, pulling him closer. Thanquil was far from being tall, but he seemed to tower over the man. "Be careful what you say, old man. We are not all the same. Arbiter Prin over there would have you whipped for calling him a witch hunter. Be thankful I am more forgiving." He finished by giving the old man a hard shove, sending him crashing to the earth in a heap and with a yelp of pain. It wasn't something Thanquil enjoyed, but he couldn't allow someone talking back to an Arbiter. If he let one off without even a warning soon they'd all be talking back.

"We are Arbiters," Thanquil hissed at the crowd. "Trained and sanctioned by the Inquisition." He let his gaze sweep over all those close by and each one averted their eyes. Then, disgusted with himself, he turned and stalked towards Arbiter Prin.

"You let him off lightly, Arbiter Darkheart," Prin said in his deep voice.

The young boy, still tied to the stake, was watching Thanquil through unnerving, calm eyes. There was no fear there, no anger. Then the boy smiled, only a slight tug at the corner of his mouth and Thanquil saw the same thing Prin did, the same thing that had condemned the entire family. Darkness.

"Get on with it, Prin," Thanquil growled, unable to take his eyes from the evil he saw in the boy. It was a terrifying thing to behold in one so young.

Arbiter Prin took a deep breath. "**NOW I CLEANSE THESE UNHOLY BODIES**," his voice rang out with unnatural volume. "**BY FIRE BE PURGED**." The Arbiter's torch burst into flame, an act that would have even the most dramatic of bards gasping in awe, and he lowered it first towards the father's pyre, then the mother's, then the daughter's, and finally the boy's. Each one took only a moment to catch light and the flames started eating at the wood, growing higher and brighter and hotter with each second as the fire rushed to consume all it could.

It didn't take long for the screaming to start. Thanquil took a few steps back and watched with a grim mask of determination. Prin joined him.

"Still think a beheading would have sufficed," Thanquil said, his voice no more than a whisper.

"Not for the boy."

Thanquil watched for a while in silence. After what seemed like an age the screaming stopped, but the flames continued to grow hotter and hotter, consuming the pyres, wood, bodies and all.

"You might be right about that."

He'd never seen a tavern so empty, even the rats seemed to be avoiding the place. Thanquil picked a dark corner of the room to avoid attention and Prin joined him. For two hours they sat there in silence and Thanquil couldn't say he was enjoying the company. Patrons entered the tavern and those same patrons left immediately after seeing the two Arbiters sitting in the corner like shades of death waiting for victims.

The tavern owner looked upset. In a usual evening the man would have been busy, but tonight he was serving just two grim visitors and Prin had been nursing the same ale for two hours now. At least Thanquil had the good grace to be on his fourth.

"Heading to Sarth, are you?" Prin asked. The question was so unexpected Thanquil had to check to make sure he hadn't dreamt it. Prin was looking at him, his face gaunt and pale, his mud-brown coat stained and missing two buttons. Thanquil rooted around in his pocket and fingered the Arbiter's button, considered giving it back, decided against it.

"Aye," he replied. He tried to think of something else to say but came up blank so took another gulp of his ale to cover the silence.

"How long has it been since you were last in the capital?"

"Three years." Part of Thanquil wished Prin would stop talking, that same part of him wished Prin would just piss off. "Give or take."

"Hasn't changed much."

"Apart from the God-Emperor being in charge of everything."

"You weren't there for his inauguration?" Prin asked. Seemed he was the type of Arbiter who liked to ask questions, as if his compulsion would somehow work on Thanquil.

"No, I wasn't."

"But weren't you..."

"Yeah, that was me."

"Hmmm." Arbiter Prin seemed to run out of questions. Thanquil sent a prayer of thanks to God and then realised the irony and almost laughed.

"Still a week's travel to Sarth," Prin continued, his deep voice loud among the deafening silence of the tavern. "Need some company on the road?"

"Not particularly."

"It's not me."

"Shame," Thanquil said with a roll of his eyes, "I was just starting to enjoy your company." He bit his tongue to stop from saying anything more and then met the open hostility in Arbiter Prin's eyes. "Sorry, Arbiter. So not you…"

"A girl. Found her a month back in a village on the border. She has potential."

Thanquil played with the button in his pocket. "She's been with you for a month; I'm surprised she hasn't set herself on fire." Again that look of hostility from Prin. Thanquil decided to give up on apologising.

"She's still a child," Prin said, his voice little more than a hiss. "Not even in her tenth year. I would think you of all people would understand, Arbiter Darkheart."

Thanquil took the button from his pocket and made sure Arbiter Prin saw it. Then he flicked it into the air, caught it, and pocketed it again.

"Fine. I'll do this favour for you, Prin. I'll be leaving at dawn tomorrow. Make sure she's ready to travel."

Arbiter Prin nodded once and then, with an ugly smile, stood from the table and walked towards the exit. Thanquil couldn't help but notice the man did not pay for his ale.

Dawn found Thanquil waiting outside the tavern standing with his little chestnut mare staring at him with dull eyes, wondering why it had been taken out of the stables only to stand around waiting. Its bags were packed and it yet here it waited, and Thanquil was in the same boat. He could have just left and let Arbiter Prin deliver the girl to the Inquisition on his own, but if he took the girl, the Arbiter would owe him a favour and he could use a few of those.

Prin arrived with the girl in tow. She looked young, skin still smooth and eyes still bright, a short crop of messy blonde curls hanging down from her head. She hurried along behind Arbiter Prin, glancing up every few steps but, for the most part, keeping her gaze locked on the earth beneath her feet.

"Sorry we're late," Arbiter Prin droned in his deep voice. He had managed to find two new buttons from somewhere and had sewn them onto his coat. "This is Arbiter Darkheart," he said to the girl. "Introduce yourself."

"G'day, sir," the girl said, her voice quiet and soft. "My name is..."

"I really don't care," Thanquil interrupted her then turned to Arbiter Prin. "She'll be walking."

"Aye, she'll do fine."

Thanquil looked at the girl. She didn't seem to own anything, just the rags that passed for clothing on her back, a sturdy-looking pair of boots, and the interesting glint of a silver chain around her neck. A necklace of some sort, a keepsake maybe.

"You owe me, Prin," Thanquil said. All he received in return was a horrific smile. With that he turned and walked away, the girl hurrying to keep up behind him.

The Black Thorn

Betrim leaned against the stone wall, eyeing the tavern. Wasn't much of a building, little more than two floors; one with a bar and kitchen, the other with a few rooms and a few beds, all encased in rotting wood with a couple of shuttered windows for air. Still, he'd seen worse. Seen much worse up close and personal. He'd been drunk in worse, he'd been hired in worse, and he'd been stabbed in worse. All part of the job.

He leaned and he waited, sometimes getting stiff and shifting his weight, then leaning some more. The other two boys with him didn't seem to like leaning. Green walked around the alley all nervous-like, glancing up and down the street, as like to give away their hiding spot as be the first to spot the target. That there was the reason they called him Green, he was new to the game and the new ones rarely lasted long. No point in naming him for real. Bones was sat on the floor, legs crossed, cleaning his bones with yellow spit and brown rag. Betrim had to admit it was a real impressive collection of bones, not quite worth killing him over though. Not yet at least.

"Oi!" Betrim hissed at Green. "Get away from the fuckin' street."

Green glanced around with a sneer and sauntered towards Betrim. He had a real nasty look about his face, did Green, the kind of look that suggested he really enjoyed hurting folk, really enjoyed killing folk. Betrim, however, would put money on Green never having killed anyone. He would, except that Betrim didn't have any money.

"Who'r you ta tell me where I should be? You ain't in charge," Green snarled as he swaggered forwards.

Betrim said nothing, his hand inching towards the dagger hidden in one of the many pockets of his coat. Boys like Green never lasted long in this game.

Bones sprang to his feet in between Betrim and Green, towering over them both. He shook his head. "None of us is in charge, but that don't make him any less right, Green. You hang back here with us. Swift'll be here when it's time ta move."

Green stopped moving but kept staring at Betrim, he snorted then hawked up a mouthful of phlegm and spat it on the ground. It landed three inches from Betrim's boot. Bones winced. The boy was lucky he missed. Betrim had only just got those boots, took them off a drunken sailor. Damned good leather too. The sailor hadn't even put up a fight he was so drunk, Betrim had only hit the sod once.

Bones put a big arm around Green's shoulder, one massive paw dangling at the end, and turned him, steering him away a little. Green sneered over his shoulder at Betrim.

"Look lad," Bones said to Green, "ya new ta this game and new ta this crew so I'm gonna impart a little bit o' my friendly knowledge, eh. Experience, ya might call it."

"What?"

Bones sighed. "Don't piss off the Black Thorn."

Green looked over his shoulder again, his sneer was gone now replaced by what looked to be worry, or fear. Betrim could never be arsed figuring out the difference between the two.

"He isn't," Green said to Bones.

"He is," Bones said to Green.

"Shit."

"Yep." Bones sat back down and looked around for his discarded spit-covered rag. "So whiles he ain't in charge, that's true. Don't piss him off."

Some men might have grinned, showing Green an almost full set of not quite pearly whites. Some men might have threatened, making sure to put the little shit in his place. Betrim Thorn was not those men. He was more than happy to go back to watching the tavern and leaning on his strip of wall.

It was the salt air, Betrim reckoned, put him in a somewhat thoughtful mood, reminded him of home. Not that salt air was pleasant. It stung the eyes, turned the throat raw, made skin all... salty. Not that home was a welcome memory either, nothing there but ghosts.

Betrim decided then that he did not like port towns. Not that Korral could really be called a town, it was little more than a large collection of decaying wooden shacks and a few better faring stone shacks all clustered around a large harbour like flies cluster around a fresh shit.

Despite that, Korral had the stones to call itself one of the free cities. All that meant was that it didn't belong to any one kingdom or another. In Betrim's mind that meant somewhere between little and fuck-all considering Korral was perched on the southern edge of the Untamed Wilds and no kingdom wanted shit to do with the Wilds anyway. Still, it was as good a place as any to get drunk, to get hired, or to get stabbed.

Green leaned against the wall not a foot away from Betrim and eyed him, nodding to himself as he did. "You really him? The Black Thorn?"

"Aye," Betrim responded, one hand still hovering over his hidden pocket, the other over the shaft of his axe. He didn't reckon Green would try anything, but he wouldn't be the first prick to try and make a name for himself by killing the Black Thorn. If Betrim had been just a little more cautious last time he might still have all nine of his fingers. And a couple more of his teeth. And a less bent nose.

"Did you really do it?" Green asked.

"Do what?" Betrim growled back.

"Did you really kill all five o' 'em?"

"Six."

"What?"

"I killed six. Everybody always forgets 'bout the first one."

"Shit." Green's sneer had been replaced by something else now, something that looked a lot like awe. Betrim reckoned he preferred the sneer. "Is that how ya got the burn?"

Betrim ran a three-fingered hand over the left side of his face. Smooth skin where it should have been rough, puckered where it should have been stubble, pitted where it should have been smooth, and tugging where it should have been slack. Not an overly large burn but large enough considering it wasn't an overly large face. "Yeah, got this from the fourth one."

"Wow."

"I told ya not ta piss him off, didn't say ya had ta lick his arse." Bones laughed from the floor.

Swift rounded the corner at break-neck speed and slowed to a halt. Bastard wasn't even breathing hard. He grinned from ear to ear, showing a full set of white teeth. Bastard had some good looking teeth.

"You boys ready then?"

"'Bout fuckin' time, Swift," Bones said, rolling onto his feet. "I'm freezin' my stones off out here."

"Ya ain't got no stones. Couple o' shrivelled pebbles, maybe," Swift shot back at the giant, still grinning.

"I'll bloody show ya I got stones!" Bones started reaching for his belt buckle so Betrim shoved himself off the wall and glanced out of the alleyway.

"Everythin' in place?" he asked Swift.

"Aye. Guards is paid off. They won't be comin' round here tonight. Boss an' Henry are inside waitin' fer us."

"Oh very fuckin' nice for them," Bones whined in a deep voice. "We sit out here in the cold while they get ta 'ave a nice drink."

"They can afford a drink," Swift muttered.

"Good point," Bones said and nudged Betrim in the ribs. "They here yet?"

"No."

"Should be here real soon. I weren't too far ahead of 'em," Swift said from behind, having taken to leaning on Betrim's spot of wall. Something about that pissed the Black Thorn off but he kept silent.

"How d'ya wanna do this?" Bones asked.

"Flip a coin?" Betrim suggested.

"You got a coin?"

Betrim grunted and turned to Green. "Gimme a coin, lad."

"What for?"

"Just fuckin' hand me a coin!"

Green grumbled and shoved his hand into a pocket, pulling out a bronze bit. He stared at it for a moment and then slapped it into Betrim's waiting five fingered hand.

"Heads or tails?" Betrim asked.

Bones squinted at the Black Thorn. "Tails?"

The coin flicked into the air, spinning and glinting in the dim lantern light before slapping back down into Betrim's waiting hand. Bones peered over.

"Shit!"

"Always bet heads," Betrim sneered and pocketed the coin.

"Hey wait a sec..."

"Shut the fuck up, Green," Bones snarled. "Target's here."

Eight men were walking down the street. Six of them were big lads, looked like they knew how to handle themselves and how to handle others if it came down to it. One was smaller, well-dressed and walking at the head of the procession. The last of them was cloaked and hooded, all in black, shuffling along in the centre of the group. Protected. None of them looked too worried about an ambush. A calm, unhurried stroll to a tavern is all it was. Except that the hooded one had a price on his head. A price large enough for the Boss to risk long odds in getting it. They entered the tavern with no rush and were gone from sight.

"Right then," Bones said, rubbing his hands together. "Five minutes?"

"Give or take," Betrim agreed.

"Good. Green, you stand outside, watch the door, and kill anyone who tries to leave who ain't us. Swift..."

"Yeah, yeah. I'll take the window." Swift strolled off towards the tavern, taking his bow from his shoulder and fingering his quiver of arrows like it were a favoured woman. Something about the sight disgusted Betrim.

"Why do I gotta stand outside?" Green complained.

"Cos me an' the Black Thorn know what we doing. First time here with us, ya get the shit job."

Green grumbled but didn't argue any further. Everyone knew their job, there was nothing left to do but wait.

"YOU SON OF A WHORE! OOOFF. CALL THAT A PUNCH?" Bones always did have a flair for the dramatic. Betrim's performances had always lacked a certain passion in comparison, something to do with not liking being hit, he reckoned.

Bones burst backwards through the door to the tavern, stumbled a few steps and caught his feet on each other and tripped, flipping a table over as he fell. The two occupants of the table sprang up from their chairs, faces somewhere between scared and confused, and backed away from the giant sprawling mess now groaning on the floor.

Betrim followed through the door a moment later, growling low in his throat as he stalked towards Bones. All eyes in the tavern turned to him, as good a distraction as he'd ever made.

"By Pelsing's golden tits! It's the Black Thorn," shouted one of the eight, the little well-dressed one. "He's here for us. Kill him."

Not the best of outcomes, but a good distraction all the same. Two of the eight were dead before they'd gained their feet, one with the Boss' axe splitting his skull from crown to jaw, the other with Henry's daggers in his neck. The crazy bitch grinned as she drew them out, cutting the man's neck open from the inside, spraying bright red gore all over the table.

Betrim roared, axe in hand, and charged at one of the eight. There was a dull thud and the man looked confused, reached up to find an arrow in his neck and stumbled a step. Betrim's axe bit deep into his face, dropping the corpse and spattering himself with blood.

He turned just in time to catch the wrist of a man swinging a heavy-looking sword at him. A punch to the face sent Betrim reeling with bright lights in his eyes and the taste of blood in his mouth, and he found himself being pushed backwards by a bigger man than him. He caught the man's other wrist just as he hit the wall hard.

Betrim spat into the face of the big man then sent a thick, metal-plated knee into his crotch and butted his scarred forehead into the man's face once, twice, three times. The big man stumbled backwards, clutching at the bloody ruined mess of his nose, and then froze. He gurgled, bloody froth issuing from his mouth, and then dropped to the floor in a messy heap. Betrim saw Henry standing there, cruel smile on her scarred lips and dark red blood dripping from her twin daggers.

"Crazy bitch," Betrim said as he started forwards, giving Henry a shove with his shoulder as he passed her. She stumbled a step then grinned up at him. Full set of teeth, some yellowing but most good.

Only two of the eight left now. One of them was a giant, towering over everyone but Bones who was, it had to be said, not a small lad. The other was the smaller, well-dressed man, the one who'd recognised the

Black Thorn.

"Don't just stand there," the well-dressed one screeched at the giant. "Fucking kill them!"

The giant looked around, didn't like the odds and tossed his sword onto the floor. "Bollocks to that," he said, holding up his hands and walking for the door.

Bones moved aside to let the man pass, watching him all the way. Henry looked as if she wanted to stab him, but she held back. The Boss was advancing on the well-dressed man.

"Shit!" he hissed as he tossed down his sword. The Boss herded him against the wall, mouth full of metal grinning out of his black-as-night face. It was a tough man that could stomach having metal teeth, Betrim reckoned, and the Boss was all sorts of tough

"Hold up," Betrim called from behind and moved forwards. "Mind if I have a word, Boss?"

The Boss looked sideways at Betrim and shrugged. "Suit ya'self, Thorn."

Betrim stared at the little well-dressed man pressed back against the wall. He was rightfully nervous and sweating dark, wet stains into his fancy clothing. His light, greasy hair was plastered to his skull and his bloodshot eyes flicked about from one member of the crew to the next.

"How is it you knew me so quick?" Betrim asked.

"You kidding me? Burnt up, scarred face like yours? Be a bloody prick not to know you." The little man sneered up at Betrim. "Inquisition is after you something fierce, Black Thorn. If I'd knew you were here I'd have told that Arbiter."

"There's one here? In Korral?"

The little well-dressed man grinned.

"Fuck! Ya need this one, Boss?"

"Nope." The Boss shrugged and turned away.

Betrim swung a heavy, five fingered fist into the little man's face, felt a satisfying crunch and a just as satisfying squeal of pain cut off as his axe chopped into the man's neck. There was a quiet hissing noise accompanied by bulging eyes and a spurt of blood as the body dropped to the floor.

"What happened ta the target? The hooded one," asked the Boss.

"Urghh."

"Ummm."

Henry just shrugged, wiping her daggers on the tunic of the tavern owner as he stared at her in horror.

"SHIT!" roared the Boss. "C'mon. We don't kill him, we don't get paid!" He began storming for the door. "Leave that, Bones."

Bones was busy collecting fingers from the two men he'd killed. He spat on the floor and hurried, unwilling to let two new additions to his collection go.

Outside, two bodies were sprawled on the floor. Tavern patrons, the two Bones had scared. They had nothing to do with the matter at hand but died just the same.

"Got them two. Big one made it half way down that way 'fore Swift took him in the back. Dumb bastard." Green had the hooded target by the neck. "But look what I found, target's a fuckin' bitch!"

Green gave the hooded figured a shove towards the Boss and she collapsed at his feet. She was terrified, but to her credit she didn't cry. Betrim hated the sound of women crying.

There was an uncomfortable silence as all looked down at the target, broken only by Henry sucking at her teeth, a cruel glint in her eye.

Betrim took a step forward and knelt by the girl. Dainty little thing, pretty little face, looked as much like a doll as a person. She glared at him through terrified eyes.

"Damn shame but here it is. Dunno what ya done, maybe nothing, ain't really important now. Chances are ya a good person, or were anyways. Certainly better 'an me. But the nature of the game means we do bad things fer bad people an' the good ones is usually the ones that get hurt... or stabbed. Thing is, we been hired fer a job an' you're that job. Ain't gonna say sorry but... well."

Betrim raised his axe and the woman's pretty green eyes went wide. A moment later and it was done. He picked up the severed head and held it out to the Boss. "Be needin' this I reckon, Boss."

"What the hell was that about?" Green asked.

Bones put one of his giant paws on the boy's shoulders again.

"Don't worry about it, kid. Black Thorn always gets all wordy when it comes ta killin' like that."

The hideout, if you could call it that, was on the outskirts of Korral. It was little more than a derelict wooden hut that Bones had found on their first day in town. Of course, what Bones meant when he'd said *found* was that he'd chucked the previous occupants, a couple of old beggars, out on their arses with a sound kicking. The result was the same, they got themselves a rat and lice infested place to hide with four walls and a patchy roof to keep out at least some of the rain. Betrim always found it funny how rain didn't bother a man until he had a roof to keep it off him, then it seemed a right nuisance.

Bones sat himself down, his large frame managing to fill one of the few dry spots, and started cleaning the flesh off the newest bits of his collection. Rats darted forwards to collect the scraps of discarded meat, coming ever closer as they decided Bones was a meal ticket instead of a threat.

Green paced about the place making stabbing motions with his dull, cheap sword. He hadn't even bothered to clean the blood off the blade. Boys like that didn't last long in the game.

Swift was perched near the window, practising some slight-of-hand trick he'd learned from a thief who'd tried to pick his pocket. It seemed to involve making a gold coin disappear up his sleeve. Betrim could think of much better uses for a gold bit.

The door slammed open making Green jump for the rafters and point his sword towards the sound. The Boss ignored him and sauntered his way into the room before sitting down on the one and only bed. Henry followed the Boss in, closing the door then eyeing the crew with savage scrutiny.

"Job went well, lads," the Boss said, cracking a metallic grin.

Henry threw one small purse at Betrim and another smaller one at Green. She dropped a third into Bones' lap, making his growing audience of rat admirers scatter, and handed a fourth to Swift. Swift grabbed at the purse and held Henry's hand with it.

"How 'bout a bonus, Henry?" he leered into her face.

Henry smiled, as sweet a smile as can be possible with a nasty scar from cheek to lip anyway, and took a step forwards, her hips swinging. She pressed herself up close to Swift and brought her knee up into his groin.

"Hard an' fast. Jus' the way I like it." She spat on him and then, with more grace than the average cat, deposited herself on the bed next to the Boss.

"Your lovin' caress is cruel as ever, Henry," Swift groaned from the floor as he rolled about, laughing through the pain. Best way to get through a knee to the stones, Betrim reckoned. You either laugh or cry, and tears would get you nowhere in this crowd.

"Boss, I got a problem," Betrim spoke from the section of wall he'd taken to leaning against. A good spot of wall, nice and dry.

"The Arbiter," the Boss growled, his bright eyes going hard in his dark face.

"Aye," Betrim growled back. "If that prick from the job recognised me, chances are others will."

"Might be time we all moved on for a spell," the Boss said with a nod. "Reckon that last target was blooded by the look o' her. Reckon her family might come lookin' fer those that did her. Best we skip town whiles we can. Good?"

Betrim nodded. "Good."

The Blademaster

Jezzet watched the river. She watched the waters moving along their lazy course. She watched the froth where the water rushed over rocks. She watched a fish battling its way up stream, an eternal struggle against the current. It felt peaceful, not a word she often associated with anything in her life.

Here in the forest, amidst the sparse trees all jutting up, reaching for the sky their branches thrusting in random directions, some growing downwards to grace the earth, some upwards towards the hot sun, others twisting and coiling around themselves. Here in the forest everything felt calm.

She started walking again, following the river up-stream. You wouldn't have thought it to look at its lazy waters but a long way away the river joined up with the furious Jorl, a crazy, thrashing mess of white rapids and currents that whipped in all directions at once. A person could get reduced to a bloody, messy pulp in moments in the Jorl. Jezzet had seen it, witnessed it first hand. Not something she'd like to experience.

The noise of the river made Jezzet smile. Not too loud, and not too quiet. Almost like a thousand tiny waterfalls all joining together in one chorus. Nice smell too; clean water, clean earth, clean trees. A far cry from the greasy, rancid stink that accompanied larger settlements, all smoke and waste.

Here a woman could almost make a decent life for herself, Jez... you know if not for the wild animals and occasional bandits. Jezzet tried not to think about those things, best just to keep on thinking happier thoughts. Dream of bandits and they'd no doubt appear. Much like dreaming of a fight. *Shame dreaming of coin never makes it appear though.*

She saw something that didn't belong sticking out of the earth near a tree. A jagged strip of rusted metal half buried in the ground. An ancient sword. No doubt this forest was the site of some old, glorious battle. Seemed everywhere people went, glorious battles weren't far behind. Jezzet had seen plenty of battles; she'd yet to see a glorious one though.

In her experience they were all just messy and painful and full of blood and shit. Still, it couldn't hurt to have a look at the sword.

Jezzet started towards the antique. As she stepped in front of a large oak she heard something. Only for a moment, only when the tree blocked out most of the sound from the river, but she definitely heard... something. Could have been a bird in the bush somewhere, Gods knew there were enough birds but...

Always best to be cautious. Better to be cautious and wrong than careless and dead.

She stopped by the ancient sword and gave it a poke with her foot. It was still sturdy but rusted beyond use. Jezzet looked around, as if searching for other artefacts, scanning the trees and the bushes for any sign of the noise she'd heard. Nothing. Nothing made her more nervous than something. Nothing usually meant something while something had a habit of being nothing.

She picked a direction away from the river, tightened the straps on her backpack and started walking. There were no leaves in the trees this time of year, they were all long since littering the dry earth, dead and rotting. Would make it hard to be silent should anything be following her. Hard but not impossible.

Not ten paces and she heard something else, it sounded like padded feet moving on leaves. That was all she needed, to be set upon by a pack of wild dogs.

What a wonderful end that would make to Jezzet Vel'urn, torn apart by a pack of mongrels, alone in a forest. Not many would weep. Not many would care.

Shit, it could be worse, could be...

"Dangerous place fer a woman t' be all alone," came a voice from somewhere in front of her.

...bandits.

The owner of the voice stepped out from behind a large tree not ten paces ahead, a mangy, grey wolf snarled at her from the man's side. He was tall and skinny, with a distinct unwashed appearance about him. Long greasy hair, yellowing teeth, dirty leathers for clothing.

Why do all bandits look the same? Is there some sort of dress code like those fancy balls the blooded folk throw?

Jezzet had been to a couple of those balls. Turns out she scrubbed up quite well when she bothered to wash, something to do with a pretty face and full figure. Didn't make her any friends among the blooded women though.

There was a rustling of some bushes to Jezzet's left and another man stepped into view and moved to stand next to the first. He grinned a yellow grin at her.

"That dog o' yers a'ways sniffs out the bes' fun," said the second man, as unwashed and uneducated as the first. Not that Jezzet could claim to be the best learned person around, or the cleanest for that matter. Truth was she could have used a bath.

Jezzet sighed. In her experience, situations such as these ended one of two ways: fighting or fucking, and if you lost the fight you were going to get fucked anyway. Two on one odds were dangerous no matter what situation you were in.

Hells, one on one odds are more than dangerous enough.

"Very dangerous place ta be," the dog man said, licking his cracked lips with a brown tongue.

Think of something smart to say, Jez.

"Do you live near here?"

Yeah, good one. Next ask them how they like their eggs cooking.

"She's alone," came a voice from behind, "checked all round, no one about." Jezzet craned her head round to look behind her. The man was a huge, bald, black-skinned bear with beady, little eyes. How he'd managed to sneak up on her was beyond her understanding.

Now the odds were three on one, four if you counted the wolf, which she did, and Jezzet liked them not at all. Did she fight and risk dying, or fuck and risk a wounded pride and catching whatever they were carrying. She was half way to dropping her trousers when her right hand found her sword and drew it from its sheath.

"HA!" shouted the second man. "I likes 'em with a bit o' fight, saves me 'aving ta smack 'em ta git 'em movin'"

Well at least I know fighting was the right choice.

"Fight?" The dog man laughed. "Look at 'er, shakin' like a week-long drunk."

He wasn't wrong. The shakes always seemed to come on at the worst possible times.

No chance of bluffing my way out of this now, I guess.

"Could still cut 'er a bit," said the second man, a nasty gleam in his eyes.

"Say what ya want, Pol," said the dog man, "I'm first."

"Ya wen' first las' time," the second man complained.

"An' I'm goin' first again."

Jezzet slipped her backpack off and turned her head to look at the giant behind her, hard to keep all three of them in view, at least he was keeping some distance. "You don't wanna wade in? Happy to be sloppy third are you?" she asked him.

"Shut it, whore!" the dog man roared at her; seemed he had a temper. "He gets whatever we don't want. You say one more word an' the dog goes first!"

"I'd prefer the dog to you." *Good one, Jez. Real smart.*

The dog man roared and started towards her, short sword drawn. He took one meaty swing and Jezzet dodged to the left and thrust with her own slim sword at the same time. The dog man teetered for a moment and then dropped, dead before he hit the floor. Jezzet's blade had entered his neck and separated his spine from his head.

The dog was the first to react. The beast bound towards Jezzet and leapt at her, teeth bared and a nasty snarl issuing forth from its maw.

"Shit!" Jezzet squeaked as she leapt left again slashing out with her blade in a wild arc. The dog landed and crumpled among a pile of twigs. She had no idea what part of it she had hit, but it must have been vital.

Never fought a dog before... or a bear!

The black giant had closed on her and swung with a heavy club. Jezzet dodged backwards right into the waiting arms of the second man. His beefy limbs wrapped around her and held her tight, too late she realised that her sword had slipped from her hands and lay at her feet. She hadn't realised how big the man was before, one of his arms wrapped round her whole body with ease.

"Now I git ta go first," the man said from behind her, his hot, wet breath on her neck, his rancid smell in her nostrils. He took one hand away and reached down in between her body and his. Jezzet heard him fumbling with his belt buckle.

Not a chance!

She flung her head backwards and felt it connect with the man's nose, something warm and wet splashed against her hair but still the man did not let go. She threw her head back again and was rewarded by a crunching noise and freedom. Jezzet didn't wait. She rolled, picked up her sword and thrust. She caught the man in his groin, just below his belt. He roared in pain through his shattered face and thrashed, but the next thrust took him through the heart.

The big black giant stared on in shock. Jezzet reached behind her head with one hand and it came back bloody, the second man's face was broken and crushed.

Not the first time you've washed your hair in blood, Jez.

The giant swished his club through the air in a menacing fashion. He had the strength to use it too. One hit from that club and Jezzet knew she'd snap like a year-old twig.

"I suppose fucking is out of the question now?" Jezzet laughed at him.

Yes, taunt the giant why don't you?

"You ain't gotta be live fer it."

"That's... urgh!" Jezzet said just before the man came at her swinging.

She dropped to the ground, flat on the earth as the blow whistled overhead. Then Jezzet pushed with her feet, trying to get behind the giant. Her feet slipped in the leaves and she went no-where. A moment later a heavy boot connected with her stomach and sent her flying. She slashed out with her sword before coming to a rolling stop next to the body of the dog man. He smelled just as bad in death as she imagined he had in life.

The giant grinned and took a step forwards, then his leg collapsed as hot, wet blood gushed from a large slash in his thigh. He took less than a minute to die, gasping and screaming right until the end.

A fight, but no fucking today, it seems.

Jezzet wasted no time in searching the bodies. Corpses wouldn't need money or food but she did. It was then she noticed that each man had a red cloth tied around his right arm. They weren't bandits, they were soldiers, or at least as close as it came in these parts.

There's only one place round here soldiers would be headed... Time to go warn him, Jez.

"By I live an' breathe, Jezzet Vel'urn. Reckoned you'd make it at least a week before coming crawling back this time."

Jezzet stepped through the gateway, glancing at the heavy gate and the soldiers on either side, then spat into the dirt, staring a vicious hole through the man in front of her.

Say it quick, get out quicker.

"Save it, Eirik, I'm only here to..."

"Oh of course we can find some use for you, eh, Jez," Eirik said with a dirty grin. "How about you get yourself up to my rooms, you know the way. Get yourself nice and naked and I'll be up soon to put you to use."

Not good odds but I could probably kill him before his men beat me senseless... would make this entire journey a waste though.

She heard creaking timbers and turned just in time to see the gates thud shut and the soldiers struggling to lift the heavy wooden cross-bar. Last thing she needed was to be stuck in this shitty little fort again.

"Open the gates, Eirik, I'm not staying. Just came to warn you of the impending attack."

In an instant the grin dropped from his handsome face, replaced by a frown. "Numbers?"

"Don't know, only met scouts. I didn't have chance to question them."

"Too busy killing them, no doubt?"

Jezzet didn't respond to the question, just stared ahead at the chief of the little fort as he chewed his lip.

"How far out?" he asked.

"Met them about two days back in the woods. Reckon you've got a day at most. Now open the gate, I got no intention of being anywhere near..."

"Oh I can't do that. Not with the threat of an attack, eh boys?"

The guards at the gate grunted back and showed no sign of unbarring it. Jezzet glared at Eirik. "I come back to warn you and this is how you repay me?"

"Never asked you to warn me of anything, Jezzet. Never needed warning of owt either." Eirik strutted around as he talked, flexing his big shoulders underneath his chain-linked armour. "Way I see it, I could use every sword, even yours."

Jezzet looked around the small square at the gathered soldiers. Twelve of them, all well-armed and well-trained, and another three hundred or so in the fort all willing to jump to Eirik's command. Not to mention she couldn't lift the bar on the gate by herself. She doubted three of her could lift it.

Shitty odds, Jez.

"You stay, help us fight off this attack, and I'll let you walk out of here, again." Then Eirik grinned. "In the mean time, we got some spare. So you get yourself ready and I'll be with you soon enough."

Fight or fuck? Sometimes, all too often for Jezzet's liking, she had no choice. She spat into the ground and glared murderous daggers at Eirik as she walked towards the clusters of buildings in the fort, towards his chambers.

Fuck!

The Black Thorn

"What is it?" Green asked and looked at Betrim.

Betrim shrugged and looked at Bones. Bones opened his mouth to speak and shut it again then looked to Swift. Swift sniffed and leered at Henry. Henry spat and walked off while scratching at something behind her ear.

"So?" Green prompted. He was still staring a Betrim, been doing that an awful lot of late, ever since Bones told the little shit that Betrim was the Black Thorn. Made sleeping a whole lot less comfortable. Betrim always slept with one eye open and a hand near a weapon, but now he had to sleep with both eyes open.

"How the fuck should I know, Green?" Betrim replied with a shake of his head.

The thing they were all gathered around was huge. Massive grey body, massive grey head, massive mouth with two massive yellow teeth in the lower jaw and lots of little yellow teeth all over the place. It had tiny, black eyes set high on its head up from its snout and tiny, round ears poking out from its skull. Its legs were short and stumpy and its tail was a thin strip of flesh poking out above its arse. All in all Betrim reckoned it must weigh as much as the entire crew put together and then some.

It looked like a giant grey pig with an oversized mouth had crawled up out of the river and died and it was, without a doubt, dead. Had the stink of death on it. Flies buzzed all around and settled on the open wound. The dead creature was huge, but Betrim didn't even want to know how big the thing had done for it was. Four jagged gashes on the creature's belly were deep and showed rotting pink flesh on the insides.

"Reckon it tastes like pig?" Swift wondered aloud. He'd stopped staring after Henry and was looking again at the dead creature.

"Reckon I'm in no hurry ta find out," Betrim said and walked away.

"You know what it is, Boss?" Green shouted.

"Or what did fer it?" Betrim added.

The Boss didn't so much as look at the creature, just fixed Green with dark eyes in a dark face surrounded by dark hair. "Don't matter what it is," he said, metal flashing in his mouth every time he spoke. "Don't matter what did fer it. Everyone stay away from the river an' keep movin'."

The Boss didn't look scared, but then Betrim had known the man for near two years now and if he was ever scared he'd never shown it. Betrim remembered their first meeting well. Not many men had the stones to introduce themselves to the Black Thorn the way the Boss had.

Betrim had been sat, nursing his last beer, studying the rest of the folk in the tavern and wondering which of them would be easiest to rob. He'd just about settled on following a couple of scrawny, merchant-looking youths out when they left and this big black bastard sat down at Betrim's table. Not the tallest man he'd ever seen, for sure, but muscled like someone who was used to swinging something heavy. Betrim had reached for his axe underneath the table, he was well used to folk starting fights with him, came with the name.

"Got an offer fer ya, Black Thorn," the Boss had said and flashed a grin. It was the metal that had made Betrim listen. He'd heard of men who changed their teeth for metal but he'd never seen it before. Chased all other thoughts away and he'd just sat there staring at those metal teeth for a long time.

When the Boss stopped smiling and started talking again Betrim listened, not saying a word until the Boss had finished. He was amazed was what it was. This big man from the far south with metal teeth had sat down and told Betrim he was putting together a crew of the most cut-throat sellswords he could find and he wanted the Black Thorn on that crew. Made sense, Betrim had one of the blackest names in the Wilds and big names always opened up big doors. Betrim had mulled it over for a while and had been about to tell the southerner to piss off when...

"Oi! Thorn." Henry poked Betrim in the ribs with a bony finger and grinned up at him. "Get back an' fetch Bones will ya."

Betrim glanced around. Bones was still staring at the dead creature near the river. Everyone else had already moved on and was well ahead. "Aye," Betrim said with a nod and started back.

"Bones," Betrim said as he got closer.

"Huh?" the big man responded as he looked away from the dead creature. Betrim nodded his head the way everyone was moving and Bones understood. "Right ya are. Sorry."

Bones fell into step beside Betrim and, not for the first time, the Black Thorn wondered at the size of the man. Betrim was not short, it had to be said, but Bones towered over him by a good head and that was with that permanent slouch of his. The giant could swing a greatsword round in one hand as if it was a wooden toy and not even the Boss could beat him in an arm wrestle.

Despite his size and strength, and the fact that he killed folk for a living, Bones was about as gentle as a damned puppy and near as friendly too. He was, in fact, the closest thing to a friend Betrim had ever had. Thorn got on well enough with Henry, that was true, but there was only so close you could be with a woman who had fucked you and then tried to kill you on your first meeting.

"Poor thing," Bones said from beside Betrim. "Food fer the maggots now I guess."

"And the lions, or the laughing dogs, vultures, or whatever the fuck is in that river." The Whitewash was big and deep. Not as big or deep as the Jorl, but big and deep enough to hide all sorts of things underneath its murky, green waters.

Betrim didn't like water. Rivers, seas, oceans. Hells, he didn't even like wells. Never knew what was under water, never knew what might be waiting for you.

They walked in silence for a while a ways back from the others. Up in front Betrim could see Henry's slinking form next to the Boss while Green listened to another of Swift's stories. Always hard to tell with Swift which of his stories were real and which were shit. Betrim tended towards believing none of them.

"Still worried about that Arbiter back in Korral, Thorn?" Bones asked as he put one big foot in front of the other. Most men walked, Bones plodded.

Betrim coughed up some phlegm and spat into the earth. Down in the far south such a waste of water was one of the worst curses a man could commit. Up here in the wilds it was just spit.

"Always. Man like me always gotta be worried 'bout 'em." He felt his burn scar tug on his face as he talked, always did when Arbiters were talked about. "Fact is that shit recognised me. Shouted my damned name."

"We didn't leave no one alive ta tell it though."

"Left the owner alive didn't we," Betrim said through gritted teeth. "Shoulda let Henry kill him."

"He'd never find us out 'ere though." Bones waved a big hand in a circular motion to indicate the plains.

The rolling plains stretched out in all directions and as far as the eye could see. Long blade-grass grew thick, covered the ground in a whispering sea of green that swayed and rippled with the wind. Soon the great herd would move through this province and strip the land bare, turn the green sea into a dusty brown expanse of barren, hilly nothing. When that happened the hunters would be out in force, both animal and human, and Korral would turn into one of the busiest port towns in the wilds.

Fact was tracking people on the plains was simple as pissing. Everywhere you went you left tracks clear as daylight to anyone with eyes to see them, and smoke from a fire could be seen for miles upon miles. If the Arbiter had a mind to follow them he could and, if he had a horse, then catch them he would. No point in worrying the giant with such logic though.

"Mhm," Bones grunted and the two went back to silence. Bones had never like silence and Betrim could see it grated on him even now.

"How long till Green turns on you, ya reckon?"

Now there was a thought. The Boss' group had always been six in number and the last three had all tried to kill Betrim at one point or another and had ended up paying for it in blood. Truth was not many who had tried for the Black Thorn lived to talk about it. Except Henry but then she was a special case.

"'Bout as long as it takes him ta grow a pair of stones, I reckon," Betrim said. The thought of sinking his axe into Green's skull brought a smile to his face. After all, the boy had a purse full of bits going to waste.

Betrim came awake at the touch and fumbled for a weapon that wasn't there. It was cold, dark, and cloudy, but not too dark to see Henry crouched in front of him holding his axe. Her fierce little face stared into his ugly scarred one and she raised a finger to her lips, then moved it to her ear, then pointed off to her left. Betrim frowned, grabbed his axe, and strained his ears. Horses. More than one, less than a lot.

Betrim's frown grew even deeper and he nodded at Henry. She was still crouched over him, straddling him almost in a way that might have got his blood going once but not anymore, not with Henry. She winked at him and stalked off to wake Bones, as silent as a cat and twice as dangerous.

Crouching down low, near crawling, Betrim followed the sounds of the horses. Less than a hundred feet and he could hear voices, soft and quiet, whispers almost. He found the Boss and Swift belly down on a slight rise and watching the little camp with the horses.

Boss had said no fires while they were travelling and now Betrim was glad. Riders following their trail could mean many things and not many of them good. He slithered up the rise on his belly and stopped next to the Boss.

Not twenty feet away Betrim could see a small camp fire, bright flames licking up at a hastily constructed spit with some small animal cooking away. He made sure not to look at the light, best to keep his night vision in case killing was needed. He counted ten horses the other side of the fire, not even tied up by the looks. They looked well-bred, but expensive horseflesh tasted no better than cheap horseflesh and Betrim had never got on with riding. All that bouncing around in the saddle gave him sore stones.

Some of the men in the little camp were sleeping, some attending the spit, and the one meant to be keeping a look out kept glancing at the fire. Chances are the fool couldn't see more than two feet in this darkness.

Betrim looked at the Boss and made the sign for *kill*. The Boss stared back for a second, deciding, then shook his head. He pointed two fingers towards the west and nodded. Betrim began slithering back down the rise and the Boss followed a few moments later. Swift would stay for a while, watching and waiting before joining up with the rest of the crew. He was the fastest of them and near as quiet as Henry.

She was waiting for them just down the rise. Her short, spiky, dust-coloured hair shooting off at all angles. Her scar, as always, tugging her lip up on the right side into a permanent sneer. Dark eyes watching them as they approached. Again the Boss made the two fingered signal for moving west and Henry nodded, turning and walking with them towards the camp.

Green was taking a piss against a dead tree stump when they got back. He yawned, shook himself a few times and then put his cock away before turning back to the others and opening his mouth to speak. The Boss grabbed the boy by the leathers and pulled him close, shaking his head in a real threatening manner. Green looked beyond scared and truth was Betrim could understand. The Black Thorn would never admit it but the Boss scared even him sometimes. Letting go of Green with a shove, the big southerner picked up his pack and started west. Henry grinned and followed. Green, no doubt glad that he'd pissed before the Boss grabbed him, picked up his own pack and shuffled off after them at a respectful distance.

Betrim found Bones sitting on a rock staring at some huge beetle he'd found from somewhere. The thing was as big as Betrim's fist, the one with a full set of five fingers. Its body had a blue-black sheen to it and a huge horn stuck out from its head and split into two at the end. It was wandering its way up Bones' arm and he seemed more than happy to sit there watching it with a big stupid grin on his face.

After watching for a few moments, Betrim poked Bones with his foot and nodded West. The big man nodded, shouldered his pack and started off, taking the giant beetle with him. Betrim waited for a minute. After a while Swift came padding along. He picked up his own pack, flashed a stolen dagger at Betrim and followed the rest of the group.

Betrim took one last look towards the faint orange glow of the camp of men and horses that had almost stumbled onto them, and hoped that the Arbiter wasn't among them. Then he picked up his pack and started off at a jog the same way the rest had gone.

The Arbiter

The capital city of Sarth. In the holy empire of Sarth. Not for the first time Thanquil wondered at the lack of originality of naming one's capital city after the kingdom, but then he supposed the original settlers had their reasons.

It was a beautiful city. Clean streets, tall white-marble buildings sprouting from the cobbles below, high walls with thousands of uniformed guard patrols all in white. Churches stood on every other street, each one towering over its neighbouring buildings while looking down on everyone through stained glass windows depicting scenes of righteous glory. Thin intersecting canals full of crystal-clear sea water and populated with long, slim boats floating along all at a calm, unrushed pace. Some were full of goods being transported to who knew where, some were full of people being transported to who knew where else, some might have just been out for pleasure given the type of day it was.

Sarth, the city of sun. A port town with little rain and constant hot sunshine beating down on all its inhabitants. Above it all, at the centre of the city, rising far up into the sky, was the imperial palace. Built of shining white-marble and glass windows and maintained by a thousand slaves, the palace and all its ten spires were the centre piece in the magnificent view that was Sarth.

A beautiful city and no mistake, as long as you stayed to the richer areas. For those not lucky enough to own a fortune or be the favoured nobility, there were the poorer areas. Wooden shacks, occasional grey-stone buildings for official purposes; guard barracks, gaols, guildhalls and the like. Streets as filthy as any backwater slum with not a hint of marble or glass in sight and patrolled by both guards and pickpockets in almost equal number. Beggars, thieves, drunkards, cripples, whores, layabouts, slaves, and thugs, not to mention the good-folk struggling to make an honest living. Sarth had a pretty face, but underneath its expensive ball gown it was a pox-ridden whore like any other.

Thanquil preferred the poorer areas of the city. They felt more honest, more real. He fit in better with the confessed criminals rather than merchants who robbed you blind and convinced you they were doing you a favour. But even down here in the slums people gave him a wide berth. Guard patrols nodded with formality and moved off. Thieves snuck away into shadows and stared through cautious eyes. Pedlars fell into an awkward silence and looked elsewhere. It was all quite comical; as if Arbiters had nothing better to do than hunt down petty criminals for petty crimes, or question the good-folk about their non-heretical inner most desires. Still, it was nice to be able to walk down the centre of a road and have people scramble to get out of your way. Thanquil would have grinned but it might have ruined the image.

"They all respect you." Thanquil had almost forgotten the girl was there. She was such a quiet little thing, barely said a word in a week, just stared at Thanquil in wonder when she thought he wasn't watching.

"They all fear me. There's a difference."

"Will they fear me?"

Thanquil stopped and turned towards the girl. He wasn't about to admit it but it was fun to force the traffic on the street to walk around him.

"Listen... um... girl," Thanquil began.

"Freya."

"Right. Freya. You have two choices here. I agreed with Arbiter Prin I would bring you to Sarth and I've done that. You're here. Congratulations."

"I..."

Thanquil interrupted her before she could start speaking. Last thing he wanted was an actual conversation with the girl. "I never agreed to take you to the Inquisition. So you can walk away right now and try to have a normal life here in Sarth." He wasn't about to point out that a ten-year-old girl on her own in the slums of Sarth would live a short and painful life, most of it on her back. "Or you can come with me and I'll hand you over to the initiate trainers."

"Arbiter Prin said..."

"Arbiter Prin no doubt told you the Inquisition is a righteous calling and you'll be bathed in holy light and every day of your life will be filled with untold joy. He lied. Initiate training is long, hard, and painful and at the end of it, IF you do manage to attain the rank of Arbiter, you'll have a lonely, bloody, violent life to look forward to. Being feared isn't all it's cracked up to be. Look around you do you see any smiles pointed my way. No. If you choose to follow the path of an Arbiter, get used to it."

"Can't be any worse than my life so far," the girl said, defiance plain in her voice. A ten-year-old girl without parents in one of the border towns would have already had a hard life.

"Don't be so sure," Thanquil replied, always having to have the last word. "I'm going to start walking now. Your choice; follow me or just walk away."

Thanquil started walking again and a moment later the girl stepped up beside him, eyes staring straight ahead and a grim set to her mouth. Already an Arbiter in the making it seemed.

"Welcome to the Inquisition," Thanquil said to the girl.

The girl looked around with her jaw well and truly dropped. She'd been staring around in wide-eyed open wonder ever since they entered the richer areas of the city, marvelling at the grandeur of it all. Now she laid her eyes upon the true heart of Sarth, the Inquisition.

Thanquil wasn't sure whether the city and the kingdom of Sarth had formed around the Inquisition or whether Volmar had chosen Sarth when he created the Inquisition. Thanquil wasn't sure it even mattered any more. What he did know was that the Inquisition compound was bloody impressive, even to someone who had lived there for twenty years of his life.

While much of Sarth was designed and built to be bright and gleaming white, the buildings in the Inquisition were built out of jagged, black rock. A huge fortress took centre stage, its single tower almost as tall as the imperial palace only without the spires. Multiple halls, some for meetings, some for training, some for storage, some for eating, some for almost any purpose imaginable. Barracks to house visiting Arbiters, those like Thanquil who rarely came back, who spent most of their time wandering the world, stamping out heresy. Countless other buildings, the purposes of which Thanquil had never discovered, all crowded the immense compound and all penned in by forty-feet walls on every side.

"Is this where I'll be living now?" the girl asked.

"No. Not yet anyway. The training compound is outside of the city but they'll probably keep you here a few days for testing."

"Testing?"

"Aptitude testing to discover your potential."

"Oh."

"This way." Thanquil started off towards one of the nearby buildings he knew to contain clerks and servants. While not true agents of the Inquisition, they would have a better idea of what to do with the girl than Thanquil did.

Servants, slaves, and other Arbiters ran to and fro on all manner of errands. It always amazed Thanquil just how many Arbiters stayed within the Inquisition's walls. At any one time there was a small army worth within the grounds, as if Arbiters had nothing better to do than laze around in the relative comfort here when there was so much heresy out in the world.

Thanquil opened the door to the building and stepped through. There, sitting behind a desk, was an old clerk Thanquil knew all too well.

"Arbiter Darkheart," the old clerk said with a sneer.

"Clerk Donic," Thanquil responded in a formal tone.

"Senior Clerk Donic."

"You are looking quite senior," Thanquil replied and it wasn't untrue. Senior Clerk Donic was tall, lean, wrinkled, had been on the hairless side of balding for at least twenty years, and had a face that looked like it was slipping to the left, as if all his features were trying to flee from his nose.

"As disrespectful as ever I see, Arbiter Darkheart," the clerk shot back.

"I assure you, Senior Clerk Donic, I have nothing but the utmost respect for all those who deserve it."

The noise that emitted from the clerk's mouth sounded a little like a growl. "Why are you here, Arbiter Darkheart?"

"New recruit, she has potential," Thanquil said with cheer and gave the girl a light push in the back so she stumbled into the room.

Senior Clerk Donic stood from behind the desk with a loud clicking of his knees and moved closer to the girl. The old clerk studied her for a moment, as if he himself could see her potential, and then nodded.

"I'll take her from here, Arbiter," the old man said and walked a few paces before turning to the girl and motioning for her to follow.

The girl looked from the clerk to Thanquil and then back again. She looked terrified. Thanquil wrestled with his conscience for a moment and lost.

"Freya," he said and the girl turned to him, the poor thing looked close to panic. Thanquil reached inside one of his pockets and his hand closed on a small piece of metal, round with a silver chain attached to it. He took the necklace out of his pocket and pressed it into the girl's hand, hoping that the clerk wasn't paying too close attention.

The girl looked at the necklace and her other hand went to her throat to check it was hers. She hadn't even noticed Thanquil taking it.

"Hide it and hide it well," Thanquil whispered. "If they find it they'll take it away."

"Thank you," the girl said with a nod.

"Don't thank me," Thanquil said, sounding far more grim than he intended. "And whatever you do don't ever thank Arbiter Prin. You may think he's done you a service but by getting me to deliver you here he's cursed you."

"I don't understand."

Thanquil snorted out a humourless laugh. "You will. Now go. Best not to keep Senior Clerk Donic waiting, has a ruthless temper does that one."

Outside, Thanquil found his dull-eyed mare staring at him with accusatory eyes. He'd have told the beast off but the last thing he needed was for other Arbiters to see him talking to his horse, so instead he just took off towards the stables, the horse following behind him, silent and obedient.

There wasn't much to do in the Inquisition for an Arbiter like Thanquil. It was one of the reasons he'd decided to become a wandering Arbiter rather than take a permanent position here. He deposited his little mare in the stables, stowed all his belongings on the first free bunk he could find, had a quick trip to the mess hall, and then took to wandering around the compound.

Outside in the courtyard he was confronted by another reason he'd taken to wandering the world. Sideways glances, hushed whispers, and plenty of dramatic head shaking all pointed in his direction by those he should have considered his brothers and sisters. It appeared, even after spending twelve years out in the world rooting out evil and purifying heretics, he was still the outcast.

"I'd heard you were back, Thanquil." Even if he hadn't recognised the voice, there was only one person in the entire Inquisition who used his first name.

"Kosh," Thanquil said with a grin and the two clasped hands in greeting. "Didn't expect to see you here. There's a whole world out there you know."

"That there is, but you don't get to be an Inquisitor without putting in some time here. I'm on guard duty these days, have been for near a year now. More boring work I've never known but I'm hoping one day it will all have been worth it."

Kosh had started initiate training at the same time as Thanquil and he'd graduated the same time as well. He was just a little bit taller and stockier to boot, blonde where Thanquil was dark brown and a good deal less scarred. Many of those scars were given to Thanquil by Kosh himself in their sparring sessions.

"What brings you back?" Kosh asked

"Three years since I was last here," Thanquil said, rubbing at the bump in his nose, the same one Kosh had broken so many years ago.

"Ah, the three year review. Inquisitors like to make sure you're still on the righteous path."

"Aye," Thanquil agreed. "No doubt they'll find some far flung corner of the world to send me to this time. Wouldn't do to have the black sheep of the family too close to hand."

"Speaking of which, you being gone for three years, you won't have met the new golden boy." Kosh nodded towards a group of young Arbiters. "The one in the middle, graduated after just six years as an initiate."

"Six years... nobody's that good."

"Fastest anyone's done it but he earned it." As Kosh spoke the Arbiter detached himself from his group and started walking away from them, straight towards Thanquil.

"Best bit," Kosh continued, "his name is Arbiter Hironous Vance."

"Inquisitor Vance's son," Thanquil said with a shake of his head. "Well that makes sense I guess."

Arbiter Vance walked past Thanquil, no doubt headed towards the mess hall, or the barracks, or maybe one of a hundred locations. It was for the best, the last thing Thanquil needed was to come to the attention of the Grand Inquisitor's son.

"Must be nice to be born with a silver spoon in your mouth." It was almost as if someone else had spoken but with his voice. Thanquil bit down on his traitorous tongue.

Arbiter Vance stopped, turned and looked their way. He was taller than Thanquil but then most people seemed to be, not skinny but then not muscled either. He wore his Arbiter coat and the robes underneath in immaculate condition. His hair was short and he had the air of a librarian about him; a librarian that moonlighted as a bounty hunter maybe. Worst of all was his eyes. Yellow eyes. Thanquil had never seen yellow eyes. They were unnerving to say the least but Thanquil refused to look away.

"I don't believe we've met," Arbiter Vance said in a calm voice, he had the gall not to look offended by Thanquil's comment in any way.

"Thanquil," Thanquil said.

"Arbiter Darkheart?" Vance said.

"Arbiter Vance," Thanquil replied, still wishing he'd never said anything in the first place.

"I'm afraid I have an appointment with my father," Vance said. "We should talk later, Arbiter Darkheart."

"Right," Thanquil said.

Vance said a formal goodbye and then turned and walked away. Thanquil noticed the man carried no weapons. Most Arbiters carried a sword or a similar metal weapon, some carried unique arms such as Kosh with his twin hand scythes, but Arbiter Vance carried none. A large tome hung by his side, locked with a metal clasp and attached to his belt by a chain.

"That was awkward," Thanquil said after a while.

"Why is it you feel the need to pick fights with the most powerful of enemies?" Kosh asked with a shake of his head. "You know he'll be an Inquisitor one day..."

"Odd eyes," Thanquil mused, interrupting his friend.

"He has the sight. Came from his mother, it's said."

"His mother is a witch?"

"Was a witch, dead now from birthing him."

"Hardly seems fair," Thanquil said with a sigh. "Why doesn't he get lumped with a name like Darkheart?"

"Because his father is Grand Inquisitor Artur Vance." Kosh pointed out. "Come on. Unless you've got somewhere pressing to be let's go get blind drunk. I know a great place just down the road. Strong spirits and clean women. Oh, and I'm going to want my ring back."

Thanquil dug into his pocket and pulled out the plain gold band. He didn't even apologise as he handed it back, those apologies had long since lost their meaning with Kosh.

"You should get out in the world more, Arbiter Kosh. Clean is overrated."

The Blademaster

Jezzet would have liked to say she wasn't the type of woman to take things lying down. However, when you had to take them, lying down was often the best way. So she lay there, on her back, staring up at the wooden ceiling and made sure her expression looked as bored and bland as possible. Eirik, on the other hand, made no attempt to hide his pleasure as he propped himself up on top of her, naked as a babe, thrusting rhythmically and being rewarded by a moist squelch and the soft *thwap* of skin on skin.

The handsome warlord grunted with each thrust and his long, red hair dangled down and tickled Jez's face. The whole thing wouldn't have been so bad but he was quite good at it and Jezzet was enjoying it, though the last thing she wanted was for him to know that. Despite her determination she could feel her treacherous heart beating too fast, her breathing becoming hot and heavy, and the familiar aching pleasure between her legs making her jaw tremble.

A wonderful and yet horrible tingle of pleasure shot through her body from her groin all the way up to her chest and escaped from her mouth as a gasp followed by a low throaty moan.

Damnit! She could feel it coming and it was the last thing she wanted right now.

Then Eirik gasped, tensed, and stopped thrusting. His mouth opened and closed like a fish on dry land and Jezzet had seen it all before. She had won again though it had been far too close for her liking this time.

The big warlord collapsed on top of her, his weight a crushing, uncomfortable force for a moment and then he rolled off to the side, breathing heavy and letting loose a contented chuckle. They were both hot and sweaty and now they both stank of sex. Jezzet would have hated herself if she'd had any pride left.

Bastard keeping me here like some sort of slave. Should have killed him months ago.

She grabbed a handful of the bed sheet and wiped between her legs then threw the soiled cloth at Eirik. "There, you can have that back," she snarled at him.

He laughed a deep, low sound that shook his entire body and the bed. "Don't be like that Jez, I know you enjoy it. Why else would you keep coming back?"

A question she'd asked herself many times over the last ten minutes. Three times she'd left this backwater fort now and each time something pulled her back, or drove her back.

The first time it had been food, or lack of it at least. One day out she'd realised she hadn't packed any. In truth she was pretty sure she had packed food, but it wasn't there when she'd checked so she'd crawled back with her tail between her legs and for two weeks had to put up with Eirik between them.

The second time she'd managed near a week before running into a group of bounty hunters with piece of paper that said, *'Dead or Alive'*. The drawing didn't hold much likeness but Jez had been fool enough to tell the bounty hunters her name. The bastards had chased her all the way back to the fort. Eirik had let her in and then stuck the bounty hunters full of arrows. Jezzet had stayed at the fort a month after.

Not this time, Jez. You're getting out of here the first chance you get. Just gotta help fight off a small army first. Easy.

She realised Eirik was staring at her, staring at her breasts. She'd been sat quiet and still for too long and he'd become bored waiting for an answer. A grin spread across his face and he made a grab for Jez's arm. As graceful as a cat she flowed up from the bed and onto her feet away from his clutching hands. She crossed to the door and cracked it open, just enough to poke her head round and look out. A lazy guard turned his head and looked at her.

"Get some water for a bath. Make sure it's hot," Jez ordered the dopey guard. His eyes sunk down from her face, trying to look around the door but she made sure her body was hidden. "Now!"

She slammed the door shut and turned, nostrils flaring in anger. Eirik was still staring at her, his eyes moved up and down and then stopped. He was staring at her scars again. It was instinct that made her react, instinct that made her look away and cover her chest with her hands. She hated herself for doing it and it wouldn't do any good anyway. The scars weren't just on her chest, they were all over her body.

"Bath sex is good. I can wait," Eirik said.

"It's not for you. I need to wash your touch off me. It would defeat the point if you were in the tub with me." Jezzet's voice was cold, her jaw locked so tight it hurt.

"You're a harsh mistress, Jez."

"I'm not your mistress. Now get out," Jez ordered the warlord in his own quarters.

Eirik made a show of shrugging his big shoulders and then stood, scooping up his discarded clothing in one hand and started for the door. He stopped next to Jezzet, reached up and grabbed a handful of breast. His thumb made slow circles around her nipple, stroking it, and he leered into her face. She stared back, defiance right in his smirking smugness. She felt her nipple stiffen, he felt it too and he grinned.

"Until later then, Jez." And with that Eirik let go of her breast and walked to the door, leaving his quarters without even dressing.

Jezzet waited until the door was shut and then spat. A thick glob of spit smacked against the wood and then started sliding downwards. She sat down on the edge of the bed with a loud sigh and waited.

There was a cold breeze out and about and it felt good. Jezzet bathed, washed herself as thoroughly as she could, dressed back into her dirty leathers and decided to take a stroll around the little fort.

Not like you're gonna be leaving anytime soon, Jez.

Soldiers and mercenaries stared at her as she walked past but they'd been doing so for months now. Jezzet wasn't tall, shorter than most of the men here. She was lean but not skinny. She had enough muscle to swing a sword, her training had made sure of that. She had a pretty face, she knew, only marred by a small snip of a scar underneath her right eye, and she wore her black hair short like a boy's. All in all she had an appearance the men in the fort seemed to like. Of course the few women in the fort seemed to take great exception to it.

There were ten other women in the fort in all and all of them were whores. Some of them had been in the fort since before Eirik had taken it, making it a permanent home for them where they were fed and paid no matter who was in control. Some of them even had children running around their heels, they were the ones who couldn't afford or didn't wait to wear a charm. Jezzet had bought her charm twelve years ago and she made damned sure it could never be taken off, lost or stolen. She'd had it sewn into her flesh underneath her skin. So the men leered at her and the whores sneered at her as if she were taking their business away from them.

They should be happy. Chances are they get more business when I'm around, just the men aren't thinking of them, Jezzet thought with a bitter grin as she endured the whores' hostile stares.

At least the wind was chill. It felt good against her skin, reddened her cheeks a little and took the breath away if you tried to breathe into the gusts. It was pleasant in a strange way but it also meant something else. A chill tended to precede rains in these parts, sometimes even storms.

The sun was dipping and darkness beginning to take hold as Jezzet walked around the fort. Soldiers hung out lamps and the whole place became lit in a warm, yellow glow.

It wasn't much of a fort. Wooden buildings for the most part. Living quarters for those in charge and the whores, barracks for the rest of the men. A mess hall, food storage, armoury. There was a well in the centre of the fort and a courtyard by the gate and all surrounded by thirty-feet walls made of strong wooden trunks sunk deep into the ground. One thing the region had in abundance was tall trees.

Eirik was a warlord only in the sense that he commanded three-hundred men. The truth of it was he was a bandit who'd managed to storm this little fort a couple of years ago. Men followed him because he was big, loud, handsome, and could swing a sword. So he'd gathered his army, took the fort and now he held it while the local governor, some blooded folk or other Jezzet couldn't name and didn't care to, paid him to hold it under the pretence of Eirik defending the governor's land.

The way Jezzet heard it, for two years Eirik hadn't defended shit. He rode out from time to time with a hundred men on horses and raided villages in the next province, but until now the fort hadn't been attacked.

She had no idea whether Eirik knew how to defend a fort against a determined force and she didn't fancy finding out. Unfortunately she was trapped here for now and had no choice but to fight alongside him because if Eirik somehow died here there was always the chance that the next commander of the fort wouldn't ever let Jez leave.

No choice but to stick close to him when the fighting starts and keep him alive. Then, if he doesn't let me leave, I'll kill him.

The biggest problem with a fort of this size, Jezzet found, was the boredom. There just wasn't anything to do when nothing was happening.

There was a nervous tension in the air. No doubt by now news of the impending battle had spread to all areas of the fort, but still everything seemed quiet and calm. For the past couple of months, in these situations Jezzet would retreat to Eirik's quarters find him waiting for her and end up having sex but that was the last thing she wanted and Eirik, for once, was busy commanding his men.

Jezzet decided to tour around the battlements. Two sets of steps winding back on themselves led up to the wooden platform that ran all the way around the fort just four feet below the top of the walls. Every five paces along the battlements the wall was shortened for bowmen to shoot from and men littered the walkway all the way around. It seemed all three-hundred of Eirik's troops were out tonight.

Here from the west side of the battlements all Jezzet could see were trees. Dark outlines against the fading light in the sky. The Red Forest, so named because of the colour of some of its trees, stretched out for miles in every direction and bordered two provinces. It was the same forest Jezzet had been in just three days ago, which meant there was a good chance the enemy would be coming from the west. The forest also stretched out towards the north where the gate was located. The enemy would have to attack there to stop a counter attack or escape. To the south were the plains and three days ride was the city of Beswith and to the east were mountains, nigh on impassable save for an old, broken trail. Any enemy attack would have to come from the forest.

"What's the chief's mascot doin' up 'ere?" The voice was cracked gravel grating against her nerves. Jezzet knew the man, a veteran of more than a few fights and he had the scars to prove it. Scars all over his face in fact. Jezzet had only ever seen one man uglier. "Bit lonely are ya? Need some company?"

You could kill him, Jez. And it was true. One flick of her sword, out of its scabbard and back in before anyone even knew what had happened and the man's throat would be laid open. Of course the rest of the men might take exception to that and the damned annoying thing was Jez could feel her hand shaking.

"You ain't got what it takes to keep me company," Jez said, putting on her best sneer.

"I got everything you need." He was close enough to smell now and Jez had to admit she'd rarely smelled much worse.

"We all know you don't. Eirik himself says you're a eunuch and all the whores agree." That earned a bark of laughter from the rest of the men but the ugly, stinking veteran only went red with anger. Jezzet always seemed to have a knack of winding up the wrong people.

"I'll bloody prove I ain't, bitch. Come 'ere," he said reaching into his britches and then stopped, a confused look on his face and an arrow through his skull. The man teetered on his feet for a moment and then dropped, his body falling down to the earth below. For a moment the soldiers behind stood motionless, looking confused. For a moment Jezzet stood motionless, looking confused.

"What the fuck?" screamed one of the men close by and as one they all looked over the battlements, Jezzet included, just in time for a scattering of arrows to hit.

Most of the arrows hit the wood of the walls and stuck there. Some flew high, completing their deadly arc somewhere inside the fort. Two hit their marks and two more men dropped, one screaming with the shaft in his shoulder, the other man already dead and slumped over the wall not two paces from Jez.

"Shit!" shouted Jez as she ducked back below the wall. Battles were always so much more dangerous than fights. You could never tell where the fatal blow was going to come from. It was hard enough to tell friend from foe.

She wasn't the only one ducked behind a wall. Men all around her had done the same, hiding from arrow fire. Taking a chance, Jez glanced over the wall and saw the men who had fired the arrows retreating back towards the woods *whooping* all the way about who had shot the killing shafts. What caught Jez's full attention, though, was the sight at the edge of the forest.

Torches. Hundreds of small flames, each one attached to a person, and more appearing from the forest all the time. Jezzet had never been too good with numbers, but even she knew it was fair to say Eirik's little army was outnumbered.

Looks like a fuck and a fight again today.

The Arbiter

Waking with a hangover that felt like your brain was two sizes too big for your head was never a fun start to a day and today was no exception. Alchemists and herbalists the world over had no shortage of remedies and concoctions for the pain and the nausea and that strange feeling of floating just outside your own body, but rarely would any of them work. The Inquisition had long ago come up with its own cure. It wouldn't look good for an Arbiter to be unable to function due to a hangover; it would no doubt lessen the fear the good folk had of them. No, it was much better that people could see Arbiters drink an inn dry and have no effect. So now one of the first things the Inquisition taught to its initiates, after the compulsion of course, was the hangover cure. It was a small charm, made from wood and carved with a powerful enchantment then hung around the neck. Simple and genius but the charm always seemed to work its way to the bottom of Thanquil's pack.

He didn't even open his eyes. To do so may well have induced vomiting and the last thing he needed was to be seen throwing up in the middle of the barracks. Instead he kept his eyes closed and rooted around in his pack with one hand while praying to Volmar that he hadn't lost his charm.

"Arbiter Darkheart," came a voice, the same voice that had awoken him. Quiet, demure, male, and with a touch of fear. Who in the Hells had decided to wake him?

Thanquil's hand closed around the charm, as always, at the bottom of his pack and he pulled it free, spilling the contents of his bag all over the floor. He hung the small wooden rectangle around his neck, waited for a few moments then sat up and pried open his eyes. The world gave one violent lurch sideways and then settled down the right side up. The pounding in his head began to slow and then fade and the nausea quieted, though his throat tasted of bile.

The man standing in front of him was dressed in the emperor's white and gold and wore a look of one part fear to two parts determination. He was young, still in his teenage years so half a man and half a boy, and had been ordered to come to the Inquisition compound and rouse a sleeping Arbiter. Thanquil was impressed.

"Hello," Thanquil said, still squinting at the man-boy and wishing the world were a couple of shades less bright.

"Emperor Frances requests your presence," the messenger said in a most imperious tone.

"Now."

"Um... yes, I think."

"I have time to bathe first," Thanquil said.

"Um..."

"I smell like a brothel, lad."

"Uh..."

"Don't worry, it won't take long. Wouldn't want to offend the God-Emperor by turning up looking and smelling like an outhouse would I. No. Exactly." With that Thanquil lurched out of bed, pushed the spilled contents of his pack under the bunk and walked for the exit, the messenger keeping up behind him while spouting a constant stream of words that Thanquil refused to listen to.

He'd never been to the Imperial palace before. Glimpsing it from afar as it rose with exaggerated majesty above the rest of the city was one thing but up close it just looked monstrously tall. How had men managed to build such a thing? Thanquil couldn't imagine it. It must have just been here all along, or maybe Volmar just willed it into existence. A God could do such a thing, but there was no way men could have built a thing so tall and yet so sturdy.

Huge, reaching spires hundreds of feet tall all white and shiny in the morning sun. Windows of all shapes and sizes, some round, some square, some rectangular, some small, some larger than any Thanquil had ever seen before and all made from expensive, clear-glass

To his left Thanquil spotted fountains taller than a man with tens of tiers where water could pool and then spill down to the one below. To his right he spied a carriage waiting to take some noble folk or other away from the palace. The carriage was bigger than any he'd ever seen with eight wheels and twelve horses all magnificent and black. Thanquil's own chestnut mare would be embarrassed to be called a horse if it stood next to the stallions that pulled that carriage.

A polite cough from beside Thanquil brought him out of his reverie and he found the Imperial messenger grinning at him. "Impressive isn't it?"

Thanquil thought he should have found something clever to say, or something fearful that reminded the messenger that he was talking to an Arbiter, but his mind was still stuck in awe of the palace.

The man-boy started walking again and Thanquil fell in beside him, trying not to stare upwards at the impossibly tall building looming over him. He tried to focus on the ground, on the messenger, on the guards and staff, on anything and found himself looking around in desperation for something to steal. He needed to calm his nerves. The grandeur of the palace spooked him for some reason. He felt as out of place here as a cat underwater.

They stopped at the main entrance just long enough for the messenger to have a word with the guards and then they were off again. The man-boy beside Thanquil with his close cropped blonde hair and pale fluff on his top lip just kept talking but Thanquil wasn't listening. He was observing the route, watching for small items, something that could fit in his pockets.

He passed expensive-looking paintings depicting some historic event or other, vases of obvious supreme craftsmanship, gaudy red carpets that looked like blood on the white marble floor, lanterns with cases of gold or silver fixed into the walls, and he passed guards. Thanquil had never seen so many guards and all of them watched him from underneath their visored helms. If he hadn't been suitably daunted before, he was now.

After a while the messenger stopped in front of a large, unassuming door of heavy wood with two guards in full, white enamelled plate either side. The messenger asked Thanquil to wait and then opened the door, disappeared inside and shut the door after him. The guards watched Thanquil. It was a shame, he was sure he could have stolen something here if not for those eight eyes following his every movement.

"You must be hot," he said to the guards as a unit, not picking any one in particular. There was no answer, not even a grunt. "I mean Sarth is a hot city and the palace, while obviously well ventilated, is still on the warm side and there you stand encased in metal. You must be sweating under there."

Silence.

Thanquil paced. Four sets of eyes followed him. He realised he was still wearing his sword. If he was to see the Emperor of Sarth they would have insisted he turn his sword in.

The door opened again and two servants and two guards filed out followed by the imperial messenger with the fluffy top lip.

"You may enter now, Arbiter Darkheart," the messenger said and stood aside.

With suspicious caution Thanquil walked into the room and looked about. The door shut behind him and it took all of his willpower not to jump for the ceiling. The room was beautiful. Austere rugs decorated the shining white floor, ornate bookshelves lined the walls each with its own collection of books and scrolls. A huge unlit hearth with a painting of the imperial palace hung above it seemed a bit indulgent but looked grand all the same. Giant glass windows at the far end of the room allowed light to stream in and there, sitting in front of them, was the God-Emperor.

On a throne, with golden hair spilling down past his shoulders and a severe look that pulled his features into the very definition of imperial majesty, the God-Emperor looked down upon Thanquil. He'd heard the Emperor was tall at over seven foot but even sat down the man looked like a giant. He wore a suit of white and gold that seemed to accentuate his muscular figure and he leaned just a little to the right, giving the impression of being relaxed. It was hard to believe that such a regal-looking figure was a poor farm boy working a field outside of Sarth just four years ago. The throne seemed to suit him as if it had been made around him. Perhaps it had. The man sat unmoving and looked like a statue of some great hero from ages past.

"You kept me waiting, Arbiter," the Emperor said from the throne, his mouth moved but the rest of him kept as still as the stone he sat on. His voice was deep, rich and resonated around the room. Thanquil realised he was the only other person in the room. It seemed strange but all the Emperor's guards and all his servants had been ordered outside.

"My apologies, your majesty. I thought it best to present myself properly," Thanquil responded with a bow of his head.

"My man tells me you stopped to bathe while he waited. I didn't invite you here to smell you, Arbiter."

"Invite," Thanquil mused aloud. "It felt more like an order."

"It was."

The silence that erupted into the room was horrific. Thanquil could hear his own breathing, could hear every creak of his leathers underneath his coat, could hear the scuff of his boots on the floor as he shifted his weight from one foot to the other and all the while the Emperor stared down at him. Thanquil glanced around the room again. There, no more than five feet away was a small table with black cloth on top and one of the largest and most impressive collections of runes Thanquil had ever seen. Each one was carved into a token of brittle wood ready to be snapped at a moment's notice to release the power contained within the rune. Thanquil had to resist the urge to walk over and take one. Stealing from the God-Emperor was bad enough, but to do so right in front of the man would be considered horribly rude.

"I've heard a lot about you, Arbiter."

"I doubt much of it good." Thanquil could feel his hand shaking in his pocket.

"No indeed," the Emperor continued. "Most of it was quite damning."

Thanquil couldn't think of a response to that so he just kept quiet.

"I hear you were the one that found my sword."

That much was true. Thanquil had recovered the sword known as '*Siege Breaker*'. A sword forged of magic and metal, with blessings inscribed into the steel. A sword fit for an Emperor, the Inquisition had decreed and had gifted it to Emperor Francis on his inauguration.

"I would very much like to hear the story of how you came upon it, Arbiter Darkheart."

"Not much to tell, your majesty. I bought it from a travelling merchant."

"Did the man realise what it was he carried?"

"Yes, your majesty. He specialised in such items."

"Where did you find this merchant of curios?"

Thanquil winced. "The Land of the Dead."

The Emperor smiled and the atmosphere in the room seemed lighter. "Interesting," he said as he stood and turned, moving to stare out of one of the excessive glass windows.

Thanquil took the opportunity to pad across to the table holding the runes and pocket one before returning to his original position. He felt better, the shaking stopped and he could concentrate again. Stealing always calmed his nerves, put him at ease.

"Must have been an interesting man indeed to be travelling those lands unmolested," the Emperor continued.

"In truth, your majesty, I can't be sure he was a man at all. Not sure what it was, but it sold me the blade all the same."

"Heh," the Emperor grunted and then fell silent for a while. Thanquil kept quiet also. He was now well aware that he was in a room with one of the two most powerful people in all of Sarth and Thanquil didn't trust himself not to anger the Emperor somehow.

"I'm going to ask a favour of you, Arbiter Darkheart. But first I think you have a question for me, don't you?"

Thanquil felt it then. The compulsion was tugging at him, trying to tear the words from his mouth. It was a physical need to answer the question. His mouth opened and his lips began to move, forming the words. But Thanquil was no commoner without knowledge of the compulsion. He was an Arbiter of the Inquisition, trained in the use of magic and with twenty years of experience. He forced his mouth shut, swallowed the words back down and forced his mind to calm.

"How did you do that?" Thanquil demanded of one of the most powerful men in Sarth. He threw the entire strength of his own compulsion along with the question. It felt like trying to break down a door with a sponge. The Emperor turned and smiled.

"I'm sorry to do that to you but I had to make sure. Ask your question."

Thanquil sighed, he felt tired, exhausted even but determined not to show it. "Are you really Volmar reborn? Are you really our God in human form?"

"The Inquisition, the council of Inquisitors has declared I am."

"I didn't ask what the council has declared," Thanquil said, determined to get his answer.

"Does it matter, I wonder? If I say I am Volmar reborn would you believe me? How would I prove such a thing?"

Thanquil thought about it, came up blank. "So you won't answer."

"My answer is this, Arbiter Darkheart. It doesn't matter if the council says I am Volmar. It doesn't matter if I say I am Volmar. What matters is whether or not you believe I am Volmar."

"Well I imagine a God would speak in such riddles," Thanquil said and the Emperor burst into laughter that even made Thanquil smile. The laughter ended abruptly and the room seemed to dim.

"I believe the Inquisition has been infiltrated, Thanquil," the Emperor said, his voice solemn. It didn't go unnoticed by Thanquil that they were now on first name terms.

"I'm not sure I understand, your majesty."

"Evil, heresy, dark magics, maybe even demons. Who knows?"

"Demons are gone from this world," Thanquil pointed out. "Volmar saw to that when he first created the Inquisition so many thousands of years ago."

"Two thousand four hundred and ninety years ago, to be exact, but demons are not gone, we both know that. Not all of them. In any case, I believe the Inquisition has been infiltrated, a part of it corrupted and I believe the culprit to be sitting on the council."

That was more than just an accusation. From anyone else it would be considered heresy, but could the man the Inquisition had decreed to be their own God reborn be capable of heresy? The very idea of it made Thanquil's head hurt despite the charm he wore around his neck to prevent such maladies.

"That is..." Thanquil searched for the right word, "an incredible accusation, your majesty."

"It's not an accusation. For an accusation I would need proof."

"Which, of course, you don't have."

The Emperor nodded, his bright blue eyes seeming darker and

worried. Thanquil paced, mindless of the company, as he considered what to do. Should he confess the Emperor's accusation to the council? It would be the wisest of things to do but what if the Emperor was right?

"I want you to find me proof, Arbiter."

"Hah! I'll just go and interrogate all twelve members of the council then." Thanquil stopped himself from saying more. "Sorry, your majesty. I have neither the right nor the power to question the council, perhaps if you..."

"The Emperor of Sarth cannot be seen to distrust the Inquisition. To do so would undermine its power throughout the world. I need you to go and find proof, discretely, and bring it back to me so I can make a move to put a stop to this."

"Why me?" Thanquil asked. "Half of the Inquisition seems to think I'm guilty of heresy myself."

"That's exactly why I've chosen you, Thanquil. You're considered an outsider. You go where you please and you're known for... sometimes travelling off the beaten path."

Thanquil rolled it around his head. It was a no win situation for him. If he turned the request down and the Emperor was right, then the entire Inquisition could well be destroyed from the inside. If he agreed to the request the best that could happen was he would save the Inquisition and be punished for going outside of the Inquisition's rules to do so. The worst that could happen involved him being tried for heresy himself.

"Because I'm expendable," Thanquil mused. The God-Emperor didn't deny it, just looked away. As much a confirmation as ever Thanquil had witnessed.

"What exactly is it you want me to do?" Thanquil found himself asking.

"My sources have brought me a name, a man somewhere in the Untamed Wilds by the name of Gregor H'ost. He is connected somehow. I need you to go to the Wilds and find him. If he can't provide proof make him tell you who can."

"The Wilds are a bit outside of my jurisdiction, your majesty. I operate within Acanthia and the Five Kingdoms."

The Emperor smiled. "Not a problem. Thank you, Thanquil. I'll not forget this."

With that the Emperor turned again and stared out of the window, dismissing Thanquil with his back. Thanquil bowed and walked to the door. He turned once. The Emperor was still standing by the window. Thanquil pushed open the door and walked through it.

Outside, the guards and the servants and the messenger with the fluffy top lip were standing waiting, but with them stood someone else.

Thanquil nodded once. "Arbiter Vance."

Vance nodded once in return. "Arbiter Darkheart."

Crushing silence descended. Again Thanquil nodded. "Glad we had this talk." With that he stalked off, the fluffy lipped messenger struggling to catch up to lead him out of the palace.

No sooner had Thanquil stepped foot into the Inquisition compound another messenger appeared in front of him. He wanted nothing so much as to find a dark corner to sit in and mull over everything the Emperor had confided in him. It did not feel like an easy task he had been given. First he would have to find a way to the Untamed Wilds. He was certain there would be boats leaving from Sarth to trade with the free cities in the Wilds, but it was a long journey and long sea journeys were never safe. Pirates were the major problem, with violent sea storms coming in a close second, and Thanquil was never sure whether to believe stories about giant sea serpents.

"Arbiter..."

"Yes, you have a message," Thanquil finished for the man.

"From the council." The messenger did not seem cowed by Thanquil's snap. "They demand your presence."

"That's why I'm here."

"Immediately."

"Of course." Thanquil was already starting to regret waking up this morning. First a private meeting with the Emperor of Sarth and now his interview with the council of Inquisitors. Thanquil couldn't think of a way the day could get any stranger. Plenty of ways it could still get worse though.

Kosh was on duty, guarding the outer doors to the council

chambers. He stood at ease but his hands rested on the shafts of his twin scythes and Thanquil knew first-hand how dangerous he was with such weapons, even more so when enhanced by blessings. His friend grinned as he saw Thanquil approaching.

"Hangover cure?" Kosh asked.

"Around my neck."

"I hear you've had a busy day."

"News travels fast here."

"Good luck in there."

The halls that led to the council chambers couldn't have been more different from the imperial palace. No carpets graced the cold stone here and Thanquil's footsteps rang out loud and clear and echoed around the black walls. No decorations of any kind in this hall. No grand paintings with gilded frames, no priceless vases, only the occasional torch sputtering in the constant and cold draft. It felt like entering a dungeon or walking to his own execution. Neither were endearing thoughts.

Then Thanquil was at the inner doors to the council chambers. Two Arbiters stood guard by the doors, neither of which Thanquil recognised. The guards nodded for him to enter and Thanquil pushed open the doors and stepped through. They shut behind him with an ominous *bang*.

The Inquisitor council chambers were built in a circle with a pit in the centre for the subject and raised seating behind a waist high barrier for the Inquisitors. All was built from cold grey stone, lifeless and dull and lit by a hundred torches positioned around the room. The torches somehow managed to project most of their light towards the pit, making it hard for Thanquil to see to the Inquisitor's seating. He heard the shuffling of robes and the scuffing of arses kissing chairs and he waited, making sure to look nowhere in particular.

"Arbiter Thanquil Darkheart," came a voice he recognised as belonging to Inquisitor Aurelus. Thanquil bowed his head and waited.

"Here you will answer for your crimes," another voice, this one from behind and belonging to a woman; either Inquisitor Heron or Inquisitor Downe.

Thanquil waited for a moment and then started. All wandering Arbiters such as himself were required to present themselves in front of the council every three years and present a list of their crimes and, if need be, explain themselves before the Inquisitors. The Inquisitors would then determine whether or not the Arbiter had been corrupted by the influences of the world outside. Thanquil didn't want to think of the consequences if they decided he had been corrupted.

His list wasn't long. Most of it consisted of petty theft and of those there were too many to name them all, too many to remember them all, and the Inquisitors were not bothered about such crimes. There were a few instances of murder, most justified, one accidental but unavoidable. Two incidents of abusing his position as an Arbiter for personal gain, while such crimes were not heresy they did earn heavy punishments but Thanquil felt justified. The gain, while not monetary in both cases, had occurred because he had run out of money and had used the fear of the Inquisition as a way of extorting free rooms in two different inns.

Through it all the Inquisitors listened and said nothing. Thanquil felt the weight of so many eyes upon him but he had been through all this before and he knew they would not punish him for his crimes. It was much more likely they'd punish him for being him.

"You have passed, Arbiter Darkheart," this was the unmistakeable voice of Grand Inquisitor Artur Vance. Thanquil squinted up towards the voice. The man looked old but that was not surprising. One hundred and fifty years was old even by Inquisitor standards and by all accounts Inquisitor Vance had passed that mark more than a decade ago. He still looked to be in good health though, and strong as an ox, which only went to further prove how powerful the Grand Inquisitor was.

Thanquil had heard the stories, read the history during his initiate training, and he knew the Grand Inquisitor's past as well as any Arbiter. The man was a hero. He had saved the Inquisition in its darkest hour.

A hundred years ago the Inquisition had gone to war against a cult of warlocks. The dark sorcerers had hunted Arbiters across the world and had dealt a serious blow to the Inquisition's numbers. The Inquisitors had marshalled and attacked the warlocks head on as they marched on Sarth. Five of the twelve Inquisitors died that day, the worst loss in the history of the Inquisition, and still the warlock army was unbroken.

An Arbiter by the name of Artur Vance had entered the battle and he alone turned the tide. The Judgement of the Righteous, the Inquisition's most powerful weapon and one usable only by Inquisitors such is its power. Magic deadly to all those with the dark stain of sin and heresy upon their soul. Arbiter Artur Vance called down the Judgement of the Righteous six times that day and stood in the centre of the searing light each time. As if calling down the judgement six times in one day wasn't unprecedented enough, the Arbiter emerged from each without injury, proving there was not a single stain of sin upon his soul. Arbiter Artur Vance was named Inquisitor that very day and only a handful of years later attained the rank of Grand Inquisitor.

By all accounts the Grand Inquisitor had lived a life of uncompromising virtue with only one questionable action, his union with a woman who had the sight. The sight was known to be an affliction of witches. In women it manifested as the ability to see into a person's past, viewing the things they had done through their own eyes. In men it manifested as the ability to glimpse a person's future, maybe even their end.

Thanquil bowed to the circle of Inquisitors and prepared to leave the chambers. Then Grand Inquisitor Vance spoke again.

"Why did Emperor Francis request your presence?" the Grand Inquisitor said and the words were like a vice closing in on Thanquil's will.

He had felt the same thing earlier, in the imperial palace, only different. The compulsion. It should not have any effect on him, a trained Arbiter, but here he was experiencing it first hand and for the second time in one day. Before, when the Emperor had used it, the compulsion had been strong but unfocused, Thanquil had managed to squirm his way free from the question. Now it was different, it lacked the same strength but the focus more than made up for it. Thanquil could think of nothing else but the words, the answer to the question the Grand Inquisitor had asked. The truth bubbled up inside of him and demanded to be set free.

He couldn't hold it back any longer. Thanquil opened his mouth to speak, gasped, and then the words fell out.

"He wished to thank me for finding his sword. He wanted to know where and how I had attained such a powerful artefact."

The pressure eased and then lifted. Thanquil gasped and sputtered. The cold room felt hot and sweaty and the weight of all those eyes on him felt heavy.

"You did well, Arbiter Darkheart," this from Inquisitor Heron. "Not many have lasted so long against the Grand Inquisitor's compulsion."

"Seems your will is still uncontested, Vance," the voice from behind Thanquil was brutish and accented. Without a doubt it came from Inquisitor Dale.

"Enough," the Grand Inquisitor's command cut through the atmosphere like a knife and left only silence behind. "If the Emperor should ever wish to talk to you again, Arbiter Darkheart, you will come to the council to explain why. Do you understand?"

Thanquil nodded. "Yes," he managed to croak. He was still shaking and could feel his heart pounding in his chest, in his ears. He couldn't remember the last time he felt so weak. It took every bit of effort he had to stop his legs from buckling.

"We have a new assignment for you, Arbiter." Inquisitor Downe. Thanquil squinted in her direction, a middle aged woman with plain features and a heavy brow. There was not an ounce of softness to Inquisitor Downe. "The free city of Chade has requested an Arbiter to question someone they have taken into custody and believe to be a dangerous heretic."

"The Inquisition has no authority in the free cities," Thanquil said, his mind struggling to catch up with the day's events.

"They have granted an agent of the Inquisition temporary rights in order to question the prisoner."

Thanquil nodded. "You're sending me to the Untamed Wilds then."

"Correct." Inquisitor Jeyne, tall and pale with eyes darker than the deepest night. "You will leave immediately. There is a boat departing tomorrow at dawn. You will be on it, Arbiter Darkheart."

Thanquil nodded again, his head searching for something witty to say and coming up blank. "Of course. With your leave."

"Go," The last word, of course, came from the Grand Inquisitor.

Thanquil turned and hurried from the room. His legs felt like jelly and it was all he could do not to collapse into the nearest dark corner and spend some time weeping. Instead he walked, aiming for his bunk in the barracks and hoping his tired feet remembered the way while his mind worked on other things.

He had learned something very important from his meeting with the council. Something he'd never known before and something he now wondered who else might know. There was a loop hole to the compulsion. The target could release it by telling only a part of the truth.

The Blademaster

The noise was one of the most terrifying things Jezzet had ever heard. Swords and spears and hammers and axes all being bashed against wooden shields and all at the same time. Sounded like thousands of them. Looked like thousands of them if the number of torches was anything to go by.

Large fires had been built up at regular intervals just beyond the tree line, just out of bow shot, and Jez could see figures moving around in front of the fires. The sun had disappeared long ago, but the moon was full and close and bright, it lit the ground between the fort and the forest well enough to see. Gave the troops in the fort some sort of hope anyway.

For hours Jez had heard axes going at wood out beyond the forest, but they had gone silent now. No doubt the ladders and rams had all been built. All the enemy were waiting for now was the call to attack. Quite why they hadn't attacked yet was a source of some confusion for Jez, unless the enemy commander wanted to scare the soldiers in the fort into surrendering. If so, it was working on Jezzet.

The clamour of weapons banging against shields died down and a single figure rode on horseback towards the front gate. Thet were holding a white flag high up in one hand. The signal to parley.

First comes the talking, then the killing. Somehow Jez doubted Eirik was the type to spend too much time talking.

She pushed her way along the battlements, moving ever closer to the front gate, closer to Eirik, closer to where the brunt of the fighting would take place. Jez couldn't say it was where she wanted to be but it was where Eirik would stay and she had to keep him alive if possible.

Or you could just hide with the whores and fuck your way out of the fort later, Jez. A bitter thought and not one she entertained for long

"Ho there, Eirik." As soon as Jezzet heard that voice drift up from below, her spirits sank. It was both masculine and feminine at the same time.

Hiding with the whores seems a good option now, Jez.

"Come to see my little fort have ya, Constance?" Eirik called back over the battlements. Jez could see the warlord she shared a bed with grinning from ear to ear through his stubble. She sank down behind the walls and prayed for a miracle, or at least she would have if she could remember the names of any of the Gods.

"The hospitality seems a little poor, Eirik. How about you just open your gates and let me in like a good host?"

"Alas, we're full up on whores at the moment, Constance. Nowhere to put you."

"Yes I can see that, Eirik. Three hundred whores my scouts tell me. Do any of them know how to hold a sword?"

Oh the banter of warlords before a battle. Like foreplay without the pay-off.

"Reckon we have least one," Eirik called out still grinning like a wolf. "Got an old friend of yours up here with me. I'm sure you remember Jezzet Vel'urn."

Why, Eirik? Why?

Silence. It seemed to stretch out for somewhere close to forever before the reply came. "Where? Show yourself, bitch."

Jezzet sighed. She wished Eirik hadn't told Constance about her. Then Jez realised all eyes on the battlements had turned to her. Hiding wasn't an option any more.

She stood up and gave a little wave towards the single figure down below.

A stupid wave. Like I'm waving to an old friend. I suppose we were once.

Constance's horse fidgeted below her, sensing the rider's anger. The woman looked as well as she ever had. As big as most men, almost as big as Eirik both in height and brawn. She wore a suit of tight ring mail armour dyed red and her long, mud coloured hair was tied up in a warrior's tail. A livid white scar ran upwards across her left eye and ended just below her hairline.

"How's the eye, Constance?" Jezzet called down.

"Don't see so good no more, Jez. Still remembers your fucking face though."

That wasn't surprising. The tip of Jezzet's sword was the last thing that eye had ever seen.

"Could be worse," Jezzet shouted back. "Could remember your partner's face. What was her name again?"

"Catherine," Eirik shouted out, his grin wider than ever.

"That's right," Jez continued. "I forget, Constance. Was she your sister, your lover, or both?"

If looks could kill then Jezzet's heart would have exploded in her chest. However, looks couldn't kill and right now, thirty feet up and behind a wall Jez felt brave enough to rub it in the warlords face. So she smiled back as sweetly as possible.

"Still opening ya legs for every man in the wilds then, Jezzet?" Constance's rock-like jaw was locked tight, thick cords of muscle writhed together as she ground her teeth. Jezzet had always been able to get under Constance's skin even before she'd killed the warlord's sister.

"Just the one at the moment." Jez nodded towards Eirik. "Why, would you like a go? Have you finally managed to grow a cock that would have matched your sister's balls?"

Eirik let out a bellow of laughter that sounded so jovial even the men around him joined in despite the sheer weight of numbers aligned against them just beyond the tree line. "Ladies," he began, "while this banter is fun an' all I believe we have a..."

"Surrender the fort, Eirik and hand over that whore trussed up like she deserves. Do that and I'll let you and yours go." Constance interrupted him.

Eirik paused and looked over towards Jezzet. Jezzet tried her damned best not to look as scared as she felt. If Constance got a hold of her, Jez could count her days left on one very painful, very humiliating hand.

"'Ost wants the fort. I want the bitch. Nobody else has to die today," Constance continued.

Terrifying silence seemed to hold for a long time. So long Jezzet wanted to scream to release the tension. Seemed Eirik was taking his time thinking about the offer. Seemed like a bad thing seeing as how it was likely his only way out of the situation that didn't involve dying.

"A tempting offer, Constance, and we all know she deserves it, but

I'm afraid I have to decline. Dolsedge would have me strung up if I surrender the fort without a fight."

"Then you all die." With that Constance whirled her horse around and set off for the tree line at a gallop. Jezzet met Eirik's eyes and he grinned at her.

Bastard he may be but at least he's a brave one.

Moments later a thunderous roar went up from the enemy camp and Jezzet could see the soldiers start to move forward. She was right about the ladders and about the ram. She counted eight ladders in all, built in a rush, no doubt, but still sturdy enough to do the job. The ram was long, carried by twenty soldiers each holding a shield in their other hand and charging forwards with the giant tree sharpened to a point.

Jez swallowed down her traitorous, fraying nerves and waited. Each moment accompanied by a deafening heartbeat drumming in her ears.

The archers charged forward in front of the enemy lines and each thrust a torch into the ground, pulled arrows from their quivers, lit them and then drew the bow string back. For a moment they all just knelt on the ground with bows ready and then someone shouted the order and a hail of flaming arrows arced towards the fort. Jezzet ducked behind the wall again as the arrows hit. Those in the wall were no problem but those that landed inside the fort could catch fire, forcing the defenders to fight the flames inside their gates as well as the army outside.

"What do we do?" a young soldier beside her shouted. He was young and pretty in a boyish way with a small strip of hair on his chin and eyes wide as the moon.

"How the fuck should I know?" Jezzet shrieked back at the stupid boy.

"ARROWS!" roared Eirik from close by and Jezzet heard bows being drawn then, "FIRE!" And the *twang* of bow strings accompanied by the screaming of men from below.

The boy beside her was still staring, wide eyed, into space. Jezzet slapped him and then crouch-walked past, unwilling to poke her head above the top of the wall, unwilling to present a target. She found Eirik shouting orders this way and that, his handsome grin replaced by a commanding frown.

"Get some damned stones on the ram," he shouted to someone and looked out towards the approaching army. His bowmen were firing at will now the enemy archers had stopped. The men carrying the ladders were reaching the base of the walls and started pushing the ladders up against them. "Repel the ladders!"

Eirik spotted Jez and took two steps towards her. For a crazy moment she thought he would try to kiss her and she was pretty sure she'd have had to punch him, but instead he stopped and his grin returned only for a moment.

"I think we pissed her off, Jez."

Jezzet didn't smile back. "I fight for you and after this you let me go. No more keeping me here just so you have someone to fuck!"

You could have left any time you wanted, Jez.

"Deal," Eirik nodded. "Long as I get one for the road after all is done."

Jezzet spun as she heard a ladder hit the wall close by. Eirik's men were already trying to push it back to the ground but there were too many holding it still at the bottom. The first man pushing on the ladder looked down just in time to take a spear thrust up through the face. The unfortunate soldier was dead before he hit the floor and then the dying started in earnest.

All around it was the same scene. Men pushed on ladders to no avail and other men climbed the ladders, trying to establish a foothold on the wall for more to rush up behind them. Arrows flew both ways now and blood and screams of pain became a constant both inside the fort and outside.

A face appeared on the ladder closest to Jezzet. Her sword, a slim longsword as sharp as a razor, slashed out and took the face just above the nose. Bone shattered and flesh sliced and the man dropped with a gurgling scream that ended with a dull thump. Another face appeared and Jez stabbed at it. This time a shield appeared and managed to block the strike but a moment later a spear thrust from the other side of the ladder and took the climbing soldier in the throat. Eirik's men had given up trying to dislodge the ladders and were attacking the men as they climbed up them.

A worrying crash of wood on wood sounded from close by, followed by a scream from Eirik to shoot arrows down on the battering ram.

A large soldier armed with a rust-spotted longsword jumped from the ladder onto the battlements, followed by another and then a third. The first man advanced towards Jezzet and muttered something about fighting a woman. Then he thrust with his sword. Jezzet spun on her feet and brushed the attack away with her own sword, a moment later her hand darted forward and her blade slid in between two of the man's ribs puncturing his liver. The man dropped to one knee screaming and with a heavy push Jezzet sent him off the battlements to the hard earth below.

The second man came at her a moment later. Jezzet twisted away, ran two steps then launched herself off the wall back towards the approaching man, parrying his sword away as she flew towards him. Small as she was, she was still heavy enough to knock the man to the floor and landed on top of him. Too close for swords, she dropped her blade and pulled her dagger from its sheath stabbing him once, twice, three times full in the face.

Definitely dead. She thought as she looked into the bloody mess she'd made.

Jez stood, her dagger still in her right hand, and picked up her sword in her left. The third man that came over the wall had been dealt with by some of Eirik's troops and they were again stabbing down at the climbers with spears.

Jezzet glanced around. Constance's forces were up on the wall in several places already and more were pouring up all the time. A loud crack signalled the gate was already on its way to giving in and Eirik was fighting with three men who had somehow scaled the wall without the use of a ladder.

All three of Eirik's assailants had their back to Jez so she rushed them. The first went down with a slash from her sword opening up his back from arse to neck. The second turned in time for Jezzet to thrust her dagger just below his armpit and into his heart, she'd long ago made sure the blade was just long enough for such a kill. The third man panicked and Eirik took his head clean off with a chop from his axe.

"Thanks for the help, Jez. I..." Eirik was cut off as an arrow thudded into his shoulder, spinning him around and sending him careening off the battlements to the ground below.

"FUCK!" Jezzet screamed as she watched him fall. No stairs close by and an unhealthy drop to the ground.

"Shit," she said and launched herself off the walkway onto the roof of a nearby building. Her ankle twisted as she landed and she fell, rolled off the roof and hit the ground with a heavy and painful *thump* that drove all the air from her lungs. Somewhere close by a great crack signalled the gate had given way and the clash of metal on metal started.

Jez pushed herself to her feet, sucked in deep breaths of air and dust through gritted teeth and limped over to where Eirik had fallen. Smoke and the smell of burning wood filled the air and the screams of the dying echoed around the fort. Jezzet realised her hands were slick with blood. Looking down she was spattered with it all over. None of it was hers though. It was never hers.

She found Eirik crumpled on the floor lying face up with arm underneath him at an impossible angle. The jagged bone of his left leg showing through skin and armour both. A steady pool of blood was leaking from him somewhere, but still he managed to open his eyes a crack as Jez approached. She'd never seen him look so pale or so young before.

"Reckon its bad," he managed to say, a weak ghost of his grin on his lips.

"Fuck," Jezzet agreed with him.

"Too late... for my one... the road."

Jezzet just stood over him. She knew she should feel sad or scared or feel something at least. Instead she just felt numb. The fort was lost. Constance had won. Jezzet would be humiliated and killed in the most painful way possible and she was damned sure Constance could think of some very painful ways.

It would be better if I just ended it now myself.

"Too late for everything I reckon, Eirik," she said.

Wonder if I can find a way to kill Constance before she kills me.

"No," Eirik said and coughed, his entire body shuddered and blood bubbled up from his mouth. "Under... shitter... my quarters... tunnel." Another cough, more blood and then nothing.

Jez should have said a prayer for him or maybe a couple of words about him being a good man or some such. Problem is she didn't feel much like lying and she didn't have the time either. She turned and ran-limped towards Eirik's quarters.

Soldiers, whores, and children ran this way and that through the buildings and courtyard. All pointless. Jez knew Constance well enough to know that if the cunt-sucking bitch was robbed of getting to kill both Jez and Eirik with her own hands, she'd murder every last person in the fort. The only way out of this alive for anyone was to get out of the fort and Jez wasn't about to take anyone with her.

She heard the shouts of surrender just as she barged her way into Eirik's quarters. The tub she'd bathed in just hours earlier still stood, the water long since cold and near brown with the sweat and dirt she'd washed off. The roof had been hit by a stray arrow and was just starting to catch fire. A good sign maybe, if the building burned to the ground Constance would never find the tunnel.

Jez flung the door to the shitter open and looked down at the circular stone she'd sat on so many times to relieve herself. She pushed her sword and her dagger back into their sheaths, took hold of the round stone and wrenched this way and that. The boards below it were loose.

Thank you, Eirik you damned bastard. She thought with a grin.

Jez sank to her knees and scrabbled at the wooden boards, tore at them with her bloody fingers until one came free. She flung the board behind her and then tore up another and then a third. There was a hole just big enough for a slim woman to squeeze through into the foul smelling tunnel below.

She wasted no time. Jezzet squeezed, pushed, wriggled, and squirmed her way into the tunnel. It was small but just large enough for her. It stank of shit and worse and was slick and vile underneath her hands in a way that made her want to vomit. Craning her head around Jez could see the tunnel extended both ways. Behind her it ran further into the fort, in front of her it led towards the east. Towards the mountains.

It was then Jezzet realised she'd left her pack up in Eirik's quarters. Everything she owned bar the clothes on her back and the sword at her side was in that pack but she'd be damned if she was going to risk going back for it. So Jezzet Vel'urn set her hands into the filthy, stinking muck in front of her and started crawling.

Shit.

The Black Thorn

Funny thing about settlements in the Wilds, they all had walls. Every village, every town, every city, every port, every fort, every manor, and every savage tribal camp. They all sported walls and Bischin was no different. It reminded Betrim of every other town on the plains he'd ever been to and he was pretty sure his count currently sat at somewhere near all of them.

Low wooden walls ringed the town and, though they would do nothing to stop a determined force, they served to keep out wild animals and disorganised raiders. The Boss' little band of sell-swords were neither, but the guards on the gate still looked at them as though they were animals

"No trouble," said one of the guards as they passed. He was a big man with bushy, overhanging eyebrows and more than a few missing teeth, the rest of his set were well on their way to browning. Yellow teeth were one thing but brown teeth struck Betrim as plain wrong.

Bones smiled as he towered over the man showing his own set of yellowing chompers. "Do I look like I could cause trouble?"

The guard paled and the Boss clapped him on the arm. "Jus' passin' through, friend. Be gone in a couple o' days." The guard nodded at the Boss' words but didn't take his eyes off Bones.

"So what we doin' here, Boss?" Swift asked as they passed through the gate. "I mean it's a bit of a shit-hole ain't it."

Betrim had to agree on that one. Low wooden buildings, half of which looked to be in the process of falling down. Scum lined the streets in droves, some of them sell-swords, some of them thieves, some of them nothings with less than nothing to their name. Seemed the good-folk were on the outnumbered side here in Bischin. Waste and garbage was piled high in some spots, as if no one could be arsed to clean it away so all were happy to just leave it lying in the streets. That made Betrim grimace. Even animals knew not to shit in their own homes.

There were a few shops selling all manner of goods. Each shop had two or three big, tough-looking guards hired by the shop owners out of their own pockets. Better that than get robbed and killed by the first scum who took a liking to whatever you were peddling.

Women with painted faces stood waving from the balcony of a large three-storied wooden shack. Their breasts hung loose and free and heavy and they whistled towards the Boss' little group of sell-swords as they passed. Nothing like a pair of tits to catch a man's attention.

"Boss," Betrim started, never taking his eyes off the jugs that hung above him. "Where we meetin'?"

"Inn called *Thieves Rest*, you know the place?"

"Aye," Betrim said and without another word walked towards the whore house.

"I'm with the Black Thorn," he heard Swift say.

"Me too," from Green a moment later.

The doors swung open to a gaudily-lit room that stank of perfume. It was almost enough to choke him, the smoke and haze was so thick. A bar at the far end of the room had a few patrons enjoying drinks and rooms upstairs were closed or open to indicate whether they were in use. Some women lounged around waiting for business while others entertained men. At the edges of the room in dark alcoves, Betrim could see women grinding their hips on top of folk. Those not rich enough to rent a room or those without the modesty to care, he reckoned. From time to time the scene was punctuated by the odd masculine grunt or a feminine giggle.

A plump lady of ageing years with more powder on her face than dust in the desert approached. The cloying scent of a hundred different perfumes clung to her but none could hide the stink of sex that trailed behind her.

"Can I help you gentlemen? We cater for all tastes," she asked in a low, throaty voice with a wide smile on her red, red lips.

"I'll take a room, a girl, and a bottle of something strong," Betrim said in a growl.

Swift laughed. "Fuck the room, I'll fuck the girl, and something to smoke wouldn't go amiss."

"Yeah, me too," Green said with all the eagerness of a boy who's never been inside a whore.

"Best make it a boy for the young'un," Betrim said, grinning his horrific grin. "Be an experience fer him."

"Fuck you, Black Thorn. I ain't no weird," Green shouted, earning himself more than a couple of looks.

The look the ageing mistress gave Betrim was far more worrying though. She studied his face for a moment, studied his collection of scars. "We don't take too kind to people messing up our girls, Black Thorn."

Swift broke into a raucous laughter. "Ya reputation is well known, Thorn," he said and then broke off as he spotted a girl he liked the look of. "I'll take that one. Come here, girl. I got something fer ya ta suck on."

Green laughed, nudged Betrim in the side and scuttled off to find a girl of his own. Never had Betrim wanted to kill the lad so much. He noticed the powdered mistress was still staring at him, studying him. Betrim stared right on back with a neutral expression.

"I don't mess up whores. I don't beat women." Betrim paused. "Well, not unless they deserve it. I want a room, a drink, an' a girl ta fuck. Don't much care what she looks like, I ain't the prettiest thing ta look at myself."

If the mistress was cowed at all by Betrim's name or reputation she didn't show an ounce of it. After a while she nodded towards the stairs. "Third door on left is free. I'll send a girl up with a bottle."

There were no smiles for Betrim anymore, he noticed. People rarely smiled at the Black Thorn. With a final stare that could have shattered a mirror, he headed for the stairs and towards the third door on the left.

By the time Betrim and the others made it to *The Thieves Rest* he felt a little less angry and a lot more relieved. The girl he'd gotten was only just prettier than he was, but she knew her way around a cock, no doubt, and Betrim had not been left wanting. She had a wonderful set of teeth on her too, all pearly white and only the one missing. The bottle of spirits he'd got were a little disappointing but had a satisfying burning sensation on the way down so he kept the whole bottle. It would serve him well when they got back out on the plains.

Swift whistled and skipped all the way from the whore house to the inn and Green wore a stupid grin and kept mumbling something about tits. Betrim tried his best to ignore the little shit lest his anger return.

They found the others sitting alone on a table in the most crowded part of the common room. Henry was nursing a pint and eyeing the collected masses with dangerous intent. A brooding Boss sat next to her, staring into his mug of beer with a dark expression. Bones looked more bored than anything else and his face lit up when he spotted the others. Seemed conversation had run a bit dry. Didn't surprise Betrim, Swift tended to do most of the talking in the crew.

"How'd it go?" Bones asked the new-comers with a knowing wink.

"Green only went an' said Black Thorn's name in the middle of the damned whore house," Swift said, grinning from ear to ear.

"An' yet he still has all his teeth," the Boss said without looking up from his mug. "The Black Thorn must like our newest recruit."

Betrim growled as he waved at the serving girl to bring a mug over and flipped a bronze bit her way. She caught it in her hand and bit it to make sure it was real before sauntering off to fill a mug.

"You boys not too drunk, I hope," the Boss said.

"Take more 'an a cheap bottle o' spirits fer that," Betrim insisted.

"Didn't touch the booze, Boss," Swift said, grinning.

"What about the smoke?"

"Didn't touch the booze, Boss," Swift repeated, still grinning.

The serving girl arrived with Betrim's beer and he took a large gulp. Tasted like watered down piss, but beer always did in the Wilds. Betrim couldn't remember the last time he had a good strong beer. Probably last time he attended one of those fancy blooded folk's parties which would put it somewhere around never.

"How come you two didn't come get yaselfs a whore?" Green asked pointing at Bones and the Boss. "Ya do like women right?"

"Oh I'd love ta," Bones said. "Unfortunately my wife says if I go around whorin' she'll know an' she'll chop my stones off."

"You married?" Green exclaimed in a loud voice. Seemed he'd had a bit too much drink or smoke or both. "Where is the bitch?"

"Fuck knows. As far away from me as possible, I hope."

"Oh right. What 'bout you, Boss?"

Everyone at the table just stared at Green. Well, everyone but Henry who broke into loud, vicious laughter. The boy would figure it out at some point. Maybe after he heard them going at it. Betrim had been in battles quieter than those two fucking.

"Fancy makin' some money, Bones?" Betrim asked the big man.

Bones looked around the common room. "Reckon we can squeeze a few bits out o' this crowd."

Betrim and Bones moved down the table a ways and Swift followed to look after the purses. He wouldn't steal from either of them, he knew better, but they'd be other purses involved in no time and there weren't quicker fingers in all the Wilds than Swift when it came to relieving purses of some of their weight.

Both men slapped their purses down on the table and that got the attention they were looking for. Nothing pulled gazes in the Wilds like the metallic *clink* of bits. So Betrim put his elbow on the table and raised his hand and opposite him Bones did the same. They clasped hands and on Swift's count of three they started pushing.

Arm wrestling against Bones was a lot like pissing into the wind, a pointless exercise that was only going to leave you worse for wear, but the giant went easy on Betrim. That was the entire point after all. Make it look like a smaller man had a chance and then pull it back from the brink and win and Bones did so with a dramatic flair and *whoop* of joy when he won.

Swift handed both purses to Bones and Betrim made a show beating the table with his fist before stalking off to the others. He knew he'd get his purse back later with interest.

"Have ya ever seen such a manly display?" Henry mocked him.

"Fuck you, crazy bitch," Betrim replied. That earned him a dark look set above a hungry grin. He gave her a shove and the grin turned into a smile. It was rare that Henry smiled, but when she did Betrim got the impression she might have been pretty if she wasn't such a murderous little imp.

"Ten bronze bits or one silver bit fer a try against the giant." Swift was saying to a big man with tree trunks for arms who sat down opposite Bones.

The walking tree slapped down a single silver bit which Swift scooped up and Bones had the good graces to look worried at least. He gave the walking tree a brief glimpse of victory before felling him hard enough to shatter the man's hand. The tree walked away swearing blind and rubbing his hand. Another man sat down for the challenge then another and another.

"Everythin' good, Boss?" Betrim asked. Dark eyes raised and met his and the Boss shook his head.

"Got a drop house in town. Get all sorts of messages left there. We got good news an' bad. Good news is I got us another job. A big job, biggest one we done yet. Bad news is that girl we killed back in Korral was blooded. Those riders passed us a few nights back on the plains were after us an' I don't reckon they jus' gonna leave us be.

"Problem is being well known as we are means people see us, people talk 'bout us. Makes us easy ta find. Ain't your fault, Black Thorn. We're all of us pretty noticeable. Well, 'cept Green here. Ain't many southern sell-swords an' my colour makes me stand out. Never seen another as big as Bones. Henry here has a name almost big as yours in parts and there ain't no mistaking the bastard blood in Swift.

"Facts are we got folk lookin' fer us with intent an' a price on all our heads. We need ta get out o' this province an' with some great haste."

"Even me?" Green asked.

"Even you."

"Never been out of Forswai before. What are the other provinces like?"

"They're jus' the same but with less folk lookin' ta kill us," Boss said and then turned back to Betrim. "We're headin' back ta Korral in the mornin'."

"Shit," Betrim cursed with some venom. "I'd rather fight a group o' hunters than an Arbiter, Boss."

"What?" Green looked confused. "The Black Thorn is scared of an Arbiter?"

Both Betrim and the Boss ignored the boy. "Fact is, Thorn, we don't know that Arbiter's after ya. Those boys passed us on the road want our heads. That an' the job I got us is in Chade."

"A boat trip an' all, Boss? S'got bad idea written all over it," Betrim said.

"I ain't askin' opinions, Thorn. Jus' tellin' it like it is. We're headed back ta Korral at first light an' not by the roads. Need ta keep as out o' sight as possible. Good."

It wasn't a question but Betrim nodded anyways. "Good."

"I'm headed to my room. Henry." The Boss looked at Thorn, his teeth flashing silver as he spoke. "Tell the other two when they done playin'."

The Blademaster

If someone had told Jezzet at the beginning of the day that she'd find herself running from Eirik's fort with only her clothes and her sword to her name with her hands, arms, feet, legs, and somehow her hair, covered in shit; well if someone had told her that she wouldn't have believed them. But then if someone had told her just two hours ago that she'd make it out of the fort alive, she wouldn't have believed them. Truth was Jezzet Vel'urn knew just how damned lucky she was and no amount of shit was going to convince her otherwise.

The tunnel ended a few hundred feet from the fort and opened up into a trickling of water that might once have been called a stream. The opening had been blocked up by earth and piled up refuse and Jez had to dig her way out. From the tunnel opening it was about a mile to the mountains, she reckoned, and so she set off right away. No sense in hanging around. Once Constance's forces had secured the fort and the warlord realised Jez wasn't among the living, or the dead, the bitch would send people looking for her. Jezzet wanted to be well away by then.

The grass between the fort and the mountains was long and the ground underfoot was lumpy and treacherous. Jezzet's twisted ankle was screaming in pain with every step but she was alive.

For now, at least, you're alive, Jez.

She glanced behind her and saw the hot, orange glow and dark, grey smoke of fire in the fort. That was a good thing. With any luck Constance's forces would be too busy putting out the fires to be looking out over the walls. With the moon so big and bright anyone who took the time to look eastwards would see her figure cutting through the grass. She'd be safer when she reached the mountains. The pass wound into and around the peaks. She'd never travelled it herself but she knew it was jagged, broken in places, dangerous and rarely travelled by anyone save the foolhardy and those with nothing left to lose. Jez was pretty sure she currently fit into both categories.

It seemed to take forever to reach the rocky base of the first mountain. Jez told herself her ankle was only twisted, hoped it was only

The Heresy Within

twisted. A broken ankle in her current situation would present a whole new set of problems.

Looking up Jez thought she could see the first ledge of the pass about twenty feet above her. That was part of the problem with the trail, in places it required almost as much climbing as walking.

Jez took one last look back towards the fort. The fires were still glowing, and she fancied she could even see a few flames. Then she placed one hand on the rock in front of her and reached up with the other hand, searching for a hold of some kind. She found one and started, pulling with her arms, pushing with her legs, scrambling up the rocky cliff face with a screaming ankle and shrieking fingertips.

One hand over the other, pulling, pushing, feet scrabbling for purchase. Pebbles, loose rocks, and dust cascaded to the ground around her. Grunting, growling and, at times, squealing Jezzet climbed, inch by painful inch.

After something close to eternity Jez pulled herself onto the ledge, rolled onto her back, and spent a good minute gasping for air. She was pretty sure she was both laughing and crying though she couldn't say why.

Her master had made her do many demanding things during her training, but never had he made her climb a mountain. She was starting to wish he had.

No time to waste, Jez. Get moving before Constance catches up.

She pushed herself to her feet and started following the trail upwards. There was no way anyone would see her from the fort now. It wouldn't be long before Constance realised Jez had escaped and the bitch would send riders in every direction to hunt her down. She wanted to be out of sight by the time those riders reached the base of the mountains. They wouldn't be able to follow her up the trail with their horses but they would be able to ride back and tell Constance where she was.

You've been in worse situations, Jez. There was that time in Korral with the Red Hands. And that time out on the southern plains being hunted by those wild dogs that laugh at you.

Truth was Jezzet Vel'urn could name a hundred bad situations she'd been in and truth was this one was climbing its way to the top.

This part of the trail was slim to say the least. One misplaced foot, one patch of loosened rock and Jez would go tumbling down the mountainside. She looked down. A bad idea. The world seemed to lurch around her as she spied the lethal drop onto vicious, jagged rocks that were waiting below. Jez flung herself backwards and pressed herself flat against the rock face trying to calm her foolish breathing. Another bad idea.

From her vantage point up on the mountain she could see Eirik's little fort burning away. It seemed Constance wasn't even bothering with putting the fires out. Her bastard of an employer didn't want the fort, he just wanted it gone and his warlord was more than happy to oblige. What was worse, though, was that from the light shining down from the moon and that of the burning fort Jezzet could see the riders. They were spreading out in all directions looking for signs of a person fleeing the fort. Looking for signs of Jezzet.

Fuck!

Jez turned back to the trail and doubled her speed. If she placed a foot wrong and tumbled downwards to her death so be it. Better that than get caught by Constance.

It wasn't often in her life that Jezzet could say luck was on her side. Truth was more often than not luck, fate, and the Gods, whatever their damned names were, seemed to be allied against her. Tonight was not one of those times.

A flash lit the sky somewhere far away and a crash of thunder that seemed to shake the earth followed just a few seconds later. A minute later and the world seemed to grow darker as clouds moved across the moon. Jez felt the first few drops of rain speckle her skin and would have *whooped* with joy would it not have given away her position. She was a dark shadow against a dark mountain with almost no light to reveal her. Only an unlucky flash of lightning could give her away now and she intended to be out of sight before that happened. The pass was already starting to bend, following the mountain edge around. Soon the fort wouldn't even be visible and neither would she.

Of course, Jez had to admit to herself, there was a problem with luck and not just that it tended to run out. It was always a double edged blade. The darker it became, the more hidden from viewing eyes she was and the more dangerous the trail became. While the rain would be welcome in washing off some of the stink of shit, it also made the rock slippery. While the thunder may help to hide any sounds of a person scrabbling up a rocky trail, it could also shake loose a small mountain of rocks which would crush Jez on the way down. Luck was ever the type of friend who showed up without warning, handed you a bag of gold bits, and then proceeded to sell you out to your closest enemy.

Another flash, another crash and the rain turned into a steady downpour. Jez took a moment, raised her head to the sky and opened her mouth. Her water skin was in her backpack which was in Eirik's quarters which were naught but ash by now. Wasn't easy drinking rain straight from the sky but it was a damned sight better than dying of thirst.

The night wore on for Jezzet. At some point she passed long out of sight of any pursuers. The trail opened out, became wider, safer. Here the path started to wind between peaks and troughs but all was black and grey to Jez in the dark and rain. Her pace slowed and Jezzet had to admit she was as miserable as she was cold, as cold as she was wet, and as wet as she was tired. So when she spotted the opening mouth of a small cave she trudged towards it, not even bothering to limp any more. At least the shooting pain in her ankle served to keep her awake and aware.

Inside, the cave was dark but dry, spacious and with a strange smell Jez couldn't quite be bothered to place. She had no dry clothes, no sleeping mat, and no wood for a fire so she found a corner, curled up in a ball and closed her eyes.

The thing about having a master who liked to sneak up on you in the middle of the night and hit you with things was that you soon learned to be a light sleeper, to wake up at the slightest creak, scuff, or wheeze. Jezzet, being the good student that she was, liked to try to turn the tables on her old master. She'd crack an eye, just enough to get a position of her assailant, and then she would wait until the very last moment before launching a counter-attack. It had never worked against her old master but then he had never been a big mountain cat. Jezzet fancied her chances against the cat a lot more.

Her eye opened just enough to let in some light and she waited for it to focus. There, padding towards her on light feet, cautious as a child stealing from its parents, was a big cat. Two feet tall at the shoulder, Jez guessed, and with a lot of damned big teeth. It had spots, not stripes. Jez tried to remember the old rhyme.

'Cat with spots... something something, cat with stripes...' No good. She remembered the point of it at least. Stripes meant a lot of cats, spots meant just the one. Luck was still playing jokes on her it seemed.

Here, Jez, have a vicious killer on four legs. Don't worry though, there's only the one of them.

Her hand tightened around the hilt of her sword. Jezzet couldn't remember the last time she'd slept without her sword in her hand. The first thing her master had ever taught her, *'A Blademaster without a blade is a master of nothing.'* Well, actually that was the second thing he'd taught her, the first had been how to fuck a man while...

The cat crouched to pounce and Jez was on her feet, sword sliding from its sheath with a reassuring metallic ringing. That made the beast pause. It had no doubt thought Jez was already dead.

Reckon you already smell like death, Jez.

Jezzet stared at the cat and the cat stared back, great golden eyes never leaving her own deep browns. Sunlight streamed in through the mouth of the cave and Jez realised it must be morning, the storm must have broken. She needed to get moving, not stand here playing with an overgrown kitten. Just as pressing a need though was she needed to eat.

Jez took a cautious step towards the cat. Her ankle held, it hurt a bit but felt more stiff than painful. That was good at least, meant it wasn't broken. The cat growled at her, a low rumbling echoing from deep within its throat. Jez hadn't known cats could growl, she thought it was something only dogs did. She was half tempted to growl back.

The beast aimed a lightning fast swipe at her but one thing Jezzet Vel'urn was known for was her speed. Her hand darted out, her sword an extension of herself. The cat had claws, Jezzet had a sword and hers was sharper. The blade skewered the cat's paw mid swipe and then Jez danced backwards.

The cat hissed in pain and tried to back away. Jezzet decided not to let it. She pressed the attack with a jab followed by a slash. The first punctured the cat's shoulder and the second laid open a long, deep gash down its back.

The creature collapsed to the floor, a sound escaping from its mouth somewhere between a mewl and a sad gurgle. For some reason Jezzet felt sorry for the beast. The damned thing had just tried to kill her and here she was feeling bad about killing it right back.

She stabbed it in the chest, hoping to put it out of its misery. Problem was the creature wasn't human so Jez had no idea where its vital parts were. Instead of dying it just cried out even more. Again Jez stepped in and stabbed it, then again, and again. By the time the beast died it had more holes in it than a sinking ship and its last breath was a great shuddering thing that made Jez feel guilty beyond belief. She went about cutting off a leg, skinning it and carving off a sizeable chunk of raw meat.

The thing about raw meat is that a person can live off of it, for a while at least, if the person can keep it down. It tasted foul, felt disgusting, sat heavy in the gut, and the blood was sticky and provoked a gag reflex that Jezzet had to fight with every mouthful. Still, she ate her fill and then left the rest of the carrion for any scavengers could find it. Then she walked outside the cave into the glorious morning sunshine.

It was good. She still felt damp from the rains of the night and now she was coated in the mountain cat's blood. The sun would soon dry her off but it would also evaporate any pools of water. Jez spotted one such pool and rushed over. A small indentation in the rock where water had collected and stood, a little cloudy but wet all the same. She put her face into the pool and sucked in as much water as she could. It tasted of blood and minerals but she'd tasted far worse things in her life.

Jez emptied the first little pool of water then found another and gave it the same treatment. Then she relieved herself over by a modest looking boulder before trying to find her bearings.

It looked to be mid-morning which would put the sun between the south and the east. Jezzet found the trail that seemed to lead the right way and set off. The good thing about owning nothing, Jez decided, was that you had nothing you had to carry. The bad thing, of course, was that she owned nothing.

Jezzet reckoned the trail would take her two days over the mountain. They'd be two hungry, thirsty, hard days, but she could manage and at least the view was nice. From the bottom of the trail it was only about seven days to get to Chade and there she could find work and get herself back on track.

I may look like a bloody savage and smell like a sewer but I'll be damned if I'm going to die and let that bitch, Constance, win.

The Black Thorn

"Back ta the matter at hand. This is gonna slow us down," the Boss said, staring out across the plains.

Bones was busy taking fingers from the men he'd just killed and storing the bloody digits in a little pouch until he was ready to clean the flesh from the bones to add to his collection. Swift took to looting the corpses. Green was measuring boot sizes from the men they'd killed, trying to find a good match for his own feet. Henry was staring at one of the two horses that hadn't run off. It was a dull-eyed creature that stared right back at her, trusting despite her having just slit its owner from navel to neck.

Betrim stood next to the Boss and joined him in his staring. A good staring was sometimes as enjoyable as a good leaning. "Knew it were comin'."

"Aye," the Boss said in a resigned voice. "Wish it'd waited another week or so though. Bloody bad luck I reckon."

Two days out of Bischin and they'd run straight into the great herd. Beasts as far as the eyes could see in front and to the side of them. Thousands upon thousands of them. Some folk gave that amount a name, a word. Weren't no words to describe the number of creatures in front of them as far as Betrim was concerned.

Some of the animals were huge, hulking things with short fur and big horns, honking to each other as they stripped the land bare of grass. Loud cracks echoed all around as two of the big males butted heads, maybe for food, maybe for mates. Smaller deer-like creatures bounced around as well. Always alert, ever watchful for any sign of danger, their heads moved with sudden jerking motions that reminded Betrim of a bird. There were the tall beasts as well, the spotted ones with long necks, long tongues, and funny little horns on top of their heads. Then there were the elephants. Huge, grey monstrosities with big ears and long snout-like noses that coiled around the grass and lifted it to their mouths. The males had dangerous tusks that could skewer a man, armour or no. Only the Boss wasn't afraid of the elephants and Betrim thought he knew why. He'd heard it said the black skins of the far south tamed and rode the monsters. Betrim was pretty sure he didn't have the stones to get close enough to touch one let alone ride one, but then the Boss had the biggest stones of anyone Betrim knew.

"At least we won't be going hungry tonight," the Boss said with a sigh.

"We gonna have a fire? Wouldn't mind cookin' my meat."

"Aye. Might as well. Don't reckon anyone else is gonna be comin' at us from Bischin an' nobody comin' at us from the herd side o' things."

"I wanna ride." Betrim and the Boss both turned to find Henry standing next to the horse. She poked its nose with a thin, bony finger and the horse nuzzled her hand. She turned to look at them with a smile. "Reckon it likes me."

"Do ya even know how ta ride one of those things?" the Boss asked.

"How hard can it be? You jus' sit on the thing, kick it a bit, an' it goes."

"That sounds more like you," Betrim said. The Boss laughed and Henry narrowed her eyes at him.

"No horses, Henry. Get rid of it." It was an order from the Boss and not even Henry would refuse an order.

"Fine, fine." One of Henry's daggers whipped out and bit deep into the horse's neck. She danced backwards with a laugh as the beast collapsed, thrashing and spraying blood everywhere.

"What the fuck?" Bones shouted, springing to his feet as a spray of blood hit him full in the face.

"I told ya ta get rid of it, not kill the fuckin' thing, Henry," the Boss shouted.

"It's got rid of. What's the difference," she replied with a shrug.

The Boss shook his head. "Swift, get ta cutting some meat off that thing. We'll move off a ways an' start a fire an' you can all thank Henry fer the horseflesh tonight."

Green and Swift groaned. Betrim shrugged. Meat was meat after all.

They all sat around the small camp fire, all except Henry who had pulled the first watch. She prowled around the camp quiet as a ghost, watching and listening for any danger. It wasn't just people they had to look out for, wild animals were a threat too. Along with the grass eaters of the great herd came the meat eaters. Predators and scavengers followed in great numbers.

Just before sun down Betrim had seen some of the big cats that stalked the plains. A whole group of them, looked to be near fifteen, had been lounging underneath the shade of a corpse tree. The trees were said to grow wherever a corpse had been buried and provided much needed shelter from the midday sun for many.

He could also hear the haunting sounds of the laughing dogs. An unnerving noise for anyone and a death sentence for everyone alone on the plains. Those dogs could smell you from miles away and would chase and hound a man till death. Snapping at his heels as he ran, trying to hamstring him and then darting away, always just out of reach of retribution.

Carrok birds were always a danger even when the great herd wasn't passing. Gigantic, winged creatures as big as a man with three times as great a wingspan and razor sharp talons and beaks that could puncture steel. They tended to prefer smaller prey but it wasn't unknown for a pair of them to attack travellers. Diving from high up in the sky, attacking from the air and then speeding away to wait and let their prey die from the wounds. Betrim was always wary when fast shadows passed over him.

There were the giant lizards too. Some called them dragons, or dragonspawn, but Betrim knew better. They weren't dragons just big lizards with dangerous turns of speed and a poisonous bite that could kill a man in hours. They didn't need to fear the lizards here though, the beasts didn't venture onto the plains, preferred the rocky areas to the grass.

For now though there was the warmth of the fire and all the horse meat he could eat and cheap spirits to burn his throat. Some of the others watched every time Betrim took a swig from the bottle but he'd be damned if they were getting any.

"How'd ya do it?" his near constant shadow, Green, asked.

The boy had chosen to sit next to Betrim and kept glancing his way. It was all Betrim could do not to shove a knife in the lad's neck. Still, the moon and stars tended to put the Black Thorn in a mellow mood. Something about the way the specks of light twinkled, he reckoned. It was pretty.

"Do what?" Betrim growled out the corner of his mouth as he tore off a strip of meat with his teeth.

"How'd ya kill 'em? The Arbiters."

Swift groaned from the other side of the fire. "He's been wantin' ta ask ya that ever since he found out who ya are, Thorn. I reckon the boy's a bit taken wit' ya."

"Which one?" Betrim asked.

"The first one," the Boss said. He knew all the stories, had asked about them himself back when Betrim agreed to join this little group of sell-swords.

Green was nodding. Swift was getting comfortable on the ground, trying to find a non-lumpy spot. Bones had finished eating and was busy cleaning the flesh off of his new bones but he was watching Betrim all the same. The big man had never heard the details either, had never asked. Only the Boss and Henry knew the details and, even then, they only knew the truth so far as Betrim had told it.

"First one turned up at my family's ranch jus' days aft' I buried my parents. Arbiter Colm he called himself." Betrim fixed Green with a cold stare. "Ya never forget ya first time. He was there ta look about my parent's death. Seems he thought they died of unnatural circumstances."

"Did they?" Green asked.

"Well seeing as how I stabbed 'em both myself. Aye."

"You killed ya own parents?" Green asked. "Why?"

"We had a disagreement 'bout a chicken." Betrim watched as Green's face went slack. It was always fun telling folk that, they were never sure whether he was shitting them or not.

"Arbiter Colm, he started askin' all the other folk on the ranch a load of questions 'bout my parents. How my da' had come by the ranch? was my ma' ever right with her future tellins? Ever been asked a question by an Arbiter, Green?"

"No."

"Ya can't lie. Ya can try as much as ya want. Try ta shit 'em. Try not ta say a thing. Don't make a difference. Ya can't lie ta an Arbiter. They force the truth out o' ya," Betrim said as he watched Bones flick the last bit of human flesh from his knife into the camp fire and take out his brown rag to start cleaning his bones.

"Thing is, though, even Arbiters need ta sleep sometimes. Not often maybe but sometimes. So I hid. Watched. Waited. Saw him question all the other folk on the ranch, heard every single one of 'em tell the Arbiter how I was the killer. None of 'em knew where I was though, hidden up in the rafters of the main house, scurryin' around the walls like a rat. Not even the Arbiter knew I was there. Thought I'd run off, he did.

"So there I waited until the Arbiter closed his eyes, locked the room. Old house like that some of the boards in the roof jus' come right up an' I was still a boy, jus' fourteen years ta my name. I slid through the gap in the roof an' into the Arbiter's room. Quiet as a ghost. Quiet as Henry sneakin' up behind you jus' now."

Green craned his neck around to find Henry staring down at him. Spiky hair standing up at all angles. Bright flames dancing in the reflection of her dark eyes. Such a sight was enough to make even Betrim shiver.

"Swift. Get ya arse up," Henry said, walking over to the Boss and taking a seat. "Your watch."

"Oh fuck me, Henry."

"Not a chance."

"I was jus' about asleep there listenin' ta that," Swift said, grinning towards Betrim and walking out of the circle of firelight. "Ya sure have led a dull life, Black Thorn."

"What happened?" Green asked, back to staring at Betrim with big, round eyes.

"Huh?"

"With the Arbiter."

"Oh right. I slit his throat in his sleep. Well, more like stabbed him in the neck a few times. I was new ta killin' folk back then, wasn't overly sure how it worked. Still, result was the same. Bled ta death pretty quick."

"Ya didn't fight him?"

Betrim laughed at that. A hard, rasping sound to be sure but the boy's question was as funny as anything he'd heard for some time. "Fight him? Fight an Arbiter? Listen up, Green. I've killed six of the fuckers an' only one of 'em did I fight. Gave me this." Betrim shoved the left side of his face towards Green, the burned side. Pitted, melted flesh. As ugly a scar as Betrim had ever seen and the reason he didn't keep a mirror. Not that he was too pretty before the burn.

"I got off easy. Ever heard of a town called Lanswitch in the Bore province?"

Green swallowed. "No."

"'Cos it don't exist no more. Burned to the ground durin' our fight. I got the blame for all of that too. A hundred folk died in that fire. Men, women, an' kids an' it all got pegged on me.

"Ya wanna kill an Arbiter do it in their sleep. Fill 'em with arrows before they spot ya. Walk past 'em in the street an' get all stabby. Jus' don't let 'em see ya coming cos if they do... ya fucked."

Silence seemed to hold for a long time. Only the crackle and pop of the fire, the low hissing of the wind, and the honking from the nearby great herd sounded in the void.

Bones spat into his rag. "That's why I never asked."

THE ARBITER

Even in the near total darkness the Inquisition compound was busy. Servants going to and fro with messages or food stuffs. A few Arbiters coming or going, but at this time most were tucked away in their bunks. Sometimes even an Inquisitor might be seen. They lived outside of the compound in large, expensive houses. They had *earned* that right through years of faithful service, so travelled each day to and from their homes.

Thanquil sat on the cold stone steps outside the barracks, smoking. Smoking casher weed was common practice among many around the world but in most places it was smoked in a pipe. Here in Sarth it was possible to purchase the expensive weed rolled in small slips of paper. A rare and costly pass-time, but Thanquil only visited Sarth once every three years and he couldn't stand smoking out of a pipe. The effect of the weed left him a little light headed but didn't impair him in any way.

It was a couple of hours before dawn and he'd have to make his way to the docks soon. If he missed the boat to the Wilds the Inquisitors would not be pleased and the last thing Thanquil needed was the displeasure of the twelve most powerful people in the Inquisition. Besides, he could still remember the feel of the Grand Inquisitor's compulsion. He could still remember how strong the old man was. The mere thought of it sent chills down his spine and Thanquil sucked in another lungful of smoke.

"Early morning, Arbiter." Thanquil looked up to see Arbiter Vance approaching. He was starting to think the young man was following him.

"Late night. Didn't feel much like sleeping."

Vance grunted and sat down next to Thanquil as if they were old friends having a pleasant chat. Nothing could be further from the truth as far as Thanquil was concerned. Hard to tell the son of the Grand Inquisitor to '*piss off*' without causing offence though, so Thanquil just sat in awkward silence.

"I hear you're going to the Wilds," Arbiter Vance said into the warm darkness.

"I hear you have the sight so why don't you tell me where I'm going."

Thanquil saw Vance smile out of the corner of his eye and conspired to *accidentally* blow smoke in his direction. It failed. A gust of wind picked up at just the wrong moment and spoiled his moment of petty victory.

"I don't look into people's futures unless they ask me to," the young Arbiter said in a soft voice. "It could be considered... rude."

"I give you my permission." The future was always a gamble, any way to stack the odds in Thanquil's favour seemed worth it to him.

"Nothing," Arbiter Vance answered far too fast. "I see nothing."

"How useful your gift is." Thanquil decided he'd had enough of the young Arbiter and he had a boat to catch. "Goodbye, Arbiter Vance."

"Be careful, Arbiter Darkheart." Thanquil turned and Arbiter Vance seemed to be staring through him with those unnerving yellow eyes. "Sometimes an enemy can be friend."

Now the boy considered them friends? Thanquil would almost have preferred them to be enemies, at least he knew where he stood with enemies. With a sigh and a shake of his head Thanquil walked away, leaving Arbiter Vance sitting on the steps.

He had never liked sea travel, it always seemed dangerous to him. Like giving your life over to someone else's hands only that someone was a vast, powerful, and sporadically vengeful body known as *the sea*.

He stood on the docks looking at the boat that was to take him to the Wilds. The slight rise and fall of it in the water as men loaded cargo up the ramp was almost mesmerising. So little wood between him and cold, wet death.

"You my passenger?" the Captain of the ship was an ageing man, grey in hair and short of teeth with a squinting left eye and a red, scabby rash that stretched from his left ear down past his collar. He wore a simple tunic and short britches that ended just below the knee. All in all he looked no different from any man on his crew save the hard stare and the air of a man in command.

"Aye, that's me. Arbiter..."

"Don't need no more than that," the Captain interrupted without so much as a flinch. "Cas, ya got a bunk spare fer the Arbiter?"

"Aye, Cap'n."

"Ya be sleeping with the crew. Ain't got no spare rooms seeing as this ain't no passenger ship. Only cabin is the captain's."

"Seems like a good boat," Thanquil said with a nod, shouldering his bags. He'd left his mare in the Inquisition compound. A shame but there wasn't room for a horse on the voyage, he'd just have to buy a new beast when he reached the Wilds. If he reached the Wilds.

"She's a ship, not a boat," the Captain said in a testy voice. It was almost refreshing to find someone not terrified of Thanquil just for being an Arbiter.

"I'm sorry. I wasn't aware there was a difference."

The Captain looked at Thanquil as if he were an ignorant child. "Ships is bigger," he said.

"I see."

"Inquisition's paid fer ya already but keep yaself out o' the crews' way, Arbiter. An' none o' ya burning crap whiles ya here. Only authority on a boat is the Captain's."

"Thought you said it was a ship," Thanquil said and immediately regretted it. "I understand, Captain. I shall refrain from burning anybody for the duration of the trip."

The Captain growled and shouted up the ramp. "Cas, get the Arbiter stowed away. Don't want him underfoot as we cast off."

"Aye, Cap'n," shouted a small lad. The boy waved Thanquil up the ramp and then darted away.

Cas was short but already turning to muscle. He wore only britches and was topless with a sun burnt torso and face. His hair was short, dark, and greasy and the boy stank of the sea, as did the entire ship, its crew, and in fact the sea itself. Thanquil was not looking forward to the voyage.

The boy led him into the bowels of the ship, skipping along with bare feet scuffing the wood. He stopped in front of a bunk. "'Ere ya go."

In truth the bunk was little more than a wooden shelf surrounded by other wooden shelves. It was short, just long enough for Thanquil, there was no mattress, no sheet to cover him and no pillow on which to rest his head. It suited him just fine. He'd slept on worse, far worse, and would be glad just to have a flat surface to sleep on. He wasn't sure what the worst part of the journey would be yet but was leaning between the constant fear of uncertain and unavoidable death, or stopping himself from stealing for the entire three week period. If things started going missing it wouldn't take long for fingers to start pointing in his direction.

So Thanquil sat down on his bunk and waited. He could feel the gentle bobbing of the ship beneath him, could hear the occasional creak of timbers and could imagine the cold water just a few short paces away. At least he wasn't sea sick. Some people couldn't handle the constant motion of being on the water. They went green and would spend the entire voyage emptying their stomachs over the side of the ship. Thanquil had no idea whether he'd be one of those people, he wasn't about to risk it, instead he wore a charm around his neck to ward off nausea.

He felt the boat begin to move. It was a strange sensation to know you were moving but not to be able to see any proof of it. Perhaps that was what caused sea sickness? Thanquil leaned back in his bunk, took out a small wad of papers and the tiny ink jar he kept and began to inscribe symbols onto the papers. It was always best to keep a wide variety at hand, never knew what would be needed and when.

"What ya doin'?"

Thanquil looked up to see Cas staring at him in wonder. It was possible the boy had never even seen paper before.

"I'm creating runes."

"Oh. The Cap'n says ya can come up on deck now if ya want. What's a rune?"

"It's a... formation of power. I inscribe the rune on paper or on wood. Then when I break the rune the power is released," Thanquil said. A simplified explanation to be sure, but it would serve.

"I don't get it," Cas said, a blank expression covering his childish features.

Thanquil grinned, glanced around to check there was no one else close by and selected a piece of paper he had recently marked, then took his dagger from its sheath on his boot. He placed the dagger against the paper and, with an easy slice, cut the paper in two, letting both pieces float to the floor. The blade of the dagger burst into bright orange flame and Thanquil was rewarded by seeing the boy's jaw drop and his eyes go wide. After a few seconds the flame, with no fuel to sustain it, gutted out.

"Not s'posed ta have fire on the ship," Cas said, his eyes still fixed on the dagger as Thanquil wiped it on his coat then placed it back in its sheath.

"In that case, you don't tell anyone and I won't do it again."

Cas nodded. Thanquil stood up, stretched and walked for the door, leaving the boy behind to gape in wonder at the two halves of paper on the wooden floor.

Outside, Thanquil was assaulted by a brisk, salty breeze that was refreshing in the face of the constant sun and heat of the region. The ship moved with constant but gentle rises and dips as it cut through the water. Sailors darted this way and that, some up on the rigging, some down on the deck, all with their own jobs to do and all going about them with no fuss. It might have been comforting except for the shadow of death following them all just waiting for the body of water below to have a violent change of mood.

Thanquil leaned on the railing at the port, or the bow, or stern... he had no idea which was which and was happy to call it the railing on the left. He could still just about see Sarth, already little more than a white blob on the coastline and getting smaller by the minute.

After a while the Captain joined him by the railing and leaned with his back against it and a wild grin on his face.

"Wind is good, fer now. If it keeps up we'll make good time, Arbiter." If Thanquil had to pick a word for the sound of the Captain's voice he would have picked *salty*.

"Aye but is it like to keep up, I wonder."

"Hard ta say. The wind does what it will, goes double for the wind at sea."

Thanquil nodded to the Captain's pointless drawl as if it was the sagest advice he'd ever heard. He'd learned long ago that often when you had nothing to say it was best to say nothing at all.

"Ya don't much like the sea do ya, Arbiter?" the Captain asked after a while.

Thanquil was always amazed by people. The Inquisition was the most feared organisation in the known world and the Arbiters were the hands that dispensed the Inquisition's righteous judgement. Most folk knew better than to talk to an Arbiter. After all, they had the authority to act as judge, jury, and executioner all in the space of one conversation. However, time and time again Thanquil found himself the subject of questions from others. Perhaps it was because he hated asking questions himself.

"I wasn't aware it was that obvious," he replied, trying to let a hint of danger creep into his voice. He failed.

"Maybe not ta most," the Captain said with a pompous tone, "but I been on the sea fer near thirty years, learn ta spot these things af' a while."

"I'm sure you do. I find it hard to like something that has so many ways to kill me indiscriminately. Storms, giant waves, pirates, sea serpents. Hard to think of a more dangerous foe than the sea."

The Captain grinned. "Aye, not ta mention whirlpools an' sirens an' ghost ships." The man laughed. "Storms are a threat, it's true, but rare this time o' year. Be no giant waves where we going, see them more nearer the Dragon Empire. Pirates are a real bother but not yet met the pirate that can outrun the *Sea's Scorn* here." He stroked the railing with the caress one would reserve for a favoured lover. "As fer sea serpents an' the rest. I been on the sea fer near thirty years an' ain't never seen any of 'em."

"Doesn't mean they don't exist," Thanquil said scratching the stubble on his cheeks. "I've never seen a dragon but I know they exist."

"I have," the Captain boasted. "Bloody impressive but not near as bad as all the stories." The man gave Thanquil a slap on the shoulder and started off. "Three weeks on board, Arbiter, give or take. Might as well make the best o' it." He seemed a different man now that he was at sea, a much happier man than the one Thanquil had met on the docks. "Besides, ain't no harm gonna come ta you. Arbiters are the chosen of ya God, ain't they?"

Thanquil nodded with a fake smile and went back to staring out to sea. Sarth was no more than a speck on the horizon now. He chanted a quick blessing of sight and could just about make out the black tower of the Inquisition and the white tower of the imperial palace. Somehow it seemed fitting.

The Black Thorn

Fact was Korral was just about the last place Betrim wanted to be. Fact was Korral was where Betrim had been stuck for the past two days. The great herd was an ever-moving mass of beasts in all shapes and sizes and after just five days the herd had passed enough for the Boss' group of sell-swords to finish their journey to Korral. There were still a great many animals on the plains but not near as many and not near as packed and the beasts were as happy to give the group of sell-swords a wide birth as the sell-swords were to be on their way again.

If anything the passing of the great herd had helped. Korral was full to bursting with people. Hunters, skinners, leatherworkers, merchants, sailors, and more all flocked after the great herd and the guards were already so hard pressed keeping the peace they didn't have time to keep a look out for folk with bounties on them. So Bones had found them a nice little hovel as near to the docks as possible and the Boss had made some inquiries as to getting a boat to Chade.

Only Green would have been safe walking around the streets of the free city, the rest of them were too well known, too easily recognised. Problem was, though, none of them trusted Green yet so the Boss ordered them all to stay in the dirty hovel until the boat was leaving.

There was only so much being cooped up with the same folk day in and out that a man could take, Betrim reckoned, and he also reckoned he was nearing his limit. If it wasn't Swift's barbed comments it was Green's doe-eyed hero worship or Bones' constant cleaning of his bones. Even Swift had taken to frowning and it took a lot to stop that one from grinning.

Today was different though. Today they were getting out of this shit hole of a free city. The Boss had all the details and they were just waiting for him to give the order. So when the southerner appeared from his and Henry's room all dressed for leaving, Betrim was about ready to *whoop* for joy.

"Time we got ourselves gone," the Boss said, flashing his shiny metal teeth at his assembled group of sell-swords. "Boat should be leavin' within the hour an' anyone not on it is gonna be missin' out on the job in Chade so..."

There was the unmistakeable tramp of boots on earth outside the hovel and the door burst open. A Korral guard attempted to rush in, another man just behind him, but Swift was too quick. A throwing knife flew past Betrim and embedded itself in the guard's neck. Betrim was only a moment behind and he pushed the guard hard, forcing the bleeding man back out of the door and then slammed it shut.

Silence.

"Weapons down and come out now. By order of the Korral guard," came the shout from outside the hovel. At least they weren't trying to storm it anymore.

Green peeked through a hole in the wall. "Shit."

"How many, Green?" the Boss asked.

"I dunno," the boy answered with a shaky voice. "Can't count that high."

Swift shouldered him out the way and peered through the hole himself. "Green's right, Boss. We're fucked. Must be least twenty out there. More out o' sight no doubt."

The Boss nodded, a grave look in his eyes. "Free city laws. If we can make it ta the boat and pay the Cap'n not ta throw us off, the guard can't take us. Bones, the back wall. Split up, make fer the docks as best ya can. Boat's called *The Whipped Gull*. Anyone not there by the time it leaves is on their own."

By then Bones had done a damned fine job of taking the back wall apart. There was plenty of space for even the big man to squeeze through. Without another word they all went through the gap and started walking away in separate directions.

"I'm with you, Black Thorn. Lead the way." Again Green had used his name and again he'd said it loud enough for folk nearby to hear. It was too damned much.

The Black Thorn grabbed Green by his hair and waved his axe in the boy's face. "If you even try ta fuckin' follow me I will take your damned foot off an' leave ya fer the guards. Get it?" he hissed into Green's face.

In reply Green only nodded, mute fear plain in his eyes. Betrim gave the boy a shove and took a quick look around. There were people staring but no guards, not yet anyway. With that he sauntered off as if he hadn't a care in the world, leaving Green behind him to do as he would.

It didn't take the guard long to find him, didn't help that the people who had witnessed his little scene with Green were still staring at him. Betrim hadn't quite gotten to the end of the street before three guards wearing the yellow and red of Korral and wielding nasty-looking iron tipped spears spotted him and gave out a cry to raise more of their friends.

Betrim wasted no time, he turned and fled. His feet pounded on the packed earth and he was glad of the boots he wore, the boots he'd stolen last time he was in the free city. He turned into an alleyway, breathing heavy with the exertion of running. The Black Thorn was built for killing folk not running around. He could hear the guards close behind him, sounded like more than three now, and that made his blood pump even faster.

Dead end. Who the hell built alleyways with dead ends? A high wall, near twenty feet, he reckoned, thrust up in front of him. There was a closed door to his left, no idea where it led, and no time to think about it. Betrim thrust his full weight against the door and it snapped open with a *crash*, the lock bursting apart. Fact was Betrim Thorn was not a small man and that had been a very flimsy door.

A slight man in an apron screamed when the door crashed open, a high girlish shriek that didn't belong in a man's throat at all. The smell of fresh baked bread assaulted Betrim's nose, a wonderful smell. At any other time Betrim would have snatched up a loaf and kept running but right now food was the least of his worries. The need to live was a far more pressing concern.

He spied a door at the back of the bakery and went for it. Jumping over a table, scattering knifes and rolling pins and other things he couldn't even name. Kicking in the door Betrim found himself confronted by stairs. The shouts of the guards were too close. A figure appeared in the doorway to the bakery and the little baker screamed as high as a girl

The Heresy Within

again and pointed at Betrim.

Up the stairs and there was a window leading out the back of the shop. Betrim ripped the wooden shutters open and looked out. A ten foot drop. Good way to break a leg, he reckoned. Still, needs must. He threw his pack out the window, heard the horrifying smash of glass as it landed on his bottle of spirits, and then followed the pack out. He landed heavy on his feet and rolled to a stop. His knees protested as he stood back up but they didn't give. Betrim scooped up his pack and started running again just as a guard poked his head out of the bakery window and started shouting.

Problem was he was still being chased and that meant he needed to run, but running down a busy street was not the most inconspicuous of getaways. Add the fact that his little escape had taken him away from the docks and there was no doubt he was in trouble. Betrim decided he needed to hide, at least until most of the guards had decided he'd buggered off somewhere else.

He started away from the docks again, ducked into another alley and then out the other side. To his left lay the docks, still a fair way away and the guards still hot on his trail. To his right he could see the market square.

This time of year the market square was packed tight with folk. Those with meat and leather and ivory from the great herd, and the constant supply of fish into Korral made it a near impenetrable, seething mass of human flesh as sellers looked to make as much money from their stock as possible and buyers looked to buy as cheaply as they could manage.

Betrim wasted no time in deciding. He sprinted off towards the market and with a great deal of pushing, shoving, elbowing, and growling insinuated himself into the masses. A man could barely find his own nose in such chaos. Let the guards try to find him. Still, he didn't have too long before the boat left and Betrim had no desire to be left behind in Korral. He'd wait in the market for a time, but not too long.

There it was, *The Whipped Gull*, a small shipping vessel if truth be told. Sat low in the water with two masts and a fat wallowing hull.

Betrim could think of a hundred reasons not to get on a boat like that but none were so pressing as the reason to get on it.

He had waited in the ever moving mass of people that was the market for near thirty minutes as best he could tell. The guards had given up but he'd wanted to make sure. Now he saw where all the bastards had gone. Thirty men stood between him and the boat he was supposed to be on. Thirty armed men with dangerous intent.

The Boss was standing on the boat within sight of the guards, not goading them, just watching. That meant Henry was there too, Betrim couldn't see any of the others though. The sergeant of the guard was standing closer to the boat than the others, calling to the ship's captain but there was nothing the man could do. Without the captain's say so the guards couldn't step foot on the boat. Those were the rules of the free city of Korral.

All Betrim had to do now was make his way past all thirty men and make it onto the boat and he was free. Sounded like a hard job in his head and he had no doubt it was even harder to put into practice. So Betrim waited, watched, hoped that an opening would appear. All the while he was all too aware that he was fast running out of time.

As Betrim watched, the sailors finished loading the cargo and started preparing the ship to set sail. He was out of time. Ropes were untied, the gang plank was removed and the boat started to move backwards, fighting to gain momentum as it was pulled by a little skiff. He was out of time.

He pulled his hood over his head and started walking forwards. Still thirty guards between him and the boat, still a stretch of pier, still no way to get on board without a ramp. Still he walked.

A guardsman with a bored expression turned and saw Betrim coming. Betrim stumbled on his feet and began to sway a little as he walked, trying to look drunk. The guard just stared at him for a moment before nudging one of his companions. The other guard was not fooled, he raised a shout and thirty faces started to turn towards the Black Thorn.

Betrim broke into a pounding run. He was on the guards in moments brushing aside their spears and shouldering through a gap between two men. The sergeant was struggling to get his sword out of his scabbard and Betrim threw a bony elbow into the man's face as he passed. Still running for the end of the pier. The Boss was watching, shouting something to someone nearby. A spear thudded into the pier just beside Betrim. It was close, too close.

The boat was still moving, faster now, gaining speed, it was almost past the pier and then it was. Betrim's foot hit the final post of the wooden pier and he leapt. For a brief and terrifying moment he was in the air with only the murky green waters of Korral bay below him. Then he hit the side of the boat, rough wood slapping him full in the body. And he was falling. His fingers managed to find purchase, the barest lip to hold onto. His feet swung below him, unable to find anything to stand on along the rounded hull of the ship.

Another spear flew at him and splashed into the water. Betrim clung on for all he was worth but he could feel his fingers slipping. Something big gripped around his right wrist like iron and started pulling. A moment later and something grabbed his left wrist and Betrim found himself rising.

First the deck, then the railing passed before Betrim's eyes and then the straining, red face of Bones as he lifted. Then Betrim was over the railing and falling forwards. He found himself lying on top of Bones and rolled off to the side breathing heavy and shaking despite himself. The Black Thorn may never admit fear to others but he'd admit it to himself and he was sweating terror through every pore of his body.

The Boss appeared over him and offered Betrim a hand. Bones was standing close by breathing heavy and grinning from ear to ear. Swift was perched on the railing with his trousers down showing his arse to Korral and Henry was there with a wolfish grin and the devil glinting in her eyes.

"Good of ya ta make it, Black Thorn," the Boss said as he slapped Betrim on the shoulder.

Betrim just nodded and looked to Bones. The big man was still grinning. Betrim had no idea a man could be that strong. "Thanks," he said in a heavy voice.

"Ya looked like ya needed a hand," Bones shot back between breaths.

The most worrying thing was they all looked happy to see him. All except Green. The boy stood at the edge of the group of sell-swords staring at Betrim with dark, murderous eyes.

The Blademaster

Jezzet arrived in the free city of Chade just short of two weeks after the battle at Eirik's fort. The trip over the mountain pass took her a little longer than she'd hoped and she'd almost walked straight into a camp of dirty, rotten-toothed bandits. Though she couldn't say she had looked or smelled any better than them at that point, she gave them a wide birth all the same. She did have to kill one of their scouts who was patrolling during the night but Jezzet knew many ways to kill a man silently, especially if you could get up behind them with a nice long knife. After that she'd scrambled down the mountain pass at double speed with the fear of an angry group of bandits riding on her heels.

The trip across the plains had taken longer as well. Jez decided to head first for the coast and follow it along until she reached the free city. She wagered there would be more food closer to the coast, never a shortage of giant land crabs the size of a dog, on the beaches in the Wilds. They weren't the easiest of things to catch with eyes that swivelled on stalks to watch you and pincers as big as a hand that could crush bone, and not to mention the rock hard armour they all possessed but Jezzet had long ago been taught the secret to killing them. It was as simple as flipping them onto their backs and stabbing them in their softer underbellies.

So with giant crabs and plenty of driftwood Jezzet didn't go hungry. The smoke from the fires was a small danger but she kept her fires to night time when the darkness would hide the smoke. The danger of starving to death seemed a lot more pressing than attracting the wrong kind of attention with a fire.

Jez even risked stripping off and bathing in the sea. It was a terrifying ordeal. Standing in the water with sea coming up to her breasts and the vastness of it stretching out before her endlessly blue, endlessly unknown. Anything could have been under those waters. Jezzet had heard stories of giant fish, with teeth as big as a hand that could bite even an armoured man clean in two. Other stories of huge jelly-like creatures with hooked tentacles that would drag a person down into the depths scared her even more.

So, with those stories in mind, Jez had washed herself, staying in the water just long enough to wash the blood and sweat and shit off her skin and out of her hair before wading, in something close to a panic, back to shore, checking over her shoulder for sea monsters all the while with her heart pounding loud in her ears.

When Jezzet reached Chade she looked almost as bad as when she had left Eirik's fort. Her skin was dirty and darkened by exposure to the sun, her hair was lank with sweat and grease. Her clothing stank like a bog and looked little more than filthy rags and she was weary beyond belief. Jez had but one thing going for her as she walked through the gates into the free city. She was still alive.

The guards on the gate watched her through smiling eyes but they wouldn't stop her. They'd seen it all before and worse. Anyone could walk into the free city but if the guard patrols found homeless scum squatting or begging those same homeless scum had a habit of disappearing. The free cities lived on gold and trade, anyone without money was wasting space but there was always money to be made from slaves.

Chade was the first free city of the Wilds and the largest. It was the second largest city Jezzet had ever been to. The first being that giant sprawling mess that the people of the Five Kingdoms called a capital. Walls ringed the entire city and all near a hundred feet high and built of stone with more than enough guards to hold off even a determined army.

The free city was ruled by a council of four and those four were some of the most powerful and richest in all the wilds. The only way onto the council was to buy your way on and replace one of the existing members, not many would have the money for such a thing as the city's laws didn't allow blooded folk to sit.

All the free cities in the Wilds were neutral islands in a sea of warring states. They abided by their own laws and played no part in the politics of the blooded. At least that was the official statement though Jezzet had long ago learned that the rich and powerful rarely stayed neutral in anything. Never had she met a more opinionated lot than those with enough money to buy the opinions of others.

So the guards watched her with dangerous interest, people moved out of her way with wary suspicion, and even the merchants who camped by the gates hoping to sell their wares to new-comers fell silent as she trudged past. All could see Jez had no money and all guessed she would be locked up in irons with a metal collar by the end of the day.

There were plenty of jobs Jez wouldn't do of course. She wouldn't rob folk for one and she would like to stay clear of whoring too. Jezzet Vel'urn still had a friend or two in the Wilds and one such friend happened to own an inn in Chade and happened to be fixer. He'd have a job or two lined up that Jez could join. The good-folk of Chade always needed sell-swords.

Guards lined the streets everywhere. Brutish looking men for the most part with metal cuirasses over red doublets and swords by their sides and clubs in their hands. Crime was done in secret in Chade because if you were caught you'd wake up a slave and, if you were a man, a eunuch. There were a few women guards but they were as mean looking as the men and no more sympathetic. People grew up hard and fast in the Wilds.

There were thieving gangs in Chade though. Jezzet could spot them a mile away. Groups of folk standing around with thinly-veiled purposes sharing slight nods and glances, trying to decide who best to pickpocket or pull down an alley and rob. One and all they ignored Jez and she was all the more glad for it.

By the time she reached her destination the sun was starting to dip and her feet felt as if they were starting to drop off. She'd been walking for weeks. Her boots were holy and reduced to leather held together by string and hope, and the blisters on her feet had developed blisters of their own. Still she stopped outside and watched the inn for a time. An old friend had long ago taught her to be cautious. He'd stop outside everywhere he went and watch for hours, making sure there wasn't anyone he knew inside. Jezzet didn't quite have his patience so she waited for all of twenty minutes, leaning against a wall and watching.

Twenty minutes and no one she knew, not that that was surprising, most of the people she knew were already dead.

Except my good old friend Constance. What a lovely surprise that would be to find her waiting for me. Might be she'd buy me a drink before killing me.

Jez pushed the thought aside and strode with feigned confidence towards the door to the inn. She noticed the name had changed just as she pushed her way through the door into the waiting warmth on the other side.

The inn used to be called *The Two Bronze Bits* but had undergone a name change and the sign outside now read *The Serpent's Tooth*. Safe to say Jez had a bad feeling about the whole situation but it was just an inn, if her friend wasn't there she'd just go looking for work elsewhere.

Inside, the common room wasn't much changed. It was as large as it had ever been though a little less populated. A group of five sailors sat over by the hearth laughing and clashing their tankards at every jest. Two men sat alone, one looked drunk with red cheeks and a red nose, and the other wore a hood covering his face and sat in shadows. Four guards populated the table farthest from the entrance, they gave Jez a quick glance as she entered then went back to ignoring everyone as the biggest of them told some story about how he'd fought three men at once in unarmed combat and beaten them all. A huge tooth adorned the wall above the fire place, easily half as big as Jez and had vicious-looking serrated edges.

Explains the name change anyway. That is a big fucking tooth. Jez thought and then found herself trying to imagine the beast it had belonged to.

She picked the table farthest from the rest of the occupants and sat down. There she waited for the owner to appear whilst wearing a dark, brooding expression she hoped would keep people away.

A plump serving maid with a huge cleavage and a soft face sauntered over with a smile. Her face curdled and her nose wrinkled when she got closer though.

Enjoying the smell?

"What can I get ya?" the woman asked, looking down at Jez over her huge tits. "Coin up front."

Jezzet fixed the girl with a mean stare. "You can get me the owner."

If the huge tits were cowed by Jez's stare they didn't show it. "He don't take payment in kind."

Bitch!

"No I don't suppose he needs to with you around," Jezzet said in a voice like ice. "Bet you give him all the kind he needs. Bends you over a table every night and pays you right up your arse." That shut the serving girl up, she went a bright red and her eyes dropped to the floor.

Close to home, Jez. She thought and allowed herself a victory smile.

"Now go fetch your master and tell him Jezzet Vel'urn is here." The serving girl spun and hurried across the room and up the stairs. Only then did she realise that if Harod didn't still own the place her name would mean less than mud to whomever was putting it up the serving girl's ample arse.

Luck was with her this time, it seemed, and a few minutes later Harod swaggered down the stairs and took a moment to look around. His bright blue eyes underneath his heavy brow rested on Jezzet and he walked towards her. Harod had always been a big man but in the past year since Jez had seen him last he'd become a fat man. He'd grown a double chin and he had the swinging walk of a man who doesn't realise his own weight. His pale-blonde hair, once long, had been cropped short but it was without a doubt him. He stopped by the table and squinted at Jez.

"By Volmar's balls it is you," he boomed. "Jezzet Vel'urn. As I live and breathe never thought to see you again. You reduced my girl to tears ya know."

"I bet you've reduced her to tears a couple of times yourself, you old bastard," Jezzet replied in a much quieter voice.

"Aye well, ya know how it is. She serves a couple of purposes." Harod grinned and Jezzet smiled back. Usually when she smiled people said she looked beautiful, she was sure that currently she looked a little crazed instead.

"Don't mean to be rude, Harod, but I'm parched."

"Aye well I don't mean to be rude, girl, but you smell like shit."

"An unfortunate consequence of crawling through a sewer."

Harod opened his mouth to reply and then laughed. "Reckon

you've got a tale to tell me."

"Reckon it'll tell easier with a drink in hand," Jez prompted again.

Harod shook his head at her. "Taking advantage of my kind nature as always, Jez. I'll get us a beer and you can tell me what the hell happened to ya. How's your sword?"

"A little dull and ready to be swung at something."

"Give it here, I'll get James to sharpen it while we talk an' then I'll set about finding something for you to do."

"Good man," Jez said with a grin and laid her sword across the table.

Harod scooped up the blade and waddled off into the back, returning a few minutes later carrying two mugs of beer. He lowered himself into the chair opposite Jez and waited while she near drained her mug.

By the Gods I could do with a few more of these. Feels like years since I was last roaring drunk.

So Jezzet started telling Harod her story. Not just about Eirik and Constance but about the rest of the past year. It felt good to talk to someone about it and Harod had always been a good listener, offering agreeing comments here and there. His serving girl reappeared at some point and by the time Jez had finished she had drained three mugs of the dark brown beer and was feeling well on her way to being merry, if not drunk.

Harod stood, showing none of the signs of being even a little tipsy, and nodded. "Well, Jez, I'll put you up for the night, get you cleaned up and tomorrow set about finding you some work so you can pay me for the room and the beer."

Nothing ever comes for free.

"You're a true friend, Harod," Jez said and went back to her beer as he swaggered away.

A warm bed and enough beer for a good night. Things are looking up.

"Jezzet Vel'urn?"

Someone knew her name and that was never a good thing. Jez craned her head around to look behind her. The four guards who been sat around were now all standing right there. The biggest of the four, the one who had been bragging to the others, had a hand on the little wooden club that hung by his belt.

"Reckon you got the wrong girl," Jez said with a smile. "Good luck to you though."

The big guard looked confused. Then his gaze shifted to stare at something across the room. "You sure this is her?"

Jez followed the big man's stare and it led straight to Harod. The fat inn keep was standing about as far away from Jez as he could with his arms crossed over his huge belly and a wary look on his face. He nodded once towards the guard but said nothing.

A hundred insults flooded through Jezzet's head and she settled with. "Bastard."

"No need for a fight," the big guard said. "Come quietly."

Four on one. Bad odds, Jez. Don't reckon I can fuck my way out of this one. Her hand reached for her sword and then she realised it wasn't there. She had trusted Harod, had given the fat fuck her sword.

The big guard saw Jezzet's hand go for an absent weapon and he started forwards. Jez kicked a chair towards him and he raised his hands to block the flying kindling. Jez rushed him and planted a kick to his knee. The big man went down with a cry but another guard, this one smaller and with a giant hook of a nose, was already on her with his little wooden club drawn.

If only I can get one of their swords.

The guard swung his club and Jez ducked the attack and stepped towards the guard, bringing a knee up into his groin. She should have felt flesh, should have sent the guard down with a groan. Instead her knee hit something hard and painful and she was the one who cried out in pain. She reached for the man's sword but his hand was already there.

Someone grabbed hold of Jez from behind and then she was off her feet, flying through the air, the inn spinning around her. She hit something back first and it collapsed underneath her. A wooden table. Broke her fall for the most part. Jez lurched to her feet and the world spun a little.

Shouldn't have drunk so much. Shouldn't have trusted that bastard,

Harod.

The big guard was coming at her again fast. He swung his club and Jezzet dodged to the side aiming a fist at his face as she did. It connected and Jez felt the satisfying crunch of a nose breaking followed by a spray of blood. She grinned.

Took three men in unarmed combat did you...

A sharp pain in the back of the head and the world went bright white. Jez had no idea where she was. Something hit her in the face, in the chest, in her entire body. The floor maybe, it was getting hard to tell. Then everything went black.

Part 2 – Secrets and Lies

The Arbiter

Chade, the largest and richest city in the Untamed Wilds. A free city abiding by its own rules and its own laws, subject only to the rule of its council and unaffiliated with any of the great kingdoms. The Inquisition had no authority in any of the free cities and Chade was no exception. Thanquil was here by the ruling council's leave to interrogate a prisoner but he was under no illusions. He would not be welcomed.

Even from a long way off Thanquil could see it was a large city, maybe even as large as Sarth, and busy. Ships and boats and vessels of a hundred different makes and origins crowded around the harbour like flees on a dog. More masts than Thanquil cared to count rose reaching into the sky, some great, some small and all bobbing up and down on the gentle waters of Rainbow Bay. Cas stopped by the railing to inform Thanquil that during the busy times, such as when the great herd was nearby, Chade could get so busy that ships had to wait for a dock to free up and sometimes the wait could extend to days. Thanquil decided he was more than thankful that the great herd was no-where near Chade at this time of year. The sooner he was back on dry land the better.

"Almost there now. Safe an' sound as promised. No pirates or sea serpents," the Captain said as he stopped by Thanquil's spot on the railing. He'd spent a lot of time leaning on that particular spot of railing during the voyage and the crew had started calling it the *Arbiter's rest*. There wasn't a single hand on *the Sea's Scorn* who hadn't come to talk to the Arbiter at one time or another. The sailors appeared to have made a daring game of it, who could talk to the witch hunter for the longest. Last thing Thanquil had wanted was company but he got it anyway.

"Wouldn't have minded seeing a sea serpent," Thanquil replied to the Captain, "just to prove you wrong."

The Captain laughed and pounded Thanquil once on the back. They had spent a fair amount of time chatting to each other over the three weeks and Thanquil had to admit he quite liked the old seaman. He was too friendly at times and had a habit of slapping people on the arms or back, but he was gruff and honest and spoke his mind and he enjoyed rolled up casher weed.

"You tell Vance my debt is paid next time ya see him, aye?" the Captain said.

"Inquisitor Vance."

"That's the one, the older one. Though the younger one's near as bad."

"Truth is I'd rather not see either of them ever again," Thanquil said with a grin. "I'll make sure to tell him I arrived quickly and without harm."

"Aye, good," the Captain said and then strode away to shout at some poor member of the crew. Thanquil had to wonder what manner of debt the Captain might owe to a man like Inquisitor Vance. He tried to imagine the Grand Inquisitor standing on this very ship, maybe leaning where Thanquil was now, tried to imagine the sailors coming and speaking to him. It was no good. If rumours were true even the other Inquisitors were afraid of Artur Vance.

As the ship floated into the dock Thanquil could see just how busy the port was. Sailors were everywhere, some working, some waiting, some collecting wages, and some wandering off in groups no doubt headed for the nearest brothel. Nothing like spending weeks cooped up on a ship with only other men for company to make you long for a bed with a young woman warming the sheets. Though Thanquil had heard it said that some whore houses in the Wilds didn't even bother with beds, the women just serviced the men in the common room, rutting like animals.

There were barrels and crates, bags and passengers, slaves and freight all being unloaded in a steady stream. Thanquil could already see some crates were full of food stuffs, some silks and other cloth, some weapons of any and all description.

Many captains were paid to bring in goods to specific merchants. Others just loaded their holds with whatever they could or whatever was cheapest, and would sell it there and then on the docks. Merchants gathered around to inspect the cargo and offer a price and demand a quantity. The captains haggled as the crew unloaded the goods and deals were struck. The merchants' men then surged forwards to take the crates into the city. All the while the proceedings were watched over by the city guard and both observed and taxed by the greedy little dock masters. The funny thing about the free cities was that nothing was ever free.

It didn't take long for Thanquil to depart once the ship had docked. The Captain was the first down the plank and was haggling with the dock master before even setting foot on the pier. After the Captain signalled the haggling was done the deckhands started unloading the cargo. Thanquil chose a time when the way was clear and hopped down from the ship. He heard Cas whistle a goodbye but ignored the boy and strode away into the free city of Chade.

Within moments of stepping off the pier Thanquil found himself surrounded by people. Some offered him services, some offered him goods, and a few offered him themselves. They pressed in close around him and there seemed to be a constant stream of them. Whenever Thanquil pushed through the crowd and left one behind another person would appear in front. To make matters worse he could feel his hand shaking in his pocket. It had been three weeks since he'd last stolen anything and now, in a new and foreign place, the need to take something that didn't belong to him was overpowering.

In the press and the noise of the crowd Thanquil felt a hand brush against the inside of his coat, a light touch and brief. Another man might have ignored it, but Thanquil knew the touch of a thief better than another man. His hand shot out and grabbed the wrist that had hold of his purse and he twisted.

There was a high squeak as the girl on the other end of the wrist collapsed on the floor, her arm twisted at a dangerous angle. One slight jerk and he could snap the wrist like a twig. The press of the crowd backed away from him, a couple of the members slinking off, disappearing into the masses.

"What's the problem here?" a loud and commanding voice called from nearby. A guard by the looks of things with a hefty crew around him.

Thanquil plucked the purse from the girl's hand and pocketed it again as the rest of the crowd dispersed and was replaced by guardsmen in red doublets with metal breastplates and wooden cudgels. He let go of the girl's wrist and she shot him a terrified look. She was young, maybe twelve at most, and wearing rich clothing though more in the style of a boy. In the Five Kingdoms or Acanthia, Thanquil might have taken her for a noble brat but here in Chade he knew there was no real nobility, just well-dressed thieves.

"Caught her stealing did ya?" the guard asked, a wicked grin on his face.

"I wonder what would happen to a thief here in Chade," Thanquil mused aloud and waited for one of the guards to answer.

"Same as anywhere. Punishment."

"Thieves is turned into slaves," the young girl blurted out, her eyes lowered.

"Quiet!" the guard warned the girl. "The nice man weren't talking ta the likes of you."

Thanquil almost groaned. He'd only just set foot off the boat and already he was condemning a girl to a lifetime of slavery. No doubt the story would spread and before long it would tell of an Arbiter sentencing a young, innocent lass just a few feet from the boat he arrived on.

"A girl like you no doubt knows the way to the Inquisition safe house," Thanquil said. "Somewhere near the craftsman terrace, near the guildhall."

"Aye," she answered in high voice, her words rushing out almost on top of each other. "I know the place. I can get ya there."

"Well then," Thanquil said with false cheer. "I'm sorry but there's been a mistake here. She wasn't thieving. Just offering her services as a guide to your wonderful city. As new as I am here I'm tempted to take her up on the offer. Thank you for your time."

The guard looked at the girl, then at Thanquil. His right hand plucked the cudgel from his belt. "Listen, friend. That's not how things work here. We seen her thieving."

Thanquil was uncomfortably aware that a large group of people had stopped to watch the scene in the middle of the docks. The girl also looked uncomfortable, though that might have been because her life was hanging in the balance. The prospect of a lifetime of slavery would make Thanquil more than a little uncomfortable.

"Arbiter," Thanquil corrected the guardsman. "My correct title is Arbiter. The coat is a dead give-away. See the buttons."

"Don't mean a thing. You can be the damned Emperor as far as I care. Got no power here," the guard said, taking a small step backwards.

Thanquil stepped forwards closing on the guard, the girl stayed close by. "Oh I have power wherever I am, believe me. As for authority, I have that too. The ruling council in Chade has granted an emissary of the Inquisition temporary authority within this free city and I just happen to be that emissary."

"He's right," said one of the other guardsmen. "Council did send fer an Arbiter. Fer her in gaol."

"We'll be going now," Thanquil told the guards, dismissing them. "Lead the way, girl."

"Aye," she squeaked and started walking, the guards moved aside to let them pass and Thanquil followed, hoping he wasn't about to feel a sharp, wooden smack to the back of his head. Seems he was in luck. With a loud grumble the guards moved back to their posts and the usual activity of the docks resumed. Noise and merchants rushed in to fill the empty space like a thunderclap.

Thanquil breathed out a sigh of relief. The girl kept glancing at him, probably wondering if she could get away with bolting. He had already decided he wasn't going to waste time chasing her.

"You really an Arbter?" she asked.

"Yes."

"Don't look like much."

Thanquil shrugged. "Neither do you. Guards were keen on taking you in though."

The girl spat into the street. "Guards get paid for every slave they take. Keeps 'em willin' ta do their jobs. They get extra fer young girls. I had a friend once who got took, she..."

"You best be leading me the right way, girl," Thanquil interrupted. He'd heard more than enough *old friend* stories on the boat, though most of those had ended in drowning, stabbing, or being eaten by krakens. One had even ended with an entire ship, complete with all hands, being dragged down to the depths by a leviathan. The idea of witnesses seemed to escape the sailor who told that particular story.

"Course I am. I ain't no..."

"I'll give you a bronze coin if you can tell me anything about that woman they have in gaol."

"You got more 'an bronze bits in that purse, I felt it."

Thanquil didn't respond. He wasn't about to haggle with a girl who had just tried to rob him. Not after he'd just saved her from a fate worse than death.

"Word is she's dangerous. Guards caught her a while back. She killed four 'em, one with her bare hands. Ben said he saw her, said she had fire in her eyes an' burnt a guard alive jus' by lookin' at him. Crazed is what they call her, fights with swords, claws, an' teeth an' the only reason they got her is 'cos she was drunk. Now they got her chained an' gagged down in gaol waitin' fer someone who knows about that sort of stuff. Which'ed be you right?"

Again Thanquil said nothing. The girl was watching him out of the corner of her eye, waiting for him to confirm. No doubt word of an Arbiter's arrival would spread through the city like wildfire soon enough. Information was, as ever, worth its weight in gold.

"Gimme my bronze bit."

Thanquil reached into one of the many pockets of his coat and pulled out a small bronze coin. He twirled it in his fingers and the girl watched it with greedy eyes. "You get the coin when I get where I'm going, girl."

Chade was not a small city and was split into four different quarters. The docks, the craftsman's terrace, Goldtown, and Oldtown. The girl explained to Thanquil that on foot it could take near half a day to walk from one side to the other. Thanquil decided he was thankful the craftsman terrace was not all that far from the docks.

They passed all manner of shops, workhouses, warehouses, dwellings, inns, and watchtowers. Guards were everywhere in abundance and all watched with a hungry eye. The girl claimed the city employed thousands of guards and Thanquil could well believe it. Slaves were in even greater abundance. Some were beaten, some were chained and all were collared and marked. The men had their owners brand seared into their left cheek while the women had it on their left hand.

Thanquil wasn't unaccustomed to seeing slaves, Sarth was built on the backs of those whose lives were owned by others, but he'd never seen folk treated so poorly before. They were dressed in rags and many went barefoot. Some were made to carry goods for their owners, some were carrying the owners themselves in huge ornate litters and all in the merciless afternoon sun. It struck Thanquil that most horses were treated better than the slaves here in Chade.

The girl didn't lie about knowing the way, she led Thanquil to his destination. The house was indeed in the craftsman's terrace and not twenty paces from the guildhall where all manner of folk were gathered in the hope of finding a day's work.

The house bore the symbol of an Inquisition safe-house and so Thanquil tossed the girl her bronze coin and she was gone before he could even say his thanks. He climbed the steps with a sigh and knocked and waited. It was a small, unassuming house built of stone but then most in the craftsman's terrace seemed to be. It had a heavy wooden door and two windows that looked to be boarded from the inside. Thanquil knocked again and again waited. Still no answer.

"You one o' them Arbiters?" A voice came from behind. Thanquil turned to find a cloaked figure staring up at him with wary eyes. The man coughed into a bandaged hand.

"I'm wearing an Arbiter's coat," Thanquil replied.

"Bit o' fancy leather don't make you nothin'. You want in there ya need ta prove ya an Arbiter."

Thanquil ground his teeth together. He hated asking questions. "And who should I prove it to?"

"Me," the man at the bottom of the steps said. Then he shivered and nodded at Thanquil. "It's been a while since I felt the compulsion. It's still just as unpleasant as ever. Sorry about the test, Arbiter. We've had people pretend to be members of the Inquisition in the past." He stood up to his full height and threw back his cloak to reveal a suit of dark red beneath.

"I am Arbiter Thanquil Darkheart. You would be the clerk assigned to Chade."

"Yes, Arbiter," the man said, his Wilds accent replaced by born and bred Sarth. He climbed the steps and put a key to the lock. "Clerk Moin. Anything you need don't hesitate to ask."

Inside, the building was well maintained but austere. It would serve its purpose, a place for Thanquil to sleep for a night.

"I will need food and a bed for the night, Clerk Moin. Tomorrow you will direct me to the council chambers, after that I will find myself an inn to sleep in for the remainder of my stay. I will return here only if I need more coin."

"As you wish, Arbiter Darkheart. Oh and welcome to Chade."

THE BLACK THORN

"Welcome to Chade."

Weren't the first time Betrim had been the Chade and fact was he was no more impressed with it this time than the last. He shoved aside the little merchant who had welcomed him and looked around. Too hot, too many guards, too many merchants, too much salt in the air, too damned busy.

"Never been ta Chade 'fore," Green said, staring in open mouthed wonder at the spectacle.

"We figured that from the first hundred times ya said so," Bones grumbled with a sigh.

Betrim had thought that two days cooped up in a building with the crew was bad, two weeks stuck on a boat with them had been far worse. Bones had somehow managed to befriend a legion of rats that had swarmed around him squeaking for food. Henry and the Boss had been going at it hammer and tongs for what seemed like the entire journey and, seeing as how the entire crew was stuck in one cabin, there was fuck all in the way of privacy. Green had spent the whole journey staring daggers at Betrim when he thought the Black Thorn wasn't watching. The boy couldn't have known that Betrim had eyes in the back of his head. Swift had been the only bearable member and that was because he spent the majority of the time absent. He had somehow managed to get his way into the beds of all four of the ship's female crew including the Captain's wife. Betrim reckon it was a miracle Swift hadn't gotten them all thrown overboard.

The Boss finished talking to the Captain, jumped down onto the wood of the pier, shouldered his way through his crew and then turned to face them all.

"Here it is. I know you all been holed up an' patient but ain't no enjoyin' the city's sights jus' yet. Bones, take Green an' find us a place ta stay. Somewhere quiet an' close ta one of the gates would be good."

"We gonna be needin' ta make a quick exit, Boss?" Bones asked in his deep tones.

"Always a possibility. Swift, go put ya ear ta the ground. I wanna know anythin' an' everythin' that's happenin' in Chade."

"Would be easier with a few bits ta grease a palm or two, Boss."

"When are things ever easy? Henry, take Thorn an' get us some supplies. We ain't got much left so use what bits ya got sparse. I gotta go meet a man 'bout a job. Ya all know *the Sailor's Penny*?"

"Aye."

"Yes, Boss."

"Mhm."

"No."

"Good. Be there at sundown."

With that the crew split up into their groups. Betrim found Henry grinning up at him. "What?" he asked giving her a push hard enough to make her stumble.

"Ya red is showin'."

Betrim ran a dirty hand through his greasy mess of hair. She was right. He hadn't dyed his hair in near a month. "Reckon we best find me some Eccan nuts then."

She shook her head, still grinning in that wolfish way, pretty teeth showing behind her scarred lips. "Boss said sparse." She started walking. "Red Thorn's got a bit of a ring ta it though."

Chade always brought back memories and not many of them the good kind. After killing his second Arbiter, Betrim stowed away on a boat and ended up in the free city. Back then he'd been nothing but a nameless boy still wet behind the ears and with only a handful of kills to his count. Off the boat for all of five minutes and guards tried to take him. Betrim stabbed one in the groin and fled. After that he spent near a year working on a heavy crew, guarding some merchant's warehouses. He was the youngest and greenest of the crew and two of the bigger lads seemed to take it personal. More than once he'd been beaten and robbed after getting paid and more than once he'd gone hungry because of it. Then one day both lads had woken up with their throats cut. That had earned Betrim some respect among that crew.

There was an Arbiter in Chade too. Betrim's fifth. Never knew the name, couldn't even remember the face but he remembered the kill. He stalked the man for two days, watching and waiting. Then, in the market, Betrim had walked up behind the Arbiter and shoved a long curved knife up under his rib cage into his chest. Left the knife in his back and walked away before anyone knew something was up. Cleanest Arbiter kill he'd ever done that one, certainly better than burning down an entire town.

"You alright?" Henry asked. She was staring at him. "Ya got a look about ya."

"Rememberin' is all. Been stabbed twice here in Chade."

"I know," she replied with a grin.

"First one was a boy 'bout same age as Green. Trying ta make a name fer himself, I reckon. Missed my vitals though, the dumb fuck, so I took his head off."

"I never miss."

"You did. Got the scar ta prove it."

Henry grinned at him again. "I never miss."

Betrim snorted. The market was just ahead, he could see it already. It was as close to one of the many Hells as he remembered. Full of people, full of smells, full of noise, full of dangers. People died all the time in the markets of Chade. Some during fights over prices or some such, some over thieving, some just tripped and got trampled though they were mostly the little ones; children or women or such.

A hundred different spices or more filled the air with their fragrance, coming together to form something close to a cloying stench. The noise was deafening, people shouting this way or that, selling, buying, accusing, it made no difference. The crowds packed in on all sides, a mass of human flesh being ground together. That was the problem with the market, or with markets in general as far as Betrim was concerned. You couldn't smell anyone coming, couldn't hear them coming, couldn't see them coming. Dangerous places were markets.

"So what're we doin' here?" he asked Henry over the clamour.

"Like Boss said, supplies."

"Food?"

Henry laughed. "You want food ask Bones ta gather ya up some rats."

Betrim nodded to that. "Meat is meat."

"We need supplies fer a job. Whatever this big one is Boss got lined up we don't have the bits ta pull it off as of now. He'll rustle us up somethin' small first, somethin' as will pay our way. Keep us supplied, keep you an' Swift in whores 'till we done."

"Ya could jus' open ya legs fer him, save some bits," Betrim said with a grin of his own, it was not returned.

"I'd rather fuck Green than that half-blood bastard."

Henry knew what they needed and knew where to go so Betrim was happy to just follow. After the first merchant it was clear why the Boss had sent them both. Henry was well known in Chade and the Black Thorn was well known everywhere and both were the type of names that commanded a healthy dose of fear. Merchants were less inclined to haggle up when the customer had a habit of killing folk for fun. Not that Betrim had ever really killed for fun but a long time ago he'd decided never to argue against his own reputation.

So it was that by sun down they had procured everything on Henry's list and for a fair deal less than they were worth. Betrim had even managed to make a merchant throw in a handful of Eccan nuts to dye his hair. The paste he'd make from them would smell like shit for a few days but it was better than having a head full of flaming, red locks as far as he was concerned.

The Boss was late and when he did arrive his scowl was even deeper than usual. "Ya find us a place, Bones."

"Aye, jus' round corner in Oldtown. One previous tenant, long since dead an' rotting. Got rid o' the corpse but Green threw up."

"Fuck, Bones. Ya said ya wouldn't say owt."

"Aye, I did say that."

"Enough," the Boss' tone was terse and dangerous. "Lead the way."

Bones wasn't wrong about their new home, had a smell to it that said *dead person* but it was nothing they hadn't all lived with before. It was a single-floored wooden shack with a secure roof and two bedrooms complete with beds. Luxury living as far as they were all concerned.

"What've ya got fer us, Swift," the Boss asked when they had all settled down.

"Lots of bad an' good. There's an Arbiter in town."

All eyes turned to Betrim, he said nothing, just continued grinding the Eccan nuts to powder.

"Might not be after you, Thorn," the Boss said.

"Will be once they find out I'm here. Best we get the job done an' get out while we can." He'd run to the Wilds to get away from the Arbiters. Seemed they were everywhere these days.

"Well good news is our escapades in Korral stayed in Korral," Swift continued. "No prices on any of us. The blooded are at war again but shouldn't make much difference here in Chade. Oh, and Bones' wife is in town."

Bones' head snapped up in an instant and Betrim saw that panicked look in his eye that Bones only got when Beth was nearby. "Any chance we can head back ta Korral, Boss?"

"I got us a job," the Boss said but even Betrim could tell he didn't seem too happy about it.

"That's why we're here ain't it?" Swift asked.

"Not the big one, gonna need some bits 'fore we can do that. Another job, a few of 'em as it happens." He paused and, for the first time since they'd met, Betrim could see the Boss was nervous. "It's working fer Deadeye."

"Boss..." Bones started.

"That ain't a good idea," Swift finished.

Betrim kept quiet and Henry did the same but she didn't look happy. Deadeye was possibly the only name in the Wilds carried more weight than Betrim's. Even Green was silent.

"She here? In Chade," Betrim asked.

"Not yet but she will be."

"Deadeye don't go nowhere without an army," Henry put in.

"Armies ain't allowed in Chade," Swift responded.

"Not all of it, no, but she'll get some of it in."

"None of us ever crossed her, have we?" Bones asked. All eyes turned to Betrim.

"I ain't. Only met her the once an' that was 'fore the whole eye thing."

"Way I hear it, not having crossed her never stopped her from killin' folk," Swift said.

"Enough." The Boss' voice was quiet but full of threat, enough threat to silence four of the biggest names in the Wilds. "I've already taken the job. It'll get us the bits an' it'll get us where we need ta be. Good."

The silence held for a while as each of them came to terms with the idea of working for Deadeye. Green was the one to break the quiet. "What's the job?"

The Boss glared at the boy. "Deadeye wants someone breakin' out o' gaol."

The Arbiter

"Arbiter Thanquil Darkheart."

Thanquil was tired of people saying his name. It should have been a heady pleasure, after all his name was said in some powerful circles these days, but he was learning the more your name was said in powerful circles the more those powerful circles wanted from him.

He ignored the announcer and strode into the audience chamber with his head held high and a crystal wine stopper in his pocket. No one would miss it for a while and they'd never suspect an Arbiter to have stolen it anyway. Besides, red wine was supposed to breathe.

The audience chamber was a long room with gaudy decorations in abundance. Blood red carpets, white silk curtains on the windows, two hearths both resplendent in their ornate golden scroll-work and both oversized, one to Thanquil's far right and the other to his far left. In front of Thanquil was a desk, a huge wooden monstrosity stacked with papers, charts, trinkets, and coins and behind the desk sat four men.

The announcer stepped up beside Thanquil and spoke again. "Lord Farin Colth." The man on the far left nodded once, setting his multiple chins wobbling. Rarely had Thanquil ever seen a man as fat as Lord Farin. He wore a rich, silk suit of blue on gold with decorative sweat stains. Golden jewellery adorned his hands and wrists and he wore a single silver bell in each ear. Thanquil knew if he could just get to shake the man's hand he could take one of the golden rings.

"Lord Xho." The man next to Lord Farin couldn't have been more different. Black skin instead of white, gaunt instead of fat, and hard instead of soft. The man wore a simple brown tunic and his only jewellery was a wooden bar through the top of his nose. He looked at Thanquil with small, dark eyes. Once, such a stare might have cowed Thanquil but after meeting with the Grand Inquisitor, Lord Xho seemed about as terrifying as a puppy.

"Alfer To'an." Tall and plump with girlish features. Thanquil would have bet all the contents of his pockets the man was a eunuch. He wore a decadent, blue robe with black lace-work and a silver ring on each finger.

He smiled towards Thanquil in a way that reminded the Arbiter of a cat smiling at a mouse.

"And speaking for Captain Drake Morrass, Belper Froth." The man on the far right was tall, lean and looked more sailor than city ruler. He wore a white sailor's shirt and no jewellery save a single stud in his right ear. His face was well tanned and tattooed around his left eye.

The announcer bowed and stepped backwards. Thanquil looked at each of the men in turn. "So Captain Morrass sends a lackey in his place." After the words were out of his mouth Thanquil decided lackey may have been a poor choice.

The eunuch giggled and then spoke in his high, feminine voice. "Oh most assuredly. Our Drake is rarely present. No doubt out pirating, or lately I hear he's managed to wriggle his way into the Dragon Empress' bed."

"Probably both knowing him," said the fat man on the far left.

"I see," Thanquil said and then bowed his head a little. "Well, my Lords. On behalf of the Inquisition, and as per your request, I am at your service."

"Never had an Arbiter at my service before," the fat man said.

"I was hopin' for an Inquisitor myself." From the pirate on the far right.

"I assure you I am much more agreeable than any of the Inquisitors. They tend to be all doom and gloom and if one of them were here at least two of you would be on fire by now." Thanquil said with a smile. It made the powerful circle in front of him pause as they started to wonder which two.

"Not here for words, witch hunter," said Lord Xho. His eyes had not left Thanquil for a moment since entering. "You have job."

"Yes, of course. You have a woman locked up and you want me to interrogate her..."

"We want ya ta tell us how ta kill her," the pirate said in his drawl.

"Oh... right." Thanquil paused. "I presume you tried all the traditional methods, stabbing her and the like."

"We did," the pirate continued. "She came back."

"Um... she came... back..."

The Heresy Within

"Aye."

The pirate seemed to think that was explanation enough. The eunuch was more helpful. "The first time she attacked four of our guards in a tavern, killed them all. It was brutal, blood everywhere and the stench was awful, so I'm told. When our reinforcements arrived they managed to bring her down, stabbed her in the chest a number of times before she died."

"So she did die," Thanquil said.

"Oh most certainly. Stabbed right through the heart. Then we gave her body to the sea. And two days later out she walks from the sea, naked and without a scratch on her."

The collective *we*, Thanquil had no doubt the eunuch had never been near the woman. "So you killed her again..."

"'Course we did," the pirate continued the story. "She murdered a few more guards so we filled her full o' arrows only this time we locked her up in the gaol. Waited ta see if she'd come back again."

"Which she did," Thanquil finished.

"Aye. Been weeks in there an' we ain't fed her none but she don't die. S'why we sent fer you."

"So you want me to kill her..."

"No," Lord Xho spoke again his voice terse and hard. "Want you to tell us how to kill her. You are... adviser, no authority here."

"I see, but why should the Inquisition do this, I wonder. You ask us for a favour in helping you to kill her and offer nothing in return."

Lord Xho leaned forward. "Eckfor no. Alabush ke'act. Fenacciun bolast."

The eunuch sighed. "He says, '*she is a witch, you hunt witches*'. Or, at least that's a rough translation without the insults."

"He did sound fairly angry," Thanquil agreed.

"Besides, the Inquisition has already agreed. You are here to do, not to negotiate."

"Very true," Thanquil said with a slight bow of his head. "I will need some time to prepare. I will see the woman first thing in the morning and report back to you once I have a solution."

There was a slight pause as each of the men looked at the others then the fat man on the far left spoke. "That is acceptable. You are dismissed, Arbiter."

Thanquil snorted and, with a shake of his head, turned and strode from the room with all the purpose he could muster. Truth was he didn't need to prepare only he didn't feel much like confronting an immortal witch right now, the prospect of finding a tavern and drinking his way through the evening was much more tempting.

The Black Thorn

"That it?" Swift asked.

"Does look very gaol-like," replied Bones.

"Aye," Betrim said. "I've been inside a couple and that's definitely a gaol."

"You wouldn't believe some of the things I've been inside," Swift said with a grin. All three of them looked at him for a moment and then burst into laughter.

The gaol was part of the guard's barracks in Oldtown. A huge stone building of two floors and plenty of barred windows. They'd walked the entire way around it and it had taken near ten minutes. The gaol itself had its own entrance but Betrim had no doubt it was connected inside to the barracks. He'd like to say getting in was going to be the hard part but he was pretty sure the guards would arrest the Black Thorn on sight. Wouldn't be his personal choice of ways to break into a gaol though.

"So how'r we gonna do this? You ever broken someone out of lockup before, Thorn?" Swift said while chewing on some sort of leaf he'd procured from somewhere. It stank like hell, though with Betrim's hair still smelling of Eccan nut paste he couldn't really make it an issue, and turned Swift's spit blue but the bastard swore it made him more alert.

"Aye, once or twice. Easiest way is jus' ta walk in with an axe swinging an' walk out a few bodies later. Bloody work but then..." He looked around at the three lads and shrugged. All of them were well used to bloody work, except maybe Green.

Bones spat onto the ground. "Reckon they'll be a few too many bodies in there, try that way an' ours will be among 'em." It would be close inside, not much space and Betrim knew Bones liked to fight with a lot of room around him, liked to get that big sword of his swinging.

"Ya can always get locked up yaself an' then break out from the inside," Betrim continued. "Though never liked the idea of that one much."

"I dunno," Green said with a sneer. "You gettin' locked up don't sound so bad."

"Shut up, Green. Dumb fuck. Other way is sneakin' in or such. Bars make it hard but not impossible."

"I once heard some boys say they did it by tying a rope round some bars, then to a horse, then they made the horse run an' when the rope ran out it pulled the bars loose," Bones said, nodding to himself.

"We don't have a horse," Betrim pointed out.

"We could steal one."

"Might work."

Swift was shaking his head. "Sounds like a noisy plan ta me. Reckon Boss wants it done quiet. No noise and no bodies."

"When was the last time we did any job without bodies?" Betrim asked. Nobody could answer but then he never expected any of them could.

"Sneak in an' sneak out then?" Green asked.

"Looks like," Swift agreed. "First thing is we should find out where's she's kept. Get in as close as possible. Last thing we want is ta break in then find we have ta get all the way ta the other side of the gaol."

Betrim rubbed at the stumps of his middle and little fingers on his left hand. He hated planning. There was always so much to think of and always they missed something. He'd much prefer to charge in axe swinging and blood spilling, but then that was why he wasn't the boss. Betrim had never much liked the idea of running his own crew and running this particular one had to be hard work. Too many big names with their own ideas and their own problems.

Betrim remembered another crew he had been in with big names, back before he'd earned his own, back when he was just as much of a shit as Green. The boss back then had been a man called Red Tooth, though fact was all his teeth were red. They'd also had the Night Blade, Alfyn Tether on the crew. The Night Blade was one of the most famous assassins in the Wilds and one of the biggest names back then. It was said he had killed more men than the sea but none could prove any of the murders were him.

Alfyn and Betrim now they'd always gotten on just fine. Betrim had been as green as Green but he wasn't so dumb as to think he could earn his name by taking out one such as the Night Blade. Some of the other boys though didn't get on so well with Alfyn, didn't hold so well having an assassin on the crew. Something about poisoners being cowards as Betrim remembered it.

Betrim had left the crew on bad terms, seems they didn't like the idea of having someone hunted by Arbiters on the team and Betrim had just killed his third. A while later he heard the rumours in a whore house, the entire crew had been found dead, all except the Night Blade, and none could say why. No cuts, no bruises, nothing. Just dead and robbed. No one ever heard of Alfyn Tether again after that.

"They got windows right?" Green asked, bringing Betrim back to the present.

"Aye, barred though," Swift said.

"Don't stop us peekin' in, finding which cell our girl's in. Can't be that many bitches bound an' gagged in there."

They all had to stop and think about that for a moment, Swift had himself a good laugh about it too. Betrim preferred his women to be willing though, even if willing meant paid.

"Green's right fer once. Get caught in Chade an' ya more likely ta be a slave than a prisoner, 'specially if you got a cunt. Shouldn't be too hard ta find her, long as they got her in a cell with a view."

"So ya want us ta go round an' check every window?" Swift asked.

"Ya don't need to check every window," Green replied with a grin. "Jus' everyone till ya find her."

"I'm fast startin' not ta like you, lad," Swift said with a punch to Green's arm.

"Got somewhere else ta be, Swift?" Betrim said, still staring at the gaol building.

"As it happens. Plenty o' whore houses in Chade not had a visit from Swift in a long time," Swift replied, still grinning. "I hear there's a place in Keflin square that has southerners, black skinned an all. It'd be like fuckin' the Boss' daughter."

"The Boss has a daughter?" Green asked.

"Hells if I know," Swift replied. "But if he did, wouldn't it be nice ta bend her over an' shove it up her arse so hard she screams?"

"The whores can wait," Betrim interrupted as he found a good-looking spot of wall in the alley and took to leaning. Swift could be an annoying prick when he tried. "Plenty of guards about an' some of 'em patrolling. Could make things tricky. We take out one of the patrols, quiet, that'll give us some time 'fore they missed. How hard do ya reckon it is ta get those bars out?"

"'Bout as hard as it would be ta take the whole wall out," Bones replied. "Which I reckon is pretty bloody hard."

They were all silent for a while. Betrim leaning, Bones sitting, Swift whistling, and Green pacing. Why the Boss sent them all for planning instead of doing it himself Betrim couldn't figure. Seemed to him they were getting close to nowhere.

"Chutes," Green said, pointing. "Old buildings like this have these chutes. See, on the ground, holes leadin' into the underground fer droppin' food an' stuff."

Betrim peered towards the building. Seemed Green was right but there was a problem. "Looks like they're barred too."

Swift had a smug look plastered all over his smug face. "Not barred. Grated an' locked. Ain't a lock made I can't pick."

"Looks a smallish gap," Bones rumbled.

"Aye," Betrim agreed. "Henry an' Swift'll fit no problem. Green too most like, maybe me. You an' the Boss ain't got a chance."

"Looks like I'll be takin' guard duty then."

"Aye, looks like," Betrim agreed. "Good?"

"Good."

They all watched from the shadows of the alley for a while longer. They'd all done similar jobs before, breaking into places and stealing stuff, or killing folk all quiet in the night; all except Green anyway. First rule is always *don't get caught* and the best way to go about that was to know where the guards would be and when.

Two patrols circled the big stone building and each one was two men strong. Wasn't much to guard given that most of the prisoners were transferred to the slavers guild soon as getting caught. Each patrol took near fifteen minutes to circle the place so if they took out a single patrol they should have... numbers never did make sense to Betrim but he reckoned they should have about thirty minutes to get in, find the bitch, free her and get out.

As far as Betrim could see it should go nice and smooth. Of course there was always the possibility of getting lost inside the building, running into more guards than expected, or even Swift not being able to pick the locks like he claimed. Always so much that could go wrong and that was why Betrim hated the planning. Again he considered the option of charging in, axe in hand and again he decided the most likely outcome of such would be certain death. Gaol breaks were never easy.

"Right then," Swift said. "I'll check the windows, Bones'll be my ladder an' Green can stand watch. Thorn, go get the Boss told of the plan."

"Wait," Betrim said. He saw something, something he hoped he was wrong about. Just a short distance away, being escorted by a couple of guards was a man. Betrim couldn't see the man's face but he didn't need to, he could see the coat and he knew those coats all too well. Instinct told him to back further into the alley, further into the shadows and the Black Thorn always obeyed his instincts.

"What ya seeing, Thorn?" Swift asked, made nervous by Betrim's backing away. Weren't often the Black Thorn backed away from anything.

Betrim ground his teeth together. "I see an Arbiter. There, between those two guards."

The other three men turned as one and peered towards the man. Bones stood up and backed away a step, Swift made a sound somewhere between a moan and sigh, and Green just scratched at his leg.

"You sure, Black Thorn? Looks a little short for an Arbiter."

"You're a bloody idiot, Green. There ain't no height requirement on being an Arbiter. Jus' so long as ya a murderous bastard who likes ta burn folk."

"Sounds fun ta me," the little shit replied with a smirk. Betrim would have knocked a few of his teeth out if Bones hadn't been standing in the way. Instead he backed away further into the alley.

"I'll go tell the Boss of the plan. You lot keep watch. Wait till that witch hunter is gone 'fore casin' the place."

"Reckon he's here fer our girl?" Bones asked, his hunched form towering over the others.

Betrim didn't have an answer for that. He just shrugged, turned, and walked away.

The Arbiter

One gaol looked much like another, or so it appeared to Thanquil. He'd been in a few during his time, never found himself locked up inside one though. They tended to consist of cold grey stone, cold metal bars, and cold angry prisoners. In this particular gaol they seemed a bit short on the prisoners.

Despite the general warmth of the city of Chade its gaol managed to remain cool and damp. There was a steady dripping sound of water throughout the entire building and many of the walls and floors seemed wet and slippery. Some of the cell bars had started to rust though none of those cells were occupied. No doubt the guards just shoved the prisoners into the better maintained cells and left the others to rot.

The tenants looked dirty and smelled worse. In fact there was an overwhelming stench of sweat, blood, and human waste throughout the building. The cells contained no beds, no furniture of any kind and only a bucket in each for the prisoner's waste. They were not intended for any sort of comfort. The few prisoners there were tended to be huddled in corners or laid out on the floors shivering in their sleep.

One prisoner, a man looking to be in his middle years and with a great shaggy beard that might once have been grey but had long since turned brown with filth, rushed forward at the sight of Thanquil and made a grab at him through the bars. The guards swatted away his hand with wooden cudgels and cursed at him. As the man fell backwards with a shriek of pain Thanquil saw what few teeth he had left were broken and brown. He'd seen that sort of abuse before, no doubt the guards kept a few prisoners away from the slavers for periodic beatings. Nothing made a weak man feel strong like someone weaker to beat upon.

"'Ave mercy," the man spluttered between his broken teeth.

One of the guards laughed and spat at the man in the cell. "Mercy from an Arbiter? You must be addled as well as a thief."

"Arbiter?" The man's eyes were bright and frantic. Again he moved forward, gripping hold of the iron bars. "I'm a heretic m'lord. I swear it. Done bad things. Deserve ta be dead."

"You ain't a heretic, just a bloody thief," the guard with the broken nose shouted and pushed the prisoner in his chest with the cudgel. The prisoner fell backwards, landed with a yelp of pain, then tried to stand up. One of his legs gave way beneath him and he crashed back to the stone floor and then lay there whimpering like a beaten dog. Both guards laughed and then herded Thanquil along. There was nothing he could do for the poor man.

Past more cells and past more prisoners some in even worse condition than first one and very few in better. The guards of Chade seemed to be little more than thugs one and all. No doubt most of them were recruited from the legion of sell-swords that littered the free cities looking for work. Those men and women were interested only in coin and paid no heed to the suffering of their fellow humans.

The steady dripping sound of water somewhere continued and the building seemed to grow even colder. The guards stopped in front of a heavy, wooden, iron-bound door. This was no ordinary cell. There were no bars, only solid stone wall. The first guard, the one with a greasy lock of straw-coloured hair falling to his shoulders and a permanently sour face, pulled back a metal shutter on the door and peered in. Then he closed the shutter again, took out a large key ring and proceeded to open three locks on the door before pulling back a heavy metal bar and pushing the door inwards, stepping back to allow Thanquil to enter.

"After you," Thanquil said with wave of his hand.

The two guards looked at each other and the man with the sour face shook his head. The broken-nosed guard then stepped forwards and, with a deep breath, walked into the room. Thanquil followed a couple of steps behind.

Inside, the cell was dark. The only light came from only a small window no more than half a foot across and even less in height and barred with more cold iron. The gloom was near complete.

"A lantern please," Thanquil said to the guard.

The broken nose shook back at him. "She can do things with fire."

"A lantern. Now," Thanquil left no doubt it was an order and, with a nod from Broken Nose, Sour Face rushed off to fetch one.

The cell didn't smell as bad as the rest of the building. It was cool and humid and there was the metallic scent of blood in the air and salt. It almost smelled of the sea.

At the far end of the cell, as far away from the door as was possible, a figure was chained against the wall. Heavy metal manacles held the woman's hands tight against the wall just above her head and her ankles were manacled to the floor out in front of her. Dried blood and blisters showed around the edges of the metal and even in the darkness Thanquil could tell the skin beneath the metal was red and raw.

The woman's mouth was wedged open with a heavily-padded leather thong strapped tight between her teeth. Blood and bile stained the thong. A bloody piece of cloth had been tied around her face to cover her eyes and her head hung limp from her shoulders. Dark black hair hung from her head in short, limp strands.

The rags the woman wore were ripped and tattered and brown, soiled with what looked like both blood and urine. They only just stretched down to her knees and hung loose off one shoulder. Her left breast was visible through one of the tears and looked small and pale but unmarked.

"She has not been raped," Thanquil said to the guard.

"Fuck no." The guard's voice was quiet, little more than a whisper. "None of us dare go near her. She's... wrong."

Sour Face returned with a small lantern and placed it on a sconce on the left wall before retreating from the cell with haste. The light flickered, casting mad, jumping shadows around the room. With light the woman looked an even more wretched thing. Her head bobbed a little at the introduction of light but there was no other movement.

Thanquil studied the woman for a time. A thin drop of spittle leaked from her mouth and dropped onto her chest, soaking into her rags but she made no sign of moving. Thanquil turned back to Broken Nose.

"She's been like this for weeks."

"Aye," the guard replied. "She's not been fed nor watered nor anything. Nobody comes in 'ere, we jus' make sure she's not gone every day. They say she's been killed twice. She jus' don't die."

Thanquil stared at the woman a while longer. She looked to be no more than twenty years of age, treated horribly and broken from the mistreatment but something didn't feel right. She felt almost like a beast playing dead, waiting to strike.

Thanquil decided to throw caution to the wind and approach the woman. Broken Nose spoke from behind. "Careful, Arbiter. She's... magical."

Thanquil glanced back at the guard. He was standing just a couple of paces behind, fear plain on his face. "I'll be fine guardsman."

He crouched down in front of the woman, she made no move. He put his hand on her forehead, still no movement. He lifted her head up, the bandage tied around her eyes was dirty with filth and dried blood. More blood had run down her cheeks like red tears. Thanquil took his hand away and the woman's head dropped. Other than her shallow breathing she seemed more corpse than living.

Thanquil lifted the bandage from around her eyes. The guardsman gasped and Thanquil heard him hit the floor. Pale blue eyes stared unfocused ahead towards the floor. The dried blood had come from wounds to her eyes, Thanquil had seen similar before, it looked almost as if...

"It's not possible," Broken Nose whispered from behind. Thanquil turned his head to find the guardsman had retreated to the door. Sour Face looked in and cursed.

"Is... Is... S'not right," Sour Face breathed and then turned and fled. Broken Nose stayed but Thanquil had rarely seen a man look so terrified.

"Her eyes..." Thanquil prompted.

"Can't be... she can't..."

"You took them." Again he prompted the guard to continue.

"Not me. Not us. Them," Broken Nose said in a high voice, his words rushing out, stumbling into each other to form a rapid slur. "When they caught her the second time they took 'em. Said she could use 'em ta... control a man. They beat her bloody, pinned her down an' scooped 'em right out. They say she didn't even scream. What sort of person don't scream when they have their eyes plucked out?"

"The sort of person who can grow new eyes," Thanquil said his voice grave even to his own ears.

Thanquil turned back to the woman. Her head was still limp, her eyes still unfocused and unseeing. Again he lifted her head so her eyes met his. Behind him he heard Broken Nose gasp but Thanquil paid him no mind. He stared into the woman's pale blue eyes but saw nothing. It was almost as if she just wasn't there. As haunting as her gaze was, it was... empty.

He poked at the leather thong strapped into her mouth. It was pulled so far back it should have been gagging her. The woman's lips were cracked and split and bloody and raw. The thong was moist with spittle.

"Her mouth," Thanquil prompted.

"She were using some sort of spell or something. Chanting it as she killed the guards. They didn't want her using it no more."

"Her tongue."

Broken Nose paused. "They cut it out, just like her eyes."

"Well. Let's see if that grew back also."

"Wait." Broken Nose started forward, his voice panicky. "What if it has? What if she casts some spell? Took eighteen guards ta bring her down second time an' ten of 'em died."

"Feel free to step outside and close the door if you're scared. But I can't very well question her if she can't talk," Thanquil replied, impatient. Broken Nose backed against the wall yet made no move to leave.

With a gentle care due to caution, Thanquil undid the clasps on the thong and slid the leather out of the woman's mouth. Her head dropped a little further and she swallowed. Signs of life at least. Then she started chanting. Foreign words Thanquil didn't understand issued from her bloody mouth in a croaking voice and she began to strain against the bonds that secured her to the wall.

"None of that, thank you," Thanquil said and his right hand slid inside his coat pocket, found the correct charm and slapped the piece of paper onto the woman's forehead.

The paper stuck and sealed to her skin. The chanting stopped and the woman's eyes rolled back into her head. Then she began to convulse, shaking and straining against her bonds. New trickles of blood leaked from old sores. Thanquil had no time for games.

He slapped the woman across the face with the back of his hand

and she stilled. Her eyelids flickered open and her eyes focused on Thanquil. Two words of some foreign tongue escaped her mouth and then she stopped, unable to remember the spell.

Thanquil stood up to stretch out his legs. "That charm is powerful magic," he explained to the woman. "When affixed it blocks magic from memory. Put simply, you can't recall the correct words, the correct symbols to draw. While that paper is there you can't use whatever magic it is you know."

The woman glared at Thanquil for a moment and then shook her head, thrashing from side to side. The charm remained in place,.iI could be peeled off but it would never fall off. Then her shaking subsided and her head went limp again, her eyes going back into the strange unfocused non-sight.

"Let's get started then," Thanquil said before focusing his attention on the woman. "Who are you?"

She didn't want to answer, Thanquil could see that, she tried to fight the compulsion but only those trained in its use could deny its effects. The words that spilled from her mouth, however, were not any that Thanquil understood. They sounded a jumbled mess of letters and sounds.

Thanquil looked at Broken Nose. Broken Nose shook his broken nose. "Any languages other than the common tongue spoken in the Wilds," he prompted the guardsman.

"No. The southerners, the blacks, they got their own language but that ain't it. I've heard it spoke an' that ain't it."

That was the problem with the compulsion. It could force a person to tell the truth but it couldn't force them to say it in the common tongue.

Thanquil sighed. An immortal witch able to regrow both eyes and tongue and who may or may not speak his language.

"Well, we may not be able to find out who you are but there's more than one way to find out what you are." He drew a short, sharp knife from his belt and advanced upon the chained woman.

The Blademaster

Jezzet's eyes snapped open. She flowed to her feet in one fluid motion and her hand reached for her sword. It wasn't there. Then she saw the bars and remembered.

Still in gaol, Jez. Still trapped and awaiting execution.

She knew why she was here, wasn't hard to guess. The guards had known her name, they'd taken her but they hadn't given her to the slavers. A woman like her would fetch a nice price from the slavers if they cleaned her up, yet there was someone willing to pay a much greater price for her. Jezzet may have been locked up in Chade's gaol but she was in no doubt that she was Constance's prisoner.

Just waiting for the bitch to arrive. Suppose I could try to kill myself in here, deny her the pleasure of doing it slowly. It wasn't the first time Jezzet had entertained the notion. She would never do it though. As long as she was alive there was a chance, however slim, of escape.

Days rolled into one but Jezzet could count the time by the light and dark that spilled in through her single barred window. At first she had complained to the guards, told them she'd done nothing wrong. That had been a mistake, all she'd earned from that was a couple of beatings. Jaxon loved his little wooden cudgel more than he'd ever loved any woman.

After that she'd tried to fuck her way out. Jez had thought to seduce the little guard with the face that was permanently turned down, Abel. When Jez was at her best men would jump at the chance to be inside her, but Jez was not currently at her best and Abel had spat at her and told her he'd rather pay a whore than fuck a dung heap. Not the most flattering of compliments she'd ever received but she had no doubt she did smell like a dung heap at the time.

"So what is she?"

"You don't need to know."

"I'd like to know. Bitch is a worry."

Jez recognised one of the voices as Jaxon and backed up against the wall of her cell and sat down on her arse, it was starting to feel very bony. Actually, most of her was starting to feel bony. Jezzet almost hoped she'd never get to look in a mirror again.

"I honestly don't care what you'd like."

The two men walked into view. One was Jaxon, the one with the boil and broken nose. The other was a shortish man, maybe half a hand taller than Jezzet, with short dark hair, short dark stubble, and a fancy brown coat. He looked to be someone of importance. Jaxon seemed a little scared of him anyway. Both men passed her cell at a steady pace, not even looking her way.

"Get me out of here," Jezzet shouted before her head could decide it was a bad idea.

"Shut it, you," Jaxon said, waving his cudgel. It was too late though, the other man had already stopped and was looking at Jezzet.

"Get me out of here and I'll do anything. Anything." Jezzet didn't move. She sat huddled at the back of her cell. Jaxon snorted but Jez ignored him. "I may not look like much right now but I'm pretty enough when clean and I know my way around a sword."

The short man in the leather coat smiled. "Literally or figuratively, I wonder."

"Both," Jez answered, ignoring Jaxon's confused look.

Idiot probably doesn't know what either word means.

She stood up and tried her best seductive walk towards the bars. It was hampered only by the fact that she looked and smelled like shit. Still, she wasn't about to let that put her off a possible escape.

You've got him, Jez. Now a bit of a throaty whisper.

She gripped hold of the bars with both hands, stared into his pretty blue eyes and whispered at him. "Anything."

"Get back or I'll beat you," Jaxon warned, waving his club from a few paces away. As idle a threat as Jez had ever heard.

"Try it and I'll take it off you and break your nose all over again," Jez replied without taking her eyes of the man in the coat.

The man in the coat smiled. "I have no need for a whore," he said and started to turn away.

"What do you need?" Jez asked. He'd stopped to look at her which meant he was interested or curious at least, Jez wasn't about to let that go. "Everybody needs something and I can be anything. What do you need?"

Jaxon looked worried. "Ar..."

"A guide." The man in the coat said over the top of Jaxon. "Someone who knows the Wilds, the towns, the people."

"I can do that," Jezzet lied. "I can be a guide and a guard and a friend and anything else you might need if you just get me out of here."

The man was still smiling, still staring at her. "You must be some sort of criminal to be locked in gaol, I would assume." His accent was strange, he might have been from Sarth but Jez couldn't be sure.

"She is..."

"I'm not. Not here in Chade anyways. Never committed a crime here." *Not recently at least.* "They've locked me up 'cos..."

"Shut up, bitch." Jaxon stepped forward, cudgel in hand. Jez was just about to reach out and disarm him when the short man in the fancy coat held up a hand between them. Jaxon backed away with a look of fear.

"I'm trying to have a conversation with the young lady, guardsman."

Lady? Jezzet would have laughed but it felt like her life was on the line here.

"She's dangerous," Jaxon said.

"So was the last one, apparently. You claim she's a criminal, she claims she's not. Who to believe."

"I'm innocent," Jez protested.

"I doubt it," the man in the coat replied with a half-smile. "You look like many things but innocent is not one of them."

"The guards are keeping me here because a bitch called Constance is paying them to. She likes to give herself the title of warlord these days and she's paying them to hold me here 'til she arrives."

"I thought with this being a free city the only crimes that mattered were the ones you committed here. That is the way it works, I believe."

Jaxon swallowed. Jezzet could see the bump in his skinny neck bobbing up and down. "Special circumstances. She's a murderer."

"And worse," Jez shouted, she could feel her anger rising. "Don't mean you got any right to keep me here."

"What sort of price could be put on such a pretty head..." the man in the coat said with that same smile on his lips.

"You ain't got no right here, Arbiter. No authority. Council said you could talk to the witch, nothing more. This one's ours."

Arbiter? Jez had never met a witch hunter before but she'd heard of them, heard of what they did, what they were capable of. *Not so sure I want to be saved now.*

The Arbiter fixed Jaxon with a stare. "How much is she worth?"

Jaxon's eyes went wide. "Fifty gold bits."

"Is that all..." The Arbiter turned to look at Jezzet again. "You're cheap."

Been called worse.

"Um..." She looked at Jaxon, the man still looked scared. "He's right. Constance would have given you a lot more for me."

"I'll give you fifty gold coins, right now, for her freedom," the Arbiter announced, reaching into his coat and pulling out a heavy purse with a strange symbol on it. Looked to be an upside down sword and a ray of light.

Jaxon looked from the Arbiter to Jezzet and back again. "I... I can't. She'd kill me. We already told Constance we captured the whore."

"Who the Hells do you think you're calling '*whore*'?" Jezzet demanded. She could sense the Arbiter was the one with the power here and she was more than willing to push her luck.

"I see," the Arbiter said in a mournful tone. The purse disappeared back inside his coat. "That's a shame but I understand."

"Wait. What?" Jezzet pressed herself close to the bars. "You can't let them have me. I can help you. I swear."

The Arbiter looked at her and shook his head. "There's nothing I can do. The guardsman is correct, I have no authority here other than that the ruling council of Chade give me. Incidentally I'll be seeing them tomorrow and I'll make sure to tell them that you're locked up here, despite having committed no crime."

Jaxon gasped. "You can't!"

"I can."

"They'll..."

"They'll have you with an iron collar around your neck before the day is out. What is your name?"

"Jaxon," Jaxon said and then clamped a hand over his mouth.

"I'll be sure to tell them." The Arbiter looked at Jezzet again. "I'm sorry but it seems I can't help you."

"Wait," Jaxon shouted.

The Arbiter stopped smiling. "Your choice is clear, guardsman. Take the gold now and she comes with me and you risk the wrath of this Constance. Or you'll get no gold and the council will find out about this."

Jaxon bit his lip then held out his hand.

"Good man," the Arbiter said, depositing the heavy purse into Jaxon's hand.

Jaxon stepped forward, took an iron ring of keys from his belt, and unlocked Jezzet's cell.

Freedom. Jezzet looked at the Arbiter. *Of a sort.* She walked out of the cell and stood next to her new captor.

The Arbiter stepped towards Jaxon and shook his hand. It was a strange farewell but one Jez had seen before in the Five Kingdoms.

I hope Arbiters ain't as bad as all the stories he told me. Jezzet thought as she followed the Arbiter out of the building. An old friend of hers had plenty of tales about the witch hunters and their deeds. Liars, murderers, thieves, and worse he'd named them all.

Outside, the sun was blinding bright after two weeks of being in a cell and Jezzet was hungry, thirsty, tired, and in desperate need of a piss.

But, damn it's good to feel the sun on my face and the wind on skin.

Even the constant clamour of people sounded something akin to heaven.

"My name is Arbiter Thanquil Darkheart," the Arbiter said as he set a quick pace.

"Jezzet Vel'urn," she replied as she hurried to keep up.

"Pleased to meet you, Jezzet. Keep moving. Quickly."

"What? Why?"

The Arbiter rounded a corner into a different street and slowed his pace just a little. They kept walking in silence for a while. So long it started to feel uncomfortable. He walked a pace ahead of her but never looked back to check she hadn't run off.

Not quite as talkative as he seemed when I was behind bars.

When the Arbiter stopped, Jezzet found she was in a market in Oldtown. Shops lined the square offering all manner of goods, and stalls occupied the centre with myriad colours and smells and tastes. Jez had never liked markets. They tended to bring out a strange sort of fear in her, all nervous and energetic, jittery. Too long surrounded by merchants and she wanted to scream.

"You smell like sewage," the Arbiter said. He was staring at her. *That was nice.*

"Reckon I look little better," Jezzet replied, smiling. She was fairly sure the smile didn't help but she tried it all the same.

The Arbiter reached into his coat and pulled out a purse. It looked familiar, exactly like the purse he'd given to Jaxon in fact. He held the purse out to Jezzet. "Buy some new clothes and a sword if you were telling the truth about knowing how to use one."

Jezzet nodded in response.

"I'll be waiting in *the Golden Fool*, it's in Goldtown. I have a room where you can bathe." He paused. "Maybe two baths."

Jezzet looked inside the purse and her jaw dropped. *That's a lot of gold, Jez.* Looked to be close to fifty bits if she was forced to hazard a guess.

"How do you know I won't just take your gold and run?"

The Arbiter grinned and turned away. "Because I'd find you. And I think the last thing you want is to be hunted by the Inquisition."

The Black Thorn

The first guard was dead with only a gurgle and soft thud as the body hit the dust and started to bleed. Betrim could say many things about Henry, not all of them good, but one thing he had to admit was the bitch knew how to kill folk. Not all that surprising given that she was one of Chade's most notorious mass murderers.

No one was sure where Henry came from or why she started murdering. A number of years back bodies started appearing in Chade, homeless folk and trash in the beginnings, but she soon stepped up to any she could find. Most people had no idea why she did it but Betrim had a theory. Henry loved the sight of blood. Betrim had seen the light in her eyes when she gutted someone and saw a splash of gore, lit her face up like nothing he'd ever seen.

When the guards caught her they ruled out slavery in an instant. People like Henry don't just stop killing because someone slaps some iron round their neck and tells them they're property. She was meant for the noose but the ruling council had bigger plans. Set her free for some job she did. Henry never would give details though, not to Betrim at least.

The second guard died with his shout still trapped in his throat. Swift's throwing dagger taking him clean in the eye, all the way up to the handle. Damn good shot if truth be told but Betrim sure as hell wasn't about to tell Swift that. Lad already had a big enough ego for three men.

"You see that?" Swift said, skipping towards the corpse. He bent down to examine his own handiwork. "Tell me someone saw that. Henry you were standing right next ta him."

Henry scowled at him.

Swift simpered and reached a tender hand out toward Henry's face. "Don't worry, my love. I'd never hit you."

Quick as a snake Henry pushed Swift's hand away then swung a heavy punch at his face. Swift didn't dodge, just took the hit and staggered away laughing and spitting blood.

"Quiet," hissed the Boss. "Both o' ya. Bones, Green get these bodies hid 'fore someone comes round here. Swift, get that grate open. Thorn, come here a sec."

Betrim moved off to the side away from the others with the Boss. He watched as Swift pulled his throwing knife from the dead guard's face, wiped the blood on his leg, and placed it back in its spot. He'd left his short-bow at the house but he always kept an arsenal of knives. The half-blood blew Henry a kiss and went to work on the grate. Weren't many better than Swift at picking locks and he'd been doing it since he was four, if you believed him. Betrim tended to believe very little that came out of his mouth though.

"Reckon you can squeeze through the chute, Thorn?" the Boss asked with an anxious look on his face. Betrim had never seen the Boss look anxious before. Weren't the most comforting of sights.

"Aye, maybe. Be tight though. Green is smaller 'an me."

"Green is green an' his bark ain't got no bite. I need someone with a name down there. I need the Black Thorn down there."

"Aye?"

"Ta stop those two from killin' each other," the Boss said with a nod towards Henry and Swift.

"Reckon they'll cause trouble?"

"I reckon this job is too important ta risk findin' out. Swift don't think much o' women, not even Henry an' she'd gut him 'fore letting him touch her. I need the Black Thorn down there ta keep the peace."

"Ain't exactly one o' my strengths but I get ya. I'll keep 'em civil." Fact was Betrim Thorn was not the type to lead folk and those he had led in the past had a poor survival rate, but he reckoned he could keep those two from each other's throats for a short while. He didn't much like the idea of squeezing through the grate though. If he got stuck halfway down they might not get him out. To be stuck there, near encased in stone, unable to move and just waiting to die. The thought scared the shit out of him, not that he'd ever admit it.

Swift finished with the lock and pulled the grate up, it made a horrible rusty scraping noise that seemed to echo around the darkness. Betrim couldn't see how a noise such as that could not have been heard. He was expecting a whole city worth of guards to come running any second and he wasn't alone in that. Most of the crew stopped and waited, looking around the street,

"Don't jus' stand around lookin' guilty. Get down there, Swift," the Boss ordered. Even in the dark he still looked anxious.

Swift grinned, stuck both legs down the chute and was gone. Betrim moved closer and looked down into the pitch-black nothing surrounded by hard, unyielding stone. Then he looked up at the dark, open night and wished the Boss had been born with smaller shoulders.

"Thorn, you're next, then Henry. Me, Green, an' Bones'll keep watch. When ya got her give us a shout up the chute, not too loud, an' Bones'll haul you up. Good?"

Again Betrim looked down the hole into the darkness. "Last fuckin' thing this is is good," he grumbled.

"You reckon you'll fit?" asked Henry with an evil grin. "Looks tight as an arsehole down there."

Betrim unfastened his cloak and dumped it next to the chute then looked down again. He took his coat off and dumped it with the cloak and then looked down again. Still looked tight. He put one leg, then the other into the chute and was just thinking of pulling out when Henry kicked him in the back.

Rough stone slipped past him on all sides, darker than black in the night. It scraped against his back, against his arms, against his legs and then he was falling. He hit the floor hard and crumpled. With groaning knees he picked himself off the floor and looked around. Was near pitch-black down in the basement, just a little sliver of light coming from underneath a door.

Something hit him in the chest and again he found himself on the floor, this time face up. After a moment he realised it was Henry. She'd come down the chute straight after him and he hadn't had time to move out the way. She was sitting on top of him, straddling him and grinning down at him.

"This seems familiar," she whispered.

Betrim patted his chest with both hands. "Nah, there's no blood."

She stood up and started looking around the room and Betrim picked himself off the floor for a second time.

Betrim glared at Swift's outline, couldn't see much else of him in the darkness but it felt good to glare. "The door, Swift."

"Unlocked an' no one on the other side, jus' a candle burnin' on a sconce."

Betrim walked over to the door and pulled on the handle. The great hunk of wood opened with a soft squeak and light spilled into the room. In the light Betrim could see Swift was grinning, Henry watched him with wary eyes and for the second time Betrim wished the Boss could have fit down the chute.

In the room with the candle was a couple of empty bunks, two cheap wooden chests, a desk with a single chair and a body. The man had a slit throat and blood was running down his neck, soaking his clothing and dripping from his hands to pool on the floor, lots of blood, thick and red and shining in the flickering candle light.

"Thought you said no one was in there, Swift," Betrim whispered.

"No, I said no one is in there. There was someone in there. I took care of him."

"Well so much for no bodies," Betrim said stepping around the pool of blood. "We move quick, quiet and careful. Kill any guards we find but do it quiet."

Henry nodded and stepped past him, reaching for the door handle. She took one last look at the blood pooling on the floor, smiled and opened the door, stepping through with Betrim just behind and Swift following last. Betrim didn't quite trust having Swift behind him, but then Betrim didn't quite trust having anyone behind him. Nor did he trust having Swift in front of him, beside him or, in truth, anywhere near him.

Most gaols Betrim had been inside were busy. Lots of prisoners, all loud and dangerous. Lots of guards, less loud but even more dangerous than the prisoners. The gaol in Chade was a different matter altogether and that was something they had to be thankful for. There weren't much in the way of prisoners. A few folk too old to be slaves or too beaten up to be of any use to anyone. Almost no guards and Betrim thanked every God he could remember for that.

They found a guard with a sour face and features that seemed to be pulled down. The fool had opened an empty cell and was busy snoring away on the straw that passed for bedding. Henry snuck into the cell, placed a hand over the guard's mouth and slid a curved dagger up under his chin into his skull. A nice, quick, clean kill. Not much blood and no noise. After that they were alone it seemed. No prisoners occupied any of the cells this far in and no guards were patrolling. Betrim was just starting to think they'd missed their target when Swift stopped and pointed to a door.

The cell was unlike the others. Stone walls instead of bars. A thick wooden door bound in iron with a number of heavy-looking locks. Betrim glanced through a shutter built into the door. Inside he could just make out a figure at the back of the cell. It was too dark for anything more.

"You sure this is the right one?" he asked Swift.

"Aye. Me n' Bones found it while you was hidin' from that Arbiter."

"Get the door open then." While Swift went to work on the locks Betrim pulled Henry to the side, just out of earshot. "You know what the Boss is up ta?"

Henry glared at him. "Eh?"

"Workin' fer Deadeye, the promise of a big job. I ain't ever seen the Boss look scared but tonight... somethin's up an' if any of us are gonna know what it'll be you."

Henry spat. She looked far from happy. "All I know is he says this big job of his will be his last job, our last job an' that we need ta work fer Deadeye fer now." She nodded behind Betrim and he turned to find Swift watching them.

"You done?" Betrim asked in a low voice.

"Of course." Swift gave the door a shove and it swung open. "After you."

Betrim set his jaw and looked into the room. It was still too dark to make much out of the figure at the far end but something about the room felt wrong. He pushed it to the back of his mind and stepped into the cell.

She was bound, hands and feet. Her hands manacled to the wall, her legs splayed out in front of her with ankles secured to the floor. She wore ripped and dirtied rags that smelled of urine and covered too little.

Her head drooped from her neck, dirty hair clumping in greasy spikes. A leather thong was wedged into her mouth and a thin strip of bandage was pressed to her forehead. Truth of it was the girl looked to be dead, or at least very close to it.

"Swift, get in here. Pick those manacles." Betrim moved closer to the woman and crouched over her. "Can you hear me, lass? We're here ta get you out. Save you as it were. Deadeye sent us."

No answer. No movement. Nothing. Only the faint hiss of her breath in and out of her chest gave away that she was still alive.

"There's no lock," Swift said. Betrim turned to find his grin gone. He was staring at the woman with a neutral expression. "These chains weren't meant to come off... ever."

Henry hadn't moved from the doorway. Betrim saw her hands twitch towards her daggers but she made no move. Her dark eyes glinted in the low light. Swift stood and stepped backwards, away from the woman.

"Now what?"

"Fuck this," Betrim looked at the short chains holding the woman. "Listen, if ya can hear me, don't move."

Standing, Betrim took his axe in hand and aimed it at the chain holding her left hand to the wall. He pulled back and swung. With a loud *ching* that echoed through the empty halls and cells the chain broke and the woman's hand flopped free. With three more practised blows she was free.

Betrim had expected her to stand up, to move, to run, to do something, anything. Instead the woman toppled sideways and hit the floor face first and lay there unmoving. Betrim looked at Swift. Swift shrugged back.

With a groan Betrim reached down, plucked the woman from the ground and lifted her up in both arms. "Let's get the hell out of here."

The journey back to the basement was less eventful. Only empty cells, empty corridors and a dead guard watched them pass. One prisoner, an old man stinking of shit crawled towards the bars and begged freedom. Henry aimed at kicked at him and the man slunk back into his cell, begging forgiveness.

The Heresy Within

Downstairs in the basement Swift didn't wait for a rope. He jumped, pulled himself up to the chute and scurried his way to the surface, leaving Betrim and Henry to stare after him in stunned silence. A moment later a rope dropped down from the black hole. Betrim tied the rope around the woman's chest, grabbing hold of a handful of tit as he did. She didn't respond at all, didn't even acknowledge she was out of her cell. Betrim called up the hole and a moment later she was hauled up into the waiting black above. Henry went next, Betrim didn't dare grab a handful as he tied the rope round her chest, not that there was much to grab. He watched as her feet disappeared above him and waited until the rope dropped down again.

By the time Betrim's head appeared up out of the chute Bones was panting and sweating as he pulled hand over hand. Betrim climbed out of the hole, turned and spat back down it. Last time he ever did anything like that again. Bones smiled at him and collapsed down onto his arse to catch his breath.

Two more bodies were sprawled out on the ground. Both were guards with their red doublets made redder by blood. Betrim nodded towards them. "The other patrol."

"Aye," the Boss said, angry. "Don't know where you learned ya numbers, Thorn, but that was not thirty minutes. More like fifteen."

Betrim shrugged. "Now what?"

"Job was ta get her out then let her go. She's free." The woman was propped up against the wall, still unmoving like some sort of life-size doll Betrim had heard that rich folk played with when they were young.

The Boss walked forwards and took the leather thong out of the woman's mouth. Betrim noticed them straight away. With her lips pulled back as they were he had a good view of her teeth and they were perfect. Bleached white and all of a size and shape, no gaps, no yellowing, none missing or broken. The most perfect set of teeth he'd ever seen.

It took him a moment to realise everyone else was also staring at the woman.

Bones was the first to speak. "She's blooded, ain't she."

Swift was the first to answer. "Looks ta be."

It didn't make any sort of sense. The blooded folk ruled the wilds.

Each family owned a province and ruled all in it save the free cities. Why would one of the blooded, a woman too, be held prisoner in Chade? And why would the ruling council be treating her so badly?

"You're free now," the Boss said. "You can go. Job was ta get ya out an' let ya go."

The woman slid sideways and toppled, again landing on her face. The whole crew just stared at her. It looked to Betrim like she was broken and he'd seen the like before. Women beaten and raped so bad that they just stopped being there, switched their minds off or something. They would eat and drink and shit and piss but apart from that they were nothing.

The Boss did not look pleased. "Fuck," he swore in a loud voice. "Bones, pick her up. Can't leave her here fer the guards ta find. We'll keep her back at the house 'til Deadeye gets here. Move. Now!"

Even as late at night as it was the streets were full of guardsman looking for folk to be taken as slaves. The doors to the slavers guild never closed and more than one drunken layabout would no doubt find themselves waking up to an iron collar. The Boss' crew was too large and too well armed to be considered for slaves but six folk carrying an unconscious woman through the streets would peak some attention.

They stayed to alleyways and shadows as much as possible. The Boss let Swift lead the way as the lad had always seemed to be part homing pigeon and they were back at the house soon enough. Back with the rats and the fleas and the stench of corpse. Now they had the body of a woman who stank of piss as well. Along with the smell of Betrim's hair dye and Swift's chewing leaf not even the dogs would come near the place.

Once inside the Boss set to examining the woman. He gave her a light slap on the cheek, poked around inside her mouth, pinched at a nipple and slid a hand up between her legs. All the while the woman did nothing, her cold blue eyes staring at the floor.

The Boss backed away shaking his head. "S'like a livin' corpse."

"Give 'er ta me fer five minutes, Boss. I'll wake her up," Green said. Everyone ignored him.

"Somethin the Arbiter did, I reckon," said Swift.

The Heresy Within

"What?"

"Word on the street is the council brought an Arbiter to deal with some woman they had in gaol."

"And this is the first I'm hearin' of this?"

"Different woman, Boss," Bones spoke up. "We saw the Arbiter leavin' the gaol with another one."

Betrim approached the woman now slumped against a wall. He lifted her head and looked at the strip of cloth on her forehead. It wasn't a bandage. It had a symbol on it.

"Ya sure about that, Bones?" Betrim grabbed a handful of the woman's hair and lifted her head to show the others the piece of cloth. "This is one of theirs or I ain't the Black Thorn."

Green opened his mouth to speak but the Boss cut him off. "Take it off, Thorn."

Betrim took hold of a corner of the cloth and pulled. It made a horrible ripping sound like it was tearing the skin but it came away easy enough. As soon as it was off the woman's head her eyes flicked up and met Betrim's.

He felt a push against his chest and then something hit him in the back and he was down on the floor, a crumpled mess against the far wall. He opened his eyes to find the woman standing up and looking about the room. Her flat gaze went to each of the six crew members in turn and then landed on Bones who was, unfortunately for him, in front of the door.

"Let her go, Bones," the Boss said but it was too late.

The woman charged the big man and shoved him aside as if he were a child. Bones hit the wall and slid down into a second crumpled mess beside Betrim. The giant groaned as he pushed himself upright.

They all stared after the woman, stared towards the gaping hole in the house where the door had once been.

"We still get paid right?" Swift asked.

The Blademaster

It had been so long since Jezzet had last been clean she'd almost forgotten what it felt like. Clean skin, clean hair, clean clothes, clean smell. It felt better than every hot meal she'd ever had. Two tubs of bath water it had taken but it was water well spent. The first had been so brown and dirty that the tub needed scrubbing before the second lot of water could be added. Jezzet waited by a low fire as a serving maid scrubbed and made disapproving noises by *tutting* and *clicking* her tongue.

She'd only spent a little of the Arbiter's money but she'd spent it well. Jezzet had bought new clothing, new leathers, a nice sharp knife to cut her hair back to a manageable length, and a new sword, plain of ornamentation but more than serviceable. Less than four gold bits she'd spent in all but when she'd tried to give the rest back to the Arbiter he had laughed and waved away the purse, producing another out of his coat which bulged even bigger.

For now she found herself sitting around in the common room of *the Golden Fool* with a mug of beer and a plate of bread, honeyed bacon, peppered egg, and tiny mushrooms. It was one of the fanciest meals Jezzet had ever eaten but she wolfed it down without a thought to how much it was costing.

After eating, Jez sat back and waited, unsure of how to occupy herself. She knew she should find somewhere to spar, to train. It had been two weeks in gaol and over moon since she was last involved in any swordplay.

Her master had once said to her: '*You are good, Jezzet, but even the sharpest blade will dull and rust over time without the proper care.*' That was just one of the many things he said to her after a hard days training. The old bastard loved to talk.

Jezzet considered returning to *the Serpents Tooth* to repay Harod for his treachery. The bastard deserved running through for a start but Jez wouldn't be the one to do it. The guards might be there again and she could well do with avoiding another encounter with them. She doubted the Arbiter would bother to free her from gaol a second time.

You could still run, Jez. Forty-six gold bits is a small fortune. You could jump a ship to the Dragon Empire. Enough to start over, a new life. The Arbiter wouldn't find you out there. Constance wouldn't find you out there. You could live as you like. A nice, simple life.

A dull life, it sounded, when she thought of it. Jez could well imagine she'd be bored after a few short weeks and everywhere she went she managed to pick up new enemies. No, the Wilds was where she belonged; fighting, scraping, clawing, killing, and fucking for every moment of life the Gods gave her.

Jezzet was still supping her beer when the Arbiter returned. He didn't bother ordering a drink for himself, spotting Jez and marching over. Despite the heat of the morning he was wearing his long brown coat with its sturdy design, many pockets, shiny buttons, and a collection of stains. The worst of it was he had the gall not to look hot. His hair was a tangled mess, his face in dire need of a shave, and he walked like a man without a care in the world. It both annoyed Jezzet and made her smile.

"Awake I see, Jezzet," the Arbiter said, sitting down opposite her on the little table. He had somehow managed to leave the room without waking Jez. She blamed it on the tiredness and relative safety of an inn after sleeping in a cell for so long, usually she woke at the slightest noise. "You slept well."

"I'd have slept better on the bed," Jez replied with none of the Arbiter's good humour.

"Only one bed I'm afraid and that's mine."

"I don't mind sharing."

The Arbiter smiled and laughed. Seemed such a good natured laugh but Jez had heard stories of Arbiters, many stories and none of them pleasant.

How can a man who burns folk for a living be so happy?

"Early morning business?" she asked, it was just past dawn and he had already been and come back.

"With the council. Seems the woman I was brought here to kill has managed to escape the gaol. As I was the last to see her they've decided to blame me."

"And yet here you sit, not in irons."

"The council wouldn't dare arrest an Arbiter for a supposed crime with no proof. To do so would be an insult to the Inquisition."

"Why did they need you to kill a woman? Couldn't they do so themselves? Pretty sure they could've killed me if they really tried." Jez took a pull of beer, she'd need another mug soon enough.

"They did kill her, she came back."

"People can do that?"

"No," the Arbiter said, shaking his head. "People can't."

"Uhh... right. So what do you need me for?" Jezzet asked. "You've sprung me from gaol, given me a small fortune and you don't seem to want me for what's between my legs. So why?"

"I need a guide. Someone who knows the places of the wilds, knows the people, how to find certain people. Arbiters are not well loved here, or anywhere for that matter, but even less here. You will be able to gather information I cannot and speak to people who wouldn't talk to me. I need you to help me."

Well that was suitably vague. "So why are you here?"

"The council of Chade asked the Inquisition to help them kill a woman. The Inquisition sent me to find a man. His name is Gregor H'ost. You've heard of him."

Jezzet had heard of H'ost alright and it was not a name she wanted to hear ever again, the very mention of it sent chills up her spine because the name H'ost went hand in hand with the name Constance.

"Sorry, Arbiter." Jezzet fished the pouch of gold from her belt and placed it on the table in front of her. "I can't help you."

"So you have heard of him."

"Of course I have. Everyone has. He's the head of the family."

"The family..."

Jezzet's mouth dropped and she stared at the Arbiter in wonder. "The H'osts. The blooded folk who own the province."

"This province..."

"Exactly. Only not Chade because it's a free city."

The Arbiter scratched at the stubble on his face, picked up Jezzet's beer and took a mouthful. "I'm not sure I understand what '*blooded*' means."

"You really don't know anything at all of the Wilds." Jezzet was starting to doubt this Arbiter's intelligence.

"It's why I need a guide. I didn't have time to study up. One minute I was suffering from a night's heavy drinking and the next I was on a ship bound for here with nothing but a name."

"The blooded are sort of royalty or something in the wilds. Descended from one bloodline. Nine provinces, nine families. Gregor is the head of the H'ost family."

"Hmmm, that could make things difficult. At least I have you as a guide."

"No, you don't." Jezzet should have been angry but she found it hard to get angry at someone who had just saved her life, even if they were trying to place it right back in danger. "H'ost has an army and at the head of that army is a bitch called Constance. Happens to be the same cunt sucker who wants me dead and worse than dead."

"You must have wronged her."

"Ya could say that. I killed her sister for a start." Jezzet looked up to find the Arbiter watching her through calm eyes. For some reason she felt the need to explain to the man as if his opinion mattered.

"About three years back Constance and her sister, Catherine, were leading H'ost's army. Constance is more like a man but Catherine was different. Bloody good with a sword and some sort of military genius or something. Constance just used to follow her older sister around like a big bodyguard.

"H'ost's army met with another of the blooded, a family named D'roan, and they agreed to settle things the old way so none of the blooded folk got hurt. They both pick champions from their army and they fight. The winner gets the land, the loser retreats. H'ost picked Catherine."

"And this D'roan picked you," the Arbiter said nodding.

"Picked would be one word I guess, sure. I was his... prisoner. He agreed to let me go if I fought and won."

"He had an entire army at his command and he picks you."

"I told you back in gaol, I'm good with a sword." Jezzet stared at the table, seemed she couldn't look the Arbiter in the face for the next bit. "D'roan told me to make a show of it. To humiliate H'ost's champion and I wanted to please him so I agreed."

Jezzet fell silent, waiting for the Arbiter to ask what happened but he didn't. He just sat there silent, watching.

"It wasn't a clean death," Jezzet said after a while. "I cut her to pieces."

Master always said, 'death should never be a spectacle. A Blademaster should always kill quick and certain.' and I ignored him.

"When Constance tried to intervene I took her left eye, left her bleeding over the corpse of her sister." It wasn't something Jezzet liked to talk about. Actually it wasn't something she had ever talked about before. Seemed some of the stories were true about Arbiters, they could force a person to speak the truth.

"I'm sorry, Jezzet," the Arbiter said in a quiet voice. "But I still need your help."

She shook her head. "You'd be better off with someone else, anyone else. Constance wants me dead and she'll stop at..."

"Even so. I need your help and you're going to help me."

Jezzet snorted. "Why would I do that?"

The Arbiter pushed the pouch of gold bits towards her. It sat there heavy on the table, felt as weighty there as it had on her belt. "Because I've already bought you, and because if what you say is true this Constance won't ever stop coming after you, and because with my help maybe you can find a way to stop her."

"Only way to stop her would be to kill her."

"I'm sure we could manage that."

Jezzet found her mouth open. Again the Arbiter ignored it. He stretched out his arms and yawned then reached forward, took Jezzet's beer and finished the drink in one big gulp.

"Time to go, Jezzet Vel'urn."

"Where?"

"To see a man about a dress."

With the sun as high and bright as it was the morning was beyond hot. Heat shimmers sprung up everywhere in front of her eyes and with not even a breath of wind the air felt thick and heavy and moist. Jezzet wore the simple set of lightweight leathers she had purchased with the Arbiter's gold but still she found herself sweating. She kept wiping the moisture from her forehead into her hair but more kept springing forth. To make matters worse the Arbiter with his long coat didn't even seem to feel the heat. It might have made her angry but truth was Jezzet was too busy feeling sticky to get angry.

He led them to the merchant's street in Goldtown and with the heat came the smells. There was no escaping the odour that hung above Chade in the heat. A constant aroma of shit and rot assaulted the occupants. Some of the more ladylike women, and indeed some of the more ladylike men, took to walking around with scented kerchiefs held to their faces and their heads high like the stink meant nothing to them.

Clearly none of them have had to crawl through a sewer on their hands and knees before. The experience might do them some good.

They attracted a few stares, though not as many as Jezzet might have thought, and the truth of it was that it was the Arbiter attracting the stares. None of them would have given Jezzet a second glance but she was walking next to a witch hunter. It still made Jez nervous to have so many eyes pointed her way.

"Doesn't it bother you?" she asked the Arbiter as they walked. "The stares and such."

He shook his head. "Being purposefully stared at is just a little bit better than being purposefully not stared at."

Jezzet couldn't say she understood what the Arbiter meant by that but it didn't make her feel any better either way. Her hand hovered near her new sword, ready to draw steel at a moment's notice. Her eyes darted everywhere, assessing every person to determine which, if any, were threats.

'A Blademaster should always know where the next strike is coming from so he will never be surprised.' Her master used to say.

"This is it," the Arbiter announced and ducked into the door of a large wooden building with a sign that stated the shop was a dressmaker. Jezzet had assumed the witch hunter was joking, a play on words or such that she hadn't understood. Now she had that terrible sinking feeling in her gut she got when she was about to be humiliated. She fixed a dark scowl to her face and followed the Arbiter inside.

It was bright inside but still a lot darker than in the sun and it took a moment for Jez's eyes to adjust. The shop was full of dresses, clothes, bolts of cloth, hats, dainty little shoes, powders, and other concoctions designed to be applied to the face. Colours Jezzet couldn't even name assaulted her eyes from all directions and she felt her lip curling up in distaste.

"This is her," the Arbiter said to an effeminate-looking man with a powdered face, big bulging eyes, a hook of a nose, and short greasy hair pulled back over his skull. The man pouted at her.

"No!" Jezzet stated in her most firm voice. Both men ignored her.

The effeminate man walked towards her and his eyes swept over her in a rudely appraising manner. The only time Jezzet felt self-conscious about her body was when people looked at her scars but the way this man looked at her... she felt her hand twitching towards her blade.

"She's skinny," the man said, his voice was as girlish as his manner.

"Recent adverse living conditions," the Arbiter spoke for her.

"Not much in the way of breasts."

"Some would say that's an advantage," the Arbiter said and Jezzet had to agree with him.

"She has the hair of a boy." Jezzet fought the urge to run her hand through her short, spiky mess of hair.

"Gives her a certain appeal I'd say."

Enough!

Jezzet looked the effeminate man up and down the same way he had done to her. "He's overly plump. Lacks balls by the looks of him, probably a eunuch, and his hair looks like it crawled out of someone's arse." She expected the man to look shocked, hoped he would. Instead he just raised a plucked eyebrow.

Jezzet turned to the Arbiter. "No!"

"It's only a..."

"Jezzet Vel'urn has never and will never wear a dress."

The Arbiter smiled at her. "You can't very well turn up to a ball wearing leathers."

"Why not? You wanted someone to tell you how things are done here in the Wilds. Well, during the rich folk's balls many important people decide to bring bodyguards with them. I wouldn't look the least bit out of place in leathers."

"Really..." the Arbiter prompted at the dressmaker.

"It's true," the dressmaker said in a resigned voice.

"Still," the Arbiter continued, "It wouldn't look right for an Arbiter to turn up with a bodyguard. One dress, one night."

"I'm not wearing a dress."

"Yes you are."

"No I'm not."

Jezzet glared at the Arbiter. The Arbiter stared back. An uncomfortable silence held the room. It seemed to stretch out forever until the silence became a living thing eating up the world around her until only her and the Arbiter remained each staring as stubbornly as the other.

"Try not to restrict her movement," the Arbiter said and Jezzet knew he was talking to the dressmaker again. "And try to stay clear of her sword arm while you're measuring."

The Arbiter started for the shop exit. "I'll be across the street, there's an interesting-looking weapon shop." He said as he walked past her.

Jezzet's hand shot out and caught the Arbiter's wrist. "No."

He leaned closer so the dressmaker wouldn't overhear. "The ball is in four days. Most people of any import in Chade will be there. Your friend the warlord arrived in Chade this morning. I think she's less likely to recognise you in a dress."

Jezzet let go of the Arbiter, her mouth had gone dry. "Why didn't you tell me earlier?"

"Didn't want you hiding in the inn all day. Come find me when you're finished." With that the Arbiter strode out the door to the shop. By the time Jezzet turned back around the dressmaker was already advancing upon her with a tape measure.

You could still run, Jez. Still got the gold, still got a sword. Just slip away before the Arbiter notices and jump on the first boat headed anywhere.

The effeminate little dressmaker started measuring her arms, and then moved onto her legs, her shoulders, her hips, and her chest. All the while Jezzet stood there scowling at the man but not running, not jumping on the first ship headed anywhere.

"Your hair is a little short but with some make-up I could make you a vision any man would..."

Jezzet glared at the man and her hand moved towards her sword. "You come anywhere near me with any of that powder and I'll paint the shop red with your blood."

The man backed away. "Of course, sorry. I meant no offence."

"We done here?"

"Yes. You can tell the Arbiter..."

Jezzet didn't listen, didn't care to listen. She stormed out of the shop and straight towards the weapon market she had seen Thanquil enter. She stopped inside and looked around. This shop was more to her liking. Blades of all types hung on the walls and more than blades besides. Hammers, maces, flails, daggers, swords, axes, spears. The shop could have supplied a small army by itself. Most of those on show were fancy works, good steel, no doubt, but jewelled and ornamented with all manner of fancy metalwork. She remembered her master's words, '*A blade should reflect its owner. Blademasters are meant for killing, not for showing off.*'

The Arbiter was busy with the shop owner being shown a small wood and metal device with a rounded handle and some sort of barrel. It looked as though it would fit in one hand but did not seem to be dangerous in any way, it didn't even have a blade.

"What is it?" Jezzet asked, curious despite herself.

"He calls it a ball shooter."

Jezzet raised an eyebrow at that. "It... shoots balls?"

"Little metal ones," the Arbiter said, holding one such little metal ball up. "See."

Jezzet took the little metal ball from the Arbiter and gave it a closer inspection. It didn't seem to be special in any way, just a small lump of rounded metal no bigger than the marbles children sometimes played with.

"It throws them like a sling?"

"No, good lady," the merchant said, his accent was not of the wilds though Jez couldn't place where it was from. "It shoots them like a crossbow but with no string."

The Pirate Isles, I reckon. They're all a bunch of thieves and this one is certainly trying to rob the Arbiter.

"How does it shoot them?" Jezzet asked.

"With black powder."

"Never heard of it."

Thanquil handed the device back to the merchant. "It's a fine black powder alchemists discovered some years ago. Ignites and explodes upon contact with fire or sufficient impact."

The merchant pointed the device with one hand at the back of the store. "You simply aim and pull on the little trigger, like a crossbow." A tiny metal hammer on the top of the device clicked against a metal plate and nothing happened.

"It doesn't work," Jezzet said.

The merchant laughed. "It is not loaded, good lady. It is accurate up to ten paces."

"That seems a little short. I've seen bows shoot twenty times that."

Again the merchant laughed. "It is not meant for range, good lady."

Jezzet hated people calling her a lady. "Have you seen it work?" she asked Thanquil.

The Arbiter grinned at her through his stubble before turning to the merchant. "I'll take it, along with some black powder and some of your little metal balls."

The merchant was all smiles and compliments after that. He charged the Arbiter eight gold bits for the device but Thanquil seemed happy to pay it. Truth was he seemed as happy as a child with a new toy. Truth was, Jezzet reckoned, the Arbiter had just been conned.

"You should have seen it work first before buying it," Jezzet said to the smiling Arbiter. "Folk in the wilds will sell you anything if you got the money and they'll happily dress something up to be a thing it ain't."

The Arbiter nodded and looked at her. "You might be right. The dress..."

Jezzet shrugged. Last thing she wanted was to be reminded about that. She'd gone her whole life without wearing one of the stupid things and just a few days after meeting this Arbiter he'd have her in one to parade her around.

Not even D'roan had tried...

"Jezzet Vel'urn?" came a harsh-sounding male voice from behind her. Jez realised she hadn't been watching the streets, hadn't been watching the people and when people knew her name it rarely turned out well.

She turned to find the ugliest man she'd ever met staring at her with something akin to a smile on his burned face though in truth it was more like a horrific tugging at the corners of his mouth.

"Thorn. Never thought to see you in Chade ever again," Jezzet said with a smile of her own, one a great deal prettier than his.

"Ya know this one then, Thorn?" asked the big black-skinned southerner beside him.

"Aye, me 'n Jezzet go way back. She helped me out when..." Thorn's voice trailed to a stop and Jezzet realised he was staring at the man beside her, staring at the Arbiter. For his own part the Arbiter looked disinterested in the whole situation but content to wait it out.

"What're you doin' with one o' them, Jez?" Thorn asked.

"Working, Thorn. The Arbiter's hired me as a guide."

"That's that short Arbiter we saw?" asked a skinny youth, looked to be half a boy still but with a nasty-looking curl to his mouth and a bit of brown fuzz on his chin. "Well don't jus' stand there, Black Thorn, kill him!"

Jezzet saw Thorn's jaw clench. The southerner behind him groaned and the biggest man Jezzet had ever seen, must have been near seven foot when stooped, gave the lad a hard smack on the back of the head.

"By all the Gods, Green. If ya don't stop sayin' his name everywhere we go I'll gut ya myself." This from the southerner.

"You're the Black Thorn," Thanquil said from beside her. "The thorn in the Inquisition's side."

In a flash steel was drawn, shining naked in the sunlight. All six folk opposite Jezzet plucked sharp metal from their belts. Thorn, the southerner, the giant, the boy, a woman just a bit smaller than Jezzet, and the handsome youth wearing a grin. Jezzet found her own sword out of its scabbard and in her hand. She also found that hand shaking.

Damnit, Jez. This isn't a fight you want to be in. Try to calm the situation.

"You don't want to fight me, Thorn," she said, putting as much command into her voice as possible.

"Ha!" barked the woman with the scar. "Bein' threatened by a girl who can't even hold a sword straight now, Thorn."

"Shut it, Henry," Thorn growled at the woman with an acidic glance.

The woman just laughed. "Don't you worry, Thorn. I'll protect ya from the little whore."

Lady. Girl. Whore! It seemed everyone was insulting Jezzet today and she'd just about had enough of it.

The guards lining the streets had taken notice of the bared steel. They wouldn't intervene, not yet. Their numbers were too few and there were too many people with weapons. The guards would wait until most of them had killed each other and then take the survivors for slaves when their own reinforcements arrived.

Jezzet realised the Arbiter hadn't yet drawn his sword. Out of all of them he was the most relaxed. His hands resting in his pockets and he stared at Thorn with an amused half-grin.

"Never thought I'd get to meet the Black Thorn," the Arbiter said from beside Jezzet. "It's a...

"You ain't takin' me," Thorn responded.

"Taking you..."

"Dead or alive. I've killed enough o' ya ta know how ta do it."

"So I hear. What's your count at now, five I think."

"Six," said the boy with the cruel mouth. "Everyone always forgets the first one." Again the giant cuffed the boy on the back of the head.

"Well I have no wish to become number seven. Besides, I have places to be."

Thorn looked confused, his entire crew looked confused, Jezzet could tell she herself looked confused. Thorn had always said the Inquisition wanted him bad, said they'd stop at nothing to take him, dead or alive.

"What sort of game you playin'?" the southerner asked.

Thanquil snorted out a laugh. "No game. I have no interest in you, Black Thorn. Nor any of your gang. Feel free to have me followed though, if it will put you at ease. Jezzet, we should go."

The Arbiter turned and walked away. Jezzet backed away a few paces, sheathed her sword and hurried after him, leaving Thorn and his crew staring after them.

"Aren't you supposed to be trying to kill him or something?" Jezzet asked Thanquil when she caught up. Now the possibility of a fight was over her hand had stopped shaking, though she hadn't quite ruled out the possibility of a knife in the back at any moment.

"Fight the Black Thorn... now there's a scary prospect," the Arbiter replied. "He's killed six Arbiters already and I wasn't joking when I said I have no wish to become the seventh."

The Black Thorn

"Follow 'em, Swift. An' don't get caught," the Boss said with even more frown than usual.

Betrim didn't like it. Didn't like the whole damned situation in fact. First they take on a job from Deadeye to free some bloody witch from gaol and now an Arbiter just happens to cross his path with Jezzet Vel'urn in tow. That there was a recipe for trouble.

"Thorn." The Boss nudged Betrim to get his attention. "That woman he was with, ya knew her?"

"Aye." Betrim watched Swift trot off after the Arbiter, always keeping his distance, always keeping behind other folk so as not to be seen. Useful lad to have about was Swift, as long as you could keep him in check. Might be Betrim was going to need useful friends sometime soon.

"Is she trouble?"

"'Bout as big as it gets. Knows her way round a sword like no one I've ever seen."

Henry snorted. "Bitch was shakin' more 'an Green."

Betrim didn't bother replying to that. Henry didn't get on too well with other women and Betrim couldn't be bothered figuring out why.

"She was quick enough ta draw steel on ya," the Boss continued and Betrim knew he'd keep at it until he had the whole story.

"That's the problem with Jezzet Vel'urn, never know which side she'll come down on in the end. Few years back was workin' a protection job here in Chade, nice easy work, easy money. Sit around an' look after some boxes 'til folk came ta pick 'em up. That was 'til some of the lads decided I'd look a better corpse. Wanted ta brag about killin' the Black Thorn most like.

"Eight o' them came at me an' only the one decided ta back me. I did fer two of 'em, she got the rest an' not one even a shade of life in 'em by the end of it. She stuck with me fer a while, right up 'til she got a better offer. Someone prettier or richer or with less folk tryin' ta kill 'em, I reckon."

"So she goes with the highest bidder?" the Boss asked.

Betrim shrugged. He had no idea how the bitch thought. Up until a few minutes ago he'd have counted Jezzet Vel'urn as an old friend, right up until he found her keeping company with the Inquisition.

He was aware that there were more guards than before, seemed some of their backup had arrived and they were all still more than passing interested in the crew. Despite no steel being naked they made for a dangerous-looking group of folk and they didn't rightly look like they belonged standing around in the middle of a street in Goldtown. Betrim reckoned the guards probably thought the crew looked like they belonged in iron collars.

"Might be about time we got movin', Boss."

"Aye." Betrim wasn't the only one who had noticed the guards, the Boss did not look happy about the situation, but then the Boss was looking less and less happy every day now. "Bones, take Green an' find us another safe-house, close ta the Oldtown gate as possible."

"Speedy exit it is, Boss," Bones said and started dragging Green away.

"Me an' Henry need ta see the contact..."

"'Bout our money? From Deadeye."

"That too," the Boss said. "Get back ta the house an' wait there, Thorn. An' try not ta run into any other old friends while ya about it."

Betrim waved the comment away and started walking, already wishing the Boss had never decided to treat them to a fancy breakfast. It had seemed a right good idea at first. They'd done the job and done it well, none of them dead and the only injury a bump on the back of Betrim's head where he'd hit the wall after the witch had thrown him. So, as no payment had been made yet the Boss took them all to a fancy tavern in Goldtown to eat as much fancy food as they could and drink some good, dark beer while they were at it. Fact was Betrim had thought himself to be on the drunk side of tipsy before coming face to face with the Arbiter. Funny how running into a man looking to kill you could sober you up so quick.

If it hadn't been for the Boss' fancy tavern Betrim would never have run into the Arbiter, or Jezzet, and would have been more than happy to spend his day drinking beer that tasted like piss in a tavern that smelled of piss until he was so drunk he could no longer feel his scars. As it was, he was about to spend the rest of his day hiding in a house like some scared no-name boy.

At least it was hot. Betrim had never liked the cold. He'd once spent a winter in the Five Kingdoms, up so far north that the rain turned white and solid it was so cold. The northerners had thought nothing of it but Betrim knew better. Water was bad enough when it was liquid, it had no cause to be solid and settle on the ground as it did there.

He was being followed. The lad was good to be sure but when you had a name like the Black Thorn and you'd been around as long as Betrim had, you tended to know when someone was paying particular attention to you and right now Betrim was getting that feeling. Like an itch he couldn't quite find to scratch. The lad crept along, keeping to the shadows where possible, ducking round corners but not quite fast enough. Betrim turned into an alley and waited. And waited. And waited.

He was just about to give up and admit he'd been mistaken when the boy's head poked around the corner of the alley. Betrim's hand shot out, fast a snake, and grabbed the boy by his ragged shirt pulling him into the alley and shoving him against the wooden wall of the bakers he was hid behind. A knife leapt into his three fingered hand and Betrim held it up against the boy's throat. He looked around to make sure there weren't any folk watching. The only spectator was a fat, ginger tom-cat that stared through lazy, golden eyes as it lounged in a patch of sunlight. It had that look that cats get, the one that makes you feel guilty because the alley belongs to them.

The boy was silent but scared. "Who put ya after me?" Betrim asked as he threatened, pressing the knife into the boys neck in a real threatening manner.

"The guards. Ones 'at saw ya back there. Said they'd gimme a silver bit if I followed an' said where ya ended."

Deadeye, Jezzet, some bastard Arbiter, and now the guards. Seemed Betrim's life was getting more and more complicated by the moment. He pressed the knife closer against the boy's throat and the lad let out a whimper as a trickle of blood loosed and ran down into his collar. A sour smell filled the air, seemed the boy had pissed himself.

Fact was Betrim would have offered the boy two silver to bugger off and never see him nor the guards ever again. Only problem was Betrim Thorn didn't have a silver bit to his name. The other option would be to kill the boy. Nobody around to see it. One quick cut and it would be over. Wouldn't be the first boy Betrim had killed and he was unlikely to be the last.

He gave the boy a shove, hard enough to knock him to the ground. "I catch ya following me again I'll cut ya up an' feed ya ta the cat."

The boy was shaking. "What cat?"

Betrim looked over towards the ginger tom-cat but it had already gone, picked itself up and left as silent as only cats can be. The boy ran while Betrim was looking the other way and was gone too. Was for the best. Betrim had no wish to kill some street trash for no reason. Acts like that had a habit of coming back a man.

It was late afternoon by the time the others started to get back. Bones and Green were the first and Betrim was busy occupying himself with nothing. He'd taken to lying on his back and staring at the roof of their little house, counting the spiders he could see up near the rafters. Some of the little bugs were pretty big too.

Betrim had once known a man who kept some spiders. Said he '*milked*' them every so often for their poisons. Seemed a damned strange word to use with spiders, '*milking*' them, but Betrim had seen the poison work all the same. The smallest of scratches from a poisoned blade and the victim collapsed in moments, unable to breathe, a couple of minutes later he'd been dead. Seemed like a shitty way to go, poisoned by a man who milks spiders, but Betrim had smiled and nodded along before promptly losing touch with the milker.

"Still hiding, Black Thorn?" Green asked with a smirk as he sauntered in. "Never thought the likes of you would be so scared of one man. Reckon they should start callin' ya Yellow Thorn."

It was about as much as Betrim could take not to hit the little shit. Actually it was a little more than Betrim could take. He pushed himself to his feet, took two steps towards Green, and swung a heavy, five-fingered fist at the boy's face. Lucky for Green the boy was fast, he saw it coming and tried to dodge. Unlucky for Green the boy wasn't fast enough, the punch caught him with a solid blow to the nose. Betrim felt the nose break, felt the spatter of blood on his knuckles and felt the sting of the punch in his own hand.

Green went down muttering curses between gurgling sobs. Then Bones was between the two of them, big man could move fast when the situation called for it. He pushed the Black Thorn away with one hand and Betrim almost went sprawling to the floor himself. He managed to stay on his feet and stood, shaking out the sting in his right hand. Funny how hitting someone with a closed fist tended to hurt so damned much.

Green crawled onto his knees. He was near gushing blood, coughing and spluttering as it ran down his face. The sight made Betrim smile. Punching Green was something he'd wanted to do since he'd first met the little bastard. He'd have liked to get in a few kicks while the boy was down, but he weren't about to fight Bones for the chance.

"Stay back, Thorn," Bones warned in very warning-like tone. "Boy's had enough."

"Reckon that's so," Betrim replied, still smiling. Wasn't often he had this much fun. "One punch is no doubt all it takes fer the likes of him." Boys like Green didn't last long in this game, something to do with their constant need to challenge men like the Black Thorn.

Green coughed, lurched to his feet, and staggered towards Betrim. Problem was Bones was in the way and the giant just pushed the boy back with one hand.

"Calm down, Green," Bones said in very calm-like tone. "Sit over there an' I'll have a look at that nose, looks like it broke."

Green spat on the straw-covered floor. Blood and spittle and, from the looks of it, a few tears. Problem for him was it just made Betrim grin all the harder.

"Fuck you, Thorn," the boy shouted. Was nice and loud, very brave of him considering he was being held back by a giant stronger than both of them put together. "I'm gonna fuckin' kill you."

That was all the invitation Betrim needed. He unhooked his hand axe with his right and plucked a dagger from his belt with his left and stood ready. "Get out the way, Bones. The boy wants ta die."

Green drew his little sword into his right hand. Now Bones looked nervous and rightly so, armed folk either side of him and each wanting to kill the other. Just another couple of moments and he'd step back, let the two of them get on with it.

"Someone fancy tellin' me what the fuck is goin' on here?" came the Boss' voice from the doorway.

Betrim glanced once towards the Boss and the look on the southerner's face was enough. Never had he seen a more stern, disapproving, and plain angry face than the Boss was wearing. Betrim put away his weapons and stepped back from the situation, slumping down against a wall, the grin slipping from his face to be replaced by his standard expressionless mess of scars and burns.

Green didn't take the hint. Seeing that Betrim had put away his weapons he made for a rush. The lad didn't get very far. Bones grabbed hold of his sword hand and pushed the boy in the chest hard. Green let go of his sword and found himself rolling arse over head into the corner where he lay on the floor, breathing heavy and still coughing blood. Bones tossed the sword towards a wall.

"What happened to Green's nose?" the Boss asked.

Bones spat and then sat himself down on the floor. "He pissed off the Black Thorn. Told him not ta long ago but the boy don't listen well."

The Boss looked at Betrim. Betrim avoided the gaze and shrugged as if the whole thing didn't matter a damn. Fact was he felt a bit disappointed. He was looking forward to shutting Green up for good.

"Henry, fix Green's nose," the Boss said and Henry skipped off towards the prone boy, grinning as she went.

"I don't know what you two got against each other an' I don't give a fuck. It stops, right now. Once we're done with the job you two can carve each other all ya like but if anythin' like this happens again 'fore we're done I'll personally hand ya both over ta the slavers guild. Good?"

Betrim nodded once. "Aye. Good."

Green howled in pain as Henry reset his nose with a loud crunch. Fresh blood ran down into his mouth and again the boy started hacking up red spittle.

"Good as new," Henry said as she stood up. Her hands were painted red with Green's blood and she stared at them with an odd fascination. Betrim remembered her looking at his blood in the exact same way, laughing just after she'd stabbed him. She looked pretty good naked as Betrim recalled even after she'd planted a knife in his side.

"What's the job?" Betrim asked from his section of wall. "And when do we get paid fer the last one?"

"As soon as Swift gets back," the Boss said, rubbing his temples with his fingers. "We got another job lined up from Deadeye."

"Boss, this ain't..."

"I don't wanna hear it, Thorn. We need ta do it so we're doin' it."

Betrim nodded but he was far from convinced. Working for Deadeye was about as dangerous as jobs came. The bitch had a nasty habit of choosing not to pay folk and killing them instead, or least that's what the rumours said. Though the rumours also said the Black Thorn had once burned an entire village to the ground, murdering everyone in it. Betrim knew first hand rumours were often made out of shit.

"What's the job?"

The Boss ground his metal teeth together and his scowl deepened even further. "We've been hired ta kill a member of Chade's rulin' council."

The Arbiter

It was never going to be the most comfortable of places, but it was spacious and well-situated and mostly empty. The warehouse still held a number of old crates, a few barrels, some rotted through and on the verge of collapse, some still serviceable, and any number of rats, many of which seemed to be verging on the giant variety. It had been occupied by some of the homeless folk that infested the city of Chade but Thanquil had seen them off. He needed privacy as much as space.

Jezzet stepped up beside Thanquil and looked around the open room. Even now she held herself like a taught bow string, ready to snap into action any moment.

"You paid money for this place? Why?"

"The Inquisition paid money for this place. We have a safe-house in the city but sometimes Arbiters require complete privacy and since I'm the only Arbiter in Chade, I have my privacy."

"Except you brought me here." Jezzet pointed out. She walked over to one of the old crates and lifted the top to look inside and then replaced it. "Might want to get rid of that one, something died in there."

From the smell of the place Thanquil had to agree on that account. "I suggest you move your gear here and keep it well hidden."

Jezzet narrowed her eyes at him, giving her an odd cat-like appearance. "You expecting we'll need to make our way from Chade in a hurry."

"Couldn't say. I like to be prepared though."

She snorted. "As long as I don't have to crawl through a sewer. Mind if I swing a sword around a bit?"

"Not at all."

Thanquil looked around the room for a suitable target. A small warehouse built of cheap wood with a small loft and a rotten ladder leading up to it. He spotted a plank of wood, no more than two foot long and a third as wide. Picking up the plank he placed it on top of a rotted barrel and walked away from it, measuring out seven paces before turning. He pulled the device that shot metal balls from his belt and armed it, measuring a small amount of black powder into the barrel and then rolling one of the small metal pellets behind it.

Thanquil took careful aim at the plank of wood closing one eye to stare down the barrel. He found himself nervous with the thought of pulling the trigger. He'd seen black powder in action before and it was known for being volatile and destructive. Even the alchemists who made the substance handled it with extreme care. People had been known to blow off limbs by mistake when experimenting with the stuff.

Wincing, Thanquil pulled the trigger on the device. Nothing happened.

"Told you. Folk in Chade love to swindle people such as yaself," Jezzet said. Thanquil glanced at her, she was stood in a low crouch with her sword reversed in her left hand, the blade pointing down her arm, but her eyes were on him and the ball thrower.

Remembering the man who had sold Thanquil the device, he pulled back the tiny hammer on top of the thing and aimed again. Again he pulled the trigger.

BANG!

Thanquil felt the recoil travel up his arm, smoke issuing from the end of the barrel. He turned to find Jezzet sprawled on the floor with eyes as wide as the moon and staring at the ball thrower.

"What the fuck was that?" she asked in a panicky voice.

Thanquil forced an uncertain smile onto his lips. "I...uh... I think it works." He placed the device on top of a nearby crate and approached the plank of wood he'd used as a target.

"Aye. Seems like." Thanquil saw Jezzet flow to her feet as she spoke and joined him to look at the target.

An arrow or a crossbow bolt would have stuck in the wood, maybe the head would have penetrated through but the shaft would have stuck. The plank of wood had a small, round hole in it where the metal ball had hit it. The pellet had burst through the target, splintering it on the way in and out. Of the ball there was no sign. Thanquil estimated it had hit the plank of wood no more than half a foot from where he had aimed.

Jezzet looked at the target through her wide eyes and then turned them on the ball thrower. "How do they put so much power into something so small?"

Thanquil was still looking for the little metal ball. "It's not the device. It's the black powder that has the power."

"A pinch of powder did that?" She looked sceptical. "I don't like it."

Thanquil wasn't sure he did either. Such a weapon could be terrible in the wrong hands though he thought it unlikely black powder would ever become readily available. The thought of an army all armed with such devices sent a shiver down his spine.

Giving up looking for the pellet, Thanquil replaced the target on top of the barrel and retrieved the ball thrower. Jezzet retreated to a safe distance and watched him as he sprinkled a bit of powder into the barrel but this time wrapped the metal ball in a strip of paper from his pocket.

"What's that?"

Thanquil grinned at her. "A rune." The one he'd chosen was a fire rune, he had to admit he was more than a little excited about seeing the effects; assuming the whole device didn't just explode in his hand.

"Magic?"

"Aye."

"Seems to me it's powerful enough without your witch hunter tricks."

"I don't much like being called a witch hunter," Thanquil said as he placed the ammunition into the device and again took aim at the target. Out of the corner of his eye he saw Jezzet place her hands over her ears and wished he could do the same. Again he cocked the hammer and pulled the trigger.

BANG!

This time the plank of wood burst into bright orange flame. Thanquil grinned wide and Jezzet backed away as the fire started to consume the plank of wood.

Still grinning, Thanquil turned to Jezzet. "It worked!"

She was standing with open mouthed wonder, staring at the flaming target. "You got one of those little rune things to put the fire out?"

The fire was spreading, moving from the plank of wood onto the rotted barrel and the flames were growing all the while. Last thing Thanquil needed was to burn down the place.

It took a good few minutes and Thanquil's coat had the distinctive smell of wood smoke by the time he smothered the fire. Jezzet didn't help, she returned to waving her sword about in dangerous arcs, slipping fluidly from one stance to another. Sometimes the strokes of her blade seemed to spin around her body and at other times they were darting, jabbing motions.

Thanquil had trained with one of the Inquisition's most renowned weapon masters but never had he seen anyone move with half as much grace as Jezzet Vel'urn when she practised with her blade. He'd watched dancers, both men and women, who had trained their whole lives but didn't possess the same fluidity of movement. He'd seen cats run along fences no thicker than a rope's width without the same surety of feet as Jezzet showed.

"How does it work?" she asked as she slipped from a two handed stance with the blade pointed downwards towards her back leg, into a side-on stance with her sword pointed in front of her, extending from her right hand as if it was another part of her body. She tried a few practice jabs and then made parrying motions, all the while dancing back and forth on the balls of her feet.

"The device is just a barrel in truth. It focuses the explosive power from the black powder and forces the metal ball to go where you point it," Thanquil explained.

"I meant your magic." Her blade flicked from one hand to the other, each seemed as sure and as deft as the other.

"The rune is transcribed onto paper, or wood, occasionally stone. When the rune is broken its power is released."

Jezzet stopped her practice and wiped a thin sheen of sweat from her forehead. "So anyone can write these runes? Seems dangerous."

Thanquil shook his head as he sat himself down on the floor and leaned his back against the rotten barrel. "The rune itself is a guide for what form the power should take, the energy to power the spell is taken from the person who inscribed the rune."

"So when you write that little scribble onto paper... you put...

power into it?"

"Yes."

"Can anyone do it?" Jezzet asked as she slipped into a new stance, this time with her sword in her right hand and a small dagger in her left.

"No. Only those with what we call potential and even then only after a great deal of training. There are other types of magic. Blessings and curses are used by chanting words with a variety of effects. Charms such as the one you wear."

He watched as Jezzet rubbed her left wrist with her right hand. "A dangerous operation," he continued, "to have a charm sewn into the flesh."

Jezzet nodded. "My old master's idea. Said he didn't ever want me losing it. Last thing I need or want is a child."

Thanquil nodded. "There are other types of magic too but each type has a counterpoint. Blessings grant... attributes, curses take away. Runes offer a burst of power, charms are a constant effect."

He had no wish to discuss magic any further lest the topic turn to the compulsion. Thanquil pushed himself to his feet, closed the distance between him and Jezzet in three easy steps and drew his own sword.

Before he knew how, his sword was no longer in his hand. Jezzet held the length of steel in her left and her own blade was pressed against Thanquil's neck. It had happened so fast he wasn't even sure how she had done it.

Jezzet backed away and looked at his sword. A long, slender, single-edged length of steel with plain hand guard and charms engraved all the way down the blade. Her own sword was shorter but not by much, lighter by the way she held it and double edged with no guard.

She snorted and tossed his sword back to him. Thanquil caught it and dropped back into stance. "You're sloppy and slow but the sword is good steel."

Thanquil didn't wait for her to finish speaking. He came on again, the first attack a wild downwards slash which she stepped away from and then he sent a jabbing thrust at her chest. Jezzet caught the blade on her own and, with a flick of her wrist, sent Thanquil's blade out of his hand and spinning across the room.

"You really are quite good with a sword," Thanquil said as he collected his blade from the floor and approached Jezzet again.

"Any blade actually. You're not."

"No. My arms master always used to tell me I was passable at best." Thanquil ran at her swinging. Jezzet reversed the grip of her sword, stepped under Thanquil's swing and his own momentum carried him onto the flat of her blade.

"That's three times you should be dead. How have you survived so long?" Jezzet mocked but she was smiling at him.

"I'm an Arbiter. We don't tend to fight fair." This time Thanquil feinted left, side-stepped to his right, and flicked a quick thrust towards Jezzet's head. His feint didn't fool her for a moment. She stepped with him, ducked his attack, and swept his legs out from under him.

Thanquil hit the ground hard, his breath rushing out of his lungs in a coughing wheeze. A moment later he found Jezzet on top of him with one knee on the wrist of his sword hand and the other knee pressing down on his chest making it even harder for him to draw a breath. Her sword tip hovered just above the bare skin of his neck.

"I doubt it's wise for a small woman like yourself to get so close to an opponent," Thanquil wheezed in a small voice after sucking in some air.

"It's not," the woman on top of him replied with a grin. "Unless I'm the stronger." She pushed herself off him knee first, causing him to cough again and then she danced backwards and waited for him to stand back up.

"I don't think I stand a chance against you," Thanquil said as he struggled back to his feet.

"You don't," Jezzet replied, the smile still playing on her lips. "But a bit of sparring will do us both good."

He lunged, parried a lazy flick from her blade, and then he slashed with all his strength. Jezzet caught Thanquil's blade on her own, twisted her wrist and stepped in close to him. He found his own blade unnervingly close to his neck. Jezzet's blade was almost as close and she almost as close again. He could smell her she was so close and she smelled clean, with a hint of sweat. It was a marked improvement from the day he had met her. His heart was beating too fast, though whether it was from the sparring or her closeness he couldn't tell.

Then she stepped away and backed off again leaving Thanquil to wonder why the hell he had decided to spar with her in the first place.

"You could at least give me some tips as you keep killing me," he said, dropping back into stance again.

"Don't pick a fight with a Blademaster," she said with a wink.

"Wait, you're a..." But she was already on him, pressing the attack.

The Blademaster

Jezzet didn't like it. She didn't like the whole damned situation. She didn't like the shoes, she liked the dress even less, she liked the people that would be attending even less, and what she liked least of all was the idea that those people might be looking at her.

It wasn't the first time she'd been to a fancy ball. D'roan used to love parading her about on his arm, those times though she'd still been dressed in leathers. The folk at these sorts of balls saw what they expected, in leathers they'd seen her as a savage to be avoided and ignored. In a dress they'd see her as one of them.

But you're not one of them, Jez. Just remember, if anyone looks at you funny, kill them. They'll be plenty of cutlery lying around.

The thought of stabbing someone with a spoon made Jezzet smile, she wasn't even sure such a thing was possible.

Maybe if it was a really sharp spoon.

"You look happy," Thanquil said from beside her. She'd let him dress her up like some blooded lady but when he'd tried to take her arm she'd very nearly twisted it off.

"Ever killed anyone with a spoon?" she asked him.

"Uhhh..."

"Me neither, but I'm thinking of trying." That shut him up, gave him that, '*is she serious?*' look.

Jezzet padded along the line in sandals. It was good to see the fancy folk have to queue. With D'roan there had been no standing in lines. Everyone knew him, everyone feared him and so he walked past the lines and past the servants with the lists at the entrance, and Jezzet walked with him. She'd never admit it but it had felt good, being low-born and all and walking past all the blooded and rich folk as if they were nothing.

Her dress was a chore and no mistake. A dark-blue silk-like cloth, but not silk, wrapped around her body so tight it constricted her and so loose it left her feeling naked. It covered her chest and back and for that she was glad. It clung to her torso in such a way that left little to the imagination and somehow managed to make her breasts look bigger than they were and without showing off any cleavage. From her hips it started to fan out a little, not much but enough to provide an ease of movement she was glad of. The dressmaker had assured her the fabric would twirl with her as she danced and dazzle every man in the room. Jezzet had almost hit him for assuming she would dance.

The dressmaker had despaired over what to do with Jezzet's hair but she had no time for it or him. Short and spiky was how she liked it so it never got in her eyes and needed no maintenance. She'd seen women take hours brushing their hair until it gleamed in the light. Seemed like a waste of time they could better spend learning to stab people which was a far more useful skill in the Wilds.

They were nearing the front of the queue now. Soon the servants would check the Arbiter's invitation and then they would be inside, among the fancy folk and the finery and Jezzet would be one of them.

Sounds like hell.

She tried to distract herself by looking around the grounds. It seemed a wonder to her that she'd been to Chade a number of times, twice on the arm of D'roan, and didn't know such a place existed. The manse, though inside the city, was as big as a castle. Walls near thirty feet high surrounded the estate and all patrolled by a number of private guard. It made sense as the city guard were, it had to be said, notorious for their disloyalty.

Crushed stone covered the courtyard and lined the pathways into the extensive and beautiful garden that, by the looks of things, surrounded the entire manor. Huge green bushes grew in straight lines and right angles, flowers of all colours she could name sprouted from select patches of dirt, artful lanterns hung over ornate benches and cast dancing shadows while attracting the flying, biting bugs that could be found near any water source.

The manor itself was huge, almost as large as D'roan's own home had been. Built entirely of stone and glass windows with creeping green vines winding their way up the walls. The entrance was covered by a huge porch that was held up by two massive white pillars of stone each as thick as a tree and a good ten feet high. Jezzet was impressed despite herself, the Arbiter just looked bored.

Likely he's seen it all and more before. No doubt Arbiters are invited to all the fancy places.

It was easy to forget this was how the fancy folk lived even here in Chade. In the Wilds, life was hard, brutal, short, messy, and bloody but there was also this. The blooded and the folk in the free cities that titled themselves '*Lord this*' or '*Lady that*' had money enough to spare and they knew how to spend it to make life grand and pretty. Still seemed a waste of bits to Jez.

"Invitation," the servant at the entrance said as Thanquil and Jezzet stepped to the front of the queue of fancy folk.

"Arbiter Darkheart and guest," Thanquil said with a pleasant smile.

The servant nodded and smiled back. "Invitation," he repeated.

"Don't have one. I wasn't invited."

Jezzet noticed guards by each of the pillars, four men in total and all of them armed and dangerous-looking. The servant stopped smiling and addressed the Arbiter in the most polite of tones. "I'm afraid this is an invitation only..."

"What's your name?"

"Elgin, sir."

"I'm no sir, Elgin. I'm an Arbiter and I'll remember to mention to Lord Xho that his servant, Elgin, is responsible for his being investigated by the Inquisition. I'm sure he'll be most interested to know why you turned me away."

Elgin looked worried. No one wanted to be the focus of an investigation by the witch hunters, even someone living in one of the free cities. The Inquisition could make anyone's life a living hell and Jezzet wagered they weren't above the odd assassination.

"Of course, Arbiter Darkheart," Elgin said in a most pleasant tone again with a nervous smile gracing his plump, hairless lips. "Feel free to enter. Uh... your sword."

"Will stay sheathed by my side."

Again Elgin nodded and then stepped aside. Thanquil grinned at the man and entered the manor with Jezzet just half a step behind. Another servant awaited them inside and, with a formal bow, started to lead them to the great hall. Jezzet stuck close to Thanquil and picked up his arm with her own. She was certain she'd rather fight every guard in Chade than step into the great hall with all the fancy folk inside.

"Would they really do that? The Inquisition. Would they investigate Xho for refusing you entry?"

Thanquil chuckled. "The Inquisition has better things to do than investigate every Lord that lacks courtesy."

Jezzet was fast realising that while it may be impossible to lie to an Arbiter, it wasn't impossible for an Arbiter to lie right back and this one seemed quite adept at twisting the truth.

When the doors to the great hall opened the blast of sound and heat and colours and revelry stunned Jez. Music filled the hall, spilling out into the corridor in waves. The big room, which seemed all the bigger given her recent confinement in a cell, was lit by a hundred different sources. Ensconced torches lined the walls at regular intervals, a large hearth sat in the far side of the hall, roaring away to itself despite the heat. Three chandeliers hung from the ceiling, each with dozens of flickering candles.

The hall was already filled with guests and they were more colourful than the flowers in the gardens outside. Women in finery with giant, frilly dresses or sleek, skin-hugging silk, some red, some blue, some yellow, some purple, some green, some orange, some colours Jezzet didn't know and didn't care to see ever again. One woman wore such a slim dress of skin colour that at first Jezzet had thought her to be naked. Only once she realised the woman had no nipples and no cunt between her legs did Jezzet notice she wore a dress.

The men were almost as bad. Suits of colours to match their partners or to match their livery. Compared to the fancy folk in the great hall she in her plain blue dress and the Arbiter in a quilted doublet of brown with his brown Arbiter's cloak looked more out of place than she could say.

Like two ducks pretending to be peacocks.

"Your mouth is open, Jezzet," the Arbiter said from her arm. "It's not very lady-like."

"I'm not a lady, Thanquil," Jezzet replied in a pointed tone but made an effort to close her mouth all the same as he escorted her into the hall.

You've seen all this before, Jez. Just been so long in the wilderness you've forgotten what it's like. They may look so very fine but put the women on their backs and they'll moan like any cheap whore, and men die just as easily in fine silks as they do armour. It's like D'roan said, 'It's all just a lie to make them think they're better than the rest of the Wilds.' The thought brought some comfort but was diminished when Jezzet had to admit that D'roan was the biggest liar of them all.

"Arbiter Darkheart and partner," the announcer announced into the hall in a voice loud enough to carry over the music.

Some sets of eyes turned to watch their entrance, more than Jezzet would have liked but by no means a lot. The women dismissed her at a glance while the men looked her up and down with appraising eyes. Jezzet Vel'urn had felt like many things before; a warrior, a thief, a murderer, a monster, but never had she felt as cheap as when the men in this room looked at her. It made her angry, angry enough to do some damage. She started looking around for some cutlery. Then their gazes were gone, back to the women they were with, to the women they weren't with, or to the men they were sharing cups with.

"That was uncomfortable," she whispered close to Thanquil's ear.

"You're the most beautiful woman in the room, Jezzet. You're going to have to get used to a few stares," the Arbiter said. He was looking about the hall through squinting eyes. "You served your purpose well."

"My purpose?" Jezzet found herself feeling angry though she couldn't say why.

Thanquil glanced at her. "You didn't think I brought you here to show you a good time did you? With you on my arm not a single man or woman even noticed me."

Jezzet felt cheap again. *He's right, Jez. He bought your life and freedom. What did you expect he wanted in return?* All the same she almost tore her arm away from him and stormed away but something in his face stopped her. He looked... nervous.

The Arbiter was sweating, his jaw was clenched, his teeth grinding back and forth, and his eyes darted about in a mad dance over the fancy folk arrayed in front of him.

"Are you alright?" she asked him.

"I... uh... need to... there." He started walking, near dragging her with him and stopped in front of a fat man in a suit of at least four different colours, each the more gaudy than the last. The fat man wore more gold than Jezzet had seen in her life. Golden rings on every finger, golden bracelets, golden studs in both his ears and nose, even a golden choker around his flabby neck. Seemed a pointless waste of wealth to Jezzet, one of those rings could feed a family for a month.

The Arbiter held out his hand to the fat man as he greeted him. Jezzet had seen the like before, in some places the grasping of hands was a traditional form of greeting. In the Wilds, however, it wasn't so. Men didn't want to touch another man, not skin to skin. The blooded folk had made such a habit of murdering each other that they had resorted to all sorts of devious tactics including rings containing a poison needle. One grasp of hands could well mean death for the unwary party.

"Arbiter Darkheart," Thanquil introduced himself. "I don't believe we met."

The fat man didn't even glance at Thanquil's hand and spent almost as little time looking at the Arbiter himself. He did, however, spend some time leering at Jezzet. The woman he was with also stared at Jez but with a great deal more hostility and great deal less lust. For a brief moment Jez considered reaching for the nearest spoon and attempting to gut them both, but they turned and walked away before she could find a weapon.

"What was that about?" she asked him in a whisper so close he must have felt her breath on his ear. It didn't faze him. He didn't even seem to hear her. His eyes were still darting about in constant motion and Jez could swear his hand was shaking.

"Wait here," he instructed her and took his arm from hers before striding away. Jezzet watched as he stepped into the path of a hurrying servant carrying a tray of empty goblets. The two men collided and the servant wasted no time in bowing multiple times, begging apologies, scooping up the scattered goblets and speeding away.

By the time Thanquil returned he had stopped sweating, stopped shaking and his eyes were calm again. His nervous, jittery energy seemed to have disappeared and he was back to his normal self.

Nothing about this man is normal, Jez.

"What was that about?" Jezzet asked again.

He smiled at her as he once again took her arm with his own. "Oh nothing, it doesn't matter." His other hand was buried deep in one of his coat's pockets. "We should introduce ourselves to Lord Xho. It is his ball after all."

Jezzet shook her head. "He won't be here, not yet. Maybe not at all. Those that throw these things tend to turn up late, after all the other guests have arrived. D'roan used to routinely not make an appearance at all. Used to just sit upstairs in his manor while the ball went on below. He used to say it showed his power over them. While it was going on we used to..." Jezzet trailed off, not wanting to talk about it and found Thanquil looking at her. "Why are we here anyway? Why am I here?"

"I'm here because I need to talk to one of the council and this is the only way I can do so without the other three."

"Lord Xho?"

"No. You're here for two reasons. The first you've already been more than successful at. With you on my arm no one has spared me even a second glance."

Flattery made Jez nervous and uncomfortable but among all these fancy folk she was already more than enough of both.

"The second reason you're here is because I may need a distraction and if I do, you're going to be it." Worrying words but the Arbiter said them with a pleasant smile.

"You want me to distract an entire room full of the richest and most powerful people in Chade?"

"Maybe, yes."

"How?"

Thanquil grinned and looked around the gathered fancy folk. "Jezzet there isn't a man in this room who hasn't spent at least some time staring at you and you're without a doubt the most graceful person I've ever seen. I'm sure you can find some way to distract them. Failing that just start... you know... killing people."

"Killing people?" *In a room surrounded by armed guards and some of the meanest looking bodyguards I've ever seen.* The bodyguards were there, keeping to the walls, trying to look inconspicuous.

"Yes. With a spoon if you like."

She shot a glare at him but he laughed it away. "And how will I know when you need a distraction?"

A shadow of doubt crossed his face. "If I need one, you'll know."

"Do you enjoy being cryptic and mysterious?"

"It's part of the Arbiter training. Over there," he said, nodding across the dance-floor. "The door on the far wall. I wonder where it leads."

Jezzet looked. Seemed to be an unassuming door. One of the servants' entrances, she guessed, maybe even leading upstairs. Getting all the way across the room would be hard with the music playing and the fancy folk dancing.

"If you ask me to dance I may have to hurt you again," she warned him.

The Arbiter laughed. "I wouldn't dream of it. No I think we'll be better splitting up here. You draw far too much attention. Remember, if I need the distraction, you're it. In the meantime, mingle, dance, and enjoy yourself, Jezzet Vel'urn."

She sent a dark scowl his way but Thanquil didn't see it, he was already striding away, skirting the dancers, heading for the door.

The Arbiter

Slipping through the door Thanquil took a quick look at his new surroundings. A long corridor leading further into the mansion and a flight of stairs that wound back on themselves before reaching the first floor of the building. He pulled the door closed and breathed a short sigh of relief for being out of the ball room. All that noise and falsity was enough to make him long for the Inquisition grounds, at least there the people didn't try to hide their hostile stares.

Nobody noticed him leave, he was certain of that. Nobody noticed him because nobody wanted to notice him. He felt bad about leaving Jezzet to her fate but certain sacrifices had to be made. She would most likely survive one way or another. He fingered the small copper band in his pocket. The stolen ring calmed him and calm was something he needed right now. He needed to find a servant or a guard, someone to question.

The stairs were carpeted, a thief's best friend and Thanquil's, though he had no intention of stealing anything further tonight. Of course that didn't mean he wouldn't if he got the chance.

His footfalls made almost no sound, just a light brushing of leather sole on pile. He mounted the stairs two at a time and waited at the top, listening. He could hear nothing but the distant sounds of music. He poked his head around the corner first one way, then the other. Another corridor and again empty.

The walls were bare of decorations. It seemed Lord Xho kept an austere home. That didn't surprise Thanquil. Xho had once owned half of the southern Wilds and was reported to have had an army of fifty-thousand black skins at the time. He had warred and pillaged and raped and butchered his way north until an alliance of blooded had crushed his army and thrown him back. Xho escaped the battle and with a fortune, enough money to buy his way onto the Chade ruling council after a previous member had mysteriously vanished. Now he was reported to own half of Chade itself and it was because he still knew the value of gold and didn't spend it rashly.

It was not Lord Xho, Thanquil had come here to see tonight. It was the fat one, Lord Farin Colth. The pig was a sot and a letch and he would be here. It had taken a fair few gold coins for Thanquil to find out where Colth would be tonight. He always turned up to these balls as a courtesy, but never stayed in the ball room. He would meet and greet and then Xho would provide him with a room and a woman. Rumours said Colth had a weakness for black skinned girls, the younger the better, and Lord Xho was willing to provide. No doubt there would be a favour somewhere down the line.

Through his bribes and eves-dropping Thanquil had discovered the politics of the Chade council were complicated and treacherous. Only the pirate Drake Morrass seemed to be free of the machinations of the others and only then because he rarely, if ever, visited Chade.

Footsteps. More than one set for certain and heading his way by the sound. Thanquil tried the handle on the closest door and found it unlocked. He slipped inside the darkness of the room and waited, his ear pressed close to the door. Three sets of footsteps he counted and making no pretence at quiet. Whispered voices as well, but he could hear no more than the hiss of breath escaping lips. Two male and one female by the sounds of it.

The footsteps came closer, passed, and receded and still Thanquil waited to make sure. He turned to look at the room he had found. Never know when there might be something worthless to steal. He almost jumped out of his coat when he saw the figure on the bed. Thanquil watched for a moment but saw no movement and decided to approach.

A man lay, stripped down to his undergarments, motionless among the sheets. He breathed and his eyes were open but he did not seem to notice Thanquil. The Arbiter waved a hand in front of the man's face, above his eyes. Still no response. There was a pipe discarded on the bed close to the man's left hand. Thanquil picked it up and sniffed. Casher weed, without a doubt, but there was something else as well, something he couldn't place. A quick search of the room turned up a uniform the guards were wearing. The guard had been drugged and Thanquil was certain he hadn't done it to himself. The casher weed was mixed with something.

Again Thanquil approached the guard on the bed. At least he was alive, and conscious. Thanquil took hold of the man's face and turned it to look into his own. He hated asking questions.

"Where is Lord Colth?" The compulsion didn't work. He could feel the man's will but it was like trying to hold onto water with an open hand, it just slipped through his grasp.

"Colth... with whore... second corridor... down... second door on... right," the guard spoke as if in a dream.

Thanquil stood, confused. "Why did you answer me?" His compulsion didn't worked, didn't taken hold. The man shouldn't have said a word.

"I... don't know..."

Thanquil looked at the man again. His pupils were wide, too wide, but his gaze was unseeing. A trickle of blood ran from his nose and another from his ear. His forehead was hot, clammy, sweating. Whatever had been done to the man seemed to be killing him. Thanquil considered for a moment trying to figure out what had caused it, but he didn't have time. He needed to get to Colth and fast. Quick enough to question the fat man.

Outside, the footsteps were long gone and the whispered voices gone with them. Still, Thanquil could hear far away music, distant and muffled but the only other sound was the faint hiss and pop of burning candles.

Second corridor down. Thanquil turned one way then the other. No choice but to pick a direction and hope. He went right, slipped past one adjoining corridor and then, with a glance to check it was clear, turned down the next. The mansion was huge, Thanquil couldn't guess at just how big from his brief view of the building but he had to wonder how many rooms it had. A prince of the Five Kingdoms had once boasted to him the royal palace had three-thousand rooms which seemed a bit excessive by any standards. Lord Xho's mansion was no palace but its rooms must have numbered in the hundreds at least.

Second door on the right. He stopped outside the door for a while, pressed his ear to it and strained to hear even the slightest of sounds. He whispered a quick blessing of hearing and noise swamped in around him.

The music, still muffled, became loud. The candles sounded close. Padded footsteps a long way away, still quiet even with the blessing. A half-whispered curse followed by *thump*, but not from this room. A bird call outside somewhere in the night. A grunting, groaning, moaning sound that could only come from sexual activities sounded close by.

Thanquil stopped whispering the blessing and twisted the door handle before slipping into the room. What he saw made him forget to close the door after him. There was blood. Blood everywhere. The bed, the floor, the walls, the furniture, even the ceiling a good ten feet above was dripping blood.

Two bodies lay on the bed, both opened up, innards pulled out. One was a huge carcass, a man and a fat one at that. Without a doubt it was Colth. The other was thinner, smaller, and younger, with black skin and, at one time, breasts but not now. Both were... gone. Where, Thanquil could not say.

He approached, careful to step over or around the blood on the floor, making sure to dodge any spots where it dripped from the ceiling, walking on his toes. Closer he went and closer, fighting the urge to gag. So much blood. He needed to investigate, to see if any clues existed as to the nature of the killing.

The bodies looked to be cut open by a blade, sharp but serrated, ragged flesh attested to that. Both must have been dead before, they could not have gone through such butchery without screaming loud enough to drown the music in the great hall. Both corpses were naked. Lord Colth's cock was missing, cut off with only a torn, bloody wound to show.

Thanquil had seen many things in his time as Arbiter. He'd seen and been the cause of burnings. He'd seen murder in a horrifying variety of forms. Bodies cut up, torn up. It never failed to affect him though, never failed to make him sick to his stomach. This was no normal murder. Someone was sending a message, he was certain of that.

Thanquil felt a drop of blood tap him on the shoulder, fallen from the ceiling, and it was all he could do not to wretch. He turned and fled from the room, leaving the slaughter behind.

The Black Thorn

Betrim pulled open the top draw, nothing. The second draw, nothing. The third, nothing. Three rooms he'd been in and each one was more fancily decorated than the last and not one had a single damned thing worth stealing. For the most part they were empty barring the furniture itself and, while he had no doubt it was worth a few bits, escaping with a wardrobe strapped to his back did not seem a good idea.

Even the sconces on the wall were ugly things made of dark grey iron. Betrim had never been in a mansion before but he was sure everything was supposed to be made from gold. As it was, Betrim owned more gold himself than he'd seen in the mansion so far and that came to a grand total of one bit. Far from a fortune.

He checked the wardrobe. Good-looking hardwood, he reckoned, imported from somewhere far off. Empty. There was a large mirror Betrim reckoned was worth a lot but it was as tall as him and he didn't like his chances of getting it out the mansion without breaking it and breaking mirrors was bad luck, everyone said. He'd had more than enough bad luck of late.

He considered bundling up the curtains and having off with them but who the hell would buy a set of curtains? No one he knew.

He hoped Swift was having a better time of it. They'd broken into the estate no problem, wasn't hard when the owner built in a secret tunnel entrance that turned out to be not so secret. The Boss left Bones to guard the entrance as it also happened to be their exit and the rest slipped across the gardens, running from shadow to shadow when guard patrols weren't looking. They climbed to the first floor and Swift opened them a window, nice and quiet. When inside the Boss had taken Henry and Green to do the job while Betrim and Swift were to steal anything worth a bit that wasn't nailed down. So far all Betrim had to show for his night of thievery was three bronze bits that he found in a discarded pair of britches in one of the rooms.

The Boss, Henry, and Green would be done with the killing by now and that meant it was time for Betrim to get out as well. Fact was he didn't want to be here when the body was found. Chances were the Boss would leave him to his fate in that case.

Betrim checked under the bed. Bare except for a shiny looking bed pan. Looked to be made out of good metal, steel maybe, and it was empty. Good steel was worth a few bits to the right people so Betrim grabbed it and gave it a quick sniff. Smelled clean, not that it would stop Betrim from stealing it even if it wasn't.

With bed pan in hand he walked to the door, opened it and stuck his head out, looking both ways down the corridor to make sure it was empty. It was. He stepped out just as another man stepped out of a doorway two doors down.

He recognised the man in a moment. Short with short hair and a short stubbly beard and the coat. The coat that identified him as an enemy of the Black Thorn.

The Arbiter stared at Betrim so Betrim just stared right back. Just like a wolf, if Betrim turned and ran the Arbiter would have to chase him, it was their way. Better to stand his ground and hope to get lucky and kill the fucker. Betrim didn't much like counting on luck, always seemed to turn on him at the last moment.

The Arbiter looked down at Betrim's three fingered hand. With a twinge of annoyance Betrim threw the bed pan away.

"Black Thorn..." the Arbiter said.

"Arbiter," Betrim replied. Didn't seem like there was much else worth saying so Betrim unhooked his hand axe from his belt and charged, a shout escaping from his lips as he did.

The Arbiter dodged the first swing of the axe as he was drawing his sword and then blocked the second swing. Then the bastard attacked. Two lightning fast jabs with his little sword. Betrim ducked the first, caught the second and then the Arbiter's left fist seemed to come out of nowhere and cracked him in the face. It felt like being hit with an anvil and might well have done for some men, but the Black Thorn was not one of those men.

Betrim steadied himself with a three-fingered hand on the wall and spat out some blood, no teeth though, he was glad for that. Last thing he needed was to be uglied up even more. He was glad for something else too, Jezzet was not with the Arbiter. There were very few people the Black Thorn was scared of fighting and Jezzet Vel'urn happened to be right near the top of that list.

Both men watched each other, Betrim with axe in hand, the Arbiter with his sword, and neither wanting to be the one to fall. Betrim almost surprised himself when he chopped at the Arbiter so he was pretty sure that bastard must have been surprised but he blocked it all the same and started muttering to himself, chanting some bloody words the Black Thorn couldn't understand.

Again Betrim chopped but this time the Arbiter brushed the attack away as if it was nothing and then started raining wild slashing blows at Betrim. Again and again Betrim blocked and blocked, falling back all the while. The Arbiter was too fast, too strong. Magic, Betrim knew for certain. Bloody witch hunters were always cheating.

He saw an opening, brief but it was there all the same. Betrim snatched a small knife from his belt and lunged at the Arbiter's face. The witch hunter tried to spin away from the attack, stumbled into a wall and then scrambled away on all fours as Betrim buried his axe in the wall where the Arbiter's head had been just a moment before.

When the Arbiter stood back up he was bleeding. A small cut on his left cheek just an inch below his eye made it look almost like he was weeping blood. Betrim found he was grinning and he knew that was never a pleasant sight, tended to scare most folk into running, but not an Arbiter.

He heard footsteps, sounded like a number of them and they sounded like heavy boots running on stone floor. Guards appeared at the end of the corridor behind the Arbiter, two of them. Betrim risked a glance backwards and saw another two. One of them spoke to his fellow and then ran off, no doubt going for more guards. The three remaining guards started forwards.

Betrim looked at the Arbiter. The man looked about as worried as Betrim felt. He glanced first at the Black Thorn, then at the approaching guards, then back again. Betrim had only one guard, the way he saw it that meant he had twice the chances of survival.

"Put down your weapons and surrender," said one of the lads

approaching the Arbiter. Then he glanced into the open door, into the room the Arbiter had come from and Betrim saw the colour drain from his face.

The Arbiter sighed.

The guard with the pale face looked at the Arbiter, then the Black Thorn, then the guard behind Betrim. "Kill them."

The guard came onto Betrim swinging a heavy sword like he was trying to chop wood with it. It was a simple thing for Betrim to brush the weapon away, smash the guard in his face with an elbow and then plant his axe in the guard's face. It bit deep into his skull right about where his eye was and the man went down in a gurgle and spray of blood.

Betrim wrenched his axe free, bits of bone and flesh came with it. He turned and chopped at the occupied Arbiter. The witch hunter saw the attack coming and managed to block with his sword. One of his guards was already down and the other attacked while the Arbiter's sword was occupied. Didn't count as one of the Black Thorn's but he'd take it. Seven Arbiters dead sounded better than six.

At the last moment the Arbiter drew something from his belt and pointed it at the guard.

BANG!

Betrim stumbled backwards shaking his head, trying to stop the ringing in his ears. The guard collapsed on the stone floor with a small hole through his breastplate, through his chest. A spatter of blood on the wall behind. The Arbiter tucked the little device back into his belt and turned towards Betrim again.

The Arbiter took a step forward. Betrim took a step backward. Killing witch hunters was always tricky. They used magic and didn't care who got hurt. Betrim had once used a woman as a hostage, the Arbiter had just stabbed both her and the Black Thorn at the same time.

Again the witch hunter started whispering some words, this time to his sword. Betrim was just getting ready to attack when the Arbiter smashed the hilt of his sword against the wall. The wall split and cracked, a huge rent in the stone sped along the wall towards Betrim. As the crack reached level with Betrim the wall exploded outwards in a hail of stone and wood and plaster. For a moment Betrim went down on one knee as a large brick hit him in the side of the head. For a moment his vision went dark and it took a few shakes of his head before he could see again.

"Black Thorn," the Arbiter said again, the cut on his face was still bleeding, fat drops of red dropped down to stain his coat. "Why did you..."

Betrim didn't give the bastard a chance to finish his question. He threw the knife in his left hand with an easy flick of the wrist. Betrim had long ago puzzled out how to throw a knife with only three fingers, only problem was it was never on target. The small blade stuck into the Arbiter's right leg and the witch hunter went down, falling backwards with a bellow of pain.

The Black Thorn's grin returned as he stalked forwards. The Arbiter struggled back to his knees, grimacing in pain.

"Thorn!" Betrim glanced behind him. Swift was stood at the end of the corridor waving like he was on fire.

"What?"

"RUN!" Then Swift was gone.

As the Arbiter pulled himself back to his feet Betrim saw the guards behind him. A corridor full of angry looking men, all armed and edging closer. Betrim was never good with numbers, but he could count to ten and then some and the guards were already closer to then some. The Arbiter glanced behind him and then back and for a brief moment Betrim thought he saw fear on the man's face.

"Good luck," Betrim said with a grin before he turned and ran, hoping that the Boss didn't decide to leave him behind.

The Blademaster

It didn't take long once the Arbiter had left for men to start presenting themselves to Jezzet. The first had been a handsome enough man though little more than a boy in truth. A thin fuzz of sand coloured hair stood out on his chin, and he had a pointed jaw, straight nose, and deep blue eyes. He bowed low and tried to take Jezzet's hand. She pulled away and almost punched the boy until she remembered men liked to kiss women's hands in some places. Seemed a dangerous prospect to her, you never knew where a person's hands had been. Her own had been in some pretty rough places.

The handsome youth straightened with an awkward smile but didn't run off straight away. He'd tookn a step closer to Jez and said, "Would the lady care to dance?"

Jezzet snorted at him and replied with. "I'd care not to dance."

The boy gave up after that, walking away with a look of utter confusion on his face as if he couldn't quite understand why Jezzet hadn't swooned at his meagre attentions. Truth was it seemed to take very little to impress these fancy ladies. One pretty-faced man seemed to get them all moist.

The second man was older, Jezzet reckoned close to his fiftieth year, but no less bold. He stepped close to Jez, too close. She stepped backwards and he followed so she stepped back again, he followed again. They continued in that strange parody of a dance for six steps before he smiled at her in a disarming fashion. Jezzet could have kept stepping away from him for the entire night, she made sure to keep track of everyone around her.

"My name is Lord Albert B'rind," the man said in voice like honey and accompanied by a blast of wine-scented air.

"Lord of where?" Jezzet asked.

"Pardon?"

"You can't be a Lord without somewhere to be Lord of and you're about as blooded as I am so..."

Again the man smiled but with a lot less warmth this time. "I'm

Lord of Ellinworth. It's a holding in Acanthia, do you know where that is?"

That might have brought a smile to Jezzet's lips if it hadn't been so patronising.

I was born in Acanthia, you stupid bastard. She'd spent the first twenty years of her life in and around the merchant town of Truridge and they were not a pleasant twenty years.

"I've never heard of it, it must be a very minor holding. I should go." She turned and almost knocked into another man. Jezzet was certain he hadn't been there a moment ago.

He must move as quiet as a ghost.

"I am shorry. Completely my fault, mish..."

"Jezzet," she replied without thinking. The man was more than a little drunk but no less handsome for it. His jaw and eyes gave away his blooded heritage and his red cheeks gave him a friendly appeal.

"Mish Jezzzzzet," he smiled.

Definitely blooded. Say what you want of the rich bastards, but they are pretty, Jez.

"Is a pretty name... and a pretty face."

"And you are?"

The man's mouth made an 'O' shape. "I'm terribly shorry. My mannersss are all over the place." He leaned towards her and she could smell the alcohol on him, it overpowered the perfume he was wearing which Jezzet counted as a good thing.

Men shouldn't wear perfume. Can't say you know why women do either, Jez. Nothing wrong with the smell of good, clean sweat.

"I think I may be a little bit drunk," he drawled at her.

"Uh huh."

"My name ish Anders and is a pleashhure... a pleashure to meet you, Jezzzzzet."

"Right." Jezzet glanced around the room and then back again, Anders was still smiling at her, swaying on his feet just a little. He was a little taller than Thanquil with long dark hair. His green, silken suit looked well-worn and stained in places, but there was something about the man that set Jezzet's nerves on edge.

"Truth ish," he said, leaning forwards a little as he swayed. "I find theesh things terribly dull. How does a beautiful, very, very beautiful, woman like yourshelf shtand them?"

Jezzet levelled a stare at him. "I count the number of armed people in the room and make sure I know where they all are."

"Really?" He sounded very surprised.

"Twelve guards, four by each wall and each carrying a longsword and wearing a plate cuirass. Three seem a little green but at least two are veterans."

Anders gazed around the room, although in his state Jezzet doubted he could see that far. They were quite near one of the walls though and a great, glass window behind Anders had a guard either side of it. "That ish quite impresshive."

"Eight others, bodyguards most like. Two mingling as guests, one armed with a shortsword, the other with a long curved knife. Six around the walls, two talking by the hearth both armed with iron clubs, and four at various spots well away from each other all armed with swords and wearing studded leather."

Anders was nodding like a bird. "I think you misshed two though."

Jezzet narrowed her eyes at the man. *Something is wrong here, Jez.*

"There ish you for a shtart."

Jez took a step away from him. "What?" She noticed a small drop of blood on the shoulder of Anders' suit.

Anders smiled at her but made no move towards her. "You have a shord... a sword. Underneath that pretty blue dresh... dres.... dress. Shtrapped to your leg." He patted his leg to show her where he meant.

Jezzet glanced around her to make sure no one was coming for her. *How did he know?*

"There's another one too. Uh... another woman... armed I mean. There'sh lots of women. She's very, very tall."

Just then Jezzet heard a *bang*. It was muffled but it sounded all too familiar to her ears. A moment later a guard burst through the door Thanquil had used just a short while back. He looked around the ball room with panicked eyes. Jezzet noticed the music had stopped, as had all the chatter.

"There's an Arbiter upstairs fighting the Black Thorn!"

Fuck! Now would be the time for that distraction he needed, Jez.

A murmur ran through the crowd of gathered fancy folk and guards started moving towards the door.

"An Arbiter ish here?" She heard Anders say.

Think, Jez. A distraction...

"The Arbiter arrived with a woman didn't he?"

"She was around here somewhere."

"A pretty little thing. I talked to her."

"She was wearing a blue dress I think."

Anders looked at her. "Your dressh ish blue."

"That's her there."

"By the window."

"Guards! Over there."

"JEZZET!" Jez knew that voice anywhere. Masculine yet also feminine. She caught a glimpse of Constance towering above the crowd, pushing her way through.

"That'sh her. The tall one."

Jezzet found herself calm despite the weight of so many pairs of eyes, despite the angry giant of a woman bearing down on her wanting her head, despite the guards watching, wondering whether they should make a grab for her.

"I'm sorry, Anders," Jez said and despite the dangerous feeling she got off him she found she meant it.

"Wha..." Jezzet grabbed hold off his suit by both hands and pushed him backwards hard. His feet stumbled as he tried to keep himself upright but Jez kept pushing and then she threw her whole weight against him.

There was a loud crash as the window shattered and then they were out in open air and falling, falling, falling. Jezzet held onto Anders and held herself close.

His body hit the floor with an unhealthy, sickening thud. Jezzet rolled off the man and gasped for air. It had been a good twenty feet and even with a soft body to take the impact it had winded her.

A face appeared at the window above her. A large, red, angry face.

Constance roared at Jezzet in fury and for a moment Jez thought the bitch would follow her out the window, but she thought better of it. It was a miracle Jez survived and she was about half the size of Constance.

"I'M GOING TO KILL YOU, WHORE!" Constance screamed out the window but Jezzet was already running, or trying to. Her dress caught in her legs and she stumbled.

With no regard for the finery of the fabric, Jezzet ripped through the bottom half of the dress to free her legs and drew her sword from the strapping on her right thigh. She risked a glance back towards the body of Anders. He wasn't moving, didn't look to be breathing but he was bleeding and it didn't surprise her.

Best distraction I could do, Thanquil and it only cost one life. Good luck.

Jez ran. She had no idea where she was running to but she ran all the same. Gravel path, green hedge, and stone wall all passed by her in a blurry haze yet she didn't slow even for a moment. Two guards stepped out in front of her, didn't look to be after her, just out on patrol.

The first man died before his sword was out of its scabbard. A deep red rend of flesh where his face used to be. The second man drew his sword and slashed at her in one motion. Jezzet caught the blade on her own and, with an easy flick of her wrist, her blade was inside the man's guard. She stepped forward and thrust at the same time and her sword went straight through the man's neck. She pulled it free with a spray of blood that soaked into the remnants of her blue dress and then she started running again.

'A Blademaster never wounds', he used to say, *'always kills. Never leave an enemy alive, don't give them chance for revenge.'*

Strange for that thought to pop into her head now but Jezzet knew why. She'd made that mistake with Constance. This entire misadventure had happened because she left Constance alive. Wounded, but alive.

Jezzet pulled up, panting from the exertion of running. The estate was huge and she already felt like she'd been running for an age. She could hear shouts from behind her somewhere, from inside the manor, from everywhere. She looked around.

High walls on every side. How the fuck do I get out? Damned

Arbiter didn't tell me this part of his fucking plan.

In the distance she saw a figure sprint across a small section of grass and then disappear into the ground. When the figure didn't reappear Jezzet knew what she'd seen. A tunnel.

It was her last chance of surviving this death-trap. She just had to hope it led out and whoever had gone in first wasn't waiting for her.

Jezzet jumped into the hole. Her stupid sandals lost purchase and she went down onto her hands and knees in the dark. Then the smell hit her and she fought to stop herself from retching.

Great. Another fucking sewer!

THE ARBITER

By the time Thanquil stumbled through the door to the old warehouse he was bleeding from a dozen different places. He was sure most were only small cuts but the stab wound on his leg, given to him by the Black Thorn, did not feel so minor. Neither did the nick taken out of his left ear for that matter, never had he known a wound to hurt so much.

Thanquil had given worse than he had received, but it turned out fighting somewhere close to twenty well-armed guardsmen was as difficult as it sounded. He'd injured at least six of them and killed two. It was unfortunate but unavoidable.

After the fighting he'd fled and discovered that running away on an injured leg, with a host of guards chasing him, was about as difficult as that sounded. Thanquil had run, chanting a mixture of speed and endurance blessings and he thanked Volmar he was able to do so. Mixing blessings was difficult, only one in fifty Arbiters ever mastered the skill and he was glad he'd taken the time and made the effort.

Now his chanting had finished though and Thanquil found himself weak, beyond tired, bloodied and in pain, angry and more than a little confused. Why had the Black Thorn killed Lord Colth and why the hell could he not have waited another hour so Thanquil could have interrogated the fat Lord first.

He stumbled, tried to catch himself on one of the old crates and went straight through the rotten wood. He found himself sprawled on the floor amidst a pile of splinters and something that smelled like it might have been alive once. His breathing was heavy and he was contemplating passing out. Even as his eyes began to close, Thanquil knew he didn't have time for sleep. There were too many things to do, not least of which was getting out of the city before the guard caught up to him. He was certain his position as an Arbiter of the Inquisition wouldn't save him if the remaining council members decided he was responsible for Colth's gruesome death.

Reaching into his coat pocket, Thanquil pulled out a small wad of papers and leafed through until he found the correct one. Each slip of paper had a different symbol on it and each charm had a different effect. Thanquil bared his left arm and slapped the paper onto his skin, it stuck there as if glued and he knew it would hurt like hell when it came time to tear it off, taking with it all the hairs beneath.

His eyes snapped open and his vision cleared a little. The sleepless charm was a dangerous one if used for too long. A person could die of exhaustion easily enough and there were other perils. Prolonged use had been known to cause a variety of symptoms including hallucinations.

Struggling to his feet, Thanquil limped towards the crate where he'd stowed his pack. He reached inside, pulled out the heavy sack, and dumped it on the dusty floor along with his coat and the brown shirt he'd been wearing, now stained with red blood.

From his pack he pulled a rough-spun wool tunic, his leathers, and the small stash of medical supplies. It was little more than some ointment and a few bandages but it would serve a purpose. He'd never been too competent at the medical studies part of his training. Thanquil set about dressing his wounds. His leg first, he cleaned the angry flesh and then wrapped the bandage around his trousers. Then his left arm where he'd taken two small cuts, followed by his right where he'd taken another. His ear he cleaned as best he could but left un-bandaged. It would do for now. He pulled the tunic over his head and sat down, resting for a short time. There was one other thing he needed to do, something unpleasant and something he had to do alone.

"Jezzet," Thanquil called out. There was no answer. "Jezzet, are you here?" Still no answer and he was thankful for that.

Thanquil pulled the box with the ink pot from his bag and a blank chip of wood. Paper wouldn't do for this rune, it couldn't hold enough power. He drew the correct symbols onto the chip with painstaking accuracy. Three runes, one for each of the seals Volmar used. When he was done, he stowed the ink pot back in his pack, stood up, and paused. Such an inscription was draining and combined with the loss of blood, his head already felt too light and his vision swam in front of his eyes. If not for the sleepless charm, Thanquil knew he'd have passed out then.

He waited until his vision cleared, took a deep breath, and hesitated. It wasn't that he was scared. Arbiter Thanquil Darkheart was scared of a number of things but this was not one of them. It was just... making contact with the void was ever a harrowing experience. The creatures there were not meant to be seen by human eyes or heard with human ears.

Thanquil snapped the chip of wood in half and dropped both pieces. Both were consumed in a low blue fire, one either side of Thanquil.

Chade was a hot place and the warehouse was no exception, but it started to grow cold, icy almost. Thanquil could see his breath misting in front of his face, could feel the bumps rippling across his skin. It grew darker too, the warehouse had not been well lit before but light from the moon shone in through holes in the roof, only not any more. An unnatural dark descended upon the interior of the building.

Then came the clinking of chains. Thanquil had never seen the chains but he heard them every time. They sounded great heavy things of thick metal, but of what metal he could not say. Volmar had never shared the secrets of how he bound them.

The face appeared out of the darkness, or formed from the darkness, Thanquil wasn't sure which. It was a vast thing almost as big as Thanquil himself, hard to see, but he could just about make it out. A darker patch of darkness among the black, it almost looked as if it absorbed the light around it. Two dots of yellow flame flickered to life in that face as the thing opened its eyes and looked upon Thanquil. When it opened its mouth it drew in a deep breath, possibly its first breath in this realm for thousands of years, and the room grew colder still as it sucked the very warmth from the room. Here was a thing not meant for this world. Here was a demon.

Thanquil stood his ground and wiped away the cold sweat from his forehead. Every time the face of the demon moved, the rattling of chains accompanied it. Thanquil stared at the monster, it was one of the biggest he'd ever seen, most appeared to be almost human in size but this one... With a face so big Thanquil couldn't imagine how big the body might be.

"Arbiter Darkheart," the demon said, its voice felt like ants in Thanquil's veins and he had the sudden urge to tear his own ears from his head. A shudder ran through him starting at the top of his head and ending in his feet.

"I have a message for the Grand Inquisitor," Thanquil shouted into the roaring darkness.

"Of course," the demon replied, its inhuman voice dripping with poisonous scorn. "We serve, as always."

Thousands of years ago Volmar had bound the demons from the void, bound them to serve the Inquisition. Nobody knew how he did it, it was a secret the God took to his grave, but the binding still stood firm. The demons still served, though grudgingly.

"I have interrogated the prisoner. She is a witch."

"Are you sure?" the demon asked. It made Thanquil pause. No demon had ever asked him a question before. They were bound to serve not to question.

"She is a witch!" Thanquil insisted. The demon did not reply, its great yellow eyes flickered at him, its mouth took another cold breath and Thanquil shivered. "The council of Chade allowed her to escape before I could carry out my judgement. I will pursue the witch into the Wilds, find her, and purge her."

The demon let forth a cruel noise that sounded something like laughter. "Is there anything else, Arbiter Darkheart?"

Thanquil thought about telling the Inquisition about the ball, telling them that he was being hunted for the murder of one of the council, telling them that he was falsely accused. He knew they wouldn't care though. They would expect him to clean up his own mess.

"No," he said into the face of the demon.

"Good," it replied, its eyes burning brighter for a moment then the face seemed to turn, the great flaming eyes saw something in the room Thanquil did not. "You are watched, Arbiter."

As the giant face faded into the darkness with another sickening laugh, the light returned to the warehouse and Thanquil heard the noise. A quiet scrambling that he might have dismissed as a rat, but the demon had known better. Thanquil started towards the noise and it turned into a crash as one of the crates collapsed under the weight of whoever it was.

It was going for the exit. Thanquil limped over towards the door as fast as he could even as he heard more scrambling and another crash. A small figure darted out from between two old crates and made for the door at a sprint. Thanquil reached out and grabbed the child by the clothing on their back and dragged them away before throwing them against a barrel.

The child was a boy, no more than nine years old by Thanquil's guess. He looked afraid and more than afraid as he pushed his back up against a barrel, shaking all over, eyes wide and dark and fearful.

"I didn't see nothin'. Nothin'. Jus' let me go, please. I won't tell nobody ya 'ere. I didn't see nothin'."

Thanquil stared at the cringing boy with his knees drawn up to his chest and his watery eyes looking around for an escape route. He wore little more than rags, his hair was long, uncut, and dirty. His teeth were stunted and crooked and his hands were covered in grime. This boy was one of the homeless for sure. Somehow he'd managed to evade the slavers all this time, an impressive feat. A boy like this would not be predisposed towards telling the truth. With a sigh Thanquil knew what he had to do.

"What did you see, boy?" Thanquil asked. He hated asking questions.

"You was talkin' ta somethin'. Somethin' dark with fire fer eyes." The boy clasped a hand over his mouth and started weeping. It wouldn't help him, it couldn't. Not now. Nothing could help him.

The poor lad had unfortunately stumbled onto the Inquisition's dirty secret and the worst thing about it was that it was Thanquil's fault. He should have checked the warehouse more thoroughly before summoning the demon. It was his fault, but the boy had to pay the price.

"I'm sorry," Thanquil said to the boy. He pulled his metal ball thrower from his belt, cocked the hammer, levelled the barrel at the boy's head and pulled the trigger.

BANG!

THE BLADEMASTER

Can't say I expected that. Jez thought as she stared at the Arbiter. Thanquil was standing over the body, his ball shooting device forgotten in his hand. His coat was discarded on the floor and he wore a pale tunic with fresh blood stains in a couple of places. Even from behind he looked tired, shaky, resigned.

You probably look worse yourself, Jez. At least he doesn't look and smell like he just crawled through a sewer... again.

She walked up behind the Arbiter on silent feet. He didn't look surprised when she appeared at his side. Didn't look much of anything apart from tired and sick. She looked down at the boy amidst the ruin of an old barrel.

Definitely dead. They don't get much deader.

Thanquil dropped the device he'd used to kill the boy and stumbled away to collapse against a beam of wood close to his back pack. He looked like he might be throwing up pretty soon, or crying, or both. She wouldn't blame him for that but Jezzet had long ago stopped getting so worked up over killing. Life in the Wilds did that to you.

"Reckon he probably deserved it," Jezzet said as she bent over to pick up the Arbiter's killing device and deposited it over by his pack.

Thanquil let out a noise somewhere between a snort and a sob. "He didn't."

"Oh." Was all Jezzet could think to say in reply.

He seemed to notice her for the first time. "Did you... see..."

"I arrived late it seems. Saw you shoot a boy in the face. Don't know why. Not sure I want to know."

"You look..." the Arbiter started to say and then stopped. "You made it out."

Jezzet nodded. "Just about. Whatever you did in there caused a mighty ruckus. Found a sewer entrance. Hence the..." She pointed at her once blue dress. It was ripped in more places than she cared to count, spattered with blood, and covered with waste. Her hands, feet, and knees looked little better. Scraped in places, covered in shit in others.

Jez pulled her own pack from its hiding spot and dragged it over to the water barrel. She pulled the remains of the blue dress over her head and discarded it on the floor. Her sandals were long since lost down in the sewer. She pulled off her undergarments, they were soiled beyond saving as well.

Funny how crawling through a sewer tends to cover you in shit. I think I should stay away from them in the future.

Jezzet knew the Arbiter was watching but she didn't care. Truth was she liked it. People had been watching her all night when she looked pretty, yet this one watched her even now, naked and covered in shit.

How long has it been, Jez? Weeks? Months? By all the Gods I'd like a good fuck. So what if he's just killed a boy. You've fucked people who've done worse, Jez.

She'd done worse herself and after the night she'd had, she needed it. She was pretty sure he needed it too. It'd get his mind off the boy, off whatever happened at the ball.

We both need it. So do it.

She cupped water in both hands and splashed it on her face. The cold liquid ran down her body. It felt good given the heat of the city. She washed her hands first, then her arms, then her knees. All the while she could feel the Arbiter watching her.

Do it. She urged him. *Make a move. We'll both be happier for it.*

Jezzet heard Thanquil push himself to his feet, heard him take a shaky step towards her.

He's tired. So are you, Jez. Fuck it, I need this. Just reach out and touch me, I'll take it from there, do the rest. Jez never initiated, that way she could claim it wasn't her fault afterwards.

She heard him take another step and he stopped. He was within touching distance, she could tell, she could feel it. She waited. And waited. The tension near unbearable.

"Those are some interesting scars," he said.

Just like that it was over. The heat, the tension, the urges, the desire. All of it gone. Now Jezzet just felt embarrassed. Felt like she needed to cover herself. She looked around for her clothing. The only thing in reach was her ripped, torn, dirtied blue dress. Her leathers had spilled out of her pack behind her.

Jezzet turned, pushed the Arbiter away with the hand not covering her scars, and stalked towards her clothing. She kept her back to him. Didn't want him to see her embarrassment as she pulled her clothing on. She heard him take a step and collapse to the floor with a heavy *thud*.

"I'm sorry," he said from the floor. "I didn't mean to..." he trailed off.

Jezzet turned to look at the Arbiter. He looked exhausted and worse. He looked like he'd done something he could never take back. Jez could still see the body of the boy motionless just a few short feet away.

How could you ever have thought he'd want to fuck after that? Would you? She asked herself, though truth was she was scared of answering.

"We all have them." She heard herself say. Already she wasn't sure why she told him that.

"All Blademasters have the same scars," he said, it wasn't a question but she felt the need to answer it all the same so she nodded.

"Far as I know anyway. My master had them, said it was part of the training." *The old bastard said a lot of things.* "Said a Blademaster has to know what it feels like to get cut so they can ignore it in battle. Flinching can cost you your life. So he'd cut me. Never let me know when, that'd remove the point. Just... when we were sparring sometimes he'd cut me."

She remembered all of them and far too well for her liking. No part of her body was safe from his blades, not her legs, not her arms, not her breasts, not even her face though he'd only cut there once and it was a small thing, only noticeable in some lights.

"Different types of cuts, some shallow, some deep, some long, some short. Different types of blade too, straight, curved, even serrated. Serrated blades really hurt and the scars they leave…" She rubbed at the raised flesh on her belly just above her navel. One of the worst scars she had, long and proud and ugly. "He even ran me through once. Said I needed to know how it felt. Missed all my vital bits but..." She showed him, couldn't say why. Jezzet hated people looking at her scars, but she showed him all the same. A small thing it was, in her side, no more than a finger width across and a matching scar on her back where it had gone all the way through. The old bastard had used a thin rapier to do it and Jez had taken months to recover.

The Arbiter was silent, watching her with eyes sunk in dark sockets. For some reason his silence made her want to say more.

You can't lie to an Arbiter, they say.

"The other one had the same scars too." She saw the Arbiter frown. "The other Blademaster. For a long time thought I was the last one, *'a dying breed'* my master used to say. But in the Five Kingdoms I met another. Some Knight... Sir... I don't remember. They all called him the Sword of the North. He had the same scars, I checked when we..."

When we fucked.

For some reason Jezzet found she couldn't quite meet the Arbiter's eyes. "Never been so scared of anyone in my life as I was of him. He was like... the shade of death given form." She shuddered just remembering him.

"I saw this Sword of the North cut down ten men. They didn't stand a chance, had him surrounded and everything and he just... afterwards he challenged me. Said he wanted to know which of us was better."

"You didn't fight him."

Jezzet laughed. "Of course not. I told him he was better. No way I was fighting him. So I fucked him instead. Now that was terrifying." She laughed but there was no humour in it. "I was so scared I just lay there with him on top thrusting away. Didn't take him long.

"Afterwards he rolled off and laughed at me. He said, *'Whores fuck their way out of fights, not Blademasters.'* Said I'll never be a real Blademaster unless I let go of the fear." Jezzet could feel the heat rising in her cheeks. "I should've killed him for that. Instead I just lay there feeling terrified and needing to piss."

And I still remember it all like it was yesterday. She'd started running from the Five Kingdoms that very same day and had never gone back. Last thing she wanted was to see the Sword of the North ever again.

For a long time the Arbiter was silent. Jezzet pulled her sword close and hugged it. Hard steel felt reassuring in her hands.

A Blademaster without a blade is a master of nothing.

"You're from Acanthia," he said. She nodded, wondering how he could tell. Jezzet had long ago rid herself of the accent though she could drop into it at will. "Vel'urn is an Acanthian name."

"It was his, my master's. Don't even remember what my name was before then. Parents made to sell me to a pleasure house at nine years." Acanthia had laws against slavery, but it had never stopped pleasure houses buying women or girls. "My master was there, bought me from them for more than the pleasure house could've paid. Said I'd have a better life with him." She snorted and spat. "They never even asked what he wanted me for."

"Do you have parents, Thanquil?" she asked after a while of silence. Jezzet couldn't say why she asked, just wanted to stop talking about herself. Seemed she'd said a lot and he'd said very little.

The Arbiter was quiet for a long time. When he spoke his voice had changed. It sounded harder, flat, cold. "No."

"Sorry, I didn't mean to..."

"You should get some rest, Jezzet. We'll be leaving in a few hours. Before dawn. We won't be stopping for a while and we won't be taking the roads."

"We're leaving Chade? Tonight?" In truth that sounded a good idea. Constance would be looking for her and she'd start looking in Chade. The sooner they left the better.

"Lord Colth is dead..."

"You killed him?"

The Arbiter laughed. "I might as well have. Get some sleep, Jezzet. I'll wake you when it's time to leave."

You're the one looks like they need sleep. But Jezzet didn't say anything. She was finding it hard to keep her eyes open.

She watched him for a while. The Arbiter just sat staring into the darkness, glancing at the body of the boy from time to time and then away again.

'Guilt is a dangerous enemy,' her master used to say. *'Guilt can stay your hand when you need to be certain. Guilt can slow your actions, slow your wits. Guilt can force you to give mercy where none is due. Guilt can kill you.'* He wasn't wrong. Guilt was trying to kill Jezzet right

now, only it called itself Constance.

The Black Thorn

"What the fuck were you doin', Thorn?" The Boss didn't shout. Rarely, even when angry, did the Boss shout, but Betrim reckoned he was on the verge. Metal flashed at the Black Thorn every time the southerner spoke.

Fact is Betrim Thorn weren't the type of person to take a tongue lashing... most of the time, but fact was Betrim Thorn fucked up good and proper and he knew it. Back in the mansion he should have run, should have turned tail fled back to the crew and through the sewer tunnel and they could've fallen upon the Arbiter on the other side. Six on one it would've been and those were good odds even against a witch hunter. Instead he stood his ground and fought.

"Sorry, Boss." Weren't many times in his life Betrim had said sorry.

"Well you've messed up my plans good, Thorn," the Boss continued, "an' the whole crew has got you ta blame fer it."

Betrim didn't like the sound of that one bit. One thing to have the Boss angry at you, another thing to have the whole crew hostile. "S'pose I could've jus' let the Arbiter take me. Reckon he'd have asked me a few questions though."

"Ya can't lie ta an Arbiter," Bones said in a quiet voice. As usual the big man had folded up on the floor cross-legged and was already cleaning his bones. He always cleaned his bones when nervous.

"Think the answers might've messed up ya plans somewhat?" Betrim continued.

"You could've let him kill ya," Green said with a sneer.

The Boss spat and continued to glare at Betrim. Bones was making sure his eyes were anywhere but on either of them. Henry was watching the street, making sure they weren't followed. Green was watching the confrontation with interest, too much interest for Betrim's liking. Swift was gone, he'd not come back with the rest of them but the Boss didn't seem too worried, like as not it was probably part of the plan.

"I was gonna give us all a few days in Chade, a chance ta spend some bits, have some fun. Can't do that no more." The Boss was still staring at Betrim with angry eyes. "Black Thorn got made fighting that damned witch hunter and now the whole fuckin' guard'll be looking fer him, fer us. They ain't gonna let the murder of a council member go unpunished."

All eyes were on him now. The crew liked only one thing better than making bits, spending them and Betrim had just stopped them from being able to spend a small fortune in a city that boasted it could accommodate any desire.

He cleared his throat. "Where are we headin', Boss?"

"I'll tell ya when ya need ta fuckin' know." Metal flashed and Betrim quieted. "We're leavin' tonight, soon as Swift gets back."

Henry spat. "Where is that half-blooded bastard?"

The Boss gave her a hard stare. "He's deliverin' a message ta Deadeye."

"What message?" Betrim asked.

"What part of '*when ya need ta fuckin' know*' didn't ya get, Thorn?" Betrim had never seen the Boss quite so angry, nor had he ever seen a jaw quite so clenched. "We wait fer Swift, and then we go. Good. Thorn, over here."

The Boss opened the door to his and Henry's room and walked through. Betrim followed, obedient, but too much following orders without knowing the why was starting to grate. Never had the Boss been so secretive before, nor had he ever been quite so testy.

"Close the door, Thorn," the Boss said once Betrim was inside. The room stank of sweat. The bed, if you could call it that, was a mess. A single mattress, stuffed with straw, ripped and torn and stained and mouldy veing propped up on a collection of wooden planks. The whole thing looked like to fall to pieces the moment anyone touched it but it held together as the Boss sat down on it, a weary look on his face.

The Boss let out a heavy sigh. "Right now, Thorn, I need ya." Betrim looked around the room, dirty discarded rags of clothing, rat droppings. Two dead rats, Bones would've been sad to see those.

"Boss?"

"More ta the fact I need ya name. Ain't no one quite so well known as the Black Thorn 'cept maybe Deadeye herself an' I need that. Right now the fixers know ya workin' fer Deadeye, more ta the fact Deadeye knows ya workin' fer Deadeye an' I need that."

"There a point ta this, Boss?"

"There is if ya let me finish. Right now I need ya. But this job I got... we got. It's bigger than you an' if you do anythin' ta fuck it up I will kill you myself an' I don't give a fuck how hard all the stories say that is."

Betrim ground his teeth a little, found a nice spot of wall to lean against close to the door and felt a tug on his burned face as his lip curled up a bit.

"Real inspirin' speech ya gave there, Boss. Take a bit more 'an an angry black-skin ta frighten me though." Not entirely truthful but the Black Thorn weren't afraid of anyone and the moment Betrim let folk think otherwise was the moment he found a dagger planted in his back, and he'd already been through that once and it fucking hurt.

The Boss glared at him for a while and then spat. "Got somethin' I need ya ta do, Thorn."

"Should be good."

"Keep an eye on Swift."

Betrim grinned. "Could be hard work seein' as ya let him run off an' all."

The Boss ignored the jab. "I mean it, Thorn. We're going to see H'ost."

That gave Betrim pause. "You don't trust him?"

"I trust Swift more than I trust Green."

Betrim snorted out a laugh. "Which is ta say not much. So ya asking a man ya jus' threatened ta kill ta watch one ya don't trust."

The Boss grinned and shook his head and for a moment he looked like the man Betrim had been recruited by years ago. "You should try runnin' a band o' cut throat, sell-sword, murderers sometime, Thorn. It's not fuckin' easy."

Part 3 – Keep Your Friends Close...

The Arbiter

Thanquil limped along as fast as he could but his right leg was agony drowning in fire. Every step was a lance of pain that seemed to travel up through his spine. He clenched his teeth so hard he felt they might shatter because it was better than crying out in pain every time his foot hit the floor.

He looked down at the wound. The bandage was red with blood, not a good sign. He'd need to change it soon, need to clean the wound again, but he dare not stop while they were still so close to Chade.

Not for the first time, he glanced at Jezzet. She looked tired but that was no surprise, at best she'd managed a couple of hours of sleep, more than Thanquil yet not enough after the night they'd had. She walked along beside him in silence but she was alert, tense, her hand never straying far from the sword hilt.

Jezzet claimed to be a Blademaster and from her skill with a sword he could well believe it. She toyed with him when they sparred and, if it had been a real fight, would have killed him in moments. But Blademasters were more like a myth these days, most everyone seemed to agree they had died out centuries ago.

He knew the history of the Blademasters as well as anyone and better than most; the libraries of the Inquisition were extensive, after all. The order was created close to a thousand years ago by a man of unequalled skill, Eliken Flameborne. He had travelled the five great empires of man and had recruited other warriors of similar skill. Two hundred they had been when Eliken decided it was enough. They had created their own weapon styles, their own training methods, and their own laws of the order. That was the first and last time all the Blademasters had met.

When they were finished Eliken sent them all over the world. That was where the history of the order started to get patchy. Some Blademasters disappeared into obscurity, others rose to greatness. Old

Blademasters vanished and new Blademasters appeared out of the ashes. One thing was certain though, over the thousand years since its creation the order was dwindling, not growing. Thanquil had believed it to be extinct but now here he was, walking beside one. She didn't seem to be much of a legend.

He glanced at Jezzet again. She was thin, not surprising after weeks in gaol, but she had a wiry strength, Thanquil could testify to that. She was both graceful and fluid, her movements controlled and precise and she was not displeasing to the eyes.

"Something you want, Arbiter?" Jezzet asked without looking at him.

Thanquil grimaced as he limped along. "The Inquisition caught a Blademaster once."

"Why?"

"You're known for your unparalleled skill with swords..."

"With any bladed weapon."

He smiled at her. She didn't so much as glance in his direction. "The Inquisition felt it needed to know whether such skill was natural or gained through... heretical means. They decided the best way was to capture a Blademaster and interrogate them. Three Arbiters were killed bringing the man in.

"It turned out hr was strangely resistant to the..." Thanquil had no wish to mention the compulsion. "To the interrogation."

"No one can lie to an Arbiter," Jezzet said in a mocking tone. "That is what people say isn't it?"

"They do and for the most part it's true and, well... the man didn't lie. He didn't say anything even after being... interrogated."

"Tortured?"

They had tortured the man, it was true, but it was not something the Inquisition liked to admit to. Not many could hide the truth in the face of the compulsion so the Inquisition had no need for torture... usually.

"You never thought just to ask him did you?" Jezzet said with a chilling look. "Instead of capturing him and torturing him, you never thought just to approach a Blademaster and ask *'are you a heretic?'*."

"No. No, I suppose they didn't."

"And what did you decide after torturing the poor man?"

"The results were... The Inquisition... They weren't sure."

Jezzet laughed, shook her head and continued walking. "So ask me. You have a Blademaster right here beside you."

"No."

"Why not?"

Thanquil ground his teeth. This was not a topic he wanted to stray onto.

"Well? Why not?"

He sighed. "I don't like asking questions."

Jezzet looked at him then, a mocking smile on her lips, and she burst into laughter. "An Arbiter who doesn't like to ask questions." She grinned at him, still laughing.

Thanquil found himself smiling back. "You don't understand. The compulsion is..." He paused, trying to find the right word.

"What's the compulsion?"

Thanquil limped along in silence for a while. Jezzet walked beside him, she didn't ask again.

"It's how we force people to tell the truth," Thanquil said. "It's magic and it's the first thing an Arbiter learns to do. It subverts a person's will, makes them unable to think about anything but the answer to the question and compels them to speak."

"So why don't you like to ask questions?"

Again Thanquil fell silent, trying to think of the right words. "The compulsion is addictive. We don't know why, something to do with dominating a person's free will, I suspect. There are Arbiters who use it all the time. It becomes a need for them, to ask questions, to feel the compulsion acting upon the target. It's..."

"Were you one of them?"

Thanquil wasn't sure how to respond to that. Actually he was, the simple answer was *'yes'*, but it was something he didn't like to admit to himself, let alone someone else.

After a long time Jezzet spoke again. "Can't you just not use it? Ask questions normally without using it?"

Thanquil shook his head. "I've tried, believe me. The compulsion is the first thing an Arbiter learns and we're... made to use it until we can't not. It is a constant, nagging need but the only way to not use the compulsion is to not ask questions so... I don't like asking questions."

"Sorry," Jezzet said in a sombre voice. "I should look at your leg."

"It's fine, just a scratch." Thanquil grimaced as he spoke and kept limping along all the same.

"It's slowing us down. You're moving no faster than a crawl."

Thanquil looked back towards Chade. Jezzet wasn't wrong. They had started out at a brisk pace, but the pain lancing through him with every step was slowing him down. They were staying away from the roads but even so, if they didn't get well away from the free city soon it was possible the guards would find them.

"I cleaned and bandaged it," he protested.

"But you didn't close it. I can tell by the blood." She wasn't wrong about the blood. "Closing a wound and bandaging one are two different things. Go and sit on that rock and drop your trousers."

Thanquil did as he was told. He dropped his pack, then his trousers and then sat with his leg stretched out on the smooth boulder. There were no rocky areas, no mountains for leagues around and Thanquil had to wonder where the boulder had come from. It sat alone on the plains, a solitary, smooth rock in a sea of grass.

Jezzet made a disapproving noise and spat on the ground as she looked at the wound. The bandage Thanquil applied had been wrapped around his clothing and had soaked up most of the blood, yet still the wound looked red and angry.

"There are some ointments and the like in my pack," Thanquil said.

Jezzet snorted. "I'll use my own."

She sniffed at the wound. It was a thin cut but deep and a good two inches long. The knife had hit him high up in the thigh, just a few more inches to the left and it could have been much worse, the wound was very close to his cock, and now so was Jezzet. She stared at the cut and Thanquil forced himself to think of disturbing images lest he get aroused by her closeness. The last thing he needed to do was poke Jezzet in the face.

All thoughts disappeared the moment she poked the wound. White hot pain shot through his leg and it was all Thanquil could do not to scream.

"Doesn't smell infected," Jezzet said as she started rummaging around in her pack.

"Wonderful," Thanquil replied, his voice strained. "This is going to hurt I think."

"Yes."

"Badly."

"Very badly."

"Let me know when you're about to start. I have a curse that will work wonders at subduing the senses."

She looked at him for a moment. "You can do that? Curse yourself to lessen pain?"

"As long as I don't forget the words."

"Huh. I'm going to clean it again. Then sew it shut, that'll hurt like all the hells. Then I'll bandage it again, properly this time."

Thanquil clenched his jaw and nodded. Jezzet had her own ointments, some fire wine to wash the wound, a thin needle and some horsehair thread for the stitches, and some white linen for the bandaging. She laid them all out ready and then nodded at him.

As he started up the chant he felt the world recede around him. The light grew dimmer, the world seeming to be lit no more than on a clear night despite the sun being high and bright. Sounds grew quieter and seemed farther away, even the sound of his own heavy breathing and heart beating in his ears seemed distant, muffled. His skin felt numbed, where before he had been able to feel Jezzet's hand on his leg, warm and calloused, now he only felt a slight tingling.

"Brace yourself," she said just before pouring fire wine into the wound.

The burning sensation was there, a deep pain that he could feel in the core of his leg, as if the very bone was on fire, but it was numbed by the curse. Still, it hurt and Thanquil could feel sweat beading on his forehead, could feel his hands, his arms, his neck, his head, and his entire body shaking.

Jezzet was looking at him with something close to sympathy. She had already dried the skin around the wound and the needle and horsehair thread had appeared in her hand.

"This is going to be the bad bit," she said with a sorry smile.

Thanquil kept whispering his curse, determined to weather the pain. All that determination fled the moment the needle pricked his skin. He gasped in pain and the curse was broken, the light of the sun, the noise of the Wilds, the pain in his leg, it all flooded back in and he screamed. He had no doubt he would have passed out had he not still had the sleepless charm on his arm. Instead he found himself lying flat on the boulder panting through the pain and choking back a sob.

"I need to keep going, Thanquil."

He took a couple of moments to collect himself, pushed back into a sitting position, recalled the words of the curse and started chanting again. Once his senses had dulled he gave a laboured nod to Jezzet and again the needle pierced his skin.

Five stitches she made and each was more painful than the last. Twice more Thanquil forgot the words to the curse and screamed in pain. By the time she was done he found himself soaked with sweat and wanting nothing more than a strong drink and a bed.

Jezzet rubbed some ointment onto the angry skin and then bandaged the leg before sitting herself down on the boulder next to Thanquil. She looked almost as shaken as he did.

"I've known men to faint from being stitched up," she said from beside him. She smelled of sweat and blood and a whiff of sewer. Thanquil found he didn't mind.

"Hah. It wasn't that bad," he lied.

She smiled. "You should try having to stitch yourself up one time. That's hard. My master used to say, *'When you're a Blademaster I won't be around to patch you up. You have to learn to do it yourself.'* So I did... every time." Jezzet fell silent and Thanquil joined her, truth was his head was still feeling slow and fuzzy and he couldn't think of any words to say.

Jezzet pushed herself off the boulder. "There's a few hours of sun left but maybe we should find some shade and make camp for the night. You need to rest."

Thanquil shook his head and pushed himself up. "No time for resting. We still need to move, get farther from Chade before they send people looking."

"You'll be alright on that leg?"

Thanquil grinned. "It's nothing really. See." He took a couple of steps and grimaced, but managed to hide the majority of his pain.

Jezzet didn't look convinced yet she nodded all the same. "Alright. You should probably put your trousers back on first though."

The Black Thorn

Betrim was on watch when he heard the voices. Truth was he was gnawing at a strip of dried salt beef that tasted a lot like a foot and was busy not paying attention to anyone that might have been trying to sneak up on them. An entire night and the following day he'd been on the receiving end of dark looks, cruel insults, and even one or two threats so right now he couldn't say he was too bothered about looking out for the others' benefit. It wasn't like the Black Thorn was the only one who ever made a mistake. They all had from time to time, so it struck him as more than a little unfair that he was getting so much heat from it.

All those thoughts fled when he heard the voices though. He could bitch and moan about his lot as well as the rest of them, but when there was a threat about they all had to stick together, assuming the threat wasn't one of them.

The voices were a ways off for now but could well be coming closer. Sound travelled a little too well over the plains at night. The laughing dogs were proof enough of that. Betrim couldn't count the amount of times he'd been kept awake at night by the damned laughing, unable to decide whether it was a long way off or right over his bloody shoulder.

Betrim gave the Boss a quick nudge with his foot, the big southerner slept light and woke easy. It took him a few seconds to figure out why Betrim had woke him and then he nodded, at least Betrim thought he did, the Boss was kind of difficult to see in dark. Henry was awake the moment the Boss moved, crazy bitch always had murder in her eyes when she woke. Frightened Betrim to tell the truth, not that he ever would.

He crawled on hands and knees away from the small camp, towards the voices. The grass was long this time of year, came up to the knees on a standing man and did a good job at hiding you when you got down low. Problem was it hadn't rained for a while and the grass was dry, made it brittle and noisy and gave it sharp edges. Seemed a strange thing to get cut by grass, but Betrim supposed that was why they were called blades of grass.

Every time Betrim put his hand down onto the ground was a near heart stopping moment for him, snakes were not uncommon out in the plains and if one managed to bite you...

Betrim had seen a man bit by a snake once. They'd killed the thing quick enough and even that was too late. Jolly Garth they used to call him on account of him always laughing and joking; not like Swift, Garth's laughing was always good natured, never had a bad word to say about anyone. He didn't laugh after the snake bit him. Within an hour his arm turned a withered brown colour and hung off his body like a piece of dead wood. He screamed too, screamed himself raw in the throat until he was coughing more than screaming. Then the brown rot started to spread to his body. It was then he pleaded for mercy so it was then they gave it to him. Harvey the Bear took his head off with one good swing from his axe.

Strange thing was, after Jolly Garth was dead his blood didn't run, just sort of seeped out a bit. It was thick and lumpy instead of runny. Blood did that in a body after a while, became almost like jelly, but with Garth it happened while he was still alive. Last thing Betrim wanted was to get bit by a snake, or a spider, or one of those land lizards that lived on the rocks. Last thing Betrim wanted was to get bit by anything.

The voices were louder now and Betrim could just about make out shapes in the distance. Seemed to be the chatter of two folk walking along, paying no mind to who might be listening or watching. The Boss crawled up beside Betrim on his right and he felt Henry brush against him on the left.

One of the two was limping a little. Injured was good, injured folk were easier to take. "What do they mean? Or what do they do?" Betrim heard a woman's voice ask.

"The charms." The voice of the second was a man.

"Aye. The ones on your sword, what do they mean?" the woman asked again. Betrim couldn't tell which one of them was the injured from this distance, still just shapes in the darkness.

The Boss waved his hand in front of Betrim's face a few times and made a walking motion with his fingers. Betrim got the idea, the two were going to pass them by if they kept on their current path, probably meant they'd just leave them be.

"There are three. The first is to keep it sharp as the day it was forged, even if some fool forgets to use a whetstone," the male voice said.

"Do you even own a whetstone?" The female voice sounded familiar. Betrim forced himself to stifle a groan.

"The second is so the sword will never break, never chip, never bend. The third is a charm of purification to help kill heretics who may survive normally fatal wounds."

Betrim knew the Boss was staring at him, knew Henry on the other side was stopping herself from laughing. He thought for sure the guards would have done for the Arbiter, after all the bastard had killed two of their own. Yet now here he was, tracking down the Black Thorn. He should have stayed back in the mansion, should have made sure the witch hunter was good and dead before running.

The Boss nudged Betrim and pointed. Betrim didn't move, just shook his head. If it was only the Arbiter, they could take him. Six on one were good odds, no matter, but he had Jezzet with him and that changed things and not for the better. Six on two odds didn't sound near so good when one of the two was an Arbiter and the other was Jezzet Vel'urn. Still, Betrim knew what needed to be done. Swift was the best bet. If they waited until the two made some sort of camp, waited until the Arbiter was sleeping, Swift could stick an arrow through him. The witch hunter would never wake. After that they could either deal with Jezzet or just leave her be. Maybe Swift could do for them both, he was damned accurate with that bow of his and quick too.

The Boss nudged Betrim again and pointed back towards their little camp. Betrim nodded and was just about to crawl back when he heard a belch. It was a loud rumbling noise that could almost have been mistaken for a peal of thunder and it was not the first time Bones had been known to burp in his sleep.

Jezzet dropped into a ready stance, hand on her sword hilt. The Arbiter just stood, looking right towards them. For a moment Betrim wasn't sure if the witch hunter would see them. They were down low in the grass, only the tops of their heads would be visible and it was dark. The three of them might even look like wild animals watching them as they were. Some wild dogs would follow travellers across the plains, watching them for leagues in case someone was split off from the group.

"It's your friend, the Black Thorn, and his gang," the Arbiter said, drawing his sword and pointing it towards them. No doubt thought he cut a right striking figure pointing a sword into the darkness like that. Truth was he just looked a fool, a fool who was about to get another knife in him. Betrim started reaching for one of the little blades he liked to keep hidden on him but the Boss was having none of it. The big southerner stood and walked towards the Arbiter. Betrim had no choice but to stand and follow, and Henry too.

"Reckon you should jus' keep on walkin', Arbiter," said the Boss in his deep, low, dangerous tones. The Boss liked to fight with both sword and axe at the same time and now he drew both. Betrim felt he had no choice but to unhook his own axe.

"Don't think I can do that, Black Thorn," the Arbiter replied, ignoring the Boss.

"You ain't talkin' ta Thorn, ya talkin' ta me."

The Arbiter glanced at the Boss and then back to Betrim. Then he pointed his sword at the Boss and drew his little string-less crossbow and pointed it at the Black Thorn.

Betrim did not much like that little thing being pointed at him. He'd seen what a mess it had made of the guard back in Xho's mansion. He took a slow step to the left, the Arbiter's aim followed him, he took a step to the right, and it followed him again. With a sigh Betrim resigned himself to getting shot.

"Six against two, Arbiter. Wouldn't much like my chances if I were you. Just keep on walkin'." The Boss didn't usually like to talk with folk for long. Betrim reckoned the big man might be near as scared as he was. Truth was the only thing Betrim liked about his situation so far was that Jezzet Vel'urn hadn't drawn her own sword yet. Seemed she was happy to stay out of the whole mess.

"Can't do it. Your Black Thorn killed Colth."

"What?" the Boss asked with a disapproving look at Betrim.

"No I didn't." Betrim was somewhat certain he'd remember killing a man as fat as Farin Colth.

"You did. I saw him, ripped open, and then I saw you sauntering out the very next room."

Betrim shook his head. "Right, but... I didn't do it. Only one I killed was that guard."

"Swift," the Boss said in his low rumble. Swift stood up from the grass not five paces from Betrim. Quiet as a shadow he'd snuck up, Betrim hadn't even known he was there.

"Yes, Boss?"

"Did you kill Farin Colth?"

"At Xho's place? No, Boss. Didn't kill no one. Was only there fer a bit of honest thievery."

Betrim snorted. "There was fuck all worth stealing."

Swift grinned. "Depends what you were looking to steal. I happened across Xho's daughter an' stole myself a ride. Turns out she was a maiden but I soon cured her of that." Another of Swift's stories, Betrim reckoned, although he was certain the bastard was capable of rape.

Henry spat towards Swift. "You were raping the daughter while we were killin' the father?"

Swift was still grinning. "Aye."

Betrim wasn't sure at that point who Henry wanted to stab more but it was looking like Swift. She was a murderous imp to be sure and it seemed Henry did not look too kindly upon rapists. Something to do with being a woman, Betrim reckoned, but he wasn't about to get into it.

The Arbiter didn't look so certain any more. "You were there to kill Xho, not Colth."

"Aye," the Boss said with a nod. "H'ost wanted Xho dead. He wouldn't want Colth dead. Everyone knows Colth was working for H'ost."

Jezzet's sword seemed to sing as it slipped from its scabbard. Her face was a dark scowl and at that moment she looked almost as murderous as Henry. "You work for H'ost."

The Boss took a step back. "Not really. We were workin' fer

Deadeye."

Betrim groaned. If the Boss knew a thing about Jezzet Vel'urn he'd have known that was the worst thing he could have said.

"You're working for Constance?" Jezzet asked and Betrim knew the question was directed at him.

"We're not workin' fer Deadeye, Jez. We jus' done a couple o' jobs fer her. Right, Boss?"

"Aye, we jus' needed ta do her a couple o' jobs so we can do the big job."

After that everyone seemed to start speaking at once. Henry started arguing with Swift. The Boss and the Arbiter started growling words at each other and Jezzet rounded on Betrim, thankfully with words and not steel.

"How could you work for Constance, Thorn? You know what she is."

"Says the bitch working fer the Inquisition," Betrim shot back.

"Well... they... pay well."

"So does Deadeye an' at least she don't burn folk."

Jezzet snorted. "I wouldn't be so sure about that. She killed Eirik, Thorn."

"Hawkeye?"

"Aye."

That gave Betrim a reason to pause. He'd never gotten on too well with Hawkeye, and his death meant there was one less name in the Wilds to fear, but it meant Deadeye was willing to kill just about anyone, might be she'd even try for the Black Thorn.

"What job?" The Arbiter's voice seemed to cut the air in two.

"We been hired ta kill H'ost," the Boss said and near bit his tongue off as he clamped his jaw down. The plains seemed to grow silent as a crypt then. Henry, Swift, Jezzet, the Arbiter, even Betrim himself just stared at the Boss.

Swift was the first to speak. "You want us ta kill H'ost?"

The Boss fixed him with a stare. "Aye. That gonna be a problem fer you, Swift?"

Swift took a moment to think about it before shaking his head. All his usual smiles and humour seemed gone. "Not a drop, Boss."

"So, working for Constance..." Jezzet started.

"Jus' needed her trust. Need a way ta get close ta H'ost."

"That's a pretty dangerous job, Boss," Henry said, her argument with Swift all but forgotten for now.

"Dangerous jobs mean big rewards an' this one's the biggest. Three hundred thousand gold bits. Split six ways is fifty thousand bits each. That's more than a lifetimes worth o' jobs right there an' no more dangerous."

Betrim didn't have a head for numbers, never had, and he had no idea how big fifty thousand was but it sounded big. Might just be big enough to be worth going up against Deadeye.

The Arbiter put away his sword. "Boss isn't it. I think we should talk."

"Aye?"

The Arbiter just nodded and started walking away into the gloom. After a moment the Boss turned to Betrim and the others and pointed at Jezzet. "Watch her." With that he stalked off after the Arbiter.

Betrim relaxed just a little, still kept hold of his axe though and Jezzet still had her sword in hand and was standing ready for a fight. "Ya good then, Jez?"

"Been worse, Thorn. Been better too. Ever had to crawl through a sewer?" she asked.

"Aye, once."

"Puts me one up on you."

At that he had to smile. Weren't a pretty sight but Jezzet smiled back all the same. Girl had been close to a friend once. Didn't mean they wouldn't kill each other when time came.

"I don't like her," Henry hissed. She had her murderous glare locked tight on Jezzet. "Why ain't we killin' the whore?"

"Cos the Boss said ta watch her," Swift replied with a sly grin. "So I'm watching her."

"You wanna call them off, Thorn," Jezzet warned, giving Betrim the impression she would like nothing more right then than to gut both Henry and Swift.

"Would that I could, Jez. Henry, Swift, this here is Jezzet Vel'urn. You might not heard of her but, well, she's the one that gave ol' Deadeye the name."

Henry looked confused, Swift caught on as fast as his name. "You the one took Deadeye's eye?"

Jezzet grinned. "Aye."

"She don't look like much," Henry said, sounding a little less confidant than before.

Betrim nodded. "Aye but neither does a woman called Henry the Red. Folk in Chade know ta fear her all the same."

Swift whistled. He was still looking at Jezzet with hungry eyes. "I think I'm in love. Sorry, Henry, my heart now belongs ta another."

"You don't have a heart, Swift. One day I'm gonna cut ya open ta prove it."

The Boss came striding back out of the darkness like some great black bear only with shiny metal teeth. His weapons were away, whether that was a good sign or bad, Betrim didn't know. The Arbiter limped behind right up to Jezzet. He put a hand on her shoulder and whispered something in her ear. A moment later Jezzet put her sword away. Didn't look too pleased about it though.

"The Arbiter an' his woman will be comin' with us fer a while," the Boss said, wearing his heavy frown.

Jezzet didn't look too happy. Swift grinned from ear to ear. Henry started cursing. Thing was, Betrim didn't give a shit what the others thought about it. "Boss, that ain't good."

The Boss rounded on Betrim like a bull about to charge. "Did I ask if it were good? Don't think I did 'cos I ain't askin', I'm tellin'. Jus' so happens we're going the same way so we're sharin' a road."

"I really have no interest in you, Black Thorn," the Arbiter said. Betrim ignored him.

"Boss, ya can't trust these fuckers. They..."

The Boss turned back to Betrim and for a moment he thought the big southerner was going to hit him. Betrim wasn't sure how he'd respond to that. No one ever hit the Black Thorn and got away with it. If he let anyone, even someone like the Boss... He'd have to hit back, and if it ever came to blows between the Black Thorn and the Boss there was only one way it could end.

Lucky for them both the Boss didn't throw a punch, just stood real close and stared until Betrim backed down with a dark glare of his own. Couldn't say he liked the way things were going these days. The Boss was starting to act strange and Betrim had to admit it might be time the Black Thorn moved on. It was a shame, he quite liked Bones and even Henry had her charms. Still, fifty thousand sounded like a real big number, might be he could stick it out a while longer at least.

"They stay with us fer a while at least," the Boss growled. "He's agreed there'll be no witch huntin' fer the time bein'. Even you, Thorn. Now back ta camp, all o' ya."

The Blademaster

There were a few times in Jezzet Vel'urn's life that she would have paid good money, and a lot of it, for a horse, and this was without a doubt one of those times. Thanquil didn't like the beasts other than to carry his own luggage, she had asked him why and the Arbiter smiled and said: *'People have been known to fall off horses and die. I don't think I've ever heard of anyone who fell off their own feet and died.'* Somehow it didn't feel like an honest answer, but then Jez had near given up trying to get Thanquil to talk plainly.

The man they called the Boss was less cryptic and a lot more blunt. He was not tall, at least not compared to the giant, but he was wide and by the looks of it he was all muscle. Thick arms, thick neck, thick legs, and a walk that hinted at barely restrained violence. His black hair was braided and hung down past his shoulders and silver flashed in his mouth every time he spoke. When Jezzet looked a little closer it seemed all the man's teeth were made of metal. The very thought made her shudder. When Jezzet asked whether they might pick up horses in order to cut down the travel time the Boss curled his lip at her and said, *'This crew don't use horses.'* After that he quickened his pace to get away from her.

It wasn't that Jez wasn't used to walking, or that she was a good horseman. The thing was that the Wilds were damned big. On horse it could take weeks to get from Chade to H'ost's estates, on foot it could take months and while she liked the Black Thorn as much as the next murderous sell-sword, she did not much like most of his companions.

The Arbiter and Jezzet travelled with and yet apart from the crew. Thanquil limped along and said little, brooding in silence and suffering dark looks from all the crew. Jezzet walked beside him and even in sullen silence she much preferred his company to the sell-swords'. They slept close and apart from the others as well, setting their own watches to make sure they weren't murdered in their sleep. The Boss seemed to have a firm grip on his crew and he wanted the Arbiter alive for now, but Thanquil had told her he didn't trust a one of them and Jezzet agreed.

There was one consolation though. The plains of the Wilds were a beautiful sight. Away from the roads, as they were, it was possible to walk where human feet rarely trod. Tall, dry grass of yellows and greens, and sometimes browns, rippled in the breeze. Here and there a corpse tree, with bark as white as bone, would spring from the earth to provide limited shelter and shade. The sky was a deep blue with only the occasional wisp of white cloud and the hot sun beat down upon them mercilessly.

Jez was not so sure of the route as the Boss. She had travelled this way before by roads. They were headed north and north would bring them to the yellow mountains, from there they would have to turn west to reach H'ost's estates. To do that they would need to cross the Jorl and the Jorl was a river like no other.

Fed by hundreds of smaller rivers and streams it was said all the water in the world had passed through the Jorl at one time or another. At its smallest it was a mere half a mile across, at its largest it stretched near four times that. Below the surface jagged rocks waited to turn the water into white foamy rapids. In places it moved faster than a horse could gallop, faster than a bird could fly. It started up past the Wilds in the God's Corpse Mountains and dipped into a cavern system below the Yellow Mountains only to re-emerge the other side and continue on its way to the sea. Hundreds of waterfalls could be found along the Jorl and the biggest of them, the Gods' Fall, could be heard thundering across the plains leagues away.

There were few ways to cross the Jorl. Only in one place this side of the yellow mountains were the waters calm enough to ford but without a horse it was a dangerous crossing and Jezzet was not convinced that all the crew could swim. There were the water lizards as well, great beasts that could grow to three or four times the size of a man with huge mouths full of row upon row of sharp teeth.

There were bridges across the Jorl, to be sure, but they were near as dangerous as the water. Swinging death-traps of rope and wood that creaked and swayed in the wind. It was not unknown for planks of rotten wood to give way, dropping crossers to their deaths or even for the rope to snap and drop a whole group into the churning waters below. The cliff sides on either side of the river were littered with the remains of such bridges. Jez had heard stories of folk who would rob those that walked the bridges. They would wait until people were half way across and then appear at the end of the bridge and threaten to cut the ropes that held it unless they were paid a toll.

Jezzet didn't relish the idea of attempting a crossing but it was either that or take a route that would lead them weeks out of the way and without horses to speed their journey it seemed unlikely the Boss would choose such an option.

"We seem to be heading in the same direction," Thanquil said as he limped up beside Jezzet.

"Still north," Jezzet said with a nod. "It'll get us there eventually. Not a short route though. How's the leg?"

"Stings a little. I can't help but shake the feeling that one of our companions stabbed me."

Jezzet snorted and grinned at him. "He scratched you is all. Anyone would think he cut your leg off the way you complain."

"From the looks I get from the Black Thorn I'd wager he'd like to."

"It could be worse. That Swift never stops staring at me," Jezzet said and Thanquil glanced behind them to where Swift was keeping pace. "He's doing it now, isn't he?"

"He's staring at a part of you."

Jezzet felt her lip curl and her hand brushed the hilt of her sword. *It would be easy just to turn and kill him. I'm sure none of the others would miss him too much.*

"We could always walk behind them," Jezzet suggested. "Stop some of the staring."

"Don't think they'd like that too much. They all seem to think that if they take their eyes off me for a second I'll light one of them on fire."

"Wouldn't you?"

Thanquil laughed, he did that a lot, she'd noticed. "We burn heretics, not petty criminals."

"Oh..." Jezzet had always assumed witch hunters just burned whoever they pleased.

"Witches, practitioners of forbidden magics, demon worshippers, Drurr..."

"The Drurr are real? I thought they were stories made up to scare children. Like trolls or giants."

"The Drurr are real but, just like Blademasters, their numbers have dwindled. The Inquisition hunts them wherever possible. They hide in places where humans have never been, in places where humans fear to tread."

"My master always used to tell me fear is a tool. A Blademaster should know fear but should never be ruled by it." *A lesson you never learned, Jez.*

"You never told me what happened to him, your master."

Jezzet spat. "I killed him."

"Oh..." Thanquil said and then fell silent for a moment. "I'm sure he deserved it."

"He did," she agreed. "I'd have killed him a hundred times if I could have. But that ain't why I did it. When a Blademaster takes an apprentice they know it can only end in one of two ways. One of them has to die.

"It took fifteen years for my master to train me and the final test an apprentice has to take is a duel with their master. If the apprentice dies, the master will know they weren't worthy. If the master dies, then the apprentice becomes a Blademaster. There were two hundred of us when the order was created and there has never been more. Now as far as I know there are only two of us left."

"You two are always whisperin'," Thorn growled. He had been walking beside them but now he kept pace just a few feet behind, glowering at the Arbiter all the while. "It's enough ta make a man nervous."

Jezzet noticed Thorn always seemed to have a weapon in his hand these days and the burnt side of his face twitched a little whenever he spoke to the Arbiter.

"And you always look like you want to stab me again, which tends to make me a little nervous. So I'd say we're even," Thanquil replied with his easy smile.

"Ya got what ya deserved fer attackin' me."

"I didn't attack you."

"Yes ya did."

"No I didn't."

Why is it men always have to get into pissing contests? Jezzet asked herself then glanced at Henry and realised it wasn't just men.

Jezzet almost walked away and left Thanquil and Thorn arguing and growling at each other, but the idea that they might dispense with the insults and get around to killing each other and leave her alone with the crew was a terrifying prospect.

"What does it matter which of you started it?" she shouted at them. "You continue this and I'll kill the both of you."

Thanquil smiled and backed down. Thorn looked worried for a moment, or at least as worried as his broken and battered face could. After that the two spent the rest of the day walking in silence, sending sullen looks at each other and making sure the entire crew was between them.

That night the Boss allowed a fire in the camp. He decided they were far enough from any of the beaten paths that the only folk likely to find them were others like themselves, and they were rare enough. Swift brought down a couple of birds with his bow during the day, the speed at which he could string the weapon and loose a shaft amazed Jezzet.

"Do ya remember Arlon Quickdraw?" he'd asked when he spotted her watching. "Not many do but some said there weren't a man in Wilds could throw an' axe half so fast or half so accurate. Well, the fool only went an' challenged ol' Swift ta a duel. Seems he'd heard about me an' my knives an' didn't take too kind on me being faster 'an him. Had all me weapons laid out on the ground an' waited fer the judge ta say 'go'. Had a string on me bow and put an' arrow through his hand 'fore he even blinked. Put one through each eye an' all, jus' ta be sure. There's a reason they call me Swift, ya know." He leered at Jez the entire time he was speaking.

Henry had padded up out of nowhere and cackled in Swift's face. "It's the whores that named ya Swift. So fast ya don't even know what a wet cunt feels like."

Swift turned his leer onto Henry. "Wet, willin', what the fuck does it matter?"

After that Henry spat at the bastard and stalked off to talk with the Boss.

The fresh meat from the birds tasted more a luxury than Jez could have imagined. There wasn't a lot of meat on either but Jezzet got a whole leg to herself and counted herself lucky. The Arbiter got none. Swift brought down the birds and so he decided who got to eat. Even Henry got a share but Swift ignored Thanquil like he didn't exist. When Jezzet had offered to share her leg with him Thanquil just smiled and shook his head.

A moody silence soon descended over the fire. The Boss and Henry retreated into the darkness. The boy, Green, had the watch and had been expelled from the circle of light. Thanquil sat staring into the fire, the flames dancing in his eyes. Swift was asleep or pretending to be and Bones was busy cleaning his bones, seems he did that a lot.

"How'd you lose the other finger, Thorn?" Jezzet asked, hoping to start some sort of conversation if just to lift some of the tension. There were times when silence could grate on Jez's nerves so that she wanted to scream.

The Black Thorn spat into the fire and for a while Jezzet thought he meant to ignore her. "Last member of the crew took it. Boy was young, pretty much like Green 'cept he knew how ta swing a sword."

"Fuck you, Black Thorn," the words drifted into the firelight but the boy stayed outside on his watch.

"Big lad an' still growing. Shoulda waited a few years 'fore testing me though. What was his name?"

"Bol," Bones replied without looking up from his bones. "Though we took ta callin' him Bull. Seemed ta fit somewhat."

"Aye well Bol decided ta try fer me at a whorehouse in Naris. I was naked as my name day with a girl sat on top of me. Pretty little wench, claimed ta be jus' fifteen an' near enough a maiden as not ta matter." Thorn let out a heavy sigh. "First swing of Bol's sword buried itself in her skull. Good job too 'cos he got it stuck an' had ta wrench it free. Gave me time ta push the corpse off me an' roll away. I swear, ya never feel yaself wither so fast as when the girl ya in turns dead. Strange feelin' ta find yaself inside a corpse, even a new one."

They were all staring at Thorn then, even Swift opened an eye and looked somewhere between disgusted and fascinated.

Then Thanquil spoke. "In some cultures it's a man's right to take his wife to bed one last time after her death. Honours her memory and allows him to say goodbye to her."

Again the Black Thorn spat. "Well this ain't there an' she weren't nobody's wife."

"What about the finger?" Jez asked.

"Got ta my gear a little too late. Managed ta block Bol's next swing, but he was a strong fucker. The swing knocked away my axe an' took my finger by the by." He held up his hand and rubbed at his middle stump.

Amazing how many situations come down to fucking and fighting.

"After that I grabbed up my dagger an' shoved it into his groin twice. As he fell away he let go of his sword so I snatched it up an' started hackin'."

"I remember the mess ya made of the lad," Bones said with a haunted look about his eyes.

"I remember the whore," Swift replied, his grin returning even as his eyes closed again. "Really was a pretty one. I wanted her but you got there first."

"Aye, shame really," Thorn sighed again. "I got the blame fer her an' all."

THE BLACK THORN

Bittersprings was a lonely town but a prosperous one all the same. It didn't survive on trade as many did. It didn't hold much of a strategic placement. The great herd never passed close by. Bittersprings had two things: sulphur and the bitter springs.

The little town sat at the foot of the first and greatest peak of the Yellow Mountains. Its walls were made from the same yellow rock that littered the mountainside and the buildings were made from the rock too. There the town had existed for near two-hundred years, sitting at the edge of H'ost's province and catering to some of the richest and most powerful folk in all the Wilds.

The people came for the springs, or at least for the healing, soothing, calming powers that they claimed to boast. The masters of the springs knew the exact ingredients in each pool of bubbling, scalding water and knew which pool would cure which ailments, which pool would soothe which ache, which pool would leech which toxins. They tended and guarded the springs and, of course, allowed others to experience the waters for a modest fee. Nothing in the Wilds came free, not even fancy water.

Betrim himself had never been to Bittersprings before. It was one of the very few towns of the Wilds he'd always managed to stay clear of. It was out of the way and, apart from the springs, which to the likes of him would always be closed, there wasn't much worth marking the journey. In fact, he had to wonder why the Boss had brought them this way at all. Seemed to be a fair distance out of the way and unless the Boss was feeling in the need of a deep soak in some foul-smelling water, the town had nothing they needed.

The smell got everywhere, was everywhere. As soon as they set eyes on the yellow walls, Betrim could smell it. Like egg left in the sun too long. Betrim himself may not have seen an egg in a good number of years, but he remembered them well enough. Back on the ranch, before his first killing, they'd had plenty of chickens and plenty of eggs.

As they got closer he could see the guards. Someone had once joked that there were more guards in the Wilds than there were beasts in the great herd. These ones were near as yellow as the walls they guarded. Dusty yellow doublets with mail over the top and a lemon-yellow cloak behind, all topped off with a high-peaked half-helm on their heads and each one of them carrying an iron-tipped spear. From such a distance they looked like toy soldiers guarding toy walls. Up close was a different matter, they looked a touch more fierce then.

The toy guards watched them through wary eyes as they approached and the more fierce types watched them with a touch of hostility as they entered through the large wooden gates. It was possible they went days or even weeks without seeing strangers and Betrim knew the Boss' crew made for a strange set at the best of times. Now with an Arbiter and a Jezzet in tow, they must look a real mystery, but they were allowed through all the same.

Inside, the town was small with squat, dirty, yellow buildings and a fair amount of dust that seemed to coat everything. It was busy enough despite that with folk moving every which way. Fewer merchants than Betrim was used to seeing, for a certainty, but then he'd spent a great deal of time in the free cities of late. Bittersprings was one of H'ost's towns and that meant they had to pay H'ost's taxes.

Not far from the gate they came across a small square whose main feature was the big well in the centre. Folk crowded around the well in droves with buckets or pails and even the occasional barrel. The water from the springs may be special but it was poisonous to drink. The Jorl was close, yet still a good few miles away, too far for the common folk to walk, they had to rely on the wells.

The Boss turned and gathered his strange crew around him. "We'll be spending a couple o' days here. Relax like we shoulda been doin' in Chade but fer these two." He pointed at Betrim and the Arbiter. "First things first. Bones, you an' Henry go find us a place ta stay, try not ta ruffle any feathers. We're keepin' a low profile."

"Jezzet and I will find a room in an inn," the Arbiter announced.

"We sometimes have ta be leavin' in a fair hurry, Arbiter. Easier when the crew's all together."

"We're not part of your crew and I'm certain no matter what hurry you're in, you'll find some time to send one of yours to find us."

Betrim had never seen the Boss back down and he had to admit he was looking forward to seeing him and the Arbiter go at it.

"I'll be staying at *the Bloody Petal*, Boss," Swift put in with a wink.

"That so?" the Boss growled back.

Swift stopped grinning and lowered his eyes. "Aye. Got family there ta see."

That seemed to make the Boss stop and think. After a while he nodded. "Bones, take Henry an' our two guests an' find us an inn."

Henry narrowed her eyes but Bones grinned. "How many rooms, Boss?" he boomed.

"One fer me an' Henry an' one fer the rest o' ya. The Arbiter can pay his own way. Green, Thorn, Swift, you're with me. Lead the way to this *Bloody Petal*."

Henry looked fit to burst and, for a moment, Betrim thought she might stab the Boss there and then. As Bones walked away chatting with Jezzet, Henry spat and stalked off with them. Betrim followed after Swift. Seemed the number of folk on the crew the Boss was pissing off of late was growing rapidly. For him to shun Henry in favour of some whore... even Betrim paled to think of the consequences and a face like his didn't pale easy.

Nothing quite said welcome to Betrim like a big pair of tits in his face and *the Bloody Petal* was pretty damned welcoming. The woman was plump, her breasts were huge and white and heavy, and she wore too much powder. Betrim found himself stiffening all the same. He grabbed hold of the plump woman by the waist and drew her closer, she didn't even seem to mind his scars too much. Then the Boss was there, tapping Betrim on the shoulder.

"Not yet, Thorn."

"I'm back!" Swift announced to the whore house with arms stretched out wide as if he could hug all the women at once.

A middle-aged woman squinted at him for a moment then walked over. She put a hand either side of Swift's face and kissed him on the lips.

"Ma," Swift said after she'd done kissing him.

"It's been too long, boy. It's on the house for my boy, Swift," she shouted to all the whores in the brothel. "Are these friends of yours?"

"Aye, near enough anyways." Swift grinned at all of them. "Find yourself a woman, lads."

Swift's mother approached Betrim. She was pretty enough, still slim despite the years and the use, though the corners of her eyes were starting to wrinkle. She wore a dark-blue dress that seemed to cover very little of her and she wasn't over powdered or over perfumed. Ageing or no, she was still attractive enough to warrant a smile. Not that Betrim would expose her to that.

"I'm Tanda," said Swift's mother. "You're the Black Thorn."

Betrim nodded. He may have never been to Bittersprings before, but everywhere he went his reputation seemed to precede him.

"Rose," Tanda called over her shoulder. The woman who stepped up was slim as a reed with long hair as black as midnight, small and perky breasts, and a beautiful face without so much as a mark on it. When she grinned Betrim could see her teeth, two perfect sets of pearly whites. It took everything he had not to smile back at her. She didn't want to see that, nobody did.

"This is Rose," Tanda was saying though Betrim was finding it hard to pay her any attention. "She's my daughter. You'll pay double and if you try to mess her up at all, she'll kill you."

That caught his attention. He looked from Rose to Tanda to the grinning Swift. "Ya daughter?"

"That's right. She's just as good with a knife as her brother too."

"Only as good?" Swift laughed. "She used ta be better."

Rose came closer, so close Betrim was poking her in the leg with his cock. She trailed a hand up his chest and spoke in a husky voice that seemed to slip out of her full red lips. "I'm sure it won't come to that but if it does," a knife appeared in her hand and she held it to his neck so close she could have shaved him with it. "If it does I'll geld you first then kill you. Fitting end for such a man as the Black Thorn."

Some men, most men, would have wilted under those conditions. Betrim was not one of those men, he found himself poking Rose in the leg even harder.

Rose smiled at him, she did have perfect teeth. "I think he gets the point, mother." She glanced down. "So will I by the looks of things. I do hope you know how to use that thing."

Betrim let out a ragged breath. It was rare any whore house gave him one of the pretty ones and he was so eager the only thing stopping him was the knife still held to his throat.

"I need ta borrow my lads an' one o' ya tables fer a few minutes, Tanda," the Boss said in his deep growl. A bottle of somethin' strong an' three glasses wouldn't go amiss. Not you, Green. You go an' find yaself some fun. Jus' need Swift an' Thorn."

Green grumbled something Betrim didn't hear and Tanda said something about a bottle. Betrim paid them no mind, his attention was fixed on Rose. Then a big hand grabbed hold of his arm, and started dragging him away.

The dagger disappeared from Rose's hand and she pouted at him as she ran a single hand down from her breasts, over her stomach, all the way down to her cunt. "Don't be too long. I get so very lonely."

Damn but the Boss was strong. If it wasn't for his iron grip, Betrim would have pulled free and then... He bumped into something and looked down. A table with some chairs. "Sit," the Boss ordered.

Betrim did as he was told but the last thing he was, was happy about it. "This best not take long, Boss."

"It'll take as long as it fuckin' needs ta. You'll get ta put ya cock in Swift's sister, don't you worry."

The big southerner waited until Tanda had brought the bottle and the glasses. He poured a shot into each glass, knocked his back and then poured another before looking around the room, making sure no other folk were listening in.

Betrim emptied his own glass and waited for the Boss to decide no one was listening. "Wasn't meanin' back on the plains ta tell everyone 'bout the job. Can't lie ta an' Arbiter though, an' now I know what that means. Never felt so..." He stopped and snapped his metal teeth together. "Fact is now we all know what we're in fer an' I need ta know if ya got any sort o' problem with that, Swift?"

Swift eyed the Boss, and then he eyed Betrim. Betrim just stared back at him, a blank look on his face. Good thing about having a ruined face, Betrim had long ago decided, that it made it easy to show no expression, no emotion. People never knew what he might do next because his face never betrayed him.

Swift downed his own drink, the Boss refilled his glass and Swift downed it again. "Only thing H'ost ever gave ma' was a silver an' a squirt in her cunt. As fer me, I got some of his blood but that's as far as his fatherin' ever went. He never wanted me an' I never wanted him so the way I see it, you just gimme the word an' it'll be my knife between his eyes."

The Boss stared at Swift for a while and for a while Swift just stared right back. Then the Boss nodded and downed his second glass. "Good..."

"I got a question, Boss," Betrim said before the talking ended. "When are we ditching the Arbiter? Here seems as good a spot as any."

This time the Boss took a swig straight from the bottle, he'd gone back to scowling. "We ain't. He's comin' with us all the way."

"Boss..."

"Seems he's after the same man we are an', if that bitch of his is as good as you say, I'd rather have them with us than against. Might not be ideal, Thorn, but as long as the target gets dead we get paid no matter if it's us or some witch hunter who deals the blow. So fer now you jus' shut up an' deal with it. After, you two can kill each other as much as ya like. Good?"

"Aye, good." Betrim didn't much like it but didn't seem like he had much of a choice.

"Go have some fun then. I best get back ta Henry 'fore she starts thinkin' I'm out whorin'. Last thing we need is her murderin' folk fer no reason."

Betrim looked around the room for Rose. He saw her leaning against the bar, watching him. That was the best thing about a good whore, Betrim decided, they always made it seem they wanted you, even when you were as ugly as he was.

Swift gave Betrim a quick tap on the arm. "Treat her good, Thorn."

"Aye."

"She likes it when you bite her nipples."

"Aye... what?" Betrim said, but Swift was already gone, half way across the room and speaking with his mother.

Betrim poured himself another shot and necked it before standing and walking towards the whore. Rose met him half way and pressed herself up close. Her breasts against his leathers, his cock poking her in her hip. Her skin was white, her hair was black, her eyes were blacker, and she smelled of sex.

She slipped a deft hand down into his trousers and gave him two long, slow strokes. Betrim shuddered and grabbed her around the waist, pulling her closer. He would've been more than happy to bend her over a table and take her right there in the middle of the room.

"I see you can pay double," she whispered close to his ear. Betrim realised she was holding his cock in one hand and his purse in the other. "I'll hold onto both of these for now. Don't worry, I'll only take what I'm worth."

"You best be worth it," he growled at her as she started leading him towards the stairs.

Rose glanced back at him, a wicked grin on her face that looked nothing like Swift's. "Oh I am."

The Arbiter

Thanquil was trying to think of a situation where he'd felt more awkward, a situation that had been more tense. He was coming up blank. Sitting between two women who seemed to hate each other was somehow worse than being questioned by the council of Inquisitors, worse than having a dozen swords pointed at him for a crime he was innocent of, worse than standing by and watching as the Arbiter passed judgement on his parents.

For her part, Jezzet wasn't making a show of it. She stared into her mug, but Thanquil could feel the anger radiating off of her like a dark haze that spurned all attempts at conversation. Henry was far less subtle, staring poisonous daggers at Jezzet and sneering with even more contempt than normal.

To make matters worse the rest of the common room of the inn was loud, jovial, and drunk. Their table was an island of moody silence among a sea of revelry and that grated on Thanquil's nerves.

The giant sighed and Henry sent him a look that could have frozen the sea. "Don't give me that, Henry. I'm bored," Bones whined. "All the others are off havin' fun an' here I am stuck here with three people all look like they want ta kill the others."

"I have no wish to kill any of you," Thanquil said.

"Not even Thorn?"

"Especially not Thorn. Trying to kill that one is dangerous work. Six Arbiters he's killed!"

Henry spat onto the reed covered floor. It landed close to a man's feet but he took one look at the table and thought better of whatever insult had been on his lips.

"He's fond of tellin' us too," Henry growled.

"Do you really burn folk?" Bones asked.

Not the sunniest of topics for a conversation but Thanquil was willing to take just about anything at this point. "I've been known to... do a few burnings."

"Why? I mean, why burnin'? Don't stabbin' work jus' as well? Or beheadin'? Or poisonin'? Or crushin'? Or drownin'? Or..."

Thanquil decided to interrupt the big man before he ran out of ways to think of killing people. "There's cleansing power in fire. I try not to burn people if possible. There are more humane ways of killing those deemed heretics."

"Huh." The giant was fumbling idly at one of the bone necklaces he kept around his neck.

"That's a grisly trophy you carry with you," Thanquil said. He had long ago discovered the best way to stop people asking questions about him was to make them talk about themselves.

Bones smiled and pulled out all three of the necklaces he wore. Crude things made of string looped through bone. Two were complete, the third only had bones half way around its length. "Took one from every man or woman I ever killed."

"Why?" Jezzet asked.

"Ta remind me. Count every night so I know jus' how many people I killed. Easy ta forget in the game we play that everyone we kill is a person, jus' like us. Each one got bones and skin, jus' like us. Each one got friends or family, jus' like us. Some folk like, Thorn an' Henry here, they like ta forget that. Not me."

"So what is your count at?"

"Forty-nine so far."

Henry snorted, Jezzet nodded, and Thanquil tried to remember how many people he'd killed. It was hard to say. He thought it would be well over fifty.

"Don't seem like that many," Jezzet said.

"Weren't always a sell-sword. Used ta be a farmer or, at least, I used ta work on a farm. The man who owned it didn't have enough bits ta buy an ox so he used me an' another lad, Jehry, from the nearby village. Used ta spend all day pullin' a plough. Now that were hard work. Mostly grew corn, but he had a small fruit orchard at the back of his house. We used ta sneak back there an' steal some sometimes, me an' Jehry. This one's Jehry, here." Bones pointed at one of his bones.

"Ya killed him?" This came from Henry.

"Didn't have much of a choice. One day group came round, armed an' mounted. They killed the owner an' then chucked a sword down between me an' Jehry an' said, '*We don't need two giants*'. Jehry got ta the sword first but he weren't never as big or strong as me so I took it an' took my first bone. After that I rode with them fer a while 'till the Hangman caught 'em."

"Hangman Yril?" Henry asked.

"Aye, chased us half way across the Wilds. The ol' bastard."

"How did ya escape?"

"Didn't. He never caught me. Was off takin' a shit when he came on our camp. Heard the commotion an' laid low. After, when I stole back into camp ta see if my stuff were still there, I found the whole gang swingin' from ropes. He hung 'em all."

"Never been so glad of a man dyin' as when I heard the Hangman had been done in by the rot. Bounty hunters is near as bad as witch hunters," Henry said.

"He weren't so bad," Bones said with a smile. "Met him a year later in Korral. Near pissed myself but he had no idea who I was. Bought me a drink."

"You could have gone back though," Thanquil suggested. "Back to your old village."

Bones laughed. "There is no going back, Arbiter. Not fer folk like us, not in the Wilds. Once ya part of the game, the game's a part of you."

"With all those people you burned, never killed an innocent one, witch hunter?" Henry asked.

Thanquil remembered the body of a boy with a hole in his head lying amongst rotted, splintered wood, he remembered the blood seeping into the soiled reeds on the floor, and he remembered Jezzet Vel'urn standing in front of him naked as a babe.

"Aye, I've killed innocents before."

Henry spat, there was something vicious and cruel about her. "See, ya no better than us."

"Never claimed to be. I'm just better spoken."

"Words? Words is jus' air, don't matter how they spoken."

Thanquil smiled at Henry, she scowled back. "Words have power with the proper application and how they're spoken is the key."

"Would words save ya if I leapt at ya with a knife?"

"With the right words... they might."

"If they didn't, I would," Jezzet said, her voice as dark and dangerous as her eyes.

"An' who are you anyway?" Henry returned the dark eyes. "Black Thorn says ya good. All I see is a scared little girl in bed with a witch hunter." She was speaking loud enough to draw attention now yet more eyes rested on Thanquil and his coat than the small woman with murder in her eyes.

"Henry..." Bones started.

"Shut it, Bones

"The Boss said..."

Henry rocketed to her feet, her chair clattering to the floor, and she spat at Jezzet. The Blademaster made no attempt to move and the spittle hit her in the face. She pushed herself to her feet, her right hand resting on the hilt of her sword. For somewhere close to a lifetime Henry and Jezzet stared at each other across the table. Then Bones stood up, towering over all of them.

"The Boss said we're all together in this. Her included. He ain't gonna be pleased if you two start killin' each other."

"Boss is off sticking his cock in some poxy whore, what the fuck do I care if he's pleased?" With that Henry turned and stalked away, men twice as large as her parting before the storm.

Jezzet sat back down, wiping the spittle from her face. Bones collapsed into his chair, Thanquil was amazed the small wooden structure didn't collapse under the weight.

The regular sounds of the common room resumed and Thanquil leaned over and picked up the fallen chair. Bones swallowed the rest of his mug of beer and motioned for the serving girl to bring him another and Jezzet echoed the request. Thanquil could see her hand was shaking, just like his did when he hadn't stolen anything for a while.

"Sorry 'bout Henry," Bones was saying. "She's... well... Henry."

"She doesn't seem to like me much," Jezzet said as she paid the serving girl for her beer.

"She jus' don't like not bein' the prettiest of the crew no more,"

Bones said with a smile and Jez smiled back. "Just don't go tellin' my wife I called ya pretty. She'd have my stones off 'fore I could say sorry."

After that Jezzet and Bones traded a few stories. Each told the other of the big names they had met and the big names they had killed. Jezzet seemed to come out on top of that contest. Bones always mentioned one crew or another he served with. Thanquil kept himself quiet for the most part, more than content to listen.

When the big southerner they called the Boss arrived, he sank down into Henry's empty chair, took a large swig of beer, and commenced scowling. "Where is she?"

Bones winced. "She um... left."

"Why?"

"Well the last thing she said had somethin' ta do with you an' whores."

"Fuck. Well we best jus' hope she don't go murderin' anyone." The big southerner looked tired and more than a little angry.

"We are moving towards H'ost, I hope. I seem to remember someone saying something about North and we seem to have moved somewhat East," Thanquil said.

The Boss nodded. "Some roads are longer than others. This one happens ta be safer, 'specially with the company we keep. Reckon it's about time Jezzet Vel'urn told us what she knows 'bout H'ost."

Jezzet's eyes flicked up to the Boss and then across to Thanquil. The Boss continued. "Aye, seems there's some folk heard of you after all. An' they reckon ya might know a bit more 'an nothin'. Some say you worked fer H'ost. Some say you crewed with Deadeye.

"Now from the way you drew steel when I said we were workin' fer her, I know ya got some sort o' involvement. Reckon it's 'bout time ya told us a tale, 'fore the others get back'd probably be best fer ya."

"Can't lie ta an Arbiter," Bones pitched in.

Jezzet looked at Thanquil and then away. "It was me gave Constance her deadeye."

"Aye," the Boss said after a mouthful of beer. "That much I know already. Did in her sister too, the one they called the Bloody Angel. Were you workin' fer H'ost or not?"

"Aye. A few years ago when I'd just come to the Wilds. I was in Solantis."

"A woman alone in Solantis is like ta end up a woman raped an' dead in Solantis."

"Maybe, but a woman who can use a sword in Solantis is like to end up very wealthy... for a time at least.

"Catherine, Constance's sister, saw me in the fighting pits. She was there gathering sell-swords, wanted to raise a new merc company and make a name for herself. She hired me on as a second bodyguard. She called us the Angel's Blades. You can imagine the talk I'm sure. A merc company led by three women. Constance was as big as a bear and stronger than most men. Me, a Blademaster, and Catherine was as good with a map as she was with a sword."

"But not as good as you," the Boss put in.

"Not with a sword, no. The other companies laughed but those who worked for her were fiercely loyal. She soon made that name for herself at Feville."

"You were the ones that sacked Feville?"

Jezzet nodded.

"Is it true what ya did there?" Bones asked.

Again Jezzet nodded. "We'd been paid to take the city. The contract was not specific as to how and their walls were fairly high. We arrived during the day when many and more of the town's people were out farming and working and such. Catherine took them prisoner, all of them, including the magistrate's daughter. Two hundred and eight townsfolk in all.

"When the rest of the company arrived she set up the siege and met with the magistrate. Told him no one had to die, no one even need get hurt. All he needed to do was open the gates and give command of the town over to us. The magistrate told her to piss off so Catherine had his daughter staked out in front of the town and gave the men free use of her. For three days and nights all you could hear was that bloody girl screaming and crying.

"Eventually one of the men took pity and slit the girl's throat. Catherine had him hanged for it. After that she had three prisoners a day brought out in front of the town's walls and had two teams of horses pull them apart. Twelve people we killed like that before the gates came open and the magistrate was marched out in chains.

"Catherine ordered the town sacked, its garrison executed to a man. After that they started calling her the Bloody Angel. Prettiest woman I've ever seen but so much blood on her hands."

"You didn't do much ta stop it yaself," the Boss put in.

"No. I didn't." Jezzet said, her face and eyes as hard as stone. "H'ost bought our contract soon after. He never was much one for military matters so he gave full command of his forces to Catherine. Our company was absorbed by H'ost's larger force."

"That doesn't tell us much about H'ost," Thanquil said.

"I really don't know that much. Only met him a few times and two of those he was in his cups. He's mad though. All the blooded families dream of reclaiming the Wilds into the empire it once was, but H'ost... he believes it, and he believes he's the man to do it."

"That it?" the Boss asked. "Nothing else?"

"Well he really doesn't like me," Jezzet added. "Not since I cost him the lands around Longwater. Or not since I won them for D'roan, more like."

"Well that's good at least," said Bones with an easy grin. All eyes turned to him. "Well I mean you're less like to betray us given that he hates you."

The Black Thorn

Rose was breathing heavy, her breasts rising and falling with each breath. Even though he only just had her, and even though that was the third time, Betrim wanted her again already.

He made a clumsy grab for one of her breasts with his five fingered hand and she swatted it away. Then she leaned over and plucked a bottle from the table beside the bed, uncorked it, and took a long, deep swallow of the sweet, amber mead inside.

"Open," she said with a smile on her lips and a brighter smile in her eyes. Betrim opened his mouth and she poured mead down his throat. Her aim was perfect.

"So, reckon I'm worth double?" Rose asked, her voice playful but not mocking.

Betrim had never been too good with women, something to do with being ugly even before the scars and the burn, but here with his cock still inside this one, he was feeling romantic. "For you I'd gladly pay triple."

Rose gasped. "You do spoil me." She took another mouthful of mead and then poured more into his mouth. "You'll run out of those lovely silver bits if you pay triple."

"Don't reckon it matters," Betrim rasped. "After this job I'll either be rich or dead. Might as well spend the bits while I can an' there ain't nothin' I'd rather spend 'em on right now than you."

"Rich or dead?" Rose said, her voice all innocent. "I do hope it's rich. Then you can come back here and pay me triple again and I can do this again. She wriggled atop of him then filled her mouth with mead and leaned down to kiss him. The honey liquid flowed into his mouth, flowed down his chin, flowed everywhere but he didn't care a bit.

The door to the room flew open with a bang. "Thorn," a familiar voice. Betrim couldn't be arsed figuring out who it belonged to. "Rose..." the voice continued with a smile. Betrim wasn't sure how a voice could smile. Then he realised it belonged to Swift.

Rose sat up, still naked, still sat atop Betrim, still with him inside of her. Golden mead ran down her chin and dripped onto her breasts.

Betrim wanted her again right there and he didn't care that Swift was watching.

"Brother, you know I'm not allowed to do you, mother says it's wrong," Rose's voice was as honeyed as the mead and ten times as sweet. A sulky pout played on her full, red lips.

"If only, little sister. But I'm here fer him," Swift sounded urgent.

Rose looked at Swift all innocent and sweet, and then looked at Betrim with wicked mischief in her eyes. "By the feel of him I think he prefers women, brother."

Betrim grunted and ran his hands up her legs towards her arse. "Piss off, Swift. We're busy."

"Fuck this," Swift said and in three long strides he was beside the bed. He grabbed Rose by the shoulders and pulled her off Betrim, off the bed. Then there was a knife at Swift's throat and another one at Rose's. Betrim couldn't quite figure out where Rose's knife had come from given that she was stark naked.

"Put it down, little sister. We don't have time fer this." Swift glanced down at Betrim's crotch as he sprawled naked on the bed. "Huh. No wonder she likes you."

"We're busy, Swift," Betrim said again, picking up the forgotten mead and taking a good long drink. "Piss off."

"Your pretty little friend, Jezzet, is down stairs, Thorn. Boss sent her. It's time ta go."

"Fuck that. He said two days an' I ain't out of bits yet."

Rose smiled a sweet smile. "Reckon he's got at least another few rides in that purse."

Swift removed his knife from her throat and she did the same. "Bounty hunters are here, looking fer us. Four o' them an' led by Big Mouth Cal."

"Bollocks," Betrim said and swung his legs off the bed already looking for his leathers. "They after us?"

"Unless another group of murderous bastards have come into town an' they also happened ta have killed one of the Chade council. Yes."

"Two."

"What?"

"Two," Betrim repeated. "We only killed the one but two are dead an' ya can bet they'll be blamin' us."

"Blamin' you," Swift said, scowling. "You're the one made himself known. Now get the fuck dressed an' let's go. Rose." Swift kissed his sister, his sister kissed him back, and then he turned and left.

As Betrim finished dressing, Rose looked at his purse, still on the table, and then at him. She was still naked and still the most beautiful thing he'd ever seen.

"Keep it all," Betrim heard himself say. "But if I survive an' come back, next ones on the house."

"Not a chance," she said, grinning. He made to kiss her but she stepped back out of his reach. Her eyes were flat, dark, emotionless pools.

Betrim turned and fled the room.

The Arbiter

Thanquil ducked another slash and then threw himself to his left just in time to dodge the jab from behind. Without his constant chanting of the blessing of speed, making his reaction times that little bit quicker, making his muscles move just that little bit faster, he would have been dead ten times over already.

Again the swords came at him. The first he blocked with his own and then pushed into the man with his blessed strength. Blessings of speed and strength were easy to combine, but using two blessings at once was a quick way to tire. The man stepped aside and Thanquil felt a sting on his right arm. He stumbled away a few steps and glanced at the pain. A new cut had appeared in his coat and a shallow wound had been opened up below. Three small cuts now and all of them hurt like hell. He couldn't help but feel the men were toying with him.

Thanquil had to admit his already quite meagre skill with a sword had gone to rust of late. Ignoring his small scuffle with the Black Thorn back in Chade, it had been well over a year since Thanquil had last truly swung a sword in anger and he wagered it showed.

One of his assailants was stony eyed and flat mouthed and the other was sporting a cruel grin. The Stoneface lurched towards him a step, raising his sword and then stepped away. A feint. The Grinner was there on Thanquil's right and he rained down blow after blow with his long sword. Thanquil caught and turned each blow but by then he had lost sight of Stoneface and the man could be anywhere. The Grinner's small, round shield rushed forwards and caught Thanquil in the chest sending him rolling over and over in the dust of the road.

"'Bout time ya used some o' that magic, Arbiter," the Boss shouted.

Thanquil coughed up some dust and looked around, searched for his opponents. Both Stoneface and the Grinner were standing together, watching him, waiting.

"Thank you for the advice, Boss," Thanquil shouted back.

The big, black southerner had his own problems. A large youth with a heavy, iron-bound staff seemed to be giving him no end of trouble.

Thanquil wished they hadn't sent Jezzet to warn the Black Thorn and Swift. He had no doubt she'd have more than evened the odds, but there was one bounty hunter missing and the Boss decided he couldn't risk the man had gone after Thorn.

"Can't ya turn 'em all inta frogs or somin'?" the Boss shouted as he spun away from an attack. The youth with the staff had the range advantage and one good crack from that heavy, wooden weapon would break bones like they were twigs. The Boss held a short sword and a hand axe but was finding it hard to get close enough to use them.

"Of course."

"Well go on then."

Thanquil let out a groan and shook his head. He could run, with a blessing of speed his assailants would never catch him. If only he could find the whore house, he'd find Jezzet and her sword. Of course it would mean leaving the Boss with three angry bounty hunters and Thanquil was certain only the stern presence of the southerner was keeping his crew together. Besides, running to the nearest whore house while screaming for help from Jezzet did not seem like the manliest of tactics and, for some reason, Thanquil found that mattered.

Stoneface smiled, his mouth stretching from ear to place where his ear should have been. His mouth was so large it made his face seem queer given his tiny, button nose.

"Black Thorn," he said with his giant mouth.

"Big Mouth." The growl came from behind Thanquil but he refused to turn and look.

"Been a while, Black Thorn."

"Not long enough."

"Been looking forward ta' killing you," Big Mouth and his companion seemed to have forgotten Thanquil for now, all their attention on the Black Thorn.

"As well look forward ta ya own grave, Big Mouth. Not that I'll be diggin' ya one."

"Thorn, help the Arbiter. Ooof." The Boss took a blow from the staff in his mid-section and stumbled away, coughing. The youth gave him no respite, following up with more merciless blows.

Thanquil heard the Black Thorn spit from somewhere behind him. "Don't reckon that's like ta happen. Reckon I'll let Big Mouth kill ya."

Turning his head, Thanquil gave the Black Thorn a withering look. The big, scarred man stared back impassively. One hand rested on his axe but he was making no move to use it. Jezzet was nowhere to be seen. Thanquil let out a sigh.

Big Mouth laughed. "We'll be taking you too, Black Thorn. Bounty on each of ya."

"Oh," the Black Thorn said and took a couple of steps forward so he was standing next to Thanquil. "Reckon that's wise? Three on three makes for even odds."

"Way I see it, your witch hunter's not worth one. What are you doing crewing with one of them anyways?"

The Black Thorn glanced at Thanquil and then back to Big Mouth. "Ya know, I've been askin' myself the same question."

"I don't see Jezzet," Thanquil said in a quiet voice, not much more than a whisper.

"Aye," the Black Thorn responded. "Gone with Swift ta fetch the magistrate. Reckon someone's been paid off. Don't see any guards about. Where's Bones?"

"Your Boss sent him to find Henry. What about the youth that was with you."

"Green? Fuck, I thought he was with you. Weren't in the whore house. Any chance we can pay ya off, Big Mouth?"

"Sure. Ya worth five thousand a piece, you an' the witch hunter both. Reckon you can afford that?"

The Black Thorn glanced down at Thanquil again. Thanquil could only laugh in response.

"Don't suppose ya take an I owe you?" the Black Thorn shouted back.

Big Mouth laughed and the Grinner next to him just grinned some more. The sun was just beginning to poke over the top of the small stone houses that surrounded them. Thanquil could hear the Boss fighting somewhere to his right yet he dared not look away, he knew his own fight would continue any moment. All he really wanted was to finish his night's sleep.

Thanquil had been sound asleep when the Boss had burst into his room in the inn. Jezzet sprung from the bed with sword drawn before Thanquil had even opened his eyes. All the big southerner said was, *'Time ta go. Hunters on us.'* Jezzet cursed and started looking for her boots while Thanquil rolled from the bed and pulled his coat on, not understanding what was happening.

"How'd ya find us anyways, Big Mouth?" the Black Thorn called. It occurred to Thanquil he might be delaying the fighting, stalling for time, and giving the others a chance to arrive.

"Chance. Luck. Just got back from Eagles' Nest. My fixer told me about a bounty on yourself an' the witch hunter, just so happens he also told me you was in town."

"News travels fast. I was hopin' we might have beaten the bounty notices."

Big Mouth laughed again. It was a loud, abrasive noise that a drowning cat would have taken offence at. "Notices went out on birds, Black Thorn. Every hunter between here and World's End is looking for ya. Lucky for me, I'm the one that found you."

"Lucky?" The Black Thorn rasped out his own laugh. "Seems ta me ya used to travel with sturdier lads. Who's that one beside ya? What's ya name boy? Chuckles?"

"Fuck you, my name's..."

"An' where's the Saint?" the Black Thorn interrupted the Grinner.

"Oh, he's around, don't you worry. Went ta look for you as it happens."

The Black Thorn spat. "That'd make him the lucky one then." He looked down at Thanquil again. "I got Big Mouth, you take Chuckles. Feel free ta get yaself killed."

Thanquil almost spat. The Black Thorn unhooked his axe from his belt with his right hand and a dagger appeared in the left hand, he stole a quick glance at the Boss, gestured to Big Mouth and then stalked forwards. A few moments later the two met with the all too familiar sound of metal clashing against metal.

Then the Grinner was there in front of Thanquil with his wide grin filling his face. It was an unpleasant sight given that the man had thick, moist lips, an ugly boil jutting out from his weak chin and blond whiskers that sprouted from the sides of his jaw. To call him ugly would have been an insult to ugly people everywhere. He bashed his sword twice against his shield.

"My name is Barry, Barry the..."

"I really don't care." Thanquil darted forwards with a burst of blessing augmented speed and jabbed at the Grinner with his sword. The attack was deflected with the small wooden shield. By the time the Grinner had recovered from the shock, his grin was long gone and Thanquil danced to his right and aimed a low slash at the man's legs.

The Grinner parried with his own sword and turned to face Thanquil. Another jab at his face and Thanquil danced right again. He remembered his old arms master telling him the best way to defeat a foe with a shield was to make the shield useless, always attack from the sword arm side and don't give the enemy a chance to block.

It didn't take long for the Grinner to figure out the tactic and, with a roar ,he charged. The shield hit Thanquil square in the chest and the man's sword came in over the top. He just managed to parry the sword as he went over backwards.

The ground slammed into Thanquil's arse with a loud grunt of pain. A moment later he was scrambling to get away as the Grinner came at him again, shield up, sword attacking around its wooden edges.

Thanquil had never been too good with a sword, but he had beaten people more skilled than him before. The trick, he found, was to cheat.

As the Grinner came on again, Thanquil kicked at the ground beneath him, sending a screen of dust at his ugly assailant.

"Argh, what the fuck?" the Grinner whined. Thanquil danced to his right and jabbed. The attack was blocked but Thanquil could see the man trying to rub at his eyes.

"What's your name?" Thanquil shouted at the Grinner. He felt the compulsion lock onto the man's will, felt the rush of heady pleasure as it subverted his will, and forced him to think of nothing but the answer.

"Barry the..." Thanquil danced right and jabbed again.

"How old are you?"

"I don't know..." Again he danced right and jabbed.

"Where are you from?"

"Korral..." Dance right. Jab.

"What's your name?"

"Barry..." Dance right. Jab.

"How old are you?"

"I don't..." Dance right. Jab. This time there was no block, no parry. Thanquil's sword point sunk deep into the Grinner's chest, past his ribs and into his lung.

The scream of pain turned into a coughing foam of blood and Thanquil wasted no time. He pulled his ball shooting device from his belt, flipped it so he was holding the barrel end and cracked the butt down onto the Grinner's skull with a burst of blessed strength. He felt, heard, and saw the man's skull crack open like a rotten egg.

The Grinner went down with a heavy *thud* and moved no more. Thick, red blood oozed from the cracked, caved in skull. Heavy drops of red dripped from the butt of the ball shooter. Thanquil stared at it for a moment then wiped it on the Grinner's clothing.

Looking up, he saw the Black Thorn still trading blows with Big Mouth. Neither seemed to hold an advantage. Both were attacking, blocking, parrying, and dodging away. The Black Thorn wore an ugly grin on his face, horrifically mirrored and enlarged on Big Mouth's features.

Thanquil took quick aim with his ball thrower. The merchant's words came back to him, '*Accurate up to ten paces*'. He judged the two men to be fifteen paces away at the very least.

BANG!

Big Mouth screamed and stumbled a step as the metal ball plunged into his arm. A moment later the Black Thorn's axe took off the lower half of his jaw in a spray of blood. Big Mouth hit the ground heavy and Thorn buried his axe deep in the man's chest. The body twitched once and was still. The Black Thorn put one foot on the corpse and pulled his axe free and then buried it in the man's neck once an then a second time, severing the head from the body.

Thanquil walked over to Thorn and the body of the bounty hunter.

The Black Thorn was bent over staring at the corpse. As Thanquil watched, he stood up straight, spat at the lifeless Big Mouth and kicked some dust over him.

"More of a burial than the bastard deserves."

Thanquil almost asked how the Black Thorn had known Big Mouth, but he caught himself. Using the compulsion so much on the Grinner had left him flushed, almost euphoric. He wanted to keep using it, needed to feel the rush again. He could feel his hands shaking and buried them in the pockets of his coat.

The Black Thorn was staring at him with that blank, expressionless look on his face. "Good shot," he growled as he walked off.

Thanquil nodded once in reply. At fifteen paces it was blind luck he hadn't hit the Black Thorn instead of Big Mouth but the sell-sword didn't need to know that.

The Boss limped over towards them through the dust in the road. He still held his axe in his right hand and his left was held across his chest. His breathing looked hard, laboured, and painful.

"Good work," the southerner wheezed at them.

The Black Thorn nodded. "You did in Little Harry. Boy was near as strong as Bones, as I hear it."

The Boss nodded. "You ain't wrong, Thorn."

"We missed all the fun?" Swift's voice called out across the street. Jezzet strode along beside him, her face as concerned as Swift's was unconcerned, though he carried his bow, already strung, in his left hand.

"Where the fuck were ya?" the Boss asked with a cough.

"Oh ya know. Breakfast with the magistrate." Swift grinned.

"You alright?" Jezzet asked Thanquil. He nodded once in reply. He didn't trust himself to speak lest questions start spewing forth.

"Right," the Boss said and looked around. "Where is he?"

"Not coming. Nor any of his guards." Swift sounded as cheerful as always. "Ya got me ma' ta thank fer that. Seems she's got the ol' man by his stones. Still, reckon it might be best ta get gone quicker rather than not."

The Boss coughed and near doubled over, holding his chest. When he stood back up straight, a dark grimace made his face even darker.

The Heresy Within

"We get ourselves ta the main gate. Bones, Henry, an' Green can meet us there. Swift, you're leadin' the way from here. We cross the Jorl first chance we get. Good?"

"Aye."

"Good."

There was a dull *thud* and the Boss went to one knee and then collapsed on the ground among the dust. A red, feathered arrow sprouted out of his broad back just below his right shoulder blade. Thanquil was still looking for the source of the arrow when he heard Swift's bowstring *thrum*.

The Blademaster

They heard the Jorl long before they could see it. Its thunder echoed across the plains for miles. Always seemed odd to Jez that water could have a sound and there was no denying the noise of the mighty river Jorl, its voice was as loud and as angry as all the Gods combined.

Four days after Bittersprings they reached the river. It shouldn't have taken four days, but the Boss was slowing them down. At the gates of Bittersprings the big man collapsed for the third time so Jez had un-shouldered her pack and set to treating the wound.

Two of his ribs were cracked, she was certain of that. Seemed he'd taken a staff hit to the chest. That wasn't so bad in itself, given time cracked ribs healed, hurt like hell but they healed all the same. The arrow wound in his back was a different matter altogether. It was in a dangerous position, too dangerous to push through so Jezzet had to cut it out. It had gone deep too and, though it hadn't hit any vital spots, the Boss was getting weaker.

At first he'd seemed alright; shaken and injured, in pain, and in need of rest, but able to go on. They waited an hour at the gates until Bones turned up with Henry and Green appeared. Henry seemed to be caught between part anger and part fear, though Jez couldn't decide whether the little woman was angrier with the man who'd shot the Boss or Jezzet for patching him up.

The archer was one of the bounty hunters. Thorn identified him as the Saint, Little Harry's big brother. No doubt he had feathered the Boss to take revenge for the southerner gutting his little brother. He'd paid dearly for that vengeance. Swift's first arrow took the Saint in his gut, the second went straight through his face. Again Swift had proved he was as fast as his name suggested.

About ten paces from the bridge across the Jorl, Bones put the Boss down.

The giant has been half carrying, half dragging him for two days now. Strong as he is there's a limit even to that one's strength. As if to punctuate her thought Bones sat down next to the Boss and his eyelids drooped closed.

"We need to rest," Jezzet said as she approached the Boss, intending to have a look at his wound.

Might be the dressings could do with changing.

"What the fuck do you know?" Henry spat at her, stepping in between Jez and the Boss. Jezzet stopped and stared at the smaller woman. Henry just stared on back.

There's murder in that one's eyes, Jez. Even more than usual. She backed away from Henry and moved to join the Arbiter.

Thanquil was stood a good two paces back from the edge of the cliff side that dropped into the Jorl, he was leaning forwards and craning his neck to try and see over the edge. Jezzet moved up beside him and gave him a very slight nudge in the back. The Arbiter near jumped out of his skin and hurried back a few more paces.

"You alright?" she asked him, grinning.

He laughed. "Not any more. That is a very big river."

Only half a mile across here, I'd say. This is where the Jorl is slimmest.

"Scared of a little water?" she teased with a smile.

"Can't say as I blame you," the Black Thorn put in. He edged only slightly closer to the cliff side than Thanquil had. "There's... things in that water, ain't right. Drownin' don't strike me as a good way ta go either. Better 'an burnin', I reckon, but still I could think of better ways ta die."

In bed, drunk, and being fucked sounds good to me.

"How about it, Arbiter? How would you like to die?" Jezzet asked.

"That sounds half a threat, Jez. Truth is I'd rather not die at all. Given the choice though... with a bottle of wine and a woman atop me."

Jezzet grinned but it was the Black Thorn who spoke first. "Ya know what, Arbiter. I'm startin' ta like the way you think."

"Did I ever tell any of you about the time I swam the Jorl?" Swift said. He was standing right at the edge of the cliff side, staring down at the waters.

Liar. No one swims the Jorl. I've seen men try, seen those same men die.

"I was still a boy," Swift continued, heedless that no one seemed to care, "no older 'an Green is now."

"Fuck you, Swift." Green had been brooding in sullen, hostile silence ever since Bittersprings. When he did talk he was always confrontational, always spoiling for a fight. Jezzet didn't know why and didn't much care to know.

"Walked down the river on this very cliff side. Passed this very bridge. Took me near a month an' I was set upon by bandits at least five times, I killed them all of course but that's another story. When I made to the very start of the Jorl, where the Toyne and the Whitewaves come together, I slipped out of all my clothes save my undergarments. Now I could go fishing with my cock, if truth be told, but I didn't feel much like having fish nibblin' away down there."

"They'd have ta find it first, Swift," Thorn said.

"Wouldn't be too hard, Black Thorn. It's the big thing attached ta the giant stones. Think yours but... well, actually yours might not be the best of examples. Think Green's but ten times the size. So I stripped down an' plunged into the Jorl. Cold waters the Jorl, despite the heat 'round here. Cold an' fast an' dangerous but not near so fast nor so dangerous as Swift.

"Took me near a week ta swim the length. I dived off waterfalls, dodged round the rocks that cause the water ta turn white. Even had ta fight off one of those bloody water lizards. Longer than Bones is tall, it was, with more teeth than he has bones an' it was easily twice as angry as Henry on one of her bad days.

"The beast dragged me down right ta the bottom of the Jorl an' there we fought an' wrestled, it with its teeth an' claws an' me with nothin' but my hands... an' a bloody great rock I picked off the bottom. Crushed its skull with that rock I did an' ate well that night, I don't mind saying.

"Finished my swim not ten miles from this spot, just down river," he gave a vague wave in the direction the Jorl was flowing. "Then I had a good two hundred foot climb on solid cliff, just like this one, 'fore I made it out. Girls of Bittersprings were so impressed I had five of 'em in my bed that night." Swift winked at Jezzet as he said the last.

"Ya know," said Bones as he sat still beside the Boss. "I half expected that one ta end with you makin' off with a mermaid."

"A mermaid..." Swift mused. "I like that, reckon I can work it in fer my next tellin'."

The Boss started to push himself to his feet and almost collapsed until Bones caught him and helped him the rest of the way up. His eyes were sunken, his flesh clammy, and he swayed on his feet even with Bones there. "Check the bridge, Swift. We follow you across."

Swift looked at the bridge then turned to Jezzet. "If I should fall an' die. Think of me when ya with the witch hunter."

Jez saw Thanquil flush red and she gave Swift a blank stare. "I'd rather think of Henry."

Swift grinned. "Now there's a thought." With that he turned and started across the bridge. For all his boasting and bravado he went slow, testing each wooden plank before putting his weight upon it.

It was a good hour before Swift made it all the way across the bridge. Jez could just about make him out waving the all clear from the other side. By then the Boss didn't even look strong enough to stand, let alone walk a half mile across a swaying collection of wooden planks held together by fraying rope. Neither did he look up for giving any more orders.

"Bones, take the Boss across," Thorn said. "We'll move across in two's. After you, me an' the Arbiter will cross, then Henry an' Jez. Green, you watch the rear, come across last."

"You ain't in charge," Green spat.

"Jus' do it, Green," Bones said as he heaved the Boss to his feet. "You can piss an' whinge 'bout it on the other side." With that he put one cautious foot on the bridge, sighed and started across, supporting the Boss with one arm while holding white knuckled onto the bridge with the other.

It took them even longer than it had taken Swift and the sun was high and hot by the time it came to Thanquil and Thorn's turn to cross. The far side of the Jorl sported a forest that crept all the way to the cliff side and the shade the trees would provide was looking more than a little tempting.

I'd happily swim the Jorl myself for a nap under those trees.

"You first, Arbiter." The Black Thorn waved at the bridge
"Can I trust you to watch my back, I wonder."
"I ain't gonna stab ya. An' the crossin' will give us some time fer a chat."

The Arbiter nodded and started across the bridge, the Black Thorn followed close behind. Jezzet watched them go for a while then sat down to wait. She couldn't help but notice Henry staring at her.

When it came time for Jezzet to cross she hesitated. Henry strutted up to the bridge, snorted out a laugh at her and began her crossing. Jez gave the little woman a good twenty paces head start before stepping onto the bridge. The wooden planks beneath her feet felt anything but safe and with every step the swaying was worse.

At least there's only a slight breeze, Jez. Trying to cross this thing in anything more would be suicide.

She edged along, one step, one plank of wood at a time. Her hand tight on the rope, never letting go. It wasn't a wide bridge, two metres at a stretch and here and there a plank was missing. Jezzet looked down.

How many people have fallen to their deaths from here? It was not a comforting thought. She considered closing her eyes as she went but that would just make things worse. If a plank did go she wouldn't see it, she'd just drop, opening her eyes just in time to see air rushing past her before...

Stop it, Jez. Don't think about it. Just keep walking. One foot after the other, slow is fine, slow is good. Don't look down. Trust your footing. Keep walking.

She was about half way across when Henry stopped and turned to face her. The first thing Jez noticed was the little woman's twin daggers were drawn. A grin and a sneer both mixed on her face, she was no more than five paces away.

"That's far enough, whore," Henry shouted over the roar of the Jorl hundreds of feet below. Her voice sounded strained, higher than normal.

"What are you doing, Henry? This isn't the place for this," Jezzet shouted back.

"What's the matter? Scared of heights?"

Yes, as it happens. Though far more scared of the Jorl, you crazy bitch.

"We fight here we're both like to die."

Henry laughed though the sound barely carried as far as Jezzet. It sounded like the rushing waters were right below them. Either that or it was Jez's heart pounding in her ears.

"Well that's your choice. Turn back or fight."

Jezzet held no illusions. If she turned back now Henry would cut the bridge the moment she reached the far side. It might be better that way. She'd be free from the crazy bitch, free from the crew, free from the insane job they were all determined to pull.

Free from the Arbiter?

Her sword was in her left hand, her right still attached to the rope of the bridge. Jez hadn't realised she'd drawn her steel but she could see her hand shaking. *Why do I always shake before a fight?*

Henry came at her with daggers and eyes flashing. First the left, then the right. Jez parried the first, blocked the second and gave ground, edging backwards far faster than she'd moved forwards.

If she gets inside my reach I'm done. Jez parried another slash and answered with one of her own, followed by a jab and another slash, her strikes dangerously close to the rope that held them both aloft. This time Henry gave ground and with the way the bridge was swaying even she looked worried.

A gust of wind slammed into the bridge and Jezzet found herself pushed up against the rope, her right hand gripping tight. Knuckles as white as bleached bone. Henry yelped and almost went over, one of her daggers fell from her hand as she clutched to the rope. Jezzet watched the short bit of metal disappear down below them into the churning waters.

With a scream Henry came at her again, her dagger thrust at Jezzet's chest.

Jez caught the smaller blade on her own, twisted her wrist and shoved an elbow into Henry's face. The bitch cried in pain and stumbled backwards, her hand grasping for the rope. Jezzet let go of the lifesaving hemp, jumped to Henry's left and slammed the smaller woman with her shoulder.

With a high-pitched scream that made her sound a small girl, Henry went over the side, hitting the rope and tumbling over. The world lurched underneath Jez's feet as the bridge gave a violent shake.

The rope snapped! Jezzet thought and clutched onto the left hand side for all her worth and the world went black. Then it passed, the bridge went back to swaying and Jez tried to calm her breathing. She prised her eyelids open.

She saw Thorn on the far side waving his three fingered hand and shouting something she couldn't hear. Opposite him, Green had started across the bridge and was moving at a snail's pace. The roar of the Jorl was still all around her, crushing in from all sides.

How is it coming from above as well as below? There was something else too, a high pitched whine. It sounded almost like crying.

Jezzet braved looking down. There, attached to one of the wooden planks was a hand, four small, pink fingers clinging onto the wood for dear life. She crossed to the right hand side of the bridge and peered over.

Henry hung by one hand, the rest of her small body swinging, swaying with the wind. Fat tears rolled down her cheeks and blew away to be swallowed up by the Jorl waiting below. She was sobbing as she clutched the wood with one hand. Her eyes were wide, fear and pleading in equal measures.

"Please," Henry squeaked.

Jez's sword still weighed heavy in her own left hand. It would be so easy. One quick stab at the bitch's hand and she would plummet down into the Jorl and Jez could sleep easier at night knowing she was less likely to wake with a knife at her throat.

Jezzet looked at Thorn still waving, looked at Green edging his way along the bridge, and looked at Henry swinging from one hand in the empty space between the bridge and the Jorl. Then she put her sword back into its scabbard and started walking to the far side. One hand still clutched at the rope, but all her fear of falling was now gone, she was too tired to be scared.

By the time Jezzet reached the far side of the Jorl the adrenaline had worn off and she was shaking so much it was all she could do to stay upright. She stumbled onto solid ground and would have collapsed had Thanquil not been there to grab her arm and steady her. Jezzet would like to have shrugged clear of him and stood on her own, but she wasn't sure she could and for that she was grateful, and more than grateful, for the Arbiter's support.

"What the hell happened out there?" the Black Thorn demanded.

Your crazy bitch of a friend tried to murder me and you should all be fucking grateful I didn't murder her right back.

"Ask her," Jezzet said, waving towards the bridge. Green had reached Henry and pulled her up and was now half supporting, half carrying her across the bridge.

Thanquil helped Jezzet to a shaded spot underneath a giant tree and lowered her to the ground. "Thank you," she said, smiling. She started to close her eyes to take that quick nap she wanted so bad when she realised there was a man sat atop a horse nearby.

The Boss was lying on the ground, unconscious by the looks of him. Bones was close, looking like he didn't even know what sleep was. Swift was gone. Betrim stood at the cliff side by the bridge and the man on the horse sat there watching them all.

"Who's he?" she asked Thanquil.

"A trader bringing spices to Bittersprings."

"On his own?"

"Seems that way."

Jezzet didn't trust that. Only fools travelled the wilds on their own. *That would make me a fool too, I guess.*

The man was grey haired, with a long grey beard and a back as straight as a pole. His face was hard and frowning and he wore old, stained riding leathers. His horse looked as old as he did. Well-fed but tired-looking, its hair the colour of dried mud.

"I think I'm gonna have a nap," she heard herself mutter.

Thanquil shook her awake. "Jezzet I need you to do something," he whispered. "I need you to check the Boss' wound. I need you to tell me if he's going to live."

"He's lasted so far," she said with an empty smile. "That's a good sign."

"Jez, the Black Thorn doesn't think the Boss is going to make it and he knows he can't hold the crew together. If the Boss dies... I need their help, Jezzet."

Can't hurt to take a look.

Jezzet nodded but she felt her eyes closing as she leaned against the rough wooden tree trunk. Her eyelids snapped open. The dim sleep that was claiming her disappeared, her vision cleared, and the fog in her head evaporated. The Arbiter held her left hand in his own, her skin tingling at his touch. He had wrapped a small piece of paper around her wrist.

"What...?"

"It's a charm. It won't stop you from being tired, but it will keep you awake for as long as you wear it. Please, just long enough to check his wound then you can sleep as long as you want, I'll watch over you."

Jezzet held up her hand and looked at the slip of paper.

He's not wrong about the still feeling tired.

Thanquil pulled her to her feet and she leaned against him for a moment before stumbling towards the Boss. The big southerner was lying on his back, his breathing shallow, his eyes closed. Jezzet waved at Bones.

"Take off his shirt and roll him onto his back." Bones hesitated. "I need to check his wound."

The giant didn't even bother struggling to his feet but did as she told him, crawling over to the Boss, lifting his thin shirt over his head and then rolling him.

Jezzet pulled her dagger from her belt and cut away the bandages. The smell was the first thing that struck her, it smelled of rot. Dead and dying flesh. The wound was angry and red, with yellow puss.

"Oh shit, that don't look good," Bones said.

Jezzet looked toward Thanquil and gave a slight shake of her head. The Black Thorn walked over, took a good long look, then he moved away and the Arbiter went with him. They stood together, out of earshot, whispering to each other.

When did those two stop wanting to kill each other?

When they were finished talking Thanquil walked over to his pack while Thorn took up his post by the bridge. Henry and Green were almost across though the going was slow with him supporting her as he was.

"Cut away the rest of the bandages," Thanquil called out as he pulled a small inkwell and a strip of paper from his pack. Jezzet did as she was told. "You'll need to clean it as best you can and be prepared to bandage it again."

Jez handed the dagger to Bones and struggled to her feet, her own pack with her bandages was near Thanquil's. He was already drawing a symbol onto the paper, beads of sweat sprung onto his forehead.

"Will that save him?" she asked.

Thanquil finished writing a second symbol on the paper, he was panting, she noticed. He put the ink pot down and looked up at her. "It will stop him from dying," he whispered just loud enough for her to hear over the ever-present roar of the Jorl.

Jezzet set to cleaning the Boss' wound as best she could while Thanquil approached the old trader sitting watching them. "We need your horse."

"S'not fer sale," the old man said, his hand straying to a small dagger on his belt.

"No one ever said we was buying." Swift appeared from the trees, a grin on his face that disappeared when he spied the Boss' wound. "Shit."

Thanquil tossed a small purse at the old trader. "Twenty gold. That's twenty times what the mare is worth."

How many purses of gold does he have?

"What 'bout my goods? Can't carry 'em all."

"Take the gold. Leave the horse an' saddle. Carry what ya can an' count yaself lucky, old man." The Black Thorn put an end to the haggling. "I'd rather keep the gold, take the horse, an' leave ya bleedin'."

Jezzet poured fire wine on the Boss' wound. He groaned but didn't wake, didn't move. *That's not a good sign. He's as good as dead, Jez.*

When she was done, Thanquil knelt beside her, the small slip of paper in his hand. He laid the paper across the wound. It almost seemed to seal itself to his skin. Jezzet looked at the charm around her left wrist.

"They can be taken off at any time. Might sting a bit though." The Arbiter said, guessing her mind.

"What are you doin' ta him?" Henry said as she sunk down to her knees just a few paces from the cliff side. Green stalked off among the trees.

"Saving his life," the Arbiter lied, though he could have said they were gutting him to look for gold and Jezzet doubted Henry could try to stop them in her condition. The little woman was barely conscious and shaking worse than Jez.

"Wouldn't be here come nightfall," the old trader said as he set his first foot on the bridge. "Unsavoury folk use this bridge at dark."

"They don't come much more unsavoury than us, old man," Swift said. The old trader just snorted in reply and started away.

Thanquil waited until Jezzet had finished with the bandaging and then took the Boss under one arm and heaved him to his feet. The Arbiter was whispering something under his breath all the while.

"Bones, help me get him onto the horse." The giant did as he was bid though it took them both a long time and a lot of struggling until they lashed the Boss onto the beast with a length of rope.

"Now what?" the giant asked.

The Black Thorn took hold of the horse's reins. "We head fer Hostown, just as the Boss planned. He'll be better by the time we get there. Right?"

"Sure," Thanquil said.

They started moving again. Swift in front with Green, Thorn leading the horse, Bones carrying the near unconscious Henry, and Jezzet came last, leaning on the Arbiter as she walked.

"You promised me sleep," she said after a while. A smile played on her lips but she lacked the energy to sustain it.

"You can sleep," Thanquil replied grinning. "Hop on my back, I'll carry you."

She laughed but the mirth was short lived. "How long will it last?"

The Arbiter let out a sigh. "Three weeks maybe, a month at best."

"What will happen when it stops?"

"It's a powerful charm but it's not a cure. It's meant to stop a wound or a disease getting worse until the afflicted can be delivered to a proper healer."

"So when it stops working..."

"He'll die."

Right then Jezzet knew that the Arbiter would sacrifice them all for the sake of his mission. Even her.

The Arbiter

Long before they could see the walls of Hostown they entered the leagues of farm land that surrounded the capital of the province. Some grew wheat, some grew corn, and some grew odd brown tubers that had to be dug from the earth for harvesting and tasted of nothing. Many and more grew various types of fruit, some green, some orange, some yellow and long, others red and round. The heart of the H'ost province was rich in farmland. Long ago they had burned the trees to make room for such crops and the land was protected from the great herd by the Jorl. Frequent storms kept the land well-watered and, in times of drought, deep wells had been dug which fed off the underground water of the Jorl.

Hostown was known all over the world for its vineyards and it produced some of the Wilds' best exports. The wine produced here was renowned for being sweet and dark, and full of body and flavour. Thanquil had tasted Hostown red wine before though, if truth be told, he found that cheap wine could get you drunk just as well as the expensive kind and he was more than happy drinking sour vinegar if it was cheaper. Or at least after a few mugs of the stuff he was more than happy.

Hostown itself was a fair size smaller than Chade. Like all towns, cities, villages, and forts in the Wilds it sported high walls thick with soldiers. These ones were all wearing the green on red that were the colours of house H'ost.

Just a half mile outside the walls Thanquil could see the tell-tale signs of an army. A multitude of tents all with coloured peaks littering the landscape. Smoke from cook fires rose into the air from a hundred different places. Scout patrols rode to and from the camp keeping watch on everything and everyone.

"That's a lot of men," Bones said in a hushed tone. The entire crew had become more and more hushed the closer they got to Hostown.

"Not just men, women too," Jezzet informed them. "Veterans from a dozen different sell-sword companies: the Angel's Blades, Catherine and Constance's old company, the Gold Caps from the far south, the Red Men from north of the Red Forest. Others too. H'ost brought them all here and turned them all from sell-swords to soldiers. His own army. The H'ost province is well populated and there are always men looking to earn money by swinging a sword."

"How many men?" the Boss asked from atop his old horse. The southerner was alive, stronger than he had been but still weak. He walked each day for as long as possible but rode the rest of the way. His flesh seemed to have been burned from his bones and even talking came hard for him. Thanquil could only hope he lasted a few more days.

Jezzet spat. "When I lef... was captured, the count stood at around eighteen thousand. Seems there might be more now. A lot more."

"Eighteen thousand sounds a big number," the Black Thorn put in. "What's he want with all them swords?"

Jezzet laughed. "He wants the Wilds. He wants the old empire back like it was in Doro's reign before his sons split the rule into the nine blooded families. He wants to be a king."

"The Wilds'll bleed 'fore they accept H'ost as king," Swift said. Even he seemed to smile less these days.

"That's the point. You don't raise an army unless you intend to use it."

"The army doesn't concern us. Just those inside the city," Thanquil interrupted.

"They'll be plenty o' men in there too, Arbiter," Swift spat and lapsed back into silence.

Thanquil didn't care how many men were in the city. He was only concerned with one. Gregor H'ost, the head of the family. He had the answers the Arbiter needed, he had to have the answers. Thanquil had crossed the Forlorn Sea and half the Wilds to question the man, to find out what he knew about the traitor in the Inquisition and know something he must, or all of it had been for nothing.

The question weighed heavy on Thanquil of late. What if H'ost knew nothing? What if the God-Emperor of Sarth had sent him here chasing phantoms and wild suspicions and false information? Thanquil had gained the service of the most murderous group of sell-swords he'd ever met with the promise that after he had asked his questions he would kill H'ost. But what if the man was innocent? True, Thanquil was already wanted for the murder of two of the four members of the ruling council of Chade, why not add the murder of the head of the richest family in the Wilds.

Thanquil had already resigned himself to his fate. If he returned to the Inquisition without any proof of the traitor the very best that could happen to him was he would have his position as a wandering Arbiter removed. He would no doubt be sent to some backwater village to live out the remainder of his days telling ignorant villagers that the old lady with no teeth was not a witch and she hadn't cursed the harvest. The worst that could happen... well he knew just how unforgiving the Inquisitors could be.

The God-Emperor had chosen him for this task because he was expendable and right now Thanquil was feeling very expendable. He only hoped the crew hadn't realised just how expendable they were.

A group of soldiers on horses trotted up to them from the town. There were ten and to a man they were armed with long spears and long swords and heavy, wooden shields. Each wore a rounded metal cuirass and a high helm and underneath was boiled leather.

"Business?" said the soldier with the bent nose, heavy brow, and thick beard.

"None o' yours," replied Henry in a sullen voice. The little woman had been quieter and even angrier since Jezzet had left her hanging from the bridge that crossed the Jorl.

"You would do well to quiet your woman before I do so myself." The soldier seemed well able to match Henry's anger scowl for scowl.

"Jus' lookin' fer a place ta rest a few days," the Boss said in a weary voice. "Pick up some more supplies. Then we'll be on our way."

The soldier peered at the Boss. "You don't look so good. You ill?"

The Boss sat as straight as possible, which was to say his shoulders stooped and he swayed in the saddle. "Let's see how good you look after takin' an arrow in the back. Jus' wounded is all."

"Bandits around the Jorl?"

"As you say."

The soldier grunted. "Stay at the *Feathered Fool* and ask ol' Bernard for the name of a healer. He'll point you good."

The Boss nodded. "Reckon I might jus' do that."

With that the soldiers turned their horses and trotted back towards the town. The crew followed at a slower pace.

"Guess they don't get too many visitors," Bones said.

"Many and more, and then some more on top," Jezzet said. "H'ost may be a madman and a sot, but he's no fool. Keeps himself and his town well-defended. Hostown has never been sacked and he doesn't intend the first time to be on his watch."

"Make for the *Feathered Fool* then, Boss?" Thorn asked.

"Aye."

The crew were silent for a moment. "Should I find us a place closer to the gates? Just in case?" Bones asked.

"Aye."

"Good."

"Aye."

The Boss was sagging in his saddle, his eyes half closed. It was late in the day and his walking in the morning had taken it out of him. Either that or the charm was losing its effect. If that was the case Thanquil would have to hope the Black Thorn could hold the crew together for long enough to get the job done.

Inside the walls Hostown was astir. Empty wagons were leaving, full wagons arriving. Slaves hurried to and fro all under the watchful eyes of their taskmasters and if any so much as missed a step the whip cracked. People gathered round a pot shop hoping for a bowl of brown stew and a heel of bread before going back out to the fields.

"Harvest time," Jezzet said. "The whole town will be busy, preoccupied."

They stopped once to ask one of the soldiers for directions to the *Feathered Fool*. There were more than enough soldiers to choose from, it seemed like half of H'ost's army must be inside the town and all of them were watching Thanquil and the crew.

The inn-keep seemed happy enough to see them. A jolly-looking fat man, red of face and possessing of at least three chins. His eyes were small, beady, and close-set. His nose was large and bulbous and his hair was a shaggy brown ponytail that made him look ridiculous, but he smiled and ushered them all to a table.

"You will want food, yes?"

"Aye," the Boss said as he sunk into a chair with a wince. "An' rooms. Two of 'em."

"Our rooms only sleep two people, there are eight of you."

The Boss was silent so Thorn answered for him. "We'll make do. Bring food, whatever you've got on an' drinks."

"We have ale."

"That'll do."

"So what's the plan, Boss?" Swift asked.

The Boss' eyelids fluttered open and he glanced around the room. Thanquil noticed yellowing around his eyes. It didn't seem a good sign.

"We'll stay here t'night. Come mornin' we'll go see H'ost. Arbiter has the plan."

The entire crew and Jezzet turned to look at Thanquil. He smiled and waited for the inn-keep to bring the ales, the plan would go down better with alcohol.

"H'ost will be in his mansion."

"His fort," Jezzet corrected.

"We're going to walk right up to the main gate where I will demand an audience with H'ost. He's not likely to turn away an Arbiter. Once inside you will create a diversion among the garrison while I question H'ost."

The table was silent, all members of the crew stared at Thanquil, some with their mugs frozen half way to their mouths. It was Swift who broke the silence.

"You never done this sort of thing 'fore have ya?"

The Black Thorn was shaking his head. "Ya plan is suicide."

Even Jezzet was no help. "Might be we need to think on this for a couple of days. Come up with something a little better."

"A little less insane," Henry put in with a scowl.

Green was grinning from ear to ear. "I like it."

"Shut up, Green," Thorn hissed. "Boss?"

The Boss lifted weary eyes from the table. "Reckon it needs some work."

"Be better goin' in at night," Swift said. "Under cover of darkness. Nip over the walls, break in, find his rooms an' slit his throat."

"How high are the walls?"

"Close to a hundred feet as I remember," Jezzet said.

"I can climb that, easy." Swift grinned. "Did I ever tell ya 'bout..."

"Without bein' spotted? With patrols above an' below?" Thorn shook his head. "What 'bout tunnels? A sewer like in Chade?"

"Oh Gods, please not another sewer," Jezzet winced at the mere suggestion.

"Might be an option at least," Thorn continued. "Worth lookin' inta."

"He must leave his little fort sometimes," Bones suggested. All eyes turned to Jezzet.

"Back when Catherine was in charge of the army he used to tour the camp once a week but now Constance is in charge... I couldn't say."

Thanquil sighed. "I need to question the man."

"Aye an' we need ta kill him," Swift hissed.

"Get me alone with him and I'll do both."

"What does the Inquisition want with him anyways?" the Black Thorn asked. Thanquil held his tongue, he wasn't about to tell a group of sell-swords that the Inquisition might have a traitor in its midst.

"What 'bout poison?" Bones said. "Ya said he likes his drink."

The argument continued for near on an hour. Swift claimed he could put an arrow through H'ost's eye from a thousand yards. They all knew it for a lie, yet he claimed it anyway. Bones suggested they pass themselves as a group of entertainers to gain entrance to the fort. Henry championed calling the whole thing off and was shot down when Green reminded them of the substantial reward for the job. Thanquil contented himself with listening and praying that the Boss would recover enough to put an end to the bickering and come up with some sort of plan. Back on the plains when they'd talked alone he claimed he was good with plans, claimed he could figure out a way inside and out again without raising suspicion. Now the man seemed uninterested, or more to the point he seemed incapable of following all the talk.

The argument ended when a score of soldiers entered the inn. They filtered into the common room and made no move to sit. The Black Thorn hissed at all the others to stay quiet.

"Arbiter Darkheart?" said the soldier with a captain's badge on his arm.

The crew fell silent. "Yes." Thanquil responded, his voice cracking a little.

"Lord H'ost wishes to talk to you."

Twenty soldiers or near as didn't matter, all well-armed and veterans by the looks of them. Thanquil doubted he could fight his way free even if the crew helped him.

"What 'bout us?" Green asked. Bones cuffed him into silence.

"You're all to come with us."

The Boss stirred from his chair, as if seeing all the soldiers for the first time. His voice was weak, strained "What's this about?"

"Not my place to say."

"Do ya need our weapons?" Green asked. Again the giant cuffed him.

The Captain smiled. "That won't be necessary. The Lordship just wants to talk."

Thanquil stood first, Jezzet followed and then the rest of the crew. The Boss struggled to his feet with Bones helping him. All of them made sure their hands did not stray too close to their weapons. None wanted to fight their way clear here.

Outside, another score of soldiers waited for them bringing their escort up to forty men, it would seem Lord H'ost was not taking any chances. The Captain instructed them to follow him and the rest of his men fell in all around Thanquil, Jezzet, and the Boss' crew. They were penned in on all sides and even if they wanted to cut their way free they would have no hope against so many.

The Black Thorn walked close to Thanquil and whispered as they went. "They knew ya name, Arbiter. Don't reckon that's a good thing."

"Just so long as it gets me face to face with H'ost," Thanquil whispered back.

"Aye."

The sun was dipping below the walls of the town as they made their way through the streets, even so there were plenty of people about to stop and watch the strange procession. Children were out in force, ever bolder than adults some of the little ones even took to marching next to the soldiers, mimicking the men, others danced about asking '*what they done?*' or '*they fer hangin'? Can we watch?*'

The only member of the crew who did not look nervous was the Boss, though, Thanquil reflected, that was because the man looked to be a walking corpse with one wasted arm over Bones' stooped shoulders for support.

"Captain," Jezzet called out. "Could you tell me, is Constance back in the city?"

The Captain glanced back at her with a cruel smile. "Deadeye got back not three days ago."

After that Jezzet fell silent, brooding. It didn't take long for them to reach H'ost's fort in the centre of his town. Sheer, grey walls rose out of the ground and Thanquil decided Jezzet might have been shy when she guessed at a hundred feet. He could see faces peering down at him from the battlements high above and the round towers either side of the gate had ten arrow slits a piece. The gate boasted an iron portcullis currently raised to allow their entry and an iron-bound wooden gate on the other side also open.

Inside they found themselves in a huge courtyard that looked as though it could accommodate a thousand soldiers. Their escort of just forty men seemed small by comparison. H'ost's mansion stood in front of them. Once it may have seemed grand, but after Lord Xho's estate in Chade and the Imperial palace in Sarth, Thanquil thought it looked a stunted, drab building. He had expected more from the most powerful blooded family in the Wilds.

The Captain turned to face Thanquil. "If you'll come with me please, Arbiter." His tone made it clear that he was to escort Thanquil alone from here on.

Thanquil hesitated. "Of course. Jezzet, you will accompany me."

The Captain narrowed his eyes. "The rest of your men will stay here. They are welcome to enjoy the hospitality of our barracks. We have food and ale."

"Two of my favourite words," Swift said with none of his usual grin. "Got a whore or two in there an' all, an' I may have ta kiss ya."

The Captain eyed Swift for a moment, then grunted and turned to march towards the mansion. The Black Thorn caught Thanquil's arm before he could follow and pulled him close to whisper in his ear. "Do ya job, Arbiter. We'll do ours."

Thanquil nodded once and followed the Captain into the mansion with Jezzet just a step behind.

The Black Thorn

An old, grizzled sergeant with long, grey hair that merged with his short, grey beard led them to the barracks mess hall. Groups of soldiers were seated all around eating and drinking, jesting and laughing, gaming and gambling. Some looked up and gave them a queer look as they entered, but most didn't even spare the crew a glance. It was a good sign as far as the Black Thorn was concerned, drunk soldiers may be more rowdy but they were also less useful if it boiled down to a fight. Though, looking at the odds, six against sixty did not fill him with confidence no matter how drunk the sixty.

The sergeant waved them to a free table and watched as they all took seats, the Boss slumped into his and his eyes sagged closed.

"Your southerner don't look so good," the old sergeant said. He had good teeth, missing one of his canines but all mostly white and not too many gaps.

"Arrow wound... in back," the Boss managed to say though his voice was thick and slurred.

"Bandits?"

"There are a lot of them around the Jorl these days, despite ya fancy army camped outside," Swift put in. "How long ya been workin' fer H'ost, old man?"

"Near four years. Used to soldier for the *Sun's Sons* free company out of Toros. Weren't a lot of us, maybe three hundred in a good year, but Lord H'ost bought us an' said we could join him for good an' all and get fed and paid an' have a home in Hostown. Cap'n Bart said we'd rather be free men than soldiers. The Cap'n didn't wake up next mornin'. Been Lord H'osts since."

"Look like ya seen ya fair share o' battle."

The old veteran laughed. "Reckon I've seen at least ten's fair share of battles. Somehow managed to come out of all them unhurt. Bless the Gods."

"Which Gods?" Betrim asked.

"Any that care to listen, lad. There's plenty of food an' help yourselves to ale. It's coming up to harvest festival time an' Lord H'ost is always free with the ale round now."

The sergeant walked off to talk with some other soldiers and was soon sat down supping at a drink of his own. This would be about the time the Boss would tell them all to be careful, not to get themselves good and drunk, but the Boss didn't seem to be in much of a condition to tell them anything. Betrim decided he should shoulder that burden himself.

"One ale a piece, ain't worth gettin' drunk. Might be we're needed fer that distraction the Arbiter wanted," he whispered.

Henry snorted. "Seems ta me this situation has gone from hopeless ta shit-storm. Look around you, Thorn," she hissed. "We're surrounded by H'ost's soldiers. The Arbiter an' his whore are gone an' the Boss... I say we cut our losses an' get the fuck out of here."

Betrim couldn't say he didn't agree if truth be told.

"No," the Boss growled through gritted teeth. "We stick ta the plan."

"What plan?"

That seemed to confuse the Boss. "The Arbiter's plan. He'll do his part an' we all walk away with a million bits."

Betrim didn't know what a million was. It sure sounded like a lot of bits though. Worth a little risk of his life. Though this seemed like more than a little risk.

Truth was, something was nagging at the back of Betrim's mind. Something about the mess hall didn't seem right. He looked around, staring at each table in turn, watching the folk drinking, laughing. It all seemed... quiet.

Betrim had been a sell-sword for the better half of his life and if there was one thing he had learned it was that put a group of men together with ale and things tended to turn loud and messy. Here there were plenty of men and the ale was free and plentiful, but the mood was sombre. Soldiers supped at their cups, talking in hushed voices. Every one of them was still armed and armoured. Then his eyes fell on the Captain, he wasn't sure when the man had returned from escorting the Arbiter, but he stood by the entrance to the mess hall and watched the crew with icy eyes.

He was just about to warn the rest of the crew when a giant stopped by the table. The big man had short, black hair, a squashed, brutish face with a heavy brow, a bulbous nose and a ruddy glow to his cheeks. His arms and chest strained against his doublet.

"Well stand up then, lets 'ave a proper look at ya," the giant spluttered at Bones.

Bones pushed the chair away from the table and stood up. He and the giant stood as tall as each other, but Bones was still stooped. Betrim guessed the bone-loving giant had a good four inches on the ruddy-cheeked giant.

"Well fuck me with a rusty spear, the boys were right. You are bigger than me." The ruddy-faced giant turned and shouted across the room. "You were right, lads. He's a damned bit bigger than me."

Bones looked right uncomfortable yet the other giant took no notice. "Never met another giant as big as me before," Ruddy Face continued, "let alone one bigger. Your father must 'ave been a bear. Hah!"

As Ruddy Face laughed a few nearby tables joined in with him. Bones wasn't fooled, big man though he may be, he was not so stupid as many folk took him for. "My ma weren't no weird. She didn't lie with bears."

The smile dropped from the ruddy faced giant's mouth. "Was only a joke, big man. How about a friendly contest of strength?"

"An arm wrestle?"

"Hell no, I mean a real test of strength. A good ol' fashioned rope pull. Two men, ten foot of rope and a line between 'em. First one to be pulled across the line loses."

"What's the point?" Bones asked.

"To prove which of us is stronger."

Bones shrugged. "Can't say I care."

The Boss struggled to his feet, keeping both hands on the table to steady himself. "Seems ta me it might make fer a welcome *distraction*."

Bones nodded. "Aye, alright then."

"Good," Ruddy Face said. "Your lads can come cheer you on. Your lady too."

Henry snorted and spat. It wouldn't have surprised Betrim if that was the first time she had ever been called a lady and she didn't look too pleased about it.

It didn't take long once they were outside for Betrim to notice the change. Before, the yard had been mostly empty save for a fair number of soldiers milling about doing very little. Now, the yard was mostly empty save for the same fair number of soldiers all pointing crossbows at the crew. It was a fairly obvious change and a none too welcome one.

"Reckon we might have been sold out," said Swift, his voice as low and dangerous as a wolf's growl.

The Captain with the icy eyes walked out behind them. "Take their weapons," he ordered his men.

None of the crew made any move to resist and they took everything. They even patted Betrim down and took the hidden blades he kept in his coat, most of them anyways. Afterwards, the Captain stood facing them, his face a cold stone mask. The Boss swayed on his feet to Betrim's left, Henry seethed on hers to his right.

"Which one of you is the Black Thorn?" the Captain asked in his quiet voice.

Before Betrim could answer Green stepped forward. "That one there," the lad pointed at Betrim.

"Good," the Captain continued. "Him we'll send back to Chade. The rest of you will be hanged once his Lordship gives the order."

"When do I get my reward?" Green asked.

"You sold us out?" Bones asked.

"Sent word we was coming back in Bittersprings. Cost all my coin fer a bird but it's like Thorn is always saying, *'folk don't last long in this game.'*"

"Actually it's boys like you don't last long in this game."

"Fuck you, Thorn. Looks like I'll be around long after you're gone eh. So when..." The back of the Captain's left hand took Green full in the face and the boy went down spitting teeth and coughing blood. Betrim always found it amazing how much damage a gauntlet could do to a face. A deep gash had torn the lad's cheek right open and Green screamed.

"Silence him," the Captain said in his quiet voice. His cold blue eyes swept over the rest of the crew as the ruddy faced giant picked the screaming Green up and delivered a thunderous punch to the lad's gut that drove all the wind out of him and left him gasping.

"Don't reckon you should start screaming again," the giant said. "For the best if you just stay quiet."

"His Lordship will decide just what kind of reward you deserve. Bind their hands, sergeant."

The old, grey-haired, grey-bearded man moved to obey, apologising even as he tied rope around their wrists.

Then the Captain smiled. "His Lordship will be done with your witch hunter soon enough. Then he will sentence you."

The Blademaster

As far as halls went it wasn't a bad one, Jezzet was sure it could fit a small house inside. Wooden floors all polished and slippery, paintings on the walls; one of H'ost himself, if Jezzet remembered what he looked like. More candles than was necessary to light a room three times the size and all were lit, seemed to give the room a thick atmosphere. One large table dominated the centre of the hall. It was long enough to seat thirty folk yet at the moment it had only four chairs.

One for me, one for Thanquil, one for H'ost, and one for Constance. Does he mean to feed us to death?

There was, as yet, no food on the table but it was all set out with plates and cutlery for four people.

Maybe he means to poison us? Jez thought H'ost was more than capable of such deception but Constance... Constance would want to kill Jezzet with her own hands.

The Captain escorted them to the room, instructed them to wait and departed. Since then Jezzet and Thanquil had been alone in the room and for all those five minutes neither had spoken. The Arbiter took a seat at the table and seemed content just to wait. Jezzet did not feel so relaxed.

She paced, she muttered, she loosened her sword in its scabbard, she made an entire circuit of the room and glared at each painting in turn. She considered smashing a very old, very expensive-looking vase. She stopped and stared into the large empty fireplace, walked to each of the windows in turn and looked out at the short drop to the ground below. Constance wouldn't baulk at following her out of these windows.

"Jez, I need you to do something for me," Thanquil said from his seat at the table. He was looking at her with those pretty blue eyes of his.

"Aye. Last time you asked me to do something for you it ended with you turning the Boss into a walking, talking corpse. Well actually he does very little of either these days but he still looks very corpse-like."

"I need you to make Constance angry."

"My breathing makes her angry."

"Then breathe a lot. I want her to attack you."

"Why? Why don't I just attack her?" Jezzet asked. She fully expected Constance to try and kill her on sight.

"They're less likely to call for more guards if she attacks you. After that, feel free to kill her." Thanquil was sporting that thoughtful, far-away look he sometimes got. Strange, but it made Jezzet want to smile.

"While you question H'ost?"

"Aye."

"What about the guards?" she asked.

"I'll deal with the guards."

Jezzet sighed and sank down into the chair next to him. Truth was he looked tired and more than a little nervous.

Reckon you look any better, Jez?

"Thanquil, what is this all about? I mean, why are we here?"

The Arbiter winced and ran a hand through his dark-oak hair. It was getting long, almost down to his shoulders.

He looks better with short hair.

"Not here, Jez. I promise you, if we both survive, I'll tell you everything."

That seemed to be about all the answer he was willing to give at the moment so Jezzet turned her attention to the table and decided to wait. There was a fork missing from the spot at the head of the table, she noticed, some poor servant would receive a whipping for that. There were plenty of spoons though.

"Ever killed anyone with a spoon, Arbiter?" she asked. Thanquil only laughed in reply.

The two big doors at the far end of the room swung open and a man in servant's garb scuttled through.

"Lord Gregor H'ost, Lord of Hostown and head of the family H'ost. Victor of Sefly's Point, Short Hill, Mooson, and Baskville. Warden of the Jorl and rightful king of the Wilds."

Rightful king of the wilds? That one's new.

The man who swept into the room was just as Jezzet remembered. Tall, handsome, short-cropped, auburn hair with a little more grey in it now. His face had sharp features that some would call hard and cold, but Jezzet had seen the man laugh and smile and she knew better. He wore a simple shirt of green on red along with similar trousers. No sword hung from his belt, only a large purse.

Still carrying around a small fortune in bits, H'ost? As if being moneyed makes you better than everyone else.

"Arbiter Thanquil Darkheart," H'ost said in a merry tone. "I've been expecting you."

That made the Arbiter pause. For a moment he looked lost. Jezzet saw Thanquil glance around the room before finding his tongue.

"Lord H'ost. On behalf of the Inquisition I am pleased to make your acquaintance."

"Of course," H'ost dismissed the Arbiter's comment with a wave of his hand. "Jezzet Vel'urn, It has been a long time. You look well... of sorts."

Constance strode in just behind her master. As much a giant ever, she stood at close to seven feet and was as muscled as the Boss. Her face had long, awkward features that Jez compared to a donkey on more than one occasion, and her hair was the colour of dirty straw, tied back on top of her head in a tight tail. She wore mail on top of boiled leather and a heavy longsword on her left hip with an equally heavy shortsword on her right. Constance's left eye, glazed and white, glared at Jezzet unseeing. Her right eye held all the fury of a particularly violent storm.

"Whore," Constance spat.

Why is everyone calling me a whore these days? I've only ever taken money for sex once and it was a long time ago. Even then it was only because the bastard was so bad at it I felt I needed some compensation.

"Catherine," Jezzet said with an easy smile. "Sorry. Constance. You two are so much alike these days now that you're the one bending over for H'ost. Tell me, Constance, does he make you squeal like he did her?"

"She never..." Constance roared, her hand on her sword hilt.

H'ost held up a hand. "Constance. Jezzet is our guest. No fighting over dinner, please. If we're ready I'll have the first course brought out." He waved to the servant and Constance backed away a step.

"Really?" Jezzet goaded. "Catherine would never have backed down so easy, but then she always did have a set of stones on her. Shame she didn't have a cock to go with them or you two could have..."

"FUCK YOU!"

"Constance," H'ost warned. "We talked about this."

Why the hell am I goading this giant with a thirst for vengeance into a fight? Jezzet glanced at the Arbiter. *For him?*

Constance saw the glance and an ugly grin managed to make her ugly face somehow uglier. "Didn't take ya long ta find another man ta fill your hole, Jezzet. At least Eirik was a man an' not a witch hunter."

Jezzet almost laughed. Catherine had tried for years to correct Constance's speech, but whenever the big woman got angry her accent slipped back into the common drawl of the Wilds. It seemed H'ost had just as little luck.

"I am most sorry about this, Arbiter. Inevitably if you put two women in a room they either fight like cocks or cluck like hens."

The Arbiter laughed though Jezzet could see his eyes remained cold and hard. "So very true, Lord H'ost. Though women do have their uses."

H'ost laughed. "Very true, very true. How are you finding our Jezzet? D'roan always said she was most pleasing."

Jezzet might have flushed red if she had any pride left, but it had all been beaten out of her long ago. Didn't seem to stop the burning anger from building up inside.

Of course D'roan talked about you, Jez. The blooded folk may all be at war but at their fancy parties it's all civilized.

H'ost continued. "He used to say he'd never known a more wet or willing ca..."

"Lord H'ost," Thanquil interrupted and Jezzet could have kissed him for it. "I wonder how it is you knew I was coming. I'm afraid I had no time to send you a message."

"After the events in Chade? I don't doubt you would be pressed for time. What with the escaping and all. Ah yes, the first course. Fried giraffe. Have you ever tried giraffe, Arbiter?"

"I must confess I do not know what a giraffe is."

"Hah! An Arbiter confessing. Brilliant. Big beast, long neck, spots, horns." H'ost sounded as if he were talking to some child ignorant of the world. Thanquil shook his head in reply. "I suppose you don't have them over in your Holy Empire. Got yourself a walking, talking, living God, but not a single giraffe. I'd prefer the beast any day. The tongue is a delicacy, but I told the cook not to waste it. Never even seen a giraffe. Hah!"

In all her life Jezzet had never met a man who loved the sound of his own voice quite like H'ost.

"So you knew we were coming..." Thanquil prompted.

"Of course I did. You may not have had time to let me know of your arrival, yet one of your hirelings did, I forget which one. Sent a bird from Bittersprings."

That wasn't good. If someone had told H'ost they were coming it was almost certain they had told him why as well. Jezzet watched as H'ost plucked a strip of fried giraffe and popped it into his mouth.

He even chews with that smug smile.

Jezzet noticed something was off. There were no guards in the room. Aside from the servant who announced the Lord and brought the food, only Constance was here to guard H'ost. Somehow she did not think that bode well. Still, it was time for Jezzet to play her part.

"Catherine once told me you weren't really sisters." Constance's eye never left Jez and she could see the woman's jaw clenching. H'ost looked intrigued. "Can't say I was surprised. Catherine was shorter, slighter, and very pretty while you... well that scar I gave you marks an improvement."

"Bitch," was Constance's only reply.

"She was drunk as a fish when she told me, to be certain, but she said she found you in Solantis rooting around with the rest of the garbage. She was... with the *Bold Men* at the time, I think." Jezzet looked at H'ost. "Old merc company used to operate out of Solantis. Catherine kept you as her... pet."

"Bitch."

"I reckon you didn't know this bit did you, H'ost," Jezzet continued. "Your mighty general Catherine used to be a slave."

"Shut up, whore!"

"The captain of the *Bold Men* bought her in Chade as a nubile girl, virgin and un-flowered. For six years she followed him around in chains to fuck him whenever he wanted. When Catherine found Constance she took her in. What was it they used to call you? Catherine told me once but I forget."

"Shut! Up!" Constance had gone bright red.

"You see, the feared Deadeye used to just be some slave whore's freakish pet, begging for scraps off her master's table." *I hope you get what you need from him, Arbiter.* "Only thing that's changed since, is now the slave whore is dead."

With a roar that was all fury and hatred, Constance pushed back her chair, sprang onto the table and leapt at Jezzet, her sword flashing from her scabbard into her hand. Jezzet tipped her own chair back and rolled arse over head as it hit the floor. She heard a crash and flowed to her feet, her own sword already in shaky hand. The chair she had been sat in was no more than splinters.

Somewhere, Jez could hear H'ost shouting, but neither she nor the big woman paid it any mind. Constance came at her swinging. Jezzet blocked, stumbled away, and blocked again.

By all the Gods I'd forgotten how freakishly strong she is.

Jez parried a stab and sent one back, Constance spun away on nimble feet that belied her size and was attacking again.

Jezzet found herself giving ground. Blocking and parrying, dodging and evading, but not attacking. The Arbiter wanted time alone with H'ost and she was determined to give it him. She was close to the wall now, Constance raining in blows from the front, the servant standing just a few feet behind, cowering in terror. Jezzet grabbed hold of one of the expensive-looking vases next to her and flung it at Constance's head. The big woman slashed it out of the air and it shattered, shards raining down on her.

All the time I need.

Jez spun around and was running by the time the first shard of vase hit the floor. She laid open the servant's throat with a single slash and barrelled into the doorway he had brought the food from, slamming it open with her shoulder. She kept running, knowing full well Constance would be just a few feet behind and all the fury of the Hells came with her.

The Arbiter

"Women," H'ost said after Jezzet and Constance had smashed their way out of the hall. Thanquil could still hear the clashing of metal on metal. Neither man moved, both still sitting at the table, though Thanquil had edged his chair away from the chaos. H'ost himself looked unperturbed by his giant of a General attacking Jezzet. "Honestly I had a feeling it might end this way. Constance is useful, a seasoned military leader, but she has a fire in her where our lovely Jezzet is concerned."

"You knew we were coming," Thanquil said as H'ost popped his last strip of fried giraffe into his mouth and started chewing. "You know why I'm here." It wasn't a question.

"Well of course I do, Arbiter. Though I must admit I'm curious as to how you managed to make her talk. I assumed she would be immune to your compulsion." Thanquil tried his best to hide his confusion, he had no idea what this man was talking about and it did not bode well that H'ost knew about the compulsion.

"Nor do I understand how you knew the language. I thought it would be quite beyond an Arbiter of your experience, but there you have it. We can't be right about everything can we."

H'ost leaned back in his chair and yawned. "You can come in now, darling."

The double doors swung open again and a woman walked through them, a woman Thanquil knew all too well. She was clad better now, tight riding leathers where before she had worn rags. She was cleaner also, her hair and skin washed. It was easy to see now that she resembled H'ost though younger and more feminine. The lack of chains were a concern, Thanquil would far preferred her to still be in chains.

He didn't hesitate. Thanquil pulled the ball thrower from his belt, aimed and pulled the trigger.

BANG!

The merchant had said accurate up to ten paces. This was more like twenty and the shot went well wide, splintering the door frame. The woman looked at where the small pellet had hit, saw the slight yellow-gold glow of the blessed bullet fading away, and then turned to Thanquil with a cruel smile. He was already reloading.

"A pistol!" H'ost said with a clap of his hands. "Wonderful. Where did you get that?"

"Chade," Thanquil answered as he finished popping the ball back into the barrel then shoved it back into his belt and stood, drawing his sword instead. The woman walked forward and stopped behind H'ost's chair. She carried no weapon but he knew how dangerous she was.

"You've met my daughter, Arbiter."

"In a cell, where they had her chained to a wall after they had already killed her twice and scooped out her eyes." Thanquil was tense, he had not planned for this. "What did you do to her, H'ost?"

The head of the H'ost family laughed while his daughter, standing behind him, stared on through cold, dead eyes. "The compulsion. Very good. It's been a while since I felt it. I must say, yours is particularly weak."

Thanquil backed away a step and tried again. "What is she?"

Again H'ost laughed. When he stopped his voice was as hard and harsh as Thanquil's own. "I am not some mindless simpleton. I am Gregor H'ost. Your pathetic compulsion will not work on me, Arbiter." He turned to his daughter standing behind him. "Kill him."

The woman came towards him, skipping from one foot to the other in a strange, jinking dance. Then she hissed something in an alien tongue and the air rushed towards Thanquil with a scream. The blast knocked him off his feet and he found himself rolling on the polished, wooden floor. The woman was coming at him fast. Her only weapons her hands, each finger sporting a sharp-looking claw.

Thanquil raised his sword to block the first attack. The noise as her claws connected with his sword sounded like metal screeching against metal. He spun out of reach, whispering blessings of speed and strength, and slashed with his sword at her head. She danced away from him and then back in with another swipe with her right hand. He blocked again and she stepped in close. As Thanquil fell away, she tore at his arm with her left hand.

He could feel blood running down his arm and the pain was agony.

It felt as though the wound both burned and froze at the same time. Thanquil clutched at his left arm, around the wound, and cried out. He scrambled backwards, pushing with his feet and glad that the floor was so well polished. The woman danced towards him again, more slowly this time, almost as if she were savouring the moment.

"Strong, isn't she?" he heard H'ost say. "And only the first of many. I intend to make an army of them."

Thanquil realised he was no longer holding his sword. He'd dropped it when she clawed his arm and now the woman was between him and the blade.

He reached into his coat pocket and pulled out a small slip of paper. The good thing about an Arbiter coat was many hidden pockets and Thanquil knew what each one contained by heart. He flung the piece of paper at the woman and she clawed it away. Thanquil curled into a ball just in time as the air exploded.

His ears were still ringing as he regained his feet. The air hung heavy with smoke and there were scorch marks on the floor. The woman was a good ten feet away, whining and writhing in pain. Her face and arms were charred, blackened ruins. Her leathers were burned and, in places, still on fire.

As Thanquil advanced on her, he had to say, she now looked a pathetic figure, wriggling on the ground, struggling to breathe through scorched lungs. The teachers at the Inquisition always warned about using rune explosions; there was always the chance you would breathe in the flames.

Thanquil stopped by the pathetic creature on the floor, pulled his pistol from his belt once more and pulled the trigger.

BANG!

The glowing bullet smashed through her skull. The body convulsed once, twice, and then stopped. A spreading pool of blood ran along the gleaming, wooden floor. Thanquil hated the smell of burning flesh.

"I don't think she will be coming back from the dead this time. I wrapped a purging rune around the bullet. Whatever she was, it's gone now."

When Thanquil looked at the H'ost he fell off his chair and

scrambled away. The Arbiter turned away to collect his fallen sword.

"I never was very good at sword play, but the teachers at the Inquisition said I more than made up for it with my skill with magic. Runes, charms, blessings and curses are my spe... H'ost stop!"

Too late, Thanquil turned back to find the terrified lord pulling a number of wooden chips from his purse. He was snapping them and throwing them to the floor. Thanquil counted ten and he recognised them right away. They were summoning runes. Already the room was starting to grow colder, darker. Already the first shade was beginning to form.

The Black Thorn

The Captain waited, his back straight and cold eyes watchful. The rest of his troops were not so diligent. Some drifted into groups and began to talk, some slipped back into the mess hall, no doubt for some ale, some stood around yawning and rubbing at their sleepy eyes. The old, grey sergeant was chatting and laughing with Bones before ten minutes had passed. The giant was well known for being an amiable bastard, even with his hands bound it seemed.

Betrim glanced to his right. The Boss was swaying, eyes half closed. "Boss," Betrim hissed. No answer. "Boss, on the off chance any of us get out o' this. Who hired us?"

The big southerner didn't give any acknowledgement of having heard. "Boss..." Betrim hissed again.

"Morrass," this came from the other side of Betrim, from Henry.

"Captain Drake Morrass?" Betrim wasn't sure why he asked, it wasn't like there were any other Morrass' it could have been. He just didn't want to believe it was true.

"Aye."

"Ahhh, Boss. Ya made a deal with the damned devil."

Captain Drake Morrass was a dangerous name not to know and an even more dangerous name to know. Betrim had heard all the stories. Morrass had drowned as a child and came back part demon. He was a pirate who had sailed on every sea in the world and tamed them all, he'd sailed through storms with waves thousands of feet high and he charmed a kraken into working for him. Morrass owned half of Chade, it was rumoured he owned some city in Acanthia and was in with the Guild there to boot. He slipped his way into the Dragon Empress' bed and that was no easy feat given it was guarded by a bloody dragon.

But those weren't even the bad stories. He raped boys and girls alike and slit their throats after to bathe in their blood so as to keep himself young. Once when one of his crew members made to mutiny, Morrass had starved the man almost to death, then gelded him and served him his own cock and balls, told the man what it was and all and watched as he ate. After, he put in close to port, close enough to swim, chopped the man's arms and legs off, threw him into the sea, and told him to swim. There were rumours he once...

BANG!

The noise wasn't as loud as Betrim had heard it before, muffled, maybe, or far away. The Captain didn't look nervous, if anything he looked a little smug.

"That'll be the end of your witch hunter now. Won't be long before you all join him," the Captain said in a tone as icy as his eyes.

Betrim spat and scratched at his cheek, the unburnt one, seemed a bit of stubble was growing through, that would need shaving. "I've been the end of a few Arbiters myself..."

"Six," Henry put in with her usual sneer.

"As she says," Betrim continued. "Been the end of six Arbiters an' that did not sound like one endin'."

There was a flicker of doubt across the Captain's face, he glanced away and then back again. Might as well have just come right out and said he was unsure. Betrim decided to push.

"Thing 'bout Arbiters is the magic. They got all sorts of spells an' shit." Betrim glanced at the Boss and himself a bit nervous his own self. The Boss was as good as gone back at the Jorl, it was only the Arbiter's charm keeping the black-skinned leader of the crew alive and the witch hunter had said it could stop working at any time.

"I saw one turn someone into a frog once," Henry said with a nod, her face so serious Betrim almost laughed, would have laughed, given how ridiculous it was, but for the situation didn't call for laughter.

"Aye?" the Black Thorn asked trying to tell Henry to shut up with his eyes alone.

"Aye."

"Aye." Betrim turned back to the Captain and took a step forward. the Captain took a step back. "So d'ya still reckon that sound was the end of our witch hunter?"

BOOM!

That was not the sound that the Arbiter's little string-less crossbow made, it was louder and... different. Less like a thunderclap and more like a rock-slide. The Captain's eyes were far less icy now, there was fear there. Fear was good, fear made folk stupid.

Betrim laughed his hard rasping laugh right in the Captain's face. "Reckon it might be time ya started seekin' alternative employment, Captain. Might wanna think 'bout lettin' us go an' all. Before our witch hunter finishes up in there."

"Sergeant, take four men and go check on his Lordship," the Captain commanded in a somewhat shaky voice.

The old, grey sergeant didn't much seem to like that idea.

BANG!

"Bugger that, Captain. You go check on him."

"I gave you an order, Sergeant!"

The sergeant was backing away, shaking his head. Betrim could hear sobbing and figured it was Green. Dumb fuck had fallen on his arse and was scrambling away from the conflict while crying.

"Them Arbiters, they burn ya. Ain't no way to die, burning" said the sergeant.

Betrim felt cold and either he was going mad or the lanterns were dimming and he could hear a strange rattling noise, sounded a bit like chains.

"What the fuck is that?" Henry said, her voice cracking just a little.

A shadow began to form in the light of the yard. At first it seemed just a floating patch of darkness, out of place in the flickering yellow light of the lanterns, but soon it seemed as if the shadow had arms and legs. Horrible, spiky limbs ending in savage claws and formed of darkness even blacker than the Boss' skin. The air seemed to shimmer where it stood and the ground froze beneath it. Then its head formed out of the darkness, near as big as its body, it sported two great horns of darkness from its crown and its mouth was a jagged line in its face, a piercing white light showing between the gaps of its teeth, each one as big as a hand. Finally, its eyes opened, two bright yellow flames amidst a sea of darkness. Hungry flames.

The shade looked nothing human. It stood as tall as Bones without the stoop. Its legs were squat things, too small for the long, thin body. Its arms were too long, reaching almost down to the ground. Its head was the worst, at least three or four feet long, Betrim guessed, and that was before the horns, it stuck out from the body on a short, thin neck. All over, the creature seemed to be covered in spikes formed from shadow, impossible to look at, each seemed to move and drift around the creature's body.

The first man to die was the bravest of them all, or maybe the most stupid. A big soldier, heavy with muscle and with long hair flowing past his shoulder, thrust a spear at the shade. As the spear point connected there was an awful screaming noise like metal grating against metal and the shaft of the spear exploded into splinters. The man died where he stood. With one casual backhand the shade turned his shouting face into a mess of bone and torn flesh and spurting blood with three deep ridges ripped from his skull. The lifeless body dropped with a heavy thud and chaos broke loose.

Some men ran at the shade, others away. Some just stood there with slack-mouthed shock on their faces. Someone somewhere was screaming. The loudest scream Betrim had ever heard and so full of pain it set his teeth on edge. There were more shades forming out of the darkness, Betrim didn't bother to count how many, he was finding it hard to think further than the steaming of his own breath in the air.

"Plan, Boss?" Bones asked.

The Boss was no help. He dropped to his knees, his eyes closed. Betrim couldn't even tell if the man was still breathing.

"Might be time fer some of that legendary strength o' yours, Bones. Get those ropes off." Betrim was rubbing his wrists raw trying to slide a hand free from the ropes.

So far the crew had been left out of the chaos. A battle was raging around them, soldiers teaming together to stab and slash at the shades, others running for the gate, trying to get away and the crew stood in a sea of calm, watching it all happening and taking no part.

Bones grunted, growled, and strained against the ropes holding his hands together, his face a bright red colour from the effort. Then Swift was there with a tiny knife cutting the bonds.

"Ol' Swift ain't never properly disarmed." The lad said with a grin. Betrim thought back to Bittersprings, to Swift's sister producing a knife from somewhere despite being naked as her name day. Then his hands were free.

Betrim gave his wrists a quick rub and walked over to the nearest weapon he could see, a discarded sword. "Not an axe but it'll do the job, I reckon."

"What do we do, Boss?" Henry asked, shaking the big man. "Boss?"

Betrim stalked past her. Someone, somewhere was still screaming.

He found Green on his knees in the dirt, staring all around him with the stink of fear coming off him. Either that or he'd shit himself. The Captain had done a real job on his face. Green's left cheek was laid open, Betrim could see teeth through the wound.

"F'horl," Green gurgled.

"Eh?"

"Thsesse sunt."

"What?"

"Thssseeese."

Thorn buried the sword in Green's neck. Didn't take the head off with one swing though, the blade stuck about half way through, hit the bone, he reckoned. Still, Green was just as dead. Betrim put a boot on the boy's chest and wrenched the steel free with a gush of red blood.

"I fuckin' hate swords," Betrim spat at Green's corpse and finished the decapitation. By the time he turned back to the chaos the crew had joined the fight, but on which side Betrim couldn't rightly say.

Bones had found himself a bloody greatsword from somewhere and was laying about himself. Two soldiers were dead close by already and four more surrounded him. Swift found his way up onto the wall somehow and was busy duelling with the Captain while more soldiers tried to work their way behind him. Henry had a dirk in one hand and was shaking the Boss' shoulder with the other, screaming in his ear. As Betrim watched the old, grey sergeant who had fought in more battles than ten men walked up behind Henry and shouted something at her. Henry spun and buried her little blade in the man's chest once, twice and then slit his throat for good measure.

All around him men were dying, fleeing, begging for their lives.

The shades didn't even seem to feel the kiss of steel, almost like their skin was made of harder stuff. Betrim watched as one shade, standing at just five feet tall, caught hold of a sword and snapped the blade in two with just one clawed hand. The soldier who had been wielding it turned to run too late. The shade tore the man's back out, breastplate, cloth, flesh, and all.

One of the creatures was no more than two feet tall, it looked like some sort of manic, black imp. It dodged attacks, slashed at legs and tore into soldiers who could no longer stand. Betrim saw it leap at a man and cling to his face, tearing into the soldier with claw and tooth until the body was a twitching mess.

The first shade that had appeared was finished with its attackers. All the brave soldiers were either dead or fled, bodies on the ground and so much blood. It began to lumber towards Henry and the Boss. Betrim guessed something like that didn't need to move too fast. Henry screamed something at it, but Betrim didn't hear what. The Black Thorn was scared of no man but right now the Black Thorn couldn't seem to make his feet move.

Henry flung her little dirk at the creature and screamed at it again. The shade just kept on walking. At ten feet away Henry started to back off, trying to pull the Boss with her. The big man just knelt there, staring at the shade. That's when Betrim realised the Boss' eyes were open again. At five feet Henry let go of the leader of the crew and fell backwards, scrambling away on her arse.

Betrim watched it all from where he stood. Bones was backed into a corner by a group of soldiers with spears, he was roaring and swinging that big sword of his, but there were too many of them. Swift was still up the wall, the Captain was nowhere to be seen but the half-blooded bastard was holding his sword and limping backwards as one of the shades advanced on him. The shade in front of the Boss calmly, almost tenderly reached out and took hold of the big man by the throat, its giant, black hand wrapping all the way around the Boss' thick neck.

Slowly, the shade lifted the Boss up so his feet were off the ground and his face was level with the creature's giant head. Then it opened its mouth, wider and wider and wider, so wide the Boss' head fit inside.

Henry was silent, watching with wide eyed horror as the shade bit down.

The Boss didn't scream. His whole body jerked but he didn't make a sound as the creature's teeth cut through his flesh and bone from the bottom of his chin to the crown of his head and blood gushed down to hit the ground below.

When it was done the shade just dropped the Boss' limp, lifeless body. The big man who had led them for years looked almost whole except the front half of his head was just missing. The Black Thorn had seen some nasty stuff in his time, he'd done a lot of it himself, but right now he felt like he needed to throw up.

Then the shade turned towards Henry. The crazy bitch was frozen on the floor, staring at the corpse of the Boss. Betrim put one foot in front of the other and then another. Before he knew what he was doing he found himself just a stone's throw from the shade and shouting.

"Fuck sake, Henry. RUN!" he screamed at her.

The shade turned to look at him, eyes blazing yellow in its huge, dark face. Betrim could feel hot water trickling down his face. He spat. The Black Thorn wouldn't go crying to his own death.

"Henry! Get the fuck up an' run! NOW!"

The shade took a step towards Betrim then stopped and turned to look at Henry as she scrambled to her feet.

The Black Thorn let out a heavy sigh. "Shit." Then he charged the shade.

The Arbiter

"Go back to the void," Thanquil hissed.

The demon seemed to smile. "We obey." With that it faded back into nothing. Thanquil turned his attention to H'ost.

"What? How did you..."

Scooping up one of the discarded runes from the floor, Thanquil advanced on the cowering lord. "The creatures of the void are bound by ancient magic to serve the Inquisition. This," he threw the broken rune in H'ost's face and the man let out a squeak of fear, "is an incomplete rune."

Thanquil grabbed hold of H'ost, spun him around and shoved him down onto the fancy dining table, sending plates and goblets scattering. There he held him. "A true transcription of summoning requires three runes. Your poor imitation was missing the rune of binding. Do you know what that means?"

H'ost shook his head. His eyes were as wide as the dinner plates now lying on the floor.

"It means the demons you summoned will not obey you. Do you hear the shouts? The sound of battle outside? They are killing your own men!" Thanquil pulled H'ost off the table and slammed him back down again.

"She... she never told me... she said."

"Tell me what you did to your daughter. What was she?"

Some clarity seemed to enter H'ost's eyes and he shut his mouth, stared at Thanquil with defiance. The sounds of battle were loud outside. H'ost might have done the Arbiter a favour by summoning the demons. Thanquil just had to hope the chaos they caused would last long enough.

"Thing about the Inquisition is, Lord H'ost, we didn't always have the compulsion as a means of making people talk. Back in the old days, a thousand years ago, we had to rely on other methods. While we don't generally employ such methods any more, we are required to learn them all the same. Just in case."

Thanquil picked up a small, silver knife lying forgotten on the table and stabbed it into H'ost's left thigh, just below the groin. The lord screamed. Blood began to well up around the small blade. The man struggled, trying to fight his way off the table and away from the Arbiter, but Thanquil was stronger and had a blessing of strength he could chant if need be. The wounded lord collapsed back onto the table and a low whine escaped his lips.

"What did you do to your daughter, H'ost? What was she?" Thanquil repeated.

Still the Lord of Hostown remained silent, refusing to answer. Thanquil reached into one of the hidden pockets in his coat and pulled out a slip of paper with a sleepless charm transcribed upon it, he slapped the charm on H'ost's arm.

"What are you..."

Thanquil held the man down with one hand and placed the other on his forehead. Then he began to whisper a blessing. H'ost screamed louder than Thanquil had ever heard anyone scream before, even burning folk didn't scream so loud. He thrashed and he clawed, he even tried to punch at the Arbiter but Thanquil held him fast. When he released the blessing H'ost was sobbing.

"Blessings and curses can be used on others, Lord H'ost. Even those unwilling. That was a blessing to augment your senses. Your leg must have felt like it was being ripped apart." Thanquil picked another silver knife off the table and stabbed it hard into H'ost's right leg. Again the man screamed but not near as loud as when Thanquil took hold of his head again and whispered the blessing.

"TELL ME!" Thanquil shouted at him when he released the blessing. The lord of the most powerful family in the Wilds smelled of sweat and blood and piss, and lay there sobbing on his own dining table. "I can do this for days, H'ost. Keep you alive and torture you. You'll not fall unconscious with that charm on you. You will feel everything a hundred times worse with the blessing."

Thanquil reached for another knife, came up with a fork. "NO! Stop... please."

"What was she, H'ost?" Thanquil hissed, the fork in his hand hovering, ready to strike.

"A demon..." he sobbed. "A creature from the void. She told me how to do it."

"How to put a demon inside a person?"

H'ost nodded, another great sob escaping from his lips. Tears and sweat ran down his face in rivers. "She said it would only work on those with potential. So I did it to her, gave my daughter the gift."

"Gift?"

"Of immortality. I made her strong, beautiful." H'ost laughed, a sad noise and mixed with pain. "And you killed her."

Thanquil spat. "You killed her, H'ost. I just sent the demon wearing the body back to where it belongs. Who taught you how to do it? Who taught you how to put a demon inside a person?"

H'ost was shaking his head, his eyes wide and fearful. "I... I don't... know."

This time the fork went through H'ost's left palm, straight through the flesh into the wood below, pinning his hand to the table. Again he screamed. Thanquil took hold of his head and whispered the blessing then twisted the knife in H'ost's leg. The scream became a guttural, raw sound, almost inhuman. It filled Thanquil's ears, made him sick to the stomach, but he continued chanting, continued until H'ost no longer had the strength to resist. No longer had the strength to scream.

"Who is it, H'ost? Who is the traitor in the Inquisition?"

H'ost sobbed and coughed, his throat no doubt raw from the screaming. From the way he smelled Thanquil guessed the man had soiled himself and blood was dripping down on the floor. If he didn't get the answers he needed soon the man might die of blood loss before confessing.

"WHO IS IT, H'OST?" Thanquil screamed at the man.

"I DON'T KNOW," the man shouted back. "I never... never met her. She sent... someone... someone else to me. A man... an Arbiter... Ke... Kessick. Arbiter Kessick."

Thanquil didn't know an Arbiter Kessick though that didn't mean much, he knew very few Arbiters if truth be told. It gave him a lead at least. If the traitor was an Inquisitor as the God-Emperor suspected then she could only be one of two; Inquisitor Heron or Inquisitor Downe. If this Arbiter Kessick was the traitor's creature, Thanquil would only have to find the man and follow him. Seemed an easy task when he thought of it that way, somehow Thanquil didn't think it would work out so easy a job.

H'ost was still sobbing, lying slack on the table. Thanquil leaned in close to the man. "Anything else, Lord H'ost?"

The man shook his head, still crying. Then his eyes flicked open, looked at Thanquil and then away.

"Last chance, my lord." Thanquil said, donning a cruel smile that he didn't feel. "What aren't you telling me?"

"The contract," H'ost said.

"What contract?"

"I don't know... not really. Something I overheard... Kessick, he... he was talking to one of the demons... said something about her contract. That's it... it's all I know. I'm sorry. I'm sorry. I'm sorry."

The man was growing weak, pale. Too much blood loss, Thanquil guessed. He started alternating between sobbing, apologising, and coughing up blood. The Arbiter judged he had learned all he would from the man and reached for another knife to finish the job. All he could find was a silver spoon.

By the time Thanquil reached the yard he felt like he needed to throw up, that and spend the next few days blind drunk. He'd passed two soldiers on his way from H'ost's dining hall and both had backed away and stared at him in mute horror. It wasn't surprising considering he was smeared with Lord H'ost's blood.

Outside was the chaos he had predicted writ in full. The demons Lord H'ost had summoned had made easy work of the garrison by the looks of things. Dead men littered the floor, bodies and bits of bodies, blood and mud, weapons and armour, much of it broken. Of the living the yard was almost deserted, only one man and one demon remained, the rest, Thanquil presumed, had fled. The demons would be in the town by now, causing as much slaughter and chaos there as they had here.

The Black Thorn was facing a demon a good foot taller than him with eyes of flame and a head as large an elephant's. As Thanquil watched, Thorn ducked inside the demon's reach, clattered two sword slashes off the creature's impervious hide and then danced backwards, blocking a swipe as he did. The force of the attack sent the Black Thorn stumbling and, as he came up, he grabbed a handful of mud and flung it at the creature. The demon laughed, a harsh, cold sound that reminded Thanquil of a peal of thunder.

Of the rest of the crew there was no sign, although a near headless body on the ground close by could have been the Boss.

Thorn darted in towards the demon again and his battered, notched sword bounced off the creature's head. "Why won't ya jus' fuckin' die?" the Black Thorn shouted at the demon.

Thanquil strode forwards. Just as the creature was about to attack he called out to it. "Demon. Go back to the void."

It stopped mid swing. Glanced at Thanquil and started to fade. "We obey."

The Black Thorn stood staring at where the demon had been just a moment before. Then he turned to Thanquil, it was hard to say what expression that burned face held but he guessed it was confusion.

"Arbiter..." Thorn began. "How the fuck?"

"I'm a witch hunter," Thanquil said with a forced smile. "I banish evil, it's what we do."

"Huh."

"The crew..." Thanquil prompted.

"Dead, I think. Green an' the Boss. Swift an' Bones I think too. Henry? Henry?" The Black Thorn spun around looking for the little woman but she was nowhere to be seen. "Might be she made it out but the rest..."

"Jez..."

"Damn, Arbiter. I thought she were with you."

Thanquil looked around the yard, looked at the bodies, at the blood. Then he looked towards the mansion. "We wait." He decided. "She'll be here."

The Black Thorn didn't look too happy about that. "What about the rest o' them shades?"

"They'll fade. In time. They can't stay in our world for long."

"But ain't they out in the city? With all them townsfolk."

Thanquil just nodded.

The Black Thorn spat. "Poor bastards."

Thanquil heard a scared whinny. "Thorn, can you ride?"

The Blademaster

Jez ducked a high slash and danced away. Constance came on strong, hot on her heels and swinging her sword in wild arcs, not caring if it bit into walls or paintings, windows or servants. Again Jezzet dodged away and again Constance followed.

Doesn't she ever tire? In truth the giant woman didn't even look to be breathing hard. *If I'm intending to wear her out I may be here all night.*

Jez blocked, parried, dodged, then dodged, blocked, and parried, all on the defensive, she made no move to attack. The end of the corridor was close behind her. She blocked a high slash, then a low slash and shouldered her way through the door. Constance's heavy sword bit into the door frame, splintering wood and causing her to pause for a moment and wrench it free. She was exposed as she would ever be. Jezzet backed further into the room.

She was in a kitchen now, the heat was oppressive and the smells were strong. Fresh bread, roasting meat, pig by the smell of it, exotic spices, something smelled of vanilla. Most days those smells would have had her mouth-watering, now they just made her want to spit. Frightened cooks scattered from the kitchen via alternative doors, one started sneaking up behind Jez with a cleaver, she saw his reflection in a pan of soup and was about to turn and gut him when Constance shouted.

"Touch her and die!" she roared. The cook startled, dropped the cleaver and ran.

"Want me all for yourself, Constance? I always knew you loved me."

Constance roared again and swung her sword, the soup pot flew towards Jez, spraying boiling hot broth everywhere. Jezzet scrambled out of the way and then ducked another two handed swing of the giant's sword.

I could have stuck her in the gut right then.

Jezzet vaulted onto a wooden counter and then dropped off the other side just as the sword sliced down behind her, cutting both a loaf of warm bread and the wooden counter in two.

As Constance cursed and struggled to pull her sword free of the wooden wreckage, Jezzet grabbed an empty iron pan and flung it at the woman's head. The warlord swatted it out of the air with one giant paw but the next one caught her in the face. She stumbled backwards cursing and spitting blood.

Jez backed away again, found another door and shouldered through it just as Constance recovered and came charging. Another slash blocked, another jab parried and all the while the Blademaster kept giving ground, backing further and further away, staying out of the giant's reach. They were now in some sort of dining hall, with crude wooden benches and tables and bodies. Lots of bodies, servants and a few soldiers by the looks of things, some pretty cut up. All this Jez took in while keeping Constance from cutting her in half. The big woman didn't even seem to notice the carnage around them until she stepped on a dismembered arm, glanced down, kicked the bloody limb aside, and came at Jezzet again.

"Stop runnin' away, whore!" Constance shouted as Jez dodged backwards yet again.

"Stop calling me a whore, you giant, freakish, cunt-eating bitch."

Insults are wasted breath. Blades speak louder than words. Her old, dead master's voice whispered in her ear.

"Why did you do it, Jez?" Constance asked, her sword pausing in front of her, her chest rising and falling as she sucked in air. "She was your friend."

Jezzet snorted. "Here in the Wilds, Constance, there's no such thing as friends. Just people ain't turned on you yet. Catherine knew that better than most, better than you. Hells, she taught it to me."

"Liar."

"You really think she was a saint don't ya?" Jez laughed. "Catherine's the one that turned on me."

"LIAR!" And with that the fight was on again.

Jez blocked a slash to her right, ducked the next one, and then spun away from the big woman's downward swipe. Up a bench and Jez mounted a table, parried Constance's sword thrust and jumped down the other side. The giant's sword bit a chunk out of the cheap wood and she wrenched her sword free and followed Jezzet over the table.

Twenty feet behind and to my left, another door. Jez turned her back to the door and started backing towards it blocking as she went.

"How do you think D'roan's men found me, Constance?"

"What?" the giant roared back.

"When they took me. I'd slipped out of the camp to find myself a tavern and get drunk and you think D'roan's men just happened upon me and knew who I was?"

"LIAR!"

"Catherine told them I was there. She wanted me gone. D'roan used to brag about it all the time when he fucked me. Used to love to tell me it was my own best friend who sold me out."

"She would never... why would she?" Constance's next swing near split a table in half and the follow up would have taken Jez's arm off if she had been a drop slower.

"Because she didn't need me anymore. Once she was in charge of H'ost's armies I was more of a threat than a friend so she gave me to our enemies hoping they would kill me."

"But they didn't kill ya."

Jez reached the door, kicked it open, and backed through it. They appeared to be on a landing. To her left the corridor seemed to stretch on forever, Jezzet glimpsed a dark shadow that way but ignored it. To her right there were some stairs down. She turned her back in the direction of the stairs and concentrated on the giant's sword.

"No, Constance they didn't kill me. It suited D'roan to keep me instead. Tied up for his amusement whenever he wanted to put his cock in something or beaten whenever he got angry.

"For three months!" Jezzet screamed at Constance. "For three months I was beaten, raped, and humiliated every day so tell me again how Catherine was my friend!"

"Lying whore!" Constance spat as she swung her sword. "You killed her."

They were at the stairs down now. Jez caught the giant's sword on her own and stepped sideways, the big woman turned with her. Constance's back was to the stairs. Jezzet planted a foot in the woman's

The Heresy Within

stomach and then she was falling away.

Constance hit the stairs with a solid crack and a cry of pain and then rolled the rest of the way down to a series of grunts and groans. Jezzet started walking down the stairs.

Steep stairs, Jez. I wouldn't want to fall.

"I didn't have a choice, Constance. When D'roan got bored of me he started threatening to give me to his men, to his whole fucking army. Then came H'ost's stupid bloody challenge and D'roan had a better idea."

Constance was struggling to her feet at the bottom of the stairs. Her left arm was hanging limp, looked broken, her face was bloodied and she was leaning on her sword. "She should never..." The giant spat out some blood. "She should never have fought you."

Jez laughed. "She should never have fought. Catherine was good with a sword, no doubt, one of the best natural fighters I've ever seen but she was never trained. D'roan had at least ten men in his camp that could have cut her to pieces but he deemed it would be best if I did it."

Constance swung a clumsy one-handed slash at Jez. She stepped aside and started circling the giant.

"He made me a deal there and then. Said If I killed Catherine, if I cut her up and humiliated her in the challenge, he'd give me my freedom. Just let me go. If I refused he'd give me to his army and make sure I died from it."

"You're lying!" Again the giant made a clumsy swing and again Jezzet stepped out of the way. "After you killed her," Constance looked to be crying from her good eye, "you were still with D'roan."

That made Jezzet pause. "Yes. He gave me my freedom and I stayed with him." *And hated myself for it. I should have killed him.*

The big woman dropped to one knee, still leaning on her sword. She was panting, clearly in a lot of pain, and shaking like a leaf in a storm. "So why tell me? You know I won't stop. I will kill you, whore!"

Jezzet nodded. "I know you won't stop, Constance." Her sword flashed out and took the giant in the face.

Constance fell to the floor screaming, clutching at her right eye with her unbroken arm. Jezzet's blade had given her a mirror of the scar she had from the day of the challenge, the day Catherine died. The day

Jezzet made herself a lifelong enemy.

The giant screamed as she writhed on the floor, blood welling up from between her fingers.

"I told you that, Constance, because I want it done with," Jezzet said, her voice sounding quiet and sad to her ears. "I want that part of my life over, done with, laid to rest. Goodbye, Constance."

Jezzet thrust her sword into Constance's chest, between the ribs, into the heart. The big woman gasped, twitched once, twice, and then relaxed into death.

On her way back to the front of the building Jezzet found a number of bodies. Servants, maids, soldiers, even a couple of folk who looked blooded. All dead and torn to shreds.

When she found the door they had entered through she could see the yard was even worse than inside the mansion. Jez had seen fewer bodies on a battlefield. Corpses were strewn everywhere and where there weren't any dead people, there was blood from one. She almost stepped on a head as she exited the building and after a moment realised it belonged to Green, half of one of his cheeks was missing, but it was him, or at least it had been.

Two men stood in the centre of the yard with three horses. Thanquil and the Black Thorn were arguing by the sounds of it but neither of them had weapons drawn, though Thorn was poking the Arbiter in the chest and pointing off towards the town. Thanquil was shaking his head in reply.

Jezzet approached. "Hell of a distraction, Thorn." *Not to mention an impressive feat, slaughtering an entire garrison.*

"Huh?" Both men turned towards her at once. Thanquil smiled and the Black Thorn's face twitched into what Jez figured was a grin.

"Oh, this." Thorn looked around the yard. "Weren't me, it were H'ost. Though I'll most likely get blame fer it."

"Are you..." Thanquil asked.

Jez smiled. "I'm alright."

"Did you..."

"I did."

Thorn spat. "Did what?"

"Constance is dead."

"Aye? So is H'ost. Tell her, Arbiter."

Thanquil winced. "I killed him with a spoon."

The Black Thorn rasped out a laugh and Jezzet couldn't help but join in. *Couldn't have happened to a more deserving bastard.*

"Horses?" she asked. The big brown one was staring at her with dull eyes. It took a step towards her and started nuzzling at her hand.

"Witch hunter's idea," Thorn said. "Reckons we need ta make a quick getaway. Reckon he might be right."

Jezzet nodded. "What about the others? I saw Green... or well his head but..."

"We're it, ain't no others."

Well I'll miss Bones at least. Truth was she might even miss Swift. Full of shit, the bastard might be, but Jez had come to like his stories.

She swung herself onto the horse and settled into the saddle. Thanquil looked comfortable enough, but the Black Thorn kept fidgeting like someone had just tried to stick something up his arse. It was near full dark and the moon was high and bright, and lanterns lit the town along the streets. They weren't the only people about; there were folk all over the roads, all looking like they were heading for the town gate. Jezzet spied a few bodies here and there, not to mention she could hear screams off in the distance.

"What the hell happened here?" Jezzet asked as they rode.

Thanquil sighed. "It's not our concern."

The Black Thorn growled. "Aye. Reckon I might get blamed fer that too though."

The Arbiter

It was two nights after Hostown when Jezzet asked the question. By then it already felt like they had been riding forever. Thanquil's rear alternated between numb and painful, and it looked as though the others were faring even worse. The Black Thorn grumbled and moaned with every bounce. Thanquil had tried to tell him to move with the horse but more than once the sell-sword had complained of, *'crushing my stones.'* Jez was more silent about the pain but he could see her wincing. They stopped from time to time, to water the horses and let them graze for a while.

Nobody had remarked on their leaving Hostown, so many of its residents were fleeing the chaos that the soldiers had been too hard pressed and confused to pay attention to three riders among a thousand.

None of the three knew the area as well as Swift, but making it to the forest that bordered the Jorl had been easy enough, from here they needed to find a safe crossing and then ride south until they reached Chade. With such a diminished party the watches were harder at night as well, each of them had to take a turn watching over the others and making sure they were not ambushed. It felt queer to trust the Black Thorn to keep him safe as he slep,t but Thanquil couldn't say he had much of a choice and so far Thorn had proved himself true.

"You said you'd explain it all if we both survived," Jezzet said just as Thanquil had been contemplating sleep. There was no fire, they would not risk it in the forest with tales of bandits what they were, but all three were sat in a circle among a copse of trees. Thanquil had his back to one, the Black Thorn leaned against another, standing watch and listening. Jezzet was sitting cross-legged on the mossy green ground, staring at the Arbiter.

"I did..." Thanquil glanced at the Black Thorn, unsure how much of the truth he was willing to tell with the sell-sword listening in.

"There is a traitor in the Inquisition..." Thanquil started. From there he told them both almost everything. He explained about how he was sent to Chade to deal with the witch in gaol, about how his true goal had been to find and question H'ost in connection with the traitor. He told them what H'ost had said, that the traitor was an Inquisitor, a woman and that she had at least one accomplice. He told them about how H'ost had been trying to implant demons from the void into human bodies and that he feared the traitor might be doing the same to Arbiters. He left out only that the demons were bound to the Inquisition, sworn to serve, and that the God-Emperor had been the one to send him on this mission.

By the end of the telling Thanquil found his jaw ached from talking. Jezzet refused to meet his eyes and the Black Thorn was staring at him with a look that might have been respect.

"So what's your plan now, Arbiter?" Jezzet asked.

The way Thanquil saw it, he only had one option available to him. "I'm headed for Chade. There I'll take a boat back to Sarth. Find Arbiter Kessick. Follow him to the Inquisitor that has betrayed us and kill them both."

The Black Thorn snorted. "Ya really gotta work on these plans o' yours, Arbiter. Why not jus' tell the rest o' ya Inquisitors 'bout this Kessick? Have them torture the truth out o' him."

Thanquil winced. "I don't know who I can trust. If Kessick gets wind that they're coming for him he'll either turn up dead or fled and then I'm back to having nothing. I need him to lead me to the real traitor."

"Do that then," Thorn said. "Find out who it is an' tell the Inquisitors which one o' them is all bad an' naughty."

"I can't just go accusing Arbiters and Inquisitors of heresy without proof, Black Thorn."

"Why not?"

Thanquil had to stop himself from sighing. "I'm not exactly well-liked in the Inquisition. They'd probably just try me for heresy instead. Most of them already believe I'm guilty."

"Why?" asked Jezzet.

"It doesn't matter." The last thing Thanquil wanted to talk about right now was his history, or his family.

Thanquil shrugged out of his Arbiter coat and started rolling the brown leather into as tight ball as it would go before shoving it into his pack. "It's too dangerous for me to be walking around as an Arbiter at the moment. Here. In Chade. In Sarth." It was strange but he felt naked without his coat.

"I need your help," Thanquil said. "Both of you. I..."

"Ya need my help ta do what?" Thorn asked.

"To do what you do best, Black Thorn. Kill Arbiters."

The sell-sword laughed, Thanquil was becoming almost used to the harsh rasping noise by now. "No."

"Um..." Somehow that was not the answer Thanquil had expected. Jezzet had yet to say anything, she just sat there in silence.

"Killin' you bastards is a risky business an' I ain't got no reason ta walk into ya midst an' risk my life like that. Strikes me I done far too much riskin' my neck recently. An' fer fuck all in the way of reward."

"What if I offered you a pardon..."

"Eh?"

"If you help me do this I'll make sure the Inquisition stop chasing you, Thorn. You'll never have to see an Arbiter again, never have to worry when the next one might catch up with you."

That seemed to peak his interest. "You could do that? Thought ya said they don't much like you."

Thanquil grinned. "Accusing an Inquisitor of heresy and convincing them the Black Thorn isn't the heretic they think he is are two different things. Help me, Thorn, and I'll get you your pardon. You'll never have to see me or another Arbiter again. I'll see you're paid as well. Two hundred gold coins in Sarth currency. More than enough for you to buy passage anywhere you might want to go and get set up there."

"Earn a pardon by killin' Arbiters." Thorn laughed again. "I'm in."

As Thanquil opened his mouth to ask Jezzet she spoke first. "I'm in. I want the same deal as Thorn. Two hundred gold bits and no Arbiters following me after we're done."

"Done."

"Might be we need ta come up with a real plan this time," the Black Thorn said with a grin

Jezzet nodded, she was staring at Thanquil. "You almost look like a normal person without that coat on."

PART 4 – TWO'S COMPANY…

THE BLACK THORN

At least they were moving again, that was something, Betrim reckoned, but not very fast. When they'd hopped on the boat from Chade it seemed it might be a quick journey. '*Strong winds.*' The captain said, '*wouldn't surprise me if we made the trip in three weeks.*' So far they'd been at sea for six weeks and two of those had been sitting becalmed.

Fact was Betrim wasn't sure he liked the idea of arriving at Sarth any better than being stuck at sea. The seat of the Inquisition was no place for a man like him. All those witch hunters walking around looking for folk to burn, looking for the Black Thorn.

For the first three weeks of his time at sea Betrim had become fast friends with the railings, leaning over and retching even when he had nothing in his stomach. He'd only been out on the open ocean twice before in his life. First when he left his home and sailed to the Five Kingdoms to spent an entire winter freezing his stones off. And second when he'd sailed from the Five Kingdoms to the Wilds where he'd spent more than a decade murdering folk for money and avoiding witch hunters. Now he was sailing back to Sarth, back to the kingdom of his birth and he was not well pleased.

The crew seemed a likeable enough sort. In between his retching Betrim had made friends with a few of them. One such sailor, a man the rest called Olly the Nose on account of his massive hawk-like bill, had taken him to the bow and shoved a bottle of rum into his hand. The sailors called the rum *Widow's Bounty* and it was close to black in colour and stronger than any spirit Betrim had ever tasted. Soon after, his retching stopped and Betrim settled into a drunken stupor for the remainder of the voyage. He counted himself lucky that the ship carried a more than healthy supply of the fiery rum.

The rest of the crew took to Betrim as well. They would drink and gamble and tell tales of women from every port. It seemed not a one of them made the connection with Thorn, the drunken seasick bastard with dark, red hair and a burned face; and the Black Thorn, a murderous sellsword on the run from the Inquisition with a reputation darker than the rum they were drinking.

They'd been chased twice by ships that the Captain reckoned were pirates, but neither had been able to keep pace with the *Blue Gull* even with only a slight breeze. They hadn't run across a single monster from the deep either, though the Arbiter insisted they existed and roamed the waters. Betrim was inclined to agree. He'd heard stories of giant creatures with eight arms all with watery suckers that could pull a man's face off, hulking leviathans that could smash a ship to pieces with one flick of their tails. And the less said about the krakens the better.

At times Betrim could swear he'd seen giant fish swimming below the surface of the deep blue, keeping easy pace with the boat. He pointed out to the Nose the shapes sliding through the water. The man had laughed and said they were Sethwith, trained pets of merfolk that followed ships, waiting for any man who fell overboard so they could steal away the poor fellow to mate endlessly beneath the waves with mermaids. Betrim wasn't sure he believed in merfolk, but he was damned sure he wasn't about to take a dip to find out.

There was a thud from the deck behind Betrim and he turned to find the Arbiter sitting on the wood again rubbing yet another bruise from his sword arm. The Black Thorn laughed and a few of the sailors close by joined in.

"Ain't the point ya supposed ta be gettin' better, Ar... Thanquil." It wasn't the first time Betrim had almost slipped up and called him by his title and he was certain it wouldn't be the last. Truth was, even without the coat, the man was a witch hunter through and through.

With a sigh and a glare in Betrim's direction the Arbiter picked himself off the deck, collected his sword, and made ready for another beating. Jezzet Vel'urn stood on the balls of her feet, watching, waiting with sword in hand and eyes focused. They'd been practising every day since they set foot on the ship. Blunted swords meant the Arbiter didn't sustain any mortal wounds, but Betrim would have put money on him being black and blue under those leathers, though at least he never complained.

The Heresy Within

At first the sailors had jeered and mocked the Arbiter for losing to a woman, some suggested they could show her how a real man uses a sword, one went so far as to make a grab for her breasts. Jez had broken the man's nose, twisted his arm, and very nearly threw him overboard before the captain roared his interruption. After that he'd decreed any man who tried to lay a hand on her would get five lashes and, if she wanted, Jezzet would be the one to swing the whip. The grin on her face said she'd be more than happy to do so.

The swords clashed, filling the air with the sweet song of metal on metal. The Arbiter was pushing the attack, driving Jezzet backwards. She blocked and parried, dodged and sometimes lashed out with her own blade. When the witch hunter was doing well she would call out encouragement, give him advice about movement and foot placement, when he should attack high or low, when to strike hard and when to feint. When the witch hunter was making mistakes she would beat him with her own sword, disarm him, and then tell him where he went wrong while giving him stern looks.

All three of them shared a cabin though Betrim rarely set foot in the room and only then to retrieve something from his pack. The rest of the time he preferred to spend up on deck, staring out at the sea with rum in his hand and in his stomach. The few times it had rained he went below deck and sat with the crew.

He still had dreams about that night at Hostown. Some men might call them nightmares, but the Black Thorn weren't the type of person to be unmanned by memories. All the same, it still made his spine shiver when he thought of how the shade had bit through the Boss' face. At how the Boss hadn't even screamed or shouted. Betrim had witnessed all sorts of carnage in his time but at Hostown... what those shades had done to folk... and the way the Arbiter had just ordered the creature to vanish.

Betrim took another swig of *Widow's Bounty* and sat back against the railing with his head swimming. The sky was bright blue, the sun was baking hot, there was only a single cloud in the sky, and the wind was a nice gentle breeze, just enough to move the ship but not enough to stir the sea into chaos. If he forgot about the endless blue water below him and all the hidden dangers it held he was quite content. Not to mention that he hadn't had to kill anyone for somewhere close to seven weeks, Betrim wasn't sure how many days that was, numbers never being his strong point, but he reckoned it was some sort of record for him.

The Arbiter hit the deck again, shaking his wrist. Jezzet had twisted his sword from his grip with a simple flick of the wrist, it was a trick she liked to use and one he fell for every time. Betrim laughed and raised the bottle of rum to the Arbiter in salute before taking another gulp.

"You laugh, Thorn, but I don't see you stepping up to give Jez a challenge," said the Arbiter from the deck.

Jezzet shot the witch hunter that stern look she used when he'd done wrong. "Get up and collect your sword, Thanquil. Else you won't be able to defend yourself when I attack."

"I ain't so stupid as to fight with Jezzet Vel'urn. Doubt she'd go as easy on me as she does you," Betrim slurred with a raspy chuckle.

"You call this going easy..."

"Well ya still ain't got ya sword an' she hasn't started hittin' ya yet, so yeah." Truth was the Arbiter was getting better and that had something to do with Jezzet having all the patience in the world. Problem was all the time in the world wasn't about to turn the witch hunter into a swordsman. Some people just didn't have the feel for it and he was one of those folk.

The Nose swaggered over and sat down next to Betrim, took the bottle from him, and gulped down a mouthful. "By the sea you go through this stuff faster 'an any man I ever known."

"Aye. Tastes like shit an' burns like fire. Better that 'an go back ta retchin'."

"Got the truth of it there, I reckon, Thorn." The song of metal clashing against metal started up again. "Do those two do anythin' but fight an' fuck?"

Jezzet caught the Arbiter's sword on her own, stepped into him and twisted herself so that he was flipped onto his back by her hip. Then she shot an acidic glare at Betrim and the Nose.

"I reckon she might have heard ya, Nose."

"Aye," the Nose said with a grin. "I reckon so. Sorry, miss V'urn. Didn't mean nothin' by it. Knew a lass like you in a port once. Land's End it was, in Five Kingdoms. Don't remember her name but when she weren't fuckin' she was practising launchin' knives at folk. Used ta be able ta skewer a thrown apple at twenty paces. Cost a pretty penny she did but was worth it. The things she could do with..."

"You're comparing me to a whore?" Jezzet asked. Thanquil was still lying on the deck, grinning like a fool. The Nose was looking worried and Betrim couldn't care less. The talk of whores had reminded him of Rose.

Might be the rum but Betrim was finding it hard to remember what she looked like, what she smelled like, what she felt like. He remembered she made his cock feel right good and that she was the most beautiful woman he'd ever been inside, not a hard boast to be sure, but everything else was fading.

Thinking of Swift's sister made his mind tumble onto thinking about Swift, how the two had kissed and then she'd refused to kiss the Black Thorn after. She'd said something too, something about their mother but he couldn't remember it. Fact was, bastard though he was, Betrim kind of missed Swift. The man always had a story to tell. Lies for the most part, to be sure, but he made them fun all the same.

Betrim missed Bones as well. The big man had been as close to a friend as he'd ever had and saved his life more than once. He didn't see the giant fall in Hostown, too focused on saving Henry from the shade to pay attention to anything else, but by the time he was finished Bones was gone, Swift too, and Henry. All three of them dead or fled and as Betrim had seen no sign of them on the road he was leaning towards thinking it was the former. He missed Henry most of all. Ever since the murderous, crazy bitch had stabbed him they'd been friends though Betrim couldn't say why.

He even missed the Boss. Betrim could see the big black southerner standing there now, swaying from side to side with eyes open and full of sadness as the darkness reached for him, took him by the neck, and lifted him off the ground. Those great black jaws opened so wide it seemed they would swallow him whole. Instead they closed around his head, slicing through flesh and bone as though it were butter. Blood gushed and flowed and the Boss' lifeless, faceless body dropped to the floor like the sack of meat it was.

"Thorn."

Betrim's eyes flicked open and he glanced around. The Nose was gone, Jezzet and the Arbiter were still there, but neither were holding swords. The captain stood with them on the bow, pointing at something. He was a well groomed man was the captain, dressed in vivid finery with dark brown eyes and an impossibly square jaw beneath a trimmed beard. He held his back so straight it looked like it hurt and his hand was never far from his sword hilt.

"Thorn," said the Arbiter. "If you're not too pickled, might be you want to come and see this."

"Aye," Betrim said as he pushed himself to his feet, took him two attempts but he made it. "I'm comin' ya bastard witch... Which one of ya said that?"

The witch hunter glared at him, Betrim shrugged as he stepped up beside him. "What? I can't help it if there's three o' ya." He went to put an arm on the Arbiter's shoulder to steady himself and caught hold of nothing. He found himself on his knees, staring at the deck. Then there was a hand underneath his arm, lifting him upwards.

"Ya too damned strong fer such a scrawny bastard," Betrim slurred into the Arbiter's face. Good thing about being drunk, he decided, was that you could get away with almost anything. "What am I lookin' at?"

"That," the captain said in a thick accent. Betrim squinted in the direction the man pointed. All he could see was blue. Blue sea, blue sky, some darker line on the horizon maybe. "The coast of Sarth. We make port in Sarth tomorrow."

"'Bout damn time."

"Sober up, Thorn," the Arbiter said.

"Last thing I want ta be when I set foot in Sarth is sober."

"Shame that," the Arbiter took Betrim by the arm and led him away, Jezzet following close behind, "because the last thing we need is you drunk as a fish."

They didn't take him to the cabin but instead led him to the mess. A small room consisting of a couple of tables, each with a couple of benches, and all nailed to the floor. The cook stood in the corner, stirring a pot of something that smelled at once delicious and disgusting.

The witch hunter pushed the Black Thorn onto a bench. Seemed he should be taking offence to being man handled as such but Betrim couldn't quite work up the bother.

"We make port tomorrow if all is well," the Arbiter said to the cook. "We need him sober. No rum."

"Aye," the cook said with a scowl. "No rum."

Betrim watched three Arbiters and three Jezzet's leave and turned to the three cooks all of whom were eyeing him. "Got any rum?"

The Arbiter

Never before in all his fifty years had Thanquil been so pleased to see Sarth, and yet at the same time he dreaded it. It felt like years since he'd set sail away from the white city, away from the Inquisition and the dark looks, away from the God-Emperor and his suspicions. Hard to believe it was just a little over five months. Now he was back though, back without the proof Emperor Francis had ordered him to find. He had the name of one traitor but it wasn't the name he needed. He had the name of an underling. What he needed was the name of the Inquisitor behind Kessick.

He could go to the God-Emperor, tell what little he knew. That the traitor was an Inquisitor and a woman narrowed the list down to two, Inquisitor Heron and Inquisitor Downe, but with no idea which and no proof, what could be done? The Emperor could not walk into the Inquisition and inform the council that he has it on poor authority one of them is a heretic any more than Thanquil could himself. No, it would be better to leave him out of this. Thanquil would find the name of the traitor and deal with her himself... And face the consequences of his actions after. Somehow he doubted whether he could rely on the God-Emperor to bail him out. He was chosen because he was expendable after all.

"That's your home then? Looks a nice place. Which one is the Inquisition, the white one or the black one?" Jezzet said. She was close. She was always close these days. It took every bit of Thanquil's restraint not to reach out and touch her but that wouldn't do. She was here to help him not to...

"The black one," he said, pointing at it as if she couldn't see which was which. "The white one is the Imperial palace, home of the God-Emperor."

They were standing on the bow of the ship, leaning on the railing and waiting. Sarth was a cautious port; all ships requesting to dock were greeted by a small skiff with a port official on board. The official would board the ship, talk with the Captain as to where he had come from and his next destination, and then tour the holds to inspect cargo. The man had already given the three passengers a brief look and decided they were no one of importance.

"It looks... dreary," Jez said, looking at the black tower of the Inquisition.

"It looks like one of the Hells," Thorn rasped from behind. "Full o' demons ready ta come pourin' out at any moment. Risin' up all dark in the middle of a white city, all that spiky-looking rock. I know why it's black. Soot an' ash from all the people burnin' is what that is."

Thanquil might have laughed but there was a kernel of truth in the Black Thorn's paranoid rambling. The tower of the Inquisition had seen more burnings, hangings, dismemberments, massacres, beatings, mutilation, and torture than any other building the human race had ever erected.

"I completely agree," Thanquil said. "With both of you. I've never thought of it as a home. Just a place I have to report to every now and then."

Thorn spat over the side of the ship. He was nervous, that much was plain. "Ya sure 'bout this, Ar... Thanquil. I mean, my hair might be goin' back ta the red side, but I got a fairly noticeable face."

"It'll be fine, Thorn. Believe it or not most of us don't know what you look like. Besides, where's the least likely place anyone would ever think to find the Black Thorn... Sarth."

"Right under their noses."

"As you say."

"What 'bout you? Takin' off that coat don't exactly make ya invisible."

"In a way it does. There are few enough in the Inquisition who would recognize me on a normal day. Without my coat even those who might, would not spare me a glance should I walk past them on the street."

"Ya can't... I dunno, sense each other?"

Thanquil laughed. "No. We can't."

"Bloody witch hunters. Struttin' around an entire fuckin' city. Bloody Sarth was never anythin' but a burden on my family an' you lot was the worst of it. I ever tell ya why that Arbiter came callin' on my folks back 'fore I killed any o' ya?"

"No."

"'Cos they refused ta pay the food tax ta your fuckin' Inquisition. So they sent a witch hunter ta look in, find out why. No doubt with the intent of burnin' my folks an' puttin' someone more agreeable in charge, eh? Well by the time he got there my folks were already dead an' the Arbiter weren't long in followin'."

"And then you ran..."

"An' then I fuckin' ran. Didn't exactly leave me much choice did ya? Barely more 'an a boy an' already on the run. Everywhere I went I had witch hunters watchin' me like they knew. Like ya could sense the presence o' someone who killed one o' ya own."

"We can't."

"Well I know that now, don't I." The Black Thorn's burned face twisted in what looked like it could have been pain. A moment later he was retching over the side of the ship.

Jezzet was still staring at the city arrayed in front of her. From here Sarth almost looked like any port town except that almost all of the visible buildings were white, built from the marble that was so abundant in the kingdom, and washed everyday by slaves to keep the city gleaming. The Imperial palace with its tower and its spires rose high above the rest of the city, from here it almost looked like two great white hands with fingers reaching towards the heavens. The tower of the Inquisition rose in bleak counterpoint, a single black, spiked spire thrusting out of the white around it like a sword driven through flesh.

"You've never been to Sarth before," Thanquil said, already knowing the answer.

"No. Never been many places if truth be told. Spent most of my life in Acanthia, around Truridge for the best part. Occasionally my master would take me with him when he went on his short journeys. Once I even visited the capital. More often than not he'd leave me though.

"After I killed him... after I became the Blademaster I went east to see the desert. Thought about trying to cross it but took a boat to the Five Kingdoms in the end. Wasn't long there, spent some time working as a merc. I soon came to the attention of that bloody Sword of the North... After that I made my way to Land's End as fast as my feet would take me and set sail to the Wilds. Seemed someone like me could make some money over there, I thought.

"When all this is done I might find a ship to take me to the Dragon Empire. Always wanted to see a dragon. You... you could come with me. It's a long journey, I hear. Might be less dull with some company."

Thanquil laughed. "When all this is done I won't be..." When all this was done he would either be dead or in an Inquisition prison cell, spending the rest of his days in darkness with only the company of rats and praying for an end to it all. "I have duties."

Jezzet nodded and went back to staring at the city.

After a while the port official and the captain of the *Blue Gull* re-emerged onto the deck; there they shook hands and the official climbed back down into his skiff looking far happier than when he had climbed on. Bribes for the more prime docking spots were not uncommon. One of the first lessons an Arbiter ever learned, *where there is power, there is corruption*. It seemed as though the lesson was doubly true when it was petty power.

As the ship lurched back into motion and began to float into port, all three passengers stood at the bow not saying a word. The Black Thorn had quit his retching for now, but looked almost green and showed no inclination towards talking, and Jezzet had lapsed into a sullen silence. Even the captain seemed to sense something was amiss as he strode up behind them and hesitated before speaking.

"Got you here safe, as promised, I did. Sorry about the delay but... well... no man can control the weather."

"Not very well at least," Thanquil said with a smile he didn't feel.

The captain frowned. "Quite. You're free to depart soon as we dock."

"Thank you, Captain Hail."

The well-dressed captain grunted, scratched once at his beard, and strutted away. They floated the rest of the way into the docks in silence.

As the crew scrambled to tie off the ship and make ready to unload the cargo, Jezzet asked the question. "So what's the plan?"

"First we get ourselves situated. There are plenty of cheap inns located far enough away from the Inquisition so no Arbiters will go to them."

"Thought ya weren't in risk o' bein' noticed, Thanquil," the Black Thorn said with a smirk.

"No point in tempting fate, Thorn. For either of us. Tomorrow we'll figure out the details of locating Arbiter Kessick."

"Got any notions o' how we're gonna manage that?"

"As it happens, I do. Jezzet is going to walk up to the Inquisition and ask for him."

The Black Thorn

"Ya know, up close it looks even more like all the Hells," Betrim said and took a deep swallow of beer. He was fast learning to enjoy the taste of beer in Sarth, it was a far cry from the piss-flavoured brown water they served you in the Wilds.

"You're not wrong," Jezzet agreed in a hushed voice.

The Arbiter said nothing.

Thanquil had found them a cheap inn in what he called the poorer section of Sarth and paid for two rooms. Betrim got one of the rooms to himself, a luxury he was not ungrateful for, while the Arbiter and Jezzet stayed in the other. Betrim quickly took to spending a good amount of time in the common room drinking himself into a comfortable stupor. He paid for it in the morning, well and good, when he'd woke with his head pounding along to the pounding on his door. The Arbiter had taken one look at Thorn and sighed. Betrim wanted nothing more than to punch the bastard at that point but he refrained. A few minutes later Thanquil handed him a necklace and told him to wear it always but keep it hidden beneath his clothing lest another witch hunter recognise it as a charm. Betrim had been sceptical at first, but just a few seconds after putting the thing around his neck his hangover had vanished, freeing the Black Thorn up for some more drinking.

Now they sat in a different inn, a fancy one not more than a few hundred paces from the Inquisition. Betrim had never seen such an inn before. The floors were clean, no straw or reeds, just wood. The tables all had chairs, not just stools and benches. The man behind the bar was dressed as fancy as one of the blooded and the serving maids were all fully clothed and had some of the best sets of teeth he'd ever seen. The place even had a balcony on the first floor for folk to sit on and drink in the open air and, just like all the other buildings in this part of town, save for the Inquisition, it was made out of some sort of white stone that took to shining in the sunlight.

The white city of Sarth in the Holy Empire of Sarth they called it, but Betrim reckoned they'd get far more folk like himself making port if they added *city of good beer and clean women*. Almost made up for the number of witch hunters he'd seen walking about. At least Thanquil had been right about them not even sparing him or the Black Thorn a second glance. Truth was Jezzet got more looks than the two men combined.

"You see the guards at the main gate," Thanquil was saying to Jezzet. "They'll stop you but they won't talk to you. Don't say a word to them, just wait. There'll be an Arbiter in the gate house who will come out to enquire about your business."

Jezzet nodded. She looked nervous and Betrim didn't blame her. Felt a lot like she was placing her head in the lion's jaws, no doubt. "What should I say?"

"The truth. You're there to speak to Arbiter Kessick."

"And the one at the gate will go fetch him?"

"He'll send someone to fetch him and keep you under watch until Kessick arrives."

Again Jezzet nodded. "What if Kessick isn't here?"

"Then we're out of luck and at a loose end."

"What if there is no Kessick?" Betrim asked. "What if your traitor jus' dressed someone up as a witch hunter and sent the man ta H'ost? What if this Kessick used a false name? Seems this plan o' yours has a lot of *'what ifs'*."

Thanquil had no reply to that. Betrim took another swallow of beer. The witch hunter claimed his dwindling supply of coin wasn't enough to keep them all in alcohol for their time in Sarth, but Betrim had looted the Boss' corpse back in Hostown and had ten gold bits to his name. A fortune if ever he'd had one and enough to keep him drunk until they were done.

"So if Kessick is real and is there... what do I tell him?" said Jezzet, frowning at Thanquil.

"Tell him H'ost is dead. Convince him you're a messenger from Hostown and that you were ordered, in the event of H'ost's death, to come to Sarth and inform Arbiter Kessick. Keep my name out of it but try to tell the truth wherever possible."

"Ya can't lie ta an Arbiter," Betrim put in.

"Exactly."

"I mean it, Thanquil. What if this Kessick asks Jez some questions? Seems he'll figure out the truth pretty quick."

"I should be able to make you a charm that will protect you from his compulsion."

"Should?" Betrim snorted. *"What ifs, maybes, and shoulds..."*

"It's OK, Thorn. I'll be fine." Jezzet looked at the Arbiter. "Maybe you should ask me some questions so I know what this compulsion feels like."

The Arbiter winced and shook his head. "I... I don't..."

"Feels like someone pokin' around inside ya head. Like someone's reachin' in, grabbin' hold of what they want ta know, an' forcin' it out o' ya mouth. Ya can't think of anythin' else, can't control yaself. Feels like bein' forced ta do somethin' against ya will. Right, Thanquil?"

The Arbiter was staring into his beer, nodding, his hand shaking somewhat. Seems the man had never used his magic on Jezzet. Come to think of it, Betrim couldn't remember him ever using it on the Black Thorn either.

Betrim waved over a serving maid to ask her for another beer. The girl stared at his face with part shock and part horror. Once that might have made the Black Thorn angry, but instead he just laughed. "Feels worse than it looks, trust me. Wanna touch it?" He ran a three fingered hand down the burned side of his face as he asked and the maid turned and near ran away.

"Do you have that effect on all women, Thorn?" Jezzet asked with a pretty smile.

"You ain't run, screaming yet."

"I'm being paid to put up with your face."

"Aye, story o' my life that." Betrim grinned, knowing full well how the muscles pulling against the burned skin would make him look even worse than normal.

The Arbiter was staring out over the street that led up to the Inquisition. Stone streets, Betrim noticed, a luxury rarely afforded in the Wilds but here in Sarth it seemed a standard. Everything seemed to be made of stone here. Would cut down on risk of fire, a useful precaution in a city full of witch hunters.

"He'll ask you about H'ost," Thanquil was saying. "To make sure you are who you say you are. Speak vaguely. You just worked for him, you didn't have access to his council. Frown when you answer his questions, try to look like you're trying to think of something else yet you can't."

Jezzet gave a practice frown, looked to be constipated to Betrim's eyes. The maid returned with the beer and the Black Thorn handed her a bit and grinned at her. Poor girl's face twisted in disgust and she ran away from the table.

They stayed at the inn for the rest of the afternoon until the light of the sun started to dip below the buildings. The Arbiter watched the Inquisition with a worried expression and gave advice here and there. Jezzet stayed silent for the most part, worried about her part in the plan no doubt. Both the others drank sparingly, Betrim, however, had no such inhibition. He ordered his mug refilled whenever it ran dry which was pretty regular if truth be told. He was merrily drunk by the time the Arbiter rose from the table and insisted it was time to leave.

Half way down the stairs they passed the serving maid again. She lowered her eyes so as not to have to look at Betrim's face again. The Black Thorn snorted, considered grabbing her face and making her look but decided against it. Folk in Sarth seemed a civilised lot. He didn't reckon they'd take too well to some scarred man scaring the hell out of a girl.

At the bottom of the stairs a man in a familiar brown coat stopped Thanquil with a hand on his shoulder. "Do I know you?"

Thanquil looked down and shook his head. "I don't think so, sir."

Betrim shouldered his way past the two. So much for none of the Arbiters recognising him without his coat. The inn was busy, three tables full of men drinking, most seemed to be merchants or tradesmen, not a single sell-sword in the entire joint.

"What's your name?" The Arbiter asked Thanquil.

"Alfred Coster, sir."

"No, that's not. I'm sure I recognise you. Are you lying to me?"

Sometimes the situation called for a distraction and the Black Thorn only knew one type. He walked up behind a group of folk drinking around a table, plucked a spare chair from close by, gripping hold of it in two hands. It was a heavy chair, looked to be well made. With a grin he slammed the chair into the back of one of the patrons. He expected it to smash into kindling, instead it hit the man's back with a heavy thud and the poor bastard slumped forward on the table.

Another man, tall as Betrim but skinny as a post, was up in a flash swinging a bony fist. The Black Thorn caught the fist with his face and went stumbling backwards into another table. One of the men from that table, a burly beast with one arm twice the size of the other and a lazy eye, stood and made to grab for Betrim.

The Black Thorn's five fingered fist flashed out and punched the blacksmith in the throat then he grabbed hold of the choking fool and pushed him at the bony man. Chaos erupted a moment later as fists started flying and folk who were just recently sitting quiet, started hitting other folk who had been sitting just as quiet.

A hoarse laugh burst forth from Betrim's lips. Seemed even the fancy folk of Sarth were just as capable of a drunken brawl as folk from the Wilds. The tall, bony man crashed into Betrim with fists flailing. The Black Thorn thrust his head into the man's face once, twice, and then picked him up and flung him across a table.

Another victim grabbed hold of Betrim by the shoulder. He turned, intending to punch the poor bastard and found himself spun around with his arm twisted behind his back. Jezzet's voice hissed in his ear. "Time to go. Now!"

Betrim took a glance at his handiwork. He spied at least ten men involved in the fight and the Arbiter who had stopped Thanquil in the midst of it trying to calm the situation down. The unfortunate bastard who had taken the chair to his back was still slumped over the table, unconscious. Thanquil was standing by the door to the inn, waving some folk in. A few seconds later a number of city guard clad in white uniforms bundled their way inside. Jezzet pushed Betrim out of the way and they slipped around the guards and followed Thanquil outside.

The Blademaster

A Blademaster without a blade is a master of nothing.
Could be worse, Jez. She told herself. *Walk unarmed to the very gates of the Inquisition and ask for a traitor by name, or spend the rest of the day with Thanquil and Thorn.* The two had been arguing almost non-stop since the Black Thorn started a brawl last night. Truth was the brawl provided the distraction they needed to slip away from an Arbiter who was close to recognising Thanquil. Truth was also that the brawl brought a lot of attention their way, attention they could well do without.

Jez rubbed her thumb across the ring on her right index finger. *A gift from Thanquil,* though '*gift*' was the wrong term. A small wooden trinket. Plain, dark-red wood on the outside but on the underside were carved the symbols of an Arbiter charm.

"It should make you immune to the effects of the compulsion though you'll still feel it trying to slip inside your head. Hopefully the Arbiter should feel it also." Thanquil said when he gave her the ring.

"Slip inside my head... sounds wonderful. What happens if it doesn't work?"

Thanquil had winced then. "It... should work."

"Well either way, reckon it's the first time a man's ever given me a ring before. Maybe you should ask me a question, to see if it works."

The Arbiter had looked pained when she suggested that. Jezzet hadn't gotten around to asking Thanquil why he was so reluctant to ask her any questions as Thorn banged on the door, stinking of last night's beer and insisting it was time to go.

A group of three slaves walked past Jezzet and she fell in a few paces behind them to hide her approach to the Inquisition gate. The slaves in Sarth were treated so differently to those in the Wilds Jez sometimes wasn't sure whether they were slaves. They wore serviceable, well-tended clothing and sandals to protect their feet, and were often seen out without a master to herd them.

There were some very strict rules as to the treatment of slaves in Sarth, so Thanquil told her, one of which being that slaves could not be used as whores, though buying a female slave to be used as a mistress was a regular occurrence among the rich and the nobility. As such, beautiful slave girls were a rare and widely sought after commodity in the white city and were often treated better than the owner's wives. Some of the richest and most powerful men in the city were even known to keep harems of slave girls, though not many could afford such a luxury.

Problem is they're still slaves, still got no freedom. Their master says, 'spread your legs' and all the slave can do is reply, 'how wide?'

The slaves in front of her now were all men and were all carrying boxes or barrels. The property of some merchant who used them as cheap labour to move goods from here to there, no doubt. In the Wilds most male slaves wore nothing more than loin cloths. Jezzet began to wonder if the male slaves here in Sarth were gelded like they often were in the Wilds.

The slaves turned off to the left and she found herself standing in front of the Inquisition compound. Up close it looked even more dark and foreboding. Jez could feel her confidence wavering but stepped up the main gate all the same.

A guardsman clad in the shiny white uniform of the city watch stepped in front of her. He shouted back to the guard house behind him and then just stood there, blocking her from proceeding and saying nothing. Jezzet treated him to stony silence right back.

A tall man with a gut as big as a barrel and a bushy brown moustache that hid most of his red face stepped out of the guardhouse and approached. He wore an Arbiter coat, just like Thanquil's, only much larger to accommodate his girth. His manner seemed cheerful but Jezzet didn't trust it.

"How may we be of service, my lady," the fat Arbiter said in a booming voice.

Seemed everyone was calling Jezzet a whore or a lady these days and she wasn't sure which pissed her off more.

"'Ere ta see Arbiter Kessick," she said, dropping into a heavy wilds drawl and staring the fat Arbiter down.

The Arbiter looked her up and down, a jovial smile on his face the entire time and then nodded and turned to one of the guards. "Go fetch,

Arbiter Kessick. Tell him... what was your name, miss?"

Jezzet felt... something. She couldn't quite explain it but it felt like something clawing inside her mind. Almost she refused to answer and punched the fat Arbiter in his fat face, but to do so would have given the game away.

"Jezzet Vel'urn," she said with a frown.

The fat Arbiter turned back to the guard. "Tell Arbiter Kessick he has a visitor, one Jezzet Vel'urn." After the guard scurried off, the fat man turned back to Jez. "Would you care to come inside? I can offer you a cool drink."

Again Jezzet felt the strange sensation in her mind.

I would care to stick a knife into one of your chins for trying to get inside my head, you slimy, fat bastard.

"Nah, reckon I'll wait jus' 'ere." She could feel her thumb rubbing at the ring on her finger. It was taking all her restraint not to attack the Arbiter in front of her.

Think I'm starting to understand why Thanquil didn't want to ask me any questions. I might have had to kill him.

When the guard returned he had another Arbiter in tow. This one was short, about of a height with Thanquil, and stocky. Everything about that man seemed hard as stone. His face looked to be carved from granite, all hard lines and tight, weather-beaten skin. His hair was black dusted with grey and cropped short, and his eyes were dark and dangerous. The man even walked like he was made of stone. *Either that or he has a particularly long stick up his arse.*

"You Kessick?" Jez asked the new arrival.

"I don't know you," the Arbiter's voice was as hard as the rest of him.

"Nah, ya don't. But if ya Kessick than I got a message fer ya," Jezzet hoped the man would pick up on the Wilds accent she was throwing in his face.

The new Arbiter turned to the fat one. "I'll take it from here. You," he pointed at Jez, "come with me."

Jezzet Vel'urn would like to have said she wasn't the type of woman to scare easy, but when surrounded by witch hunters she found it hard not

The Heresy Within

to feel like running. She hadn't realised they'd be so many. Inside the compound there were Arbiters everywhere she looked. Some were standing around in groups, talking. Others were walking from one place to another. Some even seemed to be lazing about doing very little in the afternoon sun. As Arbiter Kessick led her towards the giant black-stone tower, Jezzet hoped to all the Gods she couldn't remember that she didn't look as guilty as she felt.

The Arbiter turned right before the main entrance to the tower and walked another fifty paces before stopping. He opened a small door into the side of the tower and walked through. Inside was a small, black corridor lit with a number of ensconced torches. The corridor ended just twenty paces ahead and to each side were two doors. The Arbiter picked the second door on the left hand side, opened it and looked in, then he nodded at Jezzet.

"Get in."

The room looked almost like a cell only with a table and two chairs instead of a bed. There didn't seem to be any sort of lock on the door so Jezzet swallowed her fear and did as she was told. The Arbiter followed her in and pulled the door too.

"Sit down."

"Reckon I'll stand."

The Arbiter didn't look too pleased about that. "Sit. Down."

Again Jezzet did as she was told and the Arbiter took the seat opposite her. There he sat for a while, staring at her with his cold, dark eyes. Jezzet stared on back.

"Ya are Kessick, right?" she asked.

"Yes, I'm Kessick, and you're from the Wilds."

"I got a message. From H'ost... well... sorta a message..."

"You weren't there last I was. I'd have noticed. So either you're lying or H'ost kept you hidden."

Tread carefully, Jez.

"I ain't lying an' I weren't hidin'. I work fer H'ost... worked fer H'ost, but I worked in Chade. My orders were simple an' I'm bein' well-paid fer carryin' 'em out. If H'ost dies I'm ta come ta Sarth, find Arbiter Kessick, an' tell him."

Kessick didn't look convinced, didn't look unconvinced either. His face was as expressionless as the Black Thorn's only without the burns.

"How did he die?" the Arbiter asked. There was no feeling, no clawing inside her head, no will trying to subvert her own. There was nothing.

What the hell do I do? Do I pretend his compulsion is working or just act like I didn't feel anything?

"One o' yours did fer him," she said without dropping her stony face. "Slaughtered half the town in the doin' as I hear it."

"What was his name? The Arbiter that killed H'ost?"

"Fuck if I know. I weren't there an' bloody glad of it."

Kessick was silent for a moment. Jez could see his jaw clenched tight. "What about H'ost's daughter?" he asked.

Jezzet didn't have to feign confusion. "I don't fuckin' know. I weren't there. Paid ta tell you H'ost is dead. Job done. Now, if ya done askin' questions I don't know the answers ta, I intend ta go get stinkin' drunk."

Again Kessick was silent for a while, staring at Jezzet the entire time. It occurred to her that the Arbiter may be deciding whether or not to kill her. "Of course," he said in grave voice. "I'll escort you back to the gate."

By the time she got back to the main gate Jez was shaking so badly she had to shove her hands in her pockets to hide it. It wasn't helped by the fact that Kessick had taken to walking a couple of steps behind her and was as silent as the grave. Her nerves were frayed to the point of snapping.

"I assume you'll be departing back to the Wilds soon, Miss Vel'urn," Arbiter Kessick said from the threshold.

Jez turned and gave him a lopsided grin. "Too right. Be on the first ship I can find. Jus' as soon as I sober up on the morrow."

"Goodbye then." The Arbiter's dark, dangerous eyes never left her, never blinked. Jezzet nodded and backed away before turning and doing her very best not to look like she was fleeing.

For the rest of the day and most of the night the three of them waited and watched. It was not easy to pretend to have reasons to be there for so long and would have been a lot easier if they hadn't been involved in a bar fight at a certain inn just one night ago. Betrim found himself a nice looking spot of wall to sit by and lean on. He looked for all the world like a beggar down on his luck and in need of a few spare bits and Jezzet wasn't the only one to think so. A number of people, those who looked like they had bits to spare, tossed him the odd coin or two.

Thanquil was not quite so subtle. The Arbiter wandered around some of the shops, spending a good deal of time in each but never buying anything and always keeping one eye on the main gate of the Inquisition while trying to hide his face from the witch hunters who passed him. After the sun went down he joined Jezzet in the dirty little alley behind the bakery and let her do the watching while he paced and worried. Three times he muttered something about going to the God-Emperor and three times he shook his head, deciding against whatever plan he had laid out. Jezzet was glad of that at least, last thing she needed was to come face to face with a God whose name she couldn't even be bothered to remember.

Some nights, it seemed to Jezzet, were darker than others and this one seemed near pitch black despite the lanterns lit above the streets. Moon and stars both were hidden behind a thick blanket of cloud that stretched from one horizon to the other and even the white-stone buildings seemed to do little to keep the world from the darkness.

A fitting night for stalking someone, she thought as Arbiter Kessick stepped out from the main gate, glanced left and right, then chose right and started walking. *I could walk near enough beside him and he might not notice.*

Thorn was already up and following the man. He glanced once at Jezzet and then back to watching Kessick from thirty paces or so. Should be enough not to rouse suspicion but not so far as to lose sight of the Arbiter. Jez hissed at Thanquil to follow and then set off, keeping her distance from Thorn as he was keeping his from Kessick. Thanquil fell in beside her.

"You're sure it's him. I can't see him," Thanquil whispered.

"Thorn can. It's him."

They followed in silence as Thorn led them into and through the sleepless trade district. The sounds, smells and light in the area never truly vanished as forge fires were never allowed to go out. Merchants, even after a day of successful trading, laboured to prepare goods for the morrow and some shops never closed as there were always some folk needing supplies at all hours.

At the centre of the district was a market that did not sleep even in the dead of night. Men worked to set up their stalls for the coming day while children lurked around, always mindful and on the lookout for an easy steal. Jezzet watched a young girl charge past clutching something to her chest. A moment later an old man ran-limped after the young girl screaming profanities as he went. More children flocked to the abandoned stall to steal as much as they could before the old man returned.

Her old master used to send her into town to steal things. One morning every week he would name an item, sometimes it was something small and easy like a red apple, other times something larger like a roll of fabric, sometimes specific like the time he had sent her to steal merchant Alber's favourite beagle. If Jezzet didn't return by midday with the desired item, he would punish her and his punishments were never pleasant.

"And here I thought Sarth would be completely innocent of crime what with you Arbiters around," Jezzet said with a smile.

Thanquil never took his eyes from the Black Thorn's back. "We deal with heresy, not petty theft. The Inquisition isn't a branch of law enforcement or peace keeping. We root out and destroy evil and not just here in Sarth; all over the world in every one of the kingdoms of man."

"Except the Wilds..."

"Even in the Untamed Wilds," he corrected. "Only we're less welcome there than we are... some other places."

"Is there some place Arbiters are welcome?"

"If there is, I've yet to find it."

They lapsed back into silence and continued following Thorn. It almost felt like a pleasant late night stroll and, for a moment, Jezzet almost forgot they were following a man with the intention of murdering him and the woman he was working for.

Before long they found themselves in a very different part of the city. Wide streets, capable of moving three carriages were surrounded by gargantuan buildings all built of the same white-stone and all shining in the lantern lights despite the general gloom of the night. Some buildings had grounds that at least doubled its size. Some sported fancy gardens with a wild variety of plants, trees and flowers, others were paved over with stone. All had high stone walls many complete with iron spikes to ward off potential thieves. Most were patrolled as well, guardsmen in uniforms differing from the standard white of the city watch. Some of the guards watched as Jezzet and Thanquil strolled past, others paid them no heed.

The Arbiter caught Jezzet staring. "The Inquisitors are granted estates outside the Inquisition compound as recognition of their long service, continued diligence, and as a reward for keeping the world safe from heresy." He sounded bitter as he spat out the last few words.

"Some choose estates within the city limits, some without. The only exception being the Grand Inquisitor who resides in the top levels of the tower within the Inquisition itself."

"So which of the Inquisitors live around here?"

"I don't know. I come back to Sarth once every three years and spend a couple of weeks here at most. I've never had the time nor the inclination to learn where the Inquisitors live."

Up ahead the Black Thorn stopped, glanced backwards, and nodded for them to join him. He stood, fidgeting from foot to foot and rubbing at the burned side of his face with his three fingered hand. When they approached he pointed at an estate, somewhat smaller than most and surrounded by a black-iron fence. In the distance to their right Jez could see a gate with two white clad guards loitering around. Inside the grounds stood a small building, only two floors, built from the same white-stone as the rest of the city. Arbiter Kessick was nowhere to be seen.

Thanquil pulled up the hood of his cloak and stepped up the bars of the fence, he was whispering something under his breath but Jezzet could not understand the words.

"So... who is it?" Thorn hissed, looking like there wasn't another place in the world he wouldn't rather be.

"I don't know," Thanquil whispered. "All I saw was Kessick enter the building."

"Well we know they're both there," Jez said, "why don't we just break in and do what we came here to do?"

Thanquil almost looked like he was about to agree when they heard voices. The guards from the gate were talking to someone. All three of them backed into the shadows and watched. Jez heard Thanquil mutter a curse, wasn't often the Arbiter did that. The man at the gate was tall and handsome with sharp features and a bit of look of an eagle about him. He had the blonde hair that was so common in Sarth and he carried a set of two scythes instead of swords.

Nasty weapons, scythes. Hard to defend against and cause a lot of damage when they hit. Hurt like hell too. Jez remembered a scar just below her left breast, her old master had given her that one with a scythe when Jez had got a bit too cocky and thought she could disarm him. She remembered it felt like the entire left side of her chest was on fire but she had fought on regardless of the blood and pain.

Thanquil waited until the man with the scythes had passed through the gate then, without even so much as a word, he turned and stormed off the way they had come. Jezzet sent a confused look in the Black Thorn's direction. Thorn sent a blank look right back and as one they hurried after the Arbiter.

Back at the inn, Thanquil still refused to talk. He glared at both Jez and Thorn and then was gone, up to their room. The Black Thorn let out a loud sigh, slumped into a chair and called for a beer. Jezzet sat down opposite him and called for beer of her own.

At times like this alcohol always helps to numb the issue.

Thorn smiled at her, he was the ugliest man she'd ever met and yet somehow he just didn't seem to care. He waited until the beer arrived, took a huge mouthful, and then wiped his mouth with the back of his hand. Jezzet sipped at her own beer, staring into the murky water.

"Jezzet," Thorn began. "Me an' you, we've both been party ta a bit o' murder in our time. Some we done a'selves, some jus' watched others."

"Got a point somewhere in there, Thorn?"

"Aye, I do as it happens. We both know what murder looks like. Real murder born out o' anger an' hatred. We both seen it, in a'selves and in others. So you tell me, what was in our witch hunter's eyes jus' now?"

He was right.

"Might be ya want ta go up there an' calm him down a drop. Stop him from doin' somethin' rash an' stupid. Don't worry 'bout ya beer, I'll look after it."

Jezzet raised the mug to her lips and drained it off in one before standing and making for the stairs. Thorn's hoarse laughter rang in the common room behind her.

She found Thanquil in their room, pacing the small length over and over again. His jaw was clenched hard, his hands curled into shaking fists, and his pretty eyes were two chips of ice. He didn't speak to her when she entered, just kept pacing, his shadow dancing a mad jig in the flickering lantern light.

Jez closed the door and stood in front of it. *He looks like Constance when she saw me.* Jezzet thought she knew why he was so angry.

"Who was he? The Arbiter with the scythes?"

"Kosh." Thanquil glared at her when he spoke then went back to staring at the floor, his hands opening and closing with each step he took. "His name is Arbiter Fenden Kosh."

Jezzet waited but Thanquil didn't seem to want to volunteer any more information. "And who is he to you?"

Thanquil looked to be grinding his teeth so hard Jezzet thought it a wonder she couldn't hear them scraping against each other. "He is... was my friend. We trained together, graduated together, drank together."

Jezzet nodded. "There's a saying in the Wilds, *'There's no such thing as friends, just those who haven't turned on you yet.'*"

"We're not in the Wilds, Jezzet. We're in Sarth!" Thanquil shouted at her. It was the first time she'd ever heard him shout. "I've known him for forty years!"

"I forgot you're so much more civilised here in Sarth. I suppose you wanted him to let you know before he stabbed you in the back? Maybe a polite letter?"

Thanquil shot her an acidic warning glare, but Jez ignored it. *Never was very good at calming people down.* "So you've been betrayed. Now what?"

Thanquil stopped pacing and stalked towards her, he was taller but only just. In the face of his rage some people might have quailed. Jezzet Vel'urn was not such a person. "Now I'm going to kill him."

"How?"

"By walking into the Inquisition compound and shooting him."

Another brilliant plan. Jez almost sighed. "Then what? You kill an Arbiter and then rest of them kill you. Me and Thorn are out of a job, stuck here in Sarth, and your precious Inquisition still has a traitor in its midst."

Thanquil's breathing was a short, shaky flaring of his nostrils. "Get out of my way, Jezzet."

"No."

He reached out to move her but she brushed his hand away and pushed him in the chest. The Arbiter stumbled backwards, a look one part shock, one part righteous indignation on his face. He came at her again and again she pushed him back, this time following and grabbing him by the shirt. Her feet left the floor as Thanquil picked her up, twisted, and slammed her down onto the bed. Without thinking Jezzet leaned forwards and kissed him. There was a moment of shock in his eyes and then he was kissing her back, pushing her back down onto the bed.

Fight or fuck, Jez. Why not both?

She wriggled and squirmed underneath him, pushing herself further onto the bed as he started pulling at her clothing. She tore back at his, ripping the shirt from his body. They both pushed and slapped, twisted and wrestled, grunted and growled. It seemed to take forever before they were both naked and by the time they were Jez was wet as the sea and the Arbiter was as hard as a rock.

As he rammed himself inside her with an angry grunt, Jez gasped, whether from pleasure or pain she wasn't sure. She scratched at his arms as he started fucking her, each thrust accompanied by a grunt and a soft wet slap. One at a time he grabbed hold of her hands and pinned them back on the bed above her head.

Jez wrapped one leg around the Arbiter's arse and pushed on the bed with the other, squirming underneath him as he thrust hard into her again and again. She twisted her wrists, pulling, pushing, trying to free her hands and let a low, ragged, growling moan as she stared into his pretty blue eyes.

She snapped at him, trying to bite at his lip as his face moved above her own. Then a shiver of pleasure coursed through her and she gasped again. Then his mouth was on her own, kissing her, his lips hard and bruising so she returned in kind.

Her hands pulled free just in time and she grabbed hold of the bed post with her right while digging gouges into the Arbiter's back with her left. The shuddering pleasure started in her groin and spread outwards and upwards until her back was arched and a throaty squeal was slipping between her lips.

The Arbiter wasn't far behind. A few more hard, pounding thrusts and then he stopped, his mouth open, his breath rushing in and out in short grunts. Then he rolled off of her and collapsed onto the bed with a weary sigh.

For a long time they both lay there in silence, heavy breathing, both soaked in sweat.

"Sorry," Thanquil said. He wasn't looking at her, instead staring up at the ceiling.

Jez snorted out a laugh. "What for?"

"Didn't mean to be so rough."

Rough? It ain't rough as long as I can still walk after.

"But you did mean to fuck me?"

He hesitated. "Yes... or no... I don't know what I meant but I wanted to."

"Well that's something, I guess," Jezzet said with a grin. She rolled over and took Thanquil in hand. Short, slow strokes. Fact was Jezzet hadn't had a good night of sex since Eirik's fort months and months ago and she had no intention of leaving it at just the once.

They went at it twice more that night. The first time Thanquil kissed her cunt before sticking his cock in. Jezzet was never sure she liked the feel of a tongue between her legs but she didn't feel much like complaining. The second time she rolled on top and rode him, her hips grinding against his until they were both satisfied. Afterwards they lay there, exhausted and covered in sticky sweat. She waited until his breathing became slow and rhythmic, waited until she was certain he was asleep then closed her eyes and let the darkness take her.

The Black Thorn

For two days Betrim found himself alone in Sarth, not a single sight of either Jezzet or the Arbiter. He crawled out of bed every morning, itching from sleeping on the uncomfortable and scratchy mattress, and more grateful than he'd ever known it was possible to be that the Arbiter had given him the charm that extinguished hangovers. Betrim discovered if he never took the charm off he needn't ever feel the effects of a good night come the morning, though that didn't stop him from waking up still drunk.

After a breakfast, complete with a morning beer to wash down the food, Betrim waited around in the common room until midday. When neither of his two companions showed themselves he left in search of a more hospitable tavern with better beer and women who weren't afraid of a few scars. The latter proved to be elusive at best but at night, whether he found one or not, he would pay for a woman and if they looked at his face in disgust he'd just turn them over and take them from behind instead. Made little difference to Betrim, none of them reminded him of Rose.

When he stumbled back into his own room at night he would only be able to keep his eyes focused long enough to collapse into his bed. When he slept Betrim found himself dreaming of the dead southerner and the murderous little imp. Of that half-blooded bastard, Swift and his friend, Bones. They weren't pleasant dreams, sometimes he saw them dead, sometimes alive, but they were never pleasant dreams, always woke him sweating and shivering. The beer helped him forget though. Forget about the dreams, forget about his friends.

On the third day after they had followed Kessick, Betrim's companions left their room. Jezzet was the first to appear. Betrim had half expected her to be grinning like a thief in a safe but she looked dour striding down the stairs to the common room with purpose in her step. She sat down opposite Thorn and waved for something to eat and drink. Betrim grinned at her.

"Well I don't reckon you two were murderin' no one," he teased her. "Not unless the noises have changed since I last did it."

Jezzet stared at Betrim so he met her eyes with his usual impassive glare. "You stink of beer, Thorn."

"Aye," he agreed. "An' you stink o' sex but I ain't gonna make a deal of it."

Jezzet Vel'urn snorted out a laugh and shook her head. A short while later the Arbiter made his appearance. He looked somewhat changed. The lines of his face seemed harder, more severe. His manner seemed less casual, more purposeful. Seemed a couple of days of rutting had done them both a bit of good.

"Thorn," the Arbiter said as he sat down. It still worried Betrim how normal the witch hunter looked without his coat. Made him think Arbiters could be anywhere, there could be another in the room with him right now and he wouldn't even know it.

"Aye. Reckon I'm gonna need a few coins. Seems I gone through 'em faster than I'd hoped while you two have been... occupied. Ya got some expensive whore houses in Sarth."

"I seem to remember we already had that conversation and it ended with a '*no*'." The Arbiter's voice was severe, angry. Not enough to scare the Black Thorn.

"Aye well what have you two been bloody doin' fer the last two days?" Thorn waited for the Arbiter to look up before continuing. "'Cos I happen ta know who ya traitor is."

A strained hush fell over the table as the serving girl brought over a plate of food and a mug of dark-brown beer. Jezzet took a swig out of the mug and a moment later the Arbiter had himself a mouthful. Once the serving girl was good and gone Jezzet asked the question.

"How?"

"Well I ain't got no magical powers o' question askin', but ya might be surprised at what ya can get from a bit o' listenin' an' a well-placed comment or two."

"You're going to make me ask you who it is..."

"Inquisitor Heron is the only one that lives round there. The other one..."

"Downe."

"Aye. Her, she's got a place outside o' the city but she never leaves that big black fort o' yours."

"Inquisitor Selice Heron," the Arbiter said more to himself than to the others.

"Good lookin' woman if the drunkards at the *Sleeping Sickle* are ta be believed an' I don't see no reason why they'd lie 'bout it. Though one o' them claimed she used ta suck his cock, I reckon that one was lying.

"So how 'bout it? Reckon I can get a few o' those gold bits? Call it a loan if ya want."

The Arbiter looked up from Jezzet's beer. "Sure. On one condition. You stay sober until this thing is done."

"Well ain't that a hell of a condition." Betrim picked up and drained his mug. "Done."

The Arbiter nodded once, reached into his purse and slid five gold bits across the table. Betrim snatched them up. Staying sober didn't mean no beer at all and it didn't mean no whores.

The next two weeks Betrim counted as some of the dullest of his life. He spent a good portion of them baking in the hot, indomitable sun upon the streets of Sarth while watching the Inquisition main gate with fruitless vigilance. Arbiters came and went, messengers ran to and fro, and servants hurried about everywhere, but rarely did their three targets leave their fortress.

They took it in shifts. Watching, waiting, the occasional dabble into following. Thanquil was the worst of the two companions. Each day the Arbiter seemed a little angrier and the times when he saw the Arbiter known as Kosh he was worse. Betrim recognised the signs of barely restrained violence when he saw them. Jezzet was a far more sociable watch partner and a damn sight easier on the eyes, but even she seemed taught and high-strung. During the few times he was not on watch Betrim found himself alone and missing the company.

Fact was the whole situation stank of indecision. They discovered that the Inquisitor made for her own estate most nights just after sundown. She went in a fancy white carriage drawn by four white horses, big stallions and all of them gelded, and she was guarded by six of the city watch also clad in white. Made for a pretty sight watching all that white come from the black of the Inquisition compound, something about contrast, Jezzet said, not that Betrim knew what that meant.

The tall Arbiter with the pretty face and the scythes only left the compound one day in every three. Seemed even witch hunters got the odd day off and Kosh was partial to a bit of beer and cunt. When he did leave the compound he stopped off at a couple of inns, the *Golden Giant* and the *Merry Harpist.* Always he'd have a couple of drinks in each while folk came around and slid him the odd coin or two. Betrim had seen the like before more times than he cared to count, the Arbiter no doubt extorted money with the threats of righteous burning or the like. After collecting his ill-gotten bits the corrupt witch hunter would always visit the same place, a whore house called the *Pink Purse.* Seemed far too flowery a name considering what went on inside, but it was a fancy place all the same, the type of place a man like Betrim Thorn couldn't even get into.

Kessick on the other hand was not so free with his time. The man only ever seemed to leave the Inquisition compound to report to his heretical Inquisitor and he did that once every two days, always taking the same route and always careful to check for people following him with regular stops and the occasional waiting in alleys. Kessick would be the easiest to kill, Betrim reckoned, the man was too predictable. They could wait, ambush him three on one and Betrim could add a seventh to his list.

Still Thanquil hesitated. The Arbiter himself wasn't one for sharing his plans with the Black Thorn and while Jezzet might be on the inside, she wasn't giving much away either, counselling to be patient and wait while the Arbiter came up with a plan.

It came as a surprise when the Arbiter made a decision. Betrim was sitting down stairs in the common room enjoying some bacon and a morning beer when Jezzet appeared and asked him to follow. The Arbiter was standing at the window of their room when they entered, leaning against the wall. Looked like a nice spot with lots of light, no way for people to get behind or beside you, and a commanding view of the entire room. A real nice leaning spot and no mistake.

"Shut the door," the Arbiter said, his eyes still seemed cold and hard and his voice was flat.

Betrim did as he was asked and proceeded to lean against it. Truth was it weren't as good a spot as the Arbiter's, doors always had their problems, especially if someone was trying to break in with an axe, but it weren't far off.

"Tomorrow," the Arbiter said.

"Aye, 'bout fuckin' time, way I see it," Betrim replied. "Too much doin' nothin' an' not enough killin' makes a man edgy. So which one we doin' fer first?"

"All of them."

That gave Betrim a fair sized portion of pause. The three targets were never seen together which could only mean they were splitting up. "Ya reckon that's a good plan? Ain't never been too good with numbers but at last count only one of us here ever killed an Arbiter 'fore."

"If we kill just one and the other two find out before we get to them... we won't get another chance. It has to be all three at the same time," he paused. "Tomorrow Inquisitor Heron will be at her estate, Kessick will be making his way there to report and Kosh will be doing his rounds. We take one each and kill them before they know what's happening."

"That easy?" Betrim snorted.

"That easy."

Betrim grinned. "Reckon ya want me killin' Kessick."

The Arbiter nodded. "He already knows what Jez looks like and I... I'll be taking Inquisitor Heron."

"On ya own?"

"On my own."

Betrim sucked at his teeth, always annoyed him he had two missing, but he wasn't crazy enough to have metal ones put in their place.

"Now would be the time to voice any concerns, Thorn," the Arbiter said, still staring at Betrim.

"Aye. Ya reckon ya can do it? I don't reckon she got ta be Inquisitor on looks alone though she's sure pretty enough. Way I hear it told there's a big difference between you Arbiters an' them Inquisitors. So..."

"She's no Inquisitor. No more than if you wore a dress would you be a woman. Selice Heron may wear the title but she is nothing more than a heretic. So yes. Yes, I reckon I can do it."

Betrim held his tongue. He couldn't say he was confident and, if truth be told, the Arbiter didn't look like he was either.

"Tomorrow," said the Arbiter. "Two hours past nightfall. Thorn, you take Kessick on his way to meet with Inquisitor Heron. Jez, you'll meet up with Kosh at the brothel. I'll find the Inquisitor at her estate. After they're dead, if all goes well, we'll meet back here."

"What if all don't go well?" Betrim asked.

"Then some of us won't meet back here with the others," Jezzet said with a half-smile.

"Aye an' what if he's one o' the ones that don't come back?" Betrim asked, pointing at the Arbiter. "I ain't doin' this out o' the goodness of my own heart. If you die, Arbiter, how do I get paid?"

Thanquil paused for a moment, frowning, then walked over to his pack and started rifling through it. He tossed a small dagger, its blade no longer than a hand, to Betrim. Thorn caught it and drew the blade to get a better look at it. Seemed well-made, good steel. Not worth two hundred gold bits though. There was some sort of writing on the blade.

"That dagger has the same charms as my sword. Take it to any reputable weapons dealer in this city and you'll get more than enough gold to cover my debt to you."

"Aye?"

"Aye."

"An' what 'bout the pardon? Seems I remember something about ya stoppin' the Inquisition from chasin' me. No more Arbiters comin' after me."

"You don't need to worry about that." The Arbiter turned and looked out the window.

"I reckon I do."

"You don't." The Arbiter's voice sounded terse.

"No?"

"No."

The Black Thorn might have sighed if he was the type of man to sigh, instead he growled. "And why the hell not?"

The Arbiter turned and took two steps towards Betrim, his hands were clenched into fists and his voice was coarse and angry. "Because they've never been after you, Thorn. Not once has the Inquisition ever sent an Arbiter after you."

Betrim felt his jaw clench and his teeth grind together. "That ain't true. I been attacked by you witch hunters plenty o' times."

"Have you really, Thorn... Think back, if you can. Was there a single time the Arbiter attacked you, I wonder."

Betrim tried to remember back. Six Arbiters he'd killed and only one of them did he give a chance to fight back. "Back in Chade, you..."

"No, Thorn. You attacked me. The Inquisition has never been after you." The Arbiter snorted out a laugh. "There's actually a standing order to leave you be."

Betrim shook his head. "No..."

"Yes. You're not a heretic, Thorn, just a petty criminal with a habit of murdering Arbiters. To the Inquisition you're just a mad man not worth taking the risk to hunt down."

The Black Thorn took a menacing step towards the Arbiter, for the first time he realised just how much taller he was. He towered over the witch hunter by almost a foot. "You said, back in the Wilds, you would get me a pardon," he hissed through clenched teeth.

"I lied, Thorn. To get you here, to get you to help me. There's no pardon needed but I knew..."

The Black Thorn's right fist connected with the Arbiter's face and he went sprawling across the floor. Jezzet was on her feet with her sword drawn before Betrim could take another step.

"Don't do it, Thorn," she warned, her voice as sharp and dangerous as her blade.

The Arbiter coughed and spat out some blood and then struggled to his feet and spat again, this time a tooth hit the floor with the red spittle. He walked over to Betrim and stood there again, within striking distance. A big red mark lit the left side of his face and the Black Thorn knew it would be black and blue in a couple of hours.

"I still need your help, Thorn." Betrim had to admire the Arbiter's stones. Not many men would take a punch from the Black Thorn and then ask for his help.

"Tomorrow. Kessick. Two hours after nightfall." Betrim turned and stalked towards the door, near ripping it from its hinges as he opened it. "Don't reckon I'll be comin' back here after." The Arbiter said something but Betrim didn't hear it over the slamming of the door behind him.

By midday Betrim found himself in a tavern drinking away his dwindling coin supply. By sundown he was stinking drunk and bleary eyed. Seemed the whole world was determined to sway around him.

Drinking on your own held its perks but, if truth be told, Betrim would have preferred a drinking partner or two. Bones or Swift both liked their drink and knew how to put it away. Henry and the Boss, neither drank much around the other, but if you got them alone they would empty a few mugs. Jezzet, back when Betrim first knew her, was well known for getting so drunk she often forgot which way was up. Even the Arbiter, lying bastard though he may be, would do for a drinking partner. But the Black Thorn had none of those folk with him, he had no company but himself and the beer, and the truth was, right now he far preferred the beer's company to his own.

"I came here..." he told his beer, pointing an unstable finger at the dark-brown liquid. "I came here ta help. I thought... I dunno, maybe I reckoned I could do some good."

A man beside Betrim glanced at him, shook his head, and then said something funny to his three friends. They all laughed. Betrim ignored the drunkards.

"An' they... they lied... ta me," he slurred at the mug of beer. "They... they lied. And I never once attacked him... part from that first time but I thought... I reckoned it was him... it was all of 'em. I just... and they..." He sighed, both the best and worst thing about drinking was the fog and right now it was very foggy in the Black Thorn's head.

"The first one... the first I... well he was lookin' fer me 'cos o' what I did so I killed him first. Damned if that weren't the right thing ta do," he said to the man on the other table who appeared to be looking at him again. "First time was... well it were messy. But first times always are. Gotta get 'em out o' the way.

"The second... I didn't mean that one, I don't think. Jus' sorta bumped into him on the street. I was... where was I? Land's End, Five Kingdoms, I reckon. Jus' bumped into him... Can't remember his face but we stared at each other fer a bit. Then... then he started walkin' so I... I put my axe in his neck. Funniest thing, some folk actually cheered me."

"What are you talking about?" All four of the men on the other table were looking at him now.

"The third... I remember that one. He were followin' me fer sure. So I waited fer him that time an'..."

Betrim stared at his beer for a few moments. "The fourth. That were the bad one, the one gave me this." He tapped the scarred side of his face with his hand. "My own fault I guess. I missed, ya see. Never was too good a shot with those fuckin' crossbow things... When he came after me... he liked fire, did that one. Set the whole fuckin' town on fire ta get me. Hundreds dead an' they said it was me... I didn't light no fires though. Drowned that one in the end... they can't whisper their spells underwater... reckon that's worth knowin'.

"The fifth... quick an' clean that one. In Chade it were. Quick an' clean. Never saw me comin'... one stab an' it were done. Quick an' clean."

"I think he's talking about killing Arbiters," said a man with a pinched face and too much forehead.

"The sixth... the sixth..."

"Hey, you talking about killing Arbiters?" said the first man, the one with a bulbous nose and fat lips.

There weren't many other folk in the common room. Just Betrim, the four on the table next to his, just about within arm's reach, two men in a corner of the room looking like the last thing they wanted was to draw attention to themselves, the barkeep and a fat brown dog that couldn't seem to stop scratching at its ear. It was a dark, little shit-hole of a tavern if truth be told. Betrim had found it in the poorer district where he judged his last silver bits would go further. Sad thing was he was down to his last bit.

"You still awake there, old man?"

Betrim looked at the man, looked at all four of them: Fat Lips, Pinched Face, Pig Nose and the Pretty One. They were all younger than him, to be sure, but not by enough to call him, '*old man*'.

"Aye I'm still fuckin' awake. What the fuck do ya want?"

"Are you talking to yourself about killing Arbiters?" Fat Lips said each word loud and slow as if Betrim were deaf.

The Black Thorn grinned his most horrific stretching of scarred face. "The best thing 'bout drinkin' in a place like this... the best thing is how sturdy the mugs are."

Betrim swung his mug at Fat Lips' face as hard as possible. He was rewarded by an unhealthy crunch, a scream, and a spray of blood. Pinched Face was up and on his feet first and before Betrim. As Thorn stumbled to a standing position the man caught him with a meaty punch that sent Betrim reeling.

Pinched Face followed up with a second punch which Betrim swayed away from then answered with a fist of his own. He felt something crack, though whether it was one of his own fingers or a bone in Pinched Face's pinched face, he couldn't tell.

Pig Nose was fumbling at something on his belt but the Pretty One charged and took Betrim in the stomach pushing him back and slamming him onto a table. Big, strong hands closed around his throat. The Black Thorn knew this was the point where he should have been choking, but he found himself laughing, not an easy thing to do with someone's hands around your throat but Betrim knew something; when people were trying to strangle you they tended to leave their stones wide open.

He brought his knee up into the man's groin just as the table collapsed underneath him. Betrim heard something rip, sounded close. He rolled and found himself on top of the Pretty One. The Black Thorn grinned and rammed his head into the man's face once, twice, three times, four times, and fifth for good luck. By the time he was done he could feel blood dripping down his face and the mess that had once been the Pretty One was considerably less pretty.

A flash of shadow warned the Black Thorn something was coming and he lurched away from the broken man on the floor. Something hard caught him on his left shoulder. A flair of pain followed by a spreading numbness. Never a good sign, he knew, even in his drunken state. Pig Nose was swinging something heavy and metallic at him, a mace by the looks of things though a damned blurry one.

Betrim dodged to his left and a chair turned to kindling in his place, then he ducked and a section of the wall behind him splintered above his head. The Black Thorn rushed forwards and shoved an elbow into Pig Nose's neck. The man dropped his mace and fell backwards, coughing, spluttering, and gasping. Nothing like hitting a man in the neck to disable him, works better than the stones.

Pig Nose turned to stumble away, Betrim stepped up behind him and slid a big right arm around the man's neck. Pig Nose struggled, he was big and strong but the Black Thorn was bigger, stronger. After a while the body went limp in Betrim's arms and he let it drop to the floor.

Staggering, Betrim looked around at the tavern. Pig Nose was down, unconscious. Pinched Face was in a corner, crying. The Pretty One was a silent mess of blood and bone yet still alive. Fat Lips was gone, no doubt run off. The two shady men looked on in shady silence. The barkeep stood in open mouthed shock and the brown dog had stopped scratching to lap at a pool of blood on the floor.

"Ya all saw them..." Betrim stumbled into a table and went down on top of it. A moment later he was hauling himself back to his feet using a chair for support. "They attacked me!" he told everyone.

With that, he staggered towards the door to the tavern and out into the warm night air. Sarth was always so damned humid at night. With a drunken stumble Betrim set off to his left.

"There's gotta be a brothel round here somewhere," he looked at his last silver bit. "A cheap one."

The Blademaster

The *Pink Purse* was not a subtle building. Built out of the same white-stone as the most of the buildings in Sarth, it may be, but from every window hung a gaudy-coloured cloth each with its own crest. Inside each window hung just as gaudy draperies no doubt designed to obscure any view of what might be going on inside the room. Even from across the street where Jezzet hid, out of sight, she could smell the perfume from the place.

Thanquil suggested the plan just after Thorn's dramatic exit and Jez had almost knocked out a few more of the Arbiter's teeth.

"It's not an ordinary whore house." He told her. "The... the women there are all noble born. It's a place where those of high birth can send their daughters to..."

"To get them some experience in fucking," Jezzet finished for him in angry tones. "So as better to seduce a man above their station. Much better to have a woman who already knows how to fuck and suck than have to teach one. Right?"

Thanquil nodded. "I suppose so. Some of the nobility also send their daughters there if they... have too many."

"Of course. I forgot here in Sarth you're so damned civilized. Women are married off with dowries aren't they? So if you can't afford to pay for someone to marry her you just send her to a whore house to get fucked for the rest of her life."

The Arbiter winced. "It's more like renting them to the whore house... The family is given half of whatever is charged for the woman."

It wasn't his fault, she knew that. Thanquil didn't make the laws, didn't even live in Sarth most of the time but she'd felt like hitting someone and he was the only one there at the time. Somehow she managed to restrain herself.

"The woman who runs the place calls herself Lady Frerry," Thanquil continued. "She's well-known among the... among the thieves of Sarth."

"How do you know the thieves?"

Thanquil grinned, the new gap in his teeth showing. "The Inquisition didn't teach me everything I know. Lady Frerry is known because she can be bribed. It won't be the first time they've dealt with a body." He tossed Jezzet a purse, felt heavy at the time and later, when she checked it, she counted just over a hundred gold bits, a small fortune by most folk's count.

"Give her that," Jezzet was already shaking her head as Thanquil continued. "Tell her you want a room and you want Kosh."

"You want me to be his whore?" She almost hit him again.

"No..."

"How about I just ambush him in the street and kill him, like Thorn and Kessick?"

"You're good, Jezzet, with your sword, probably the best I've ever seen, but Kosh. Our old master at arms used to say Kosh was the best warrior the Inquisition had ever produced and he's an Arbiter on top of that. I don't want you to do anything but pretend you're there to... until..."

"To fuck him."

"Until he puts aside his weapons. Then," Thanquil stood and handed Jezzet her sword, "you're going to need this."

The rest of the day had been awkward. They'd had awkward conversation, awkward sex, and awkward silence. It was like neither of them could think of anything to say to the other. Eventually Jezzet fled with sword and gold in hand. That was yesterday, she hadn't seen Thanquil for a full day. Might be he thought she'd just gone, took the gold and left him.

Could you blame him for thinking that? You just got dressed, took the gold and ran, Jez. Not exactly a fond farewell. At least he wasn't dead though, you have a habit of leaving men dead. It was a discomforting thought considering what she was about to do.

Two guards stood at the entrance to the *Pink Purse* both armed and armoured. One was thick of neck the other looked thick of head and both looked ready for a fight.

Places like this always have their own guards and both look like they've seen a few fights, the stupid one maybe a few too many.

Jez sauntered up to the entrance with a look on her face she hoped made her look official; it wouldn't do for them to guess that she was here to murder one of their patrons. She stopped in front of the two guards and let them look at her. They were both big men, both towered over her and both weighed twice as much as her. Still, Jezzet held her ground and didn't flinch as they leered and grinned.

The thick-necked one pointed at Jezzet's sword, it would look little more than a toy in one of their beefy hands, and laughed.

"It's not the size that matters, it's where you stick them," Jez said with a sneer.

The one with the thick neck laughed and waved her in. Jezzet nodded and walked inside, it was unlikely they got many female visitors; no doubt they weren't certain whether they should let her in or turn her away.

Inside the smell was a cloying stench of stale sex and sweet perfume. *Think I preferred the smell of the sewer... both of them.* The room was dimly lit with covered lanterns lending a seedy feel to the disgusting smell. Jezzet hated whore houses almost as much as she hated being called a whore.

Cushioned couches and sofas scattered the floor, some had women lounging on and others were vacant. Each woman wore a light-coloured dress to contrast against the dark-coloured cushions and each dress looked like it could slip from their shoulders at a moment's notice. Some of the women looked Jez up and down the way a predator might stare at its prey, others just watched her with dull, vacant eyes.

Should I pity them or despise them? Or should I just put them all out of their misery? Problem was not all of them looked miserable. *How could any woman enjoy this lifestyle?*

There were two more guards just inside the door, both as big and weighty as those outside, but these two looked like they had some intelligence about them. Jezzet wagered she could kill them both before they even touched their weapons.

"Um... We don't service women... or well... Alexis does but she doesn't take payment," Jez turned to find a petite girl with big, brown eyes and long, blond hair that flowed down to her arse. She didn't even look old enough to bleed and the green dress she wore was more or less transparent, Jez could clearly see her tiny, budding breasts beneath.

Presumptuous little whore! Jezzet wondered how hard she had to stare at someone before they exploded. The little whore did not explode, but she did wilt and back off a few steps. Jezzet became aware of the guards closing in behind her.

"No, no, no, no, Faren," came a voice to Jez's right, spiced with an accent she had only heard once before back in the Five Kingdoms. "This one is not here for that. I am right, I am."

The woman was older than Jez but not by a lot. Her skin was the colour of a dark olive and her hair was black as midnight. She had full, red lips, fine features barely touched with powder and lively, dark eyes. She wore a light-red dress of silk, which hugged the curves of her body while remaining as transparent as the little whore's green shift.

"You're a desert dweller," Jez said with narrowed eyes.

The woman crossed her arms underneath her heavy breasts. Jez had never seen such large nipples before. Everything about the woman screamed, *'whore'*.

"A westerner from the Five Kingdoms I am, yes." Her voice was as sweet and choking as the perfume in the air. "And you have something for me, you do."

"After we set terms."

"No, no, no. I will have the payment now, whether we agree or not," her voice became less sweet and more dangerous.

Jezzet gritted her teeth and sighed. "Perhaps we should continue this conversation in private?"

The whore mistress grinned and stepped up to take hold of Jez's arm. "Mmmmm," she purred, "I thought you'd never ask, I did."

If you try to touch me I will stab you, Jezzet thought as she allowed the whore to lead her away by the arm. They passed a number of other women who stared at Jez in mute fascination as they reclined on sofas. She fought the urge to spit.

You were almost sold to a whore house, Jez. She reminded herself and thanked all the Gods she couldn't remember that her old master had saved her from that, even if he had made her pay for it every day she was with him.

It appeared there were no private rooms on the bottom floor of the *Pink Purse* so the whore mistress led Jezzet to a secluded alcove. She took a seat on one side and Jez sat down on the other. As the whore leaned forwards Jez pushed herself back into the cushioned seat.

"Do I scare you?" the whore mistress asked.

"No."

"Ahhhh." The woman's voice was husky.

No doubt men go wild for that when she moans in their ears.

"Then it is something else, it is. You do not agree with what we do here?"

Jezzet stared at the woman in silence. *I'm going to knock out another of Thanquil's teeth after this. He could have sent Thorn, that bastard would have loved it here. Maybe a little too much.*

"Your purse..." the whore mistress hinted. Jezzet plucked it from her belt and almost threw it at the woman. Instead she placed it on the cushion between the two of them. The whore picked it up, opened it and made throaty moans as she looked through the contents. "So, you come to me in men's armour with men's weapons and you ask of me?"

I'd ask you to go fuck yourself but you'd probably just enjoy it.

"You have a regular," Jezzet said, her voice as hard as stone. "An Arbiter."

"Ahhh, yes. Arbiter Kosh. The things he does with some of my women. Mmmmm. You wish to experience them?"

"I wish to kill him."

"Oh, that would explain the small fortune I have between my legs." Jezzet hadn't failed to notice the whore had placed the gold purse between her thighs. "What could he have done to you, I wonder, to make you want him so dead so bad."

Again Jezzet stared at the woman in harsh silence.

"It matters not, I suppose. You want to use one of my rooms, to draw him in, to strip him of his faith's armour and then. You know how to kill, you do."

"Yes," Jez bit off the word.

"Mmmmmm," the whore mistress purred. "Murder and sex so often go hand in hand. We haven't much time. You will need to bathe and be dressed appropriately if you wish for him to pick you. Come, come. We shall have you ready in time, we shall."

Jezzet had never been bathed before. No sooner had she settled into the hot water than the little girl with the big brown eyes took a sponge to her. Jez snapped. She grabbed the sponge, twisted the girl's wrist, and was on the verge of drowning her when the whore mistress entered the room.

The woman took one look at the scars all over Jez's body and her expression changed into one of sympathy. That made Jezzet angry all over again.

"Faren, out." The whore mistress walked over to the bed and laid out a slim, blue dress. "Some women... you will want to bathe alone, you will. Be quick, your Arbiter will be here soon, he will."

My Arbiter may already be dead. Jez thought as she watched the whore mistress retreat from the room and shut the door.

She bathed, surprised as always by the amount of dirt that came off her, and patted herself dry with the towelling cloth they left her. There was a full sized mirror in the room but Jezzet had no time for such things. She slipped the blue dress on over her head, it was so light it almost felt like she was wearing nothing and it hugged her figure much like the whore mistress' red counterpart.

She caught a glimpse of herself in the mirror as she turned and her expression soured. *You look like a fucking whore, Jez. If only Constance could see you now, might be then she'd rather fuck you instead of kill you.* Through the dress Jezzet could see her small breasts and her soft pink nipples, she could see the hair between her legs, and she could even make out the faint outlines of some of her scars. *If only breaking mirrors wasn't bad luck.*

Jez hid her dagger and her sword, she couldn't be seen with them but she'd have need them soon enough, she placed her normal clothing under the bed as well. Then she walked over to the door, took in a deep breath and made her way down stairs.

As soon as she stepped out onto the landing, eyes all over the greeting room turned to her. Half a dozen different whores stared at her, some with harsh eyes, and some with dull, vacant expressions. A man, a customer by the looks of things, watched her with a hungry smile on his face as he stared at her breasts. The guards looked on as well, one giving her a gap toothed smile while the other winked, stuck out his tongue and gave it a waggle. The worst bit was the whore mistress' stare though. The olive-skinned woman stared at Jezzet with frank appraisal, as a merchant might stare at a barrel of fish, and gave an approving nod at the result.

Jez felt her heat rising into her face as she descended the stairs. *Jezzet Vel'urn is not the type of woman to blush at a few stares.*

"Such a wonderful colour in your cheeks, you should show it more often, you should," the whore mistress sang as she met Jez on the last of the stairs. The whore reached out a hand to cup her cheek but stopped short, thinking better of it.

"A stare that has frightened many a man, I'm sure. But we are not hoping to frighten today, we aren't. You would do better to soften the eyes, pout the lips. Open just a little, like so. The man wants to imagine the lips around him, not barred to him. A whore does not..."

"I. Am. Not. A. Whore," Jezzet forced out between her barred lips.

The mistress smiled in reply. Her hands waved in front of Jezzet, tracing the lines of her body beneath the dress without touching her. "But such a pretty one you would make." She waved a hand at Jez's head. "Though the hair... will do, I suppose." Then she waved a hand at Jez's crotch. "Perhaps though we should trim you a little."

Jez focused her angriest glare at the woman. "You take a blade anywhere near my cunt and I'll gut you with it."

The whore mistress sighed. "Such anger. When your man arrives I shall do the talking, I think. Direct him to you. You can smile, I hope."

Jezzet took a moment to calm herself, let out a sigh and then smiled.

"Oh yes," the whore mistress said with a smile of her own. "He will pick you. How could he not. Why I am tempted to pick you myself. Over here, come." She led Jez to one of the sofas, a gigantic, green-cushioned monstrosity that looked like it could swallow Jezzet whole if she relaxed on it.

"Here, lounge. Hmmm, try one knee cocked. Keep your legs open, crossed legs never let any man in. Take your arms away from your chest, many men like small breasts but they need to be seen. Yes, that is good, it is."

Jezzet felt like a fool lying in the position the mistress had cajoled her into but she lay there all the same, hoping it wouldn't take too long.

"I will greet your Arbiter, direct him to you. He will pick you, he will. Take him to the room. After, we will deal with the..."

"The body," Jezzet finished for the mistress, the woman nodded in reply. "You do this a lot, don't you?"

The whore mistress smiled and lowered her voice to a whisper. "I did not come here all the way from my desert to be a whore. There is money in what we women have between our legs, but there is more money in using it to kill men."

After that the mistress moved away. She greeted two men as they entered, the first a huge, fat man with more chins than hairs on his head. He focused his beady little eyes on Jezzet and a wet grin spread across his face but the mistress turned him away, directed him to a girl even smaller than Jez.

He'll likely crush her beneath that weight. At least it won't last very long. Fat men, in Jezzet's experience, rarely lasted very long.

The second man to enter the brothel looked as plain as plain could be with nervous, jittery hands that he constantly squeezed together. He greeted the mistress before angling straight for a black-skinned beauty lounging at the back of the room. The woman greeted the man as if they were old friends.

Jezzet recognized the third man to enter. Kosh was tall, handsome in a clean way with sharp features. He had the blonde hair and blue eyes so prevalent in Sarth. *Dark, dangerous eyes but not near as pretty as Thanquil's.* He wore the coat as well, the brown-leather coat that marked him as an Arbiter. It was clean and well-looked-after whereas Thanquil's was ragged and stained. Jezzet noticed the scythes as well, two of them, one hanging either side of his hip.

The whore mistress greeted him with a beaming smile and a kiss on the lips that allowed her to press her breasts against him. He was red faced and grinning by the time she released him. "Mistress Frerry," Kosh said, his voice as handsome as his face. "Am I finally to experience you instead of one of your girls?"

She giggled back at him. "Why Arbiter Kosh you dare too much, you do. You know I save myself for your Emperor."

"You may be saving yourself a very long time."

"What is a woman to do? He will come to his senses eventually, he will. I have a new one for you to enjoy today. She is rare and well-trained."

Jezzet fought the urge to gag and instead put on the same smile she used to give to D'roan.

"Huh," Kosh grunted with a grin. "She is..."

"Beautiful, no? I bought her from Acanthia, expensive but worth every coin I am assured. Though. if truth be told. no one has had the chance to experience her yet. Only arrived today, she has."

"Acanthia?" Kosh mused. "A slave?"

The whore mistress *tutted* at the Arbiter. "No, no, no. Slavery is outlawed in Acanthia. I merely... purchased her contract."

Arbiter Kosh licked at his lips. "We'll settle accounts after. Does she speak?"

Yes, I do. I'll say 'FUCK YOU' as I slit your throat.

"Only when commanded to. She will say whatever you wish her to."

"Good, lead the way then, Acanthia."

Jezzet caught the whore mistress' anxious stare and ignored it. She took hold of Arbiter Kosh's hand and began leading him up the stairs.

'Once he puts aside his weapons.' Thanquil had said. Until then Jezzet would continue the act though she could feel her anger bubbling up inside.

Kosh couldn't even wait till they were inside the room. As Jezzet went to open the door she felt him press himself up against her. She felt his cock, hard through his trousers, poking at her backside. With a grunt she pushed open the door and stepped through. Kosh followed her in, slamming the door in his haste. Once inside, his dark eyes moved over every inch of her body. Jezzet kept her own eyes down and fought the urge to scream.

"Take off your dress," he commanded. Jezzet shrugged out of the piece of cloth and let it puddle on the floor at her feet. "Scars... do they cut all the whores like that in Acanthia?"

Jezzet found her hands shaking. She wanted to cover herself, wanted to scream, wanted to stab someone, wanted to fuck someone. Instead she lowered her voice to a whisper and said. "Only the disobedient ones."

The glint she saw in Arbiter Kosh's eyes told Jez she had guessed right about him. He liked the idea that she had been beaten for being disobedient to her masters. Some men liked women who had been hurt.

"Come here," he ordered.

Just a little longer, Jez.

She did as she was told. Kosh grabbed her, squeezed at her breasts, pressed his wet lips against her own, and started fondling at his belt buckle. Jezzet suffered his clumsy attentions and then helped him with his buckle. His scythes hit the floor with a metallic thump. Then she pushed the coat off his shoulders and that too hit the floor. His trousers were next and then his undergarments. Jezzet ripped at his shirt and flung it aside.

Her target, Arbiter Kosh stood there, naked and weapon-less in front of her. *Now!*

Jezzet pushed him backwards on to the bed. He lay there staring at her, a curious grin on his face. Jez climbed on top of him, took hold of his cock and guided it inside of her as she lowered herself down.

He's smaller than Thanquil.

At first she began to move her hips. Up and back, forward and down. Faster and faster. She knew she should be smiling, men liked it when she smiled, instead she found herself staring at Kosh in disgust. Either the Arbiter inside of her didn't notice or he didn't care, staring back at her with a hungry face, red and panting, grunting and groaning. Jezzet continued to grind her hips.

Jez had fucked many men in her life. Some were fat, some were thin. Some smelled of stale alcohol and sweat, others of flowery perfume. Some had worn armour, some had worn silk. Some were rich, some didn't have a single bit to their name. Some of them had names, others had been nameless drunken fucks. Most times it had been willing but sometimes it had been rape. Never before had she felt truly disgusted in herself though.

Fight or fuck, Jez? You always choose fuck. She remembered what the Sword of the North had told her, '*Whores fuck their way out of fights, not Blademasters.*'

Kosh was panting now, his breath coming out as grunts of pleasure. His hands squeezed painfully at her small breasts and then ran down her body and they gripped hold of her arse. Still she moved her hips. Up and down, she could feel him inside of her, but took no pleasure of it.

A Blademaster without a blade...

Jezzet leaned down to kiss the Arbiter and slid her right hand underneath the pillow at the head of the bed. Her fingers closed around the hilt of the dagger she had hidden there.

"Oh God yes!" Kosh wheezed out.

Jezzet sat up and drove her dagger through the Arbiter's heart.

THE BLACK THORN

Betrim sat at the camp fire staring into the flames as they danced and fought to see which one could reach furthest into the darkness. He chewed on a strip of charred horse flesh, tasted like shoe but meat was meat. He took a swig of the bottle in his hand, cheap spirit, tasted like fire and vomit. That seemed a little odd, alcohol tended to taste like vomit coming up not going down.

Bones sat cross legged on the bare earth cleaning his bones with yellow spit and brown rag. The giant grinned as he went about his grisly business and bled from half a hundred small cuts. Swift lay on the ground, one leg twisted at a horrific angle, snoring. Betrim didn't reckon the bastard was really asleep, Swift liked to play stupid games like that.

The Boss tore a strip of seared horseflesh from the spit and shoved it into the bloody mess of jagged bone and raw flesh that had once been his face. Betrim could see muscles twitching there but there was no face, no nose, no eyes, no mouth. Just spurting blood and a horrible squelching noise.

"How'd ya do it?" came Green's voice. Betrim found the boy's body sitting across from him, he could see it through the flames. Green's head was laying on the floor just a couple of feet away.

"Do what?" Betrim asked the head.

"How'd ya kill 'em? The Arbiters?"

How a decapitated head could speak should have been a matter for concern, Betrim knew, instead he just ignored it and looked for Henry. The little imp was nowhere to be seen. Fled or dead he didn't know but she wasn't here amongst this gruesome company.

Somewhere Betrim heard the laughing dogs of the wilds laughing at him. Seemed they were laughing at him, at least. They'd be here soon enough to feast upon the corpses of his dead friends... and Green.

"Get up," the bloody mess of the Boss' head said in a voice that wasn't his. "Get up!"

Betrim felt something tapping his foot, he looked down to find Green's head had rolled closer and was bumping against his boot.

Pushing itself with his tongue.

"Get up!" the Boss' faceless face insisted.

Betrim tried to open his eyes. Felt like the weight of the world was pulling his eyelids back shut. He started to drift off again.

"Get up! By Volmar if you don't get up I'll call the guard."

Again Betrim tore his eyelids open and let out a groan. It felt like someone was stamping on his head... from inside his skull. Every bit of him felt heavy, sluggish, and painful.

He was lying on something hard and wooden, felt a lot like floor and Betrim had slept on enough floors to know what one felt like. There was something wet and foul smelling under his mouth, up by his nose.

"Vomit..." Betrim said to himself.

"Yes, vomit! Vomit which I will have to clean before the next person wants to stay here."

"Here?" Betrim asked as he scrabbled at the wooden floor with his hands and pushed himself up. It felt like trying to lift a small house.

"Yes. Here. Get up and go. Now! You've already stayed here too long. I should have called the guard."

"Too long..." Betrim said. Fragments of memory were coming back to him. He had stumbled into this inn, slapped his last bits on the counter and demanded a room. He glanced at the window, it was still dark.

"Yes! Too long! Now go!"

Betrim looked at the tall, skinny, ugly man. "It's still night. I paid for..."

"You paid for a night. You've been here a night and a day."

"What?" Betrim's head screamed in pain with each pounding thump. His hand went to the Arbiter's charm around his neck, the one that should keep away the hangover, it was gone. "Ya sayin' it's tomorrow... already?"

"Tomorrow. Tonight. Get out!"

"Fuck! I gotta... go." Betrim lurched to his feet and stumbled as the world spun around him. He hit the wall and caught himself on it then fumbled his way to the door.

"Arrgh." He doubled over and retched. Vile, burning acid spattered the floor and Betrim caught a whiff of urine. Seems he'd pissed himself at some point.

"GET OUT!"

Betrim stumbled his way to the stairs and started down them, his head pounding all the way down. He tripped on the last two steps and hit the ground face first, only at the last moment did he think to turn his head to stop the fall from breaking his nose.

He pushed himself back to his feet, stumbled into a table and staggered towards the door. Outside, the night was cool and crisp. Something seemed wrong about that, Sarth was never cool. "It's night..."

Betrim spun, the world spun the other way and he crashed into someone. A woman hit the stone with a gasp of pain. Betrim fought the urge to vomit again, swallowed it down. By all the Gods he wished he still had that charm. Someone grabbed Betrim by his leathers. A man, tall and broad.

"How dare you..."

"What time is it?" Betrim asked.

"What?"

Betrim shrugged the man's hands off and grabbed him by his fancy cloth shirt, and shook him. "What fuckin' time is?"

"Uhh... umm... About two hours after dusk."

"Fuck!" Betrim shouted, blasting the man with sour breath. "Which way to the Inquisition?"

"I...uh..."

"WHICH FUCKIN' WAY?"

The man pointed, Betrim shoved him to the floor next to the woman, and turned in the direction he had pointed and started running.

His feet pounded on the stone ground in a steady rhythm with the beating inside of his head. Despite the darkness the world felt so bright Betrim found himself squinting as Sarth spun past him in a drunken blur. Buildings loomed over him in towering white silence. People stared at him or ignored him, it made no matter, some even shouted after him but their words were lost, drowned out by the deafening drum inside his skull.

He was looking for something he recognised, anything, a landmark, a tavern, a shop, a brothel, a church. The second time he stopped to retch up what little was left in his stomach Betrim had the idea to look up. The black tower of the Inquisition loomed above the city of Sarth, swaying and bending over the white buildings below it like some great drunken tower about to vomit over the pristine...

Betrim shook himself, there was no time. He had to find Kessick. Had to kill the Arbiter before he reached the Inquisitor's estate. Too many of Betrim's friends had died of late. Bones, the Boss, Swift, Henry, all gone, dead or fled, all gone. He wasn't about to let that happen again. He had few enough friends left in this world he wasn't about to let the last two die because he was too drunk to hold up his end of the bargain.

The Black Thorn tried to figure out where he was and where he needed to be. The Inquisition tower was close, crowding the sky above him like a dark monolith. Kessick went right out of the gates so Betrim could cut him off by going left. It seemed to make sense so he stumbled into another run and cut left through alleys and byways, hoping he didn't come across one of the Sarth canals. Not that a dip in some water wouldn't do his smell the world of good.

Betrim stumbled out into a large street. In front of him was a bakery he recognised. He'd been this way before many times, always while following Kessick. He turned to his right and ran. Sprinted. The world focused in around him until the Black Thorn was watching through a muted, painful blur of a tunnel.

Up ahead he saw a coat, the coat. Betrim unhooked his axe from his belt and gritted his teeth. Fifteen paces from Kessick the Black Thorn slid to a halt and launched his hand axe.

"KESSICK!" Betrim roared.

The Arbiter just started to turn as the axe head bit into his back with a solid *THUMP*. The body hit the stone floor face first.

THE ARBITER

Thanquil stood outside Inquisitor Heron's estate and waited in the shadows, hidden from view by the trunk of a large, ancient oak. He waited and he watched. She was there. He had seen her enter an hour ago, no doubt sitting down to an evening meal by now.

He twisted a small, pewter necklace around his fingers. Necklaces were one of the hardest things to steal from a person. To take something from around a woman's neck without her noticing was a skill not many possessed. It had taken Thanquil years to learn but learn it he did, much to the shock of some of the other thieves.

It was nerves, he decided then. He was nervous and it was scaring him into inaction. By now Jez should have killed Kosh and the Black Thorn, assuming he hadn't just fled, should have taken care of Kessick. Only Inquisitor Heron remained and she needed to be dealt with before she heard of the other's deaths.

He slipped his arms through the sleeves of his coat and tugged the leather garment straight. If he was going to do this he was going to do it as an Arbiter of the Inquisition. He stashed the necklace in one pocket and checked the others, making sure he remembered where each of his runes were hidden, where the charms were secreted away. It had been months since he'd last worn his Arbiter's coat. Now he was it felt right, almost as if a part of him had been missing but was now restored.

Thanquil made one final check of his preparations. A sleepless charm wrapped around his left arm, it wouldn't do to be knocked unconscious, his sword loosened in its scabbard, his pistol loaded and tucked away in his belt.

The guards blocked him at the gate. Two big men in white and both looked more than a little nervous. Thanquil stared at each of them in turn.

"Arbiter Thanquil Darkheart here to see the Inquisitor. Stand aside."

"Uhh," the bigger of the two guards bit his lip. A brown lip, Thanquil noticed. The man chewed too much casher weed. "Do you... have an appointment?"

Thanquil spat, a nasty habit he'd picked up from somewhere. "Wasn't aware I needed one. Move aside or I will move you."

The guard looked pained. "Yes, sir." He stepped away and Thanquil strode past them both, through the open gate and into the Inquisitor's grounds.

It was a beautiful estate, Thanquil couldn't deny. Flower beds in every colour he could imagine all lit by the ruddy, orange glow of hanging lanterns. Short grass, a gardener's worst nightmare. An eight-tiered fountain with crushed white marble in each bowl to allow the water to filter and drain.

Thanquil approached the main door, took a deep, steadying breath and knocked. It took only a few moments before the door was opened. A thin, balding man stood on the threshold, bathed in the warm light that spilled out from behind him.

"Arbiter Thanquil Darkheart here to see the Inquisitor," Thanquil said in his most officious tone.

"Regarding?"

Thanquil stared at the man in silence.

"Of course. If you'll follow me, Arbiter..."

"No. I'll wait out here. Go fetch your master."

"You want me to... Of course."

The servant turned and hurried away. Thanquil walked back down the path a short way. If he was going to fight an Inquisitor he'd rather not do it in a confined space.

It didn't take long for the Inquisitor to respond to his summons. She walked out of the doorway to her mansion with an easy grace and a warm smile that lit up her already beautiful face even in the dim lantern light.

Inquisitor Selice Heron looked to be only a little older than Thanquil himself but the truth, he knew, was that she had lived for close to eighty years. The slightest hint of crow's feet was beginning to show at the corners of her eyes, but other than that she looked no older than the first time he had seen her forty years previous. Her face was soft and caring, beautiful in a kind way that belied her position as an Inquisitor. Her hair was long and blonde, tied into a braid that reached down to the small of her back. Her eyes shone with a blue light even in the darkness.

She wore a light set of cotton trousers and a matching shirt underneath her Inquisitor's coat; identical to an Arbiter's except for being white instead of brown. Somehow it all made her seem pure and holy and for a moment Thanquil was unsure.

"Arbiter Thanquil," her voice soft and fluid. "We have been worried. It has been months since you last contacted the Inquisition. We feared the worst."

His hands were shaking a little, just like when he needed to steal something. Inquisitor Heron was standing right there in front of him. He knew he should attack, not give her chance to defend herself. The Black Thorn had said, *'The way ta kill an Arbiter is not ta let 'em know ya comin''* and that went doubly true for an Inquisitor. But she was Inquisitor Heron, the kindest of the Inquisitors, the only one who ever had a good word to say about him. The only one who didn't look at him like he was a heretic.

"Arbiter, are you alright?" she asked in a sweet voice. There was no compulsion there, no will trying to subvert his own. In training the Inquisition forced an Arbiter to use the compulsion until they were unable to ask questions without using it. There was no way around it, even the Grand Inquisitor was bound by it. But the compulsion was a power given to them by their belief in Volmar. If an Arbiter or an Inquisitor turned away from the faith...

Thanquil noticed Inquisitor Heron was armed. A cruel-looking, black-steel sword hung from her belt, its jagged blade unsheathed and waiting.

"Why?" Thanquil asked, his own compulsion crashing against the Inquisitor's will like a wave hitting a cliff. The question was too broad, too unfocused, even if she hadn't been protected it would not have worked.

"Why what, Arbiter?"

"Why betray the Inquisition?"

"What are you talking about, Thanquil? I would never..."

"I know about you and H'ost. I know about Kessick. I know about the contract, Inquisitor," Thanquil interrupted her plea of innocence.

Inquisitor Heron sighed. "Did H'ost at least put up a fight? He shouldn't even have known about the contract. That must have been Kessick's fault."

The Inquisitor took a step forwards off the porch of her mansion and towards Thanquil. She smiled at him, a predator's smile. "But how much do you know?"

Thanquil backed away. "I know you're putting creatures from the void into people's bodies. Is that how you turned Kosh?"

She giggled. "Kosh? He came to me on his own. He saw the truth. All I did was confirm it for him. You, of all people, should see it too, Thanquil Darkheart."

"What truth?"

"Do you remember when Arbiter Yellon brought you in, Thanquil?" she asked him. "He was a very pretty man that one, but such a vicious streak. I was a newly graduated Arbiter myself and I saw him walk you in, one hand on your shoulder. He stopped in the middle of the compound and said, *'This boy's name is Thanquil Darkheart'*. Do you remember? The day he gave you that name. I do. All around you Arbiters and servants alike stared at you in disgust or laughed at you. Yet you met all of their stares head on and didn't flinch. All they saw in you was a child of two heretics burned for their evil, but not me. I saw something else in you, potential."

Thanquil barely remembered that day. He had been somewhere close to eight years old, half-starved and he'd just watched his own parents burning, screaming. He remembered very little of that day or of the weeks that followed, but he remembered the scorn, the derision. He was the first Darkheart in the Inquisition for near a thousand years. After all, a child born of heresy was more like to turn to the darkness.

"Do you have a reason for bringing that up, Inquisitor?"

"The Inquisition has grown stagnant. Too bogged down in tradition and prejudice, unable to see power even when it is in front of them." She looked up at the sky and took a deep breath then exhaled slowly.

"A thousand years ago all the Inquisitors were as powerful as our Grand Inquisitor Vance. Now? Now he is dying remnant of the past. Too stubborn, like the rest, to realise that their time is at an end. The Inquisition isn't strong enough to stand up to the darkness that's coming,

Thanquil.

"Kosh saw it as I do, how could he not? One as powerful as him could easily see the others around him were not his match. He came to me for guidance, seeking answers that he already knew, but asking the wrong questions. I showed him the truth..."

"By putting a demon from the void in his body?" Again Thanquil's compulsion crashed against her will, impotent and powerless.

"I can show you the truth as well, Thanquil. I can show you what's coming. It's time to choose a side."

"I already have."

She laughed. "They don't even realise what they have in you, do they. They mock you, scorn you, fear you. And yet you are the one that's here fighting for their survival like some sort of paragon of misguided justice."

Thanquil drew his sword and held it in front of him, edging forwards a step. "Kosh and Kessick are both dead, Inquisitor."

"What?" For the first time uncertainty crossed her beautiful face. "You couldn't have..."

"I didn't come back to Sarth alone."

"Tell me, Arbiter Darkheart, once you are dead, do you think even a single one of them will believe you were anything more than a heretic? Even if you should succeed in killing me the Inquisition will execute you for it."

"Once you're dead they'll find the proof, they'll find the contract," Thanquil pressed for information.

Inquisitor Heron laughed. "Do you believe I'd leave such a dangerous artefact lying around, Arbiter? No. The contract is safe. I am the only person who could ever retrieve it."

"The void," Thanquil said.

She smiled. "Yes. The demons of the void are sworn to obey the Inquisition and I ordered them to take the contract and never speak of it to anyone but myself."

If that was true then there was no proof. The Inquisitor was right. Thanquil would be killed by the Inquisition on suspicion of heresy even if he should win.

Then Inquisitor Heron's sword was in her hand and with a silent grin she came at him.

The Blademaster

She watched the blood well up around the blade of the dagger. A thin, red line ran down the Arbiter's skin and soaked into the silk bed linen. She needed to get dressed, put on some real clothing, and fetch the whore mistress to deal with the body.

Then I need to go check on Thanquil. He might need my help.

Jez pushed herself up onto her knees and wiped between her legs with a corner of the bed sheet.

Arbiter Kosh's eyes flicked open.

Wha...

The Arbiter's knee crashed into Jez's crotch and she realised the scream of pain was her own. Then there was a foot on her belly. Kosh grunted as he pushed and Jez found herself crashing against the far wall and dropping to the floor, winded and whimpering in pain.

"Never been through that before." Jez looked up at his words, still gasping for air. Kosh rolled from the bed and stretched, the dagger still lodged in his chest.

It should be right through his heart!

"It told me death might hurt, but I never thought... who are you?" Kosh took hold of the dagger and pulled. The blade slipped out of his skin with a small squirt of blood and the wound sealed itself closed. After just a moment only a thin, red line remained to prove there had been any wound at all.

Jezzet didn't answer. She gathered her legs underneath her and made ready to move.

A Blademaster without a blade...

Kosh dropped the dagger and moved towards his discarded clothing. "So? Who are you? Why did you kill me?"

As the Arbiter knelt down to take hold of one of his scythes Jez made her move. She leapt towards the small dresser, shoved her hand behind it and pulled out her sword.

"Your dagger couldn't kill me, what makes you think your..."

As Jez drew her sword from its scabbard two small slips of paper floated to the floor.

"Huh," Kosh grunted, he was staring at her sword. It took Jez a moment to realise why. The steel blade was glowing. It wasn't much of a glow, just a slight sparkle along the metal, but it was unmistakable.

Kosh snatched up one of his scythes and ran. A moment later he crashed through the window, glass, wood and all. Jezzet was already moving when she heard the thud of the Arbiter hitting the ground outside. She looked out the window to see the dead man running up the street away from the whore house. Jez looked at her sword again and she remembered Thanquil handing it to her and saying, *'You're going to need this.'*

He would have told me if he had known...

Jezzet leapt out the window and for a brief moment she was falling. Then she hit the ground, rolled to a stop, and sent a silent prayer of thanks to the Gods that the building wasn't any taller. Then she turned and started sprinting after the fleeing Arbiter.

Not for the first time in her life Jezzet was glad of having small breasts. She'd seen big women try to run and it looked a painful and dangerous affair. Fact was she'd much prefer to be fully clothed, but she knew if she'd have wasted the time she'd have lost Kosh. The Arbiter was in front of her but not by much and she was quicker than him and gaining.

He turned a corner and was lost from sight, two seconds later Jezzet turned the same corner and saw him again, still running. There weren't many people on the streets but those there were stared and pointed and shouted. Jezzet tried her best to ignore them. She wanted to cover herself, cover her scars.

She was just a few paces behind Kosh when he slid to a halt and spun around, his scythe cutting through the air towards her. Jezzet had no time to stop. She leapt to her left, trying to avoid the razor sharp blade. The weapon's edge passed by her arm, she felt the air rush past but the blade itself missed. Jez rolled again and came up in a half crouch facing the Arbiter.

Kosh stood facing her, naked as the day he was born with only a single scythe as his protection. Jez crouched, just as naked, holding her

The Heresy Within

glowing sword in one hand. All around them people stared.

"Who are you?" Kosh asked again. "Why are you trying to kill me? You're no Arbiter."

His eyes on her made Jez's skin crawl. *You need to end this before reinforcements arrive, Jez.*

She sprang at him slashing her sword at his face. The Arbiter raised his scythe and the blades sang as they clashed together. He was already moving, trying to get on Jezzet's left side, trying to get on her weak side. Jezzet was already moving too, attacking.

A high slash, a low jab, a leap to the left, feint further left then slash at the right. Each attack was blocked by singing steel. Then the Arbiter attacked. He came on hard and fast, his scythe slashing first one way then the other. Jezzet dodged each time.

Dangerous things scythes. Even when blocked the blade can hit you and up close they're fucking deadly.

Kosh was muttering something as he attacked, the same way Thanquil did.

Blessings! Explains why he's so fast.

And he was fast. Each attack flew at her and each one was followed by another just as quick, just as deadly. Jezzet danced and dodged, ducked and weaved, blocked and fell back, but what she needed to do was attack. She didn't know much about runes yet she knew the magic affecting her sword wouldn't last forever.

The blade of the scythe angled towards her head, she blocked with her sword even as she leapt to her right. The scythe crushed through her defence and passed within an inch of her neck. Jezzet found herself shaking. Again Kosh was moving, trying to get on her left side.

The Arbiter was still talking, still muttering, still saying something. But his wasn't the only voice. There were others, a lot of others. Jez risked a glance and found people all around her, lots of them all standing and staring and talking, and staring. Before she could stop herself she found she was covering her scars with her left arm even while trying to defend against the Arbiter with the sword in her right.

Too many people, too many eyes. She couldn't cover the scars on her back, not even all the ones on her chest, let alone her arms and her legs and they were all staring at her. Her movements had become sluggish, slow. She blocked another attack from the scythe and staggered from the impact. The Arbiter pushed and Jez found herself falling, she landed hard on the cold stone ground and grunted in pain then rolled away just as the scythe cut through the air where her head had been a moment before. She scrambled to her bare feet and backed away. The Arbiter came on smiling.

He smiles like the Sword of the North. Like he knows he's already won.

She still remembered everything that man had said: '*Whores fuck their way out of fights, not Blademasters. We're not chosen, not trained. We're born. Some people are born to be Blademasters, born to be the shades of death and until you let go of that fear you'll never be one of us.*'

Jezzet felt the heat rising in her. She dodged another slash from the scythe. She wasn't sure what made her more angry; that the Sword of the North had said that to her, that she hadn't done anything about it, that he was right, or that she was about to lose her life to the naked man she'd just fucked and murdered.

Jez took her left hand away from her chest and gripped hold of her sword in both hands. The next attack came and she brushed it aside and answered with two lightning-fast slashes of her own. Kosh blocked one and stumbled away from the other, surprise showing in his eyes. Jezzet gave him no time to recover, she pushed the attack, slashing here, jabbing there. Dodging to the side and cutting at the Arbiter, not giving him a moment to collect himself.

Kosh started whispering under his breath again. He dodged away from Jez then back in close with near inhuman speed. The scythe flew towards her face. Jezzet caught the blade on her own, twisted it and pushed. The shock on the Arbiter's face was a beautiful thing to see as he found the flats of both his own scythe and Jezzet's glowing sword pushed up against his naked chest. Jezzet shifted the grip on her sword and spun away. There was a spray of blood and a scream and Kosh's scythe bounced off the stone ground, his hand still attached.

The Arbiter was clutching at the bloody stump of his right arm with his left. Jezzet danced around and thrust her sword up underneath his left armpit. She knew the exact placement of the sword, her old master had made her memorise all the vulnerable locations on a person's body. The blade slid through flesh and for the second time that night the Arbiter's heart was pierced. She gave the blade a twist and then pulled it out in a gush of wet, red blood. Kosh's body slumped to the floor and gave a final twitch.

"My name is Jezzet Vel'urn. Thanquil Darkheart sent me to kill you," she told the corpse, but it was too late.

No sense in talking to a dead man.

Jez looked down at herself, naked and spattered with blood she looked half a demon herself.

Lots of blood, none of it mine though. It's never mine.

All around her people were still watching, still whispering, still staring. She ignored them all.

Let them look, let them see what a shade of death looks like.

Men clad all in white and armed with spears surrounded her. Ten of them. One of them said something but Jezzet didn't hear him, couldn't hear him over the roaring in her ears demanding for more blood. The ten men started to close in around her as one, edging their way forwards with spears lowered.

Jezzet grinned.

They think to take down a shade of death with just ten men? They should have brought an army.

The Black Thorn

Betrim staggered over to the body. He was dripping sweat. It weren't a bad shot, he had to congratulate himself. Head pounding, arm shaking, and a moving target and he still managed to hit it square. Fact was it were a damned good shot.

He put his foot on the Arbiter's back and reached down to pull his axe free. It had bitten deep, severed the spine by the looks of things and Betrim had to wrench to pull the thing out. Drops of blood came free with the axe and the Black Thorn felt them spatter his face.

"Best make sure ta finish ya off," he said to the corpse as he rolled it over to get a in a clean chop at the Arbiter's neck. Betrim couldn't wait to see the look on Thanquil's face as the Black Thorn dropped Kessick's head at his feet.

The face staring back at him was young, smooth-skinned with a dusting of hair on the top lip. Almost reminded Betrim of Green if truth be told. One thing was for sure though, the body was not Kessick. The Black Thorn had killed the wrong Arbiter.

A hand grabbed Betrim by the shoulder and wrenched him to his feet, a moment later a fist connected with his face turning his vision a bright, blinding white. He hit the floor still blind and scrambled away, moaning with the pain. He pushed himself to his feet just as the light began to dim and his vision returned. A man stood over the body of the dead boy, staring at Betrim with cold, icy eyes.

"Kessss.... aarrgh." Betrim near screamed at the pain in his face. Didn't take much of a feel with his hand to realise his jaw was broken. Seemed Kessick had one hell of a punch to him. Still, the Black Thorn had suffered far worse and come out kicking. It wasn't like a broken jaw could make him any less pretty, might be it even improved his looks.

Kessick just stood there, watching Betrim. No Arbiter coat, seemed he'd given it to the dead boy and had no intention of taking it back. The Black Thorn tightened his grip on his axe and made ready to attack. Kessick held no weapons but an Arbiter was never easy prey, he might have any number of magical tricks hidden away.

The Heresy Within

"I've had a feeling of late I was being followed. Never thought it would turn out to be the Black Thorn," Kessick said in a cool, emotionless voice.

Betrim might have grinned but he already knew how much that would hurt with a broken jaw. "'Ookin' 'a 'ake it 'even," he managed with a lot of wincing.

The Black Thorn was a good foot taller than Kessick. He had the reach and the weight advantage and was armed. He started forwards.

"I don't think I'm a random target," Kessick said, still standing over the body of the dead boy. "Someone sent you. Was it Arbiter Darkheart?"

That made Betrim pause. He might have asked a question himself but his jaw didn't feel up to it.

"Yes. I think it was. I've heard he's back. He was the one that killed H'ost wasn't he? And the woman, the one who told me H'ost was dead, also one of his?"

The Black Thorn didn't like how much this Arbiter seemed to know. He loosened his grip on his axe a little and charged.

Kessick didn't move. He waited while Betrim charged him, waited as the axe fell towards his skull. At the last moment the Arbiter moved with inhuman speed, grabbing hold of the Black Thorn's wrist and twisting with such force that Betrim roared in pain despite the broken jaw. The axe clattered to the floor and Betrim received a heavy push in the back that sent him stumbling over the dead body on the floor.

"I wasn't finished, Black Thorn," Kessick said in a reproachful tone. "So you and the woman are working for Arbiter Darkheart. Are there any more or is it just the three of you?"

Betrim made no move, nor did he answer, just stared at the Arbiter in mute anger.

"Yes. Just the three of you. Not the most dangerous force ever assembled. So if you're here to kill me... He sent the woman to kill Kosh, didn't he? You do know about Kosh? Yes. I think you do."

It didn't make sense to Betrim. He wasn't answering any of Kessick's questions but the man seemed to know the truth anyway. His axe was on the floor at the Arbiter's feet. He drew the dagger, the blade Thanquil had given him as payment, '*enchanted*' he said. Might be that was just what was needed to kill the bastard.

"So that would mean Arbiter Darkheart himself has gone to confront Inquisitor Heron," Kessick concluded. "I wonder if she'll kill him or if he'll join us."

Betrim whipped his left hand out and a throwing knife flew at Kessick. The Arbiter made no move to dodge and the knife buried itself in his left leg. The Black Thorn was only a second behind the knife, his enchanted dagger whipped at Kessick three times. The first Kessick ducked, the second cut a scratch into his arm, but the third the Arbiter caught.

Kessick had hold of Betrim's right hand, the dagger tip just inches from the Arbiter's heart. The Black Thorn punched at the man's face with his three fingered left hand but Kessick didn't even flinch. Betrim thrust his head towards the man face. A hand shot up and grabbed the Black Thorn by the throat. Squeezing, choking him.

Arbiter Kessick twisted Betrim's right hand around until the dagger was between them. The bastard was so damned strong the Black Thorn couldn't move, couldn't breathe.

"That's a very nice dagger," Kessick said, his voice as flat and cold as his eyes. Then his hand was gone from Betrim's throat and the blade was gone from Betrim's hand. The Black Thorn felt the dagger go in and out, in and out, in and out, in...

Kessick let go and Betrim stumbled backwards, tripped over the body at his feet and hit the floor hard, his head cracked against the stone and his vision went white again. It cleared into a fuzzy haze and Thorn looked at his chest. Blood was seeping into his leathers, the dagger stood up, proud and silver, but it didn't hurt. Fact was he didn't feel much, just... numb.

Thorn coughed and felt blood on his face. He was staring at the sky, at the stars, at the moon, at the endless black above him. Then Kessick was there, standing over him, looking down at him in the same way he had looked at the boy, the boy he'd killed... or had Betrim killed him. It was getting hard to remember.

The Black Thorn coughed again and tried to move, tried to get away from the Arbiter but his limbs were so heavy, they just twitched at his commands.

"Fuck." Betrim tried to say but all that came out was a cough and more blood.

"You are an impressive man, Black Thorn. To still be clinging to life after that. Most would just die, give up, but not you. You like living, don't you? Yes. Yes, you do. Pity really. I'm wondering, though, just how much pain will it take before the Black Thorn does give up?"

The last thing Betrim saw was Kessick's fingers reaching into his eye socket.

The Arbiter

On the ship, during the voyage to Sarth, Jezzet had beaten the hell out of Thanquil every day with a blunted sword and every day he had gone to bed wondering if it was an exercise in futility. Now, though, he was glad and more than glad that he'd gone through the ordeal. Thanquil was certain Inquisitor Heron would have cut him in two more than once already if Jez hadn't trained him.

He blocked a savage downward cut, stepped back and then stepped forwards again, closing the distance between himself and the Inquisitor. Their blades met with a hiss of steel on steel and a shower of sparks. Two enchanted swords each driven by the augmented strength of a blessing seemed to make for an impressive display. Thanquil just wished he wasn't the one fighting so he could have enjoyed the spectacle.

The Inquisitor wrenched both swords to the side then slapped Thanquil in the face. Something stuck to his cheek. A charm. Thanquil found he couldn't remember the words to any of the blessings. He tore the charm away with a stinging scrape but too late the words came back to him. Inquisitor Heron was already upon him, her speed inhuman, her strength overpowering. He blocked as best he could but her blows sent him reeling first one way then the other. He started whispering the blessings again and they were back on level footing. Although Thanquil's actual footing appeared to be in a flowerbed full of red and white roses.

Inquisitor Heron whispered something to her sword and then drove the point into the earth below their feet. Thanquil readied himself for the effect. Magic could do many things. Thanquil had seen it make the earth shake, he had forced the sky to open up and rain, he'd seen apparitions and illusions, and he'd seen fire burst into an inferno from nothing. What he'd never seen was plants bending to a person's will.

Something thin and wiry crawled up his ankle and held fast, sharp points poking into his skin. The flowers beneath him had coiled their way around his legs, holding him. He tried to free himself but the plants seemed unusually strong and then the Inquisitor was there and her sword was flying towards him.

The Heresy Within

Thanquil barely had time to think. He reversed his own sword and thrust it downwards towards his right leg. Hot, wet pain sprang forth on his ankle, but he was free. He stepped into the Inquisitor's attack with his free leg, twisting his other ankle. Her sword skimmed his left side, opening a shallow wound near his ribs and he was inside her guard. A crazy thought sprang into Thanquil's mind, '*what would the Black Thorn do? He would butt the woman with his head*' and so that's what Thanquil did.

Inquisitor Heron staggered backwards with a scream of pain and put a hand to her face, blood dripped between her fingers onto the earth below. Blood dipped from her blade as well and that was Thanquil's. He put a hand to his side where her sword had scored him, it hurt like the Hells, but it wasn't too serious, at least not for now. His ankle, however, was more serious. It screamed as he tried to put weight on it and Thanquil found himself wishing he knew more about medicinal charms.

He cut away the remaining plants restraining him and limped towards the Inquisitor. She was staring at the blood in her hand. As she looked up at Thanquil he could see her nose was bent, broken, her small mouth and delicate, pointed chin were stained red, her eyes held all the fury of a raging fire. If Thanquil hadn't been trying to kill her he would have liked very much to run away from those eyes.

The Inquisitor dug a hand into a pocket of her coat and pulled out a small chip of wood. She snapped it between thumb and fingers and threw the two pieces of wood at Thanquil. He crouched down ready to spring into action and waited. Nothing happened. Slowly he shifted his weight from his bad ankle to his good one, breathing heavily from the tension. Sucking air into his lungs and out like a bellows.

Inquisitor Heron pointed her black, serrated sword at Thanquil and he wheezed in a breath, waiting for the rune to take effect. The way the light caught her sword made it look as if the colouring on the surface of the metal was shifting, moving. A swirling darkness within the blade. She charged.

Thanquil sucked in another breath, panicking. There was no air. He was suffocating out in the open. He dropped to one knee, gasping. His limbs felt so heavy, so slow, almost like the whole world was pressing in around him, on top of him, crushing him.

The Inquisitor's first swing sent Thanquil's sword spinning out of his hand into the darkness of the night, her second almost took off his left arm, but he managed to stumble backwards just in time, not fast enough to stop a new cut opening. Her third attack would have skewered him yet Thanquil stepped around it and close to her again. He put both hands on her chest and with his last breath whispered a blessing of strength and pushed. The Inquisitor flew away from him into the unnatural darkness waiting behind. Thanquil stumbled backwards, looking for his sword. There in the distance he saw a glint of light on metal and crawled towards it, when he'd fallen to his hands and knees, he wasn't sure.

All of a sudden he could breathe again. Cool, crisp air rushed into his lungs making him cough and sputter but he was glad of it. Life flooded back into his limbs. The world no longer closed in around him, crushing him. He looked back at the rune on the earth behind him, powerful magic and far beyond his own capabilities. He had the sinking feeling he was over-matched in this fight. Still he crawled over to his sword and stood, blade in hand, ready to face the Inquisitor's next attack.

She was nowhere to be seen. Darkness closed in thick around the Arbiter and he glanced first one way then the other yet there was no sign of the Inquisitor. He looked up to see thick black-grey clouds had gathered, arraying themselves above to shut out all light. Even the hanging lanterns only seemed to illuminate small patches of the darkness.

"I'm disappointed, Thanquil." The voice echoed from behind him. Thanquil spun around and squinted into the darkness. He whispered a blessing of sight and there she was, no more than twenty paces away, staring at him as if the darkness was as bright as a summer's day. A sad smile graced her face making her look like a ghoul with the crimson mask of blood running from her nose.

"They told me you excelled with runes and charms and blessings, but here you are falling for child's tricks and relying on brute force." Her voice floated out of the darkness at him.

Thanquil might have laughed at her calling that rune a child's trick. He hadn't even known it was possible to do such a thing. He wasn't even sure what it had done, but he'd be damned if he was falling for it a second time.

He was preparing for an attack of his own when he noticed the chip out of his sword. An enchanted blade with a charm that should mean the edge never dulled, the blade would never break. But there it was, a small chip of metal missing.

"What in Volmar's name is your sword made from?" Thanquil called out.

Inquisitor Heron laughed a warm, merry sound that might have made Thanquil smile had the two of them not been trying to kill each other. "You've noticed that have you?"

A knife flew out of the darkness towards Thanquil. He raised his sword to deflect it away and broke the paper rune wrapped around the knife. Both his sword and his entire right arm burst into flame.

With a yell Thanquil dropped his sword and fell backwards. He started rolling on the ground, trying to put the out flames but succeeded only in lighting more of his coat on fire. He struggled out of the burning leather and scrambled away.

His right hand was a mass of pain, red-black skin and blood and blisters, so Thanquil scooped up his sword in his left and stood, trying to find the Inquisitor in the darkness. He glanced back at his coat once, still burning away. All his carefully prepared charms and runes were in the pockets of that coat. All of his runes!

He lurched into a sprint, not caring where he ran to as long as it was away from the coat.

BOOM!

The world turned upside down and inside out as the explosive runes inside the coat activated all at once. Thanquil found himself rolling to a stop on the grassy earth, his eyes wet with tears from the pain in his hand. Smoke and dust filled the air. Bits of earth and mud rained down from above and his ears were a cacophony of ringing. The Arbiter tried pushing himself to his feet but his left leg collapsed under him, a small circle of metal embedded in the flesh of his calf. It took him a moment to realise it was one of the buttons from his coat. He pushed himself to his feet again, this time putting most of his weight on his right leg and looked around for the Inquisitor.

Where he had run from was now a giant, burning crater in the earth, bright from the flames. Not ten paces from the crater Thanquil saw the Inquisitor. She was limping towards him with eyes full of fury. The left side of her face was blackened and bloody. Her hair was all but gone, burned away by the explosion. Her left ear was missing, nothing more than a bloody, burnt stump of flesh. Blood ran down her left arm and dripped onto the earth, soaking into the soil. She may have been caught in the blast, but Thanquil could tell she was far from finished and the look in her eyes told him she was done playing with him.

Thanquil raised his sword, ready to fight. The blade was spotted black from where the fire had engulfed it and it looked near as battered as he did. His left leg still couldn't support his weight but he couldn't risk ripping the button out.

The Inquisitor's first attack seemed to jar Thanquil down to his very bones and he fought to stay upright while blocking the next strike. Left to right, right to left, and over again. With every swing of the sword the Inquisitor seemed to be getting stronger despite her left arm hanging limp by her side. Thanquil stepped backwards onto his bad leg and screamed in pain just the Inquisitor's sword shattered his own.

He hit the ground, dropped the useless shard of metal that had been his sword, and started scrambling backwards, still cradling his right arm against his chest. Inquisitor Heron advanced on him, her once-beautiful face a charred, bloody ruin. Yet there was no pain in her eyes, only anger.

"It's over, Arbiter Darkheart," she slurred, the burnt side of her mouth twisting into a grimace.

Thanquil had no choice, he snapped the chip of wood he kept hidden, sown into his trousers. The same rune he had stolen from the God-Emperor of Sarth half a year ago. It was as likely to kill him as it was her, but at least neither of them would die alone. He could already feel the power building around him. Arbiter Darkheart looked up at Inquisitor Heron and smiled.

"Mine is the Judgement of the Righteous, Inquisitor."

Thanquil was rewarded with her eyes going wide with fear just as the sky opened up and the light of judgement bathed him and everything around him in its cleansing fire.

The light was so bright it blinded Thanquil even with his eyes closed. The fire so hot he could feel his flesh searing, burning, melting from his bones. Three voices screamed in pain out into the light: his, hers, and another; a voice with no traces of humanity. Thanquil could no longer tell if he was standing or lying down. Up and down no longer mattered, all was light and fire and pain as the Judgement of the Righteous burned away all the sins, all the heresy from his soul.

Then it was over. The light was gone, the fire was gone. But the pain remained, his flesh was still burning. Thanquil pried his eyes open and let the bright spots of colour clear. He was kneeling on the earth, his arms hanging limp by his sides, and his head slumped down against his chest. He could see the skin on his arms, his right hand was a blackened, bloody mess but his left was fine, it wasn't burnt at all despite the feeling still coursing through his flesh.

He was so tired he couldn't move. Truth was Thanquil was certain he'd have passed out if it hadn't been for the sleepless charm still sealed to his left arm. He was so tired he couldn't even take pleasure in his survival. Part of him wanted to giggle, part of him wanted to cry, all of him wanted to sleep.

Someone laughed. A woman's voice, hoarse and raw and cackling, a horrible sound that sent a wave of despair through Thanquil. She shouldn't have been able to survive. He picked his head off his chest. Not two metres away Inquisitor Heron knelt opposite him, her entire left side still a bloody, burnt mess. Her right arm raised into the sky, her sword held above her, black and smoking. She threw her head back and laughed into the night sky.

"The sword..." she laughed. "MY sword!"

The merchant had said accurate up to ten paces, Thanquil remembered. "How about point blank?" he asked of no one just as Inquisitor Heron's head rolled forward to look at him.

BANG!

Thanquil never saw the result of the shot. He saw Inquisitor Heron fall backwards, or maybe it was just him falling backwards. He knew he hit the floor and he knew he couldn't summon the energy to move anymore and he knew he should be unconscious, but instead he just lay there, eyes closed, his mind awake but not aware.

At some point he heard voices, He wasn't sure when. It might have been a few minutes, a few hours, days... He knew there were a lot of them, some hurried and frantic, others slow and thoughtful. One sounded like it might belong to the Grand Inquisitor but he couldn't be certain.

"What do we do with him?" a voice asked.

"Is he still alive?"

"I think so... yes."

"Finish him off. It's what she'd have wanted."

"No."

"Sir?"

"Take him back to the Inquisition, to the infirmary. He will be tried for his crimes."

"Sir."

Thanquil thought he felt arms on him. He had the strange sense of moving, or being dragged or carried, but his mind refused to process any of it.

"There's something on his arm."

"What?"

"I don't know. I'm not one of them."

"Take it off."

"But what if it..."

The Arbiter

Four guards escorted him from his cell to the council chambers. It would have seemed excessive even had Thanquil been uninjured, unfettered, and armed. As it was, he had no doubt a single novice could take him down right now. Still, he supposed it helped them all to feel safer.

He shuffled along, little more than a crawl with his hands and feet chained together giving him a permanent stoop while standing. The guards around him were silent and unyielding, setting a slow pace and he was glad of that. Any faster and they'd have had to carry Thanquil to the council chambers.

At least they were doing it discretely. They could just have paraded him across the Inquisition compound for all to see. He had no doubt every Arbiter in Sarth would have come to see the traitor.

Four days, they told him. Four days he'd been unconscious. The medic, a grumpy old Arbiter with too much skin to his face and a permanent scowl, told Thanquil he was starting to doubt if he'd ever wake up. That hadn't stopped them chaining him to the bed though. The old man had done his best to heal Thanquil's arm, but confided there was only so much could be done with a burn like that.

"It'll heal, most likely, given time. Assuming you have any. Doubt you'll ever have full movement again though. Burns tend to scar," the old Arbiter croaked at him.

His right arm was swathed with bandages up to the elbow and the bandages had been soaked in some sort of oil that made them feel greasy to the touch. Still the hand hurt like every one of the Hells and Thanquil could feel the skin red and raw underneath whenever he tried to move a finger. It also didn't help that the guards insisted on chaining both his hands despite the injury. The metal cuff rubbed against his wrist setting it on fire all over again. The guards would hear none of it though, so he suffered in silence.

Thanquil thought of Jezzet and Thorn. Mainly of Jezzet. No one had brought him any news on the status of Kessick or Kosh so he had no idea whether the others had succeeded with their targets, no idea whether the others had even survived. He chose to believe they had. They would have met at the inn after the job was done, waited for Thanquil for a couple of days, realised he wasn't coming, and then they would have fled. Thorn would no doubt run back to the Untamed Wilds and Jezzet... Jezzet would go with him. If they were lucky they would already be on a ship sailing back to Chade. At least they wouldn't have to share in Thanquil's execution.

The walk seemed longer than every time before. It might have been because of the crawling pace, or maybe because of the dread anticipation, Thanquil couldn't tell. When the doors to the council chambers loomed up in front of him, coming out of the darkness like the gates to a Hell, he stumbled and very nearly fell; he would have if it weren't for one of the guards behind him catching his arm and helping him upright.

Thanquil turned to thank the Arbiter for the help, but the look on the man's face convinced him not to. There was hatred there and he had little doubt as to why. Inquisitor Heron had been well-loved among the Inquisition and Thanquil had left her an almost unidentifiable corpse. The fact that she was the heretic who was trying to bring down the entire Inquisition was not yet widely accepted, except by Thanquil himself.

Two more Arbiters stood guard this side of the door. They watched the prisoner and his escort with cold, hard eyes. Seems they were taking no chances of Thanquil escaping. No doubt there would be more guards inside the chambers along with the remaining eleven Inquisitors. Rarely had anyone ever commanded such a powerful audience.

The doors opened with an ominous boom and the two guards stood aside to let Thanquil and his escort through. Both men were armed with short swords on their hips and both men kept their hands on the hilts as he shuffled past.

"Do I really look so dangerous?" Thanquil said. He rattled his chains for effect and winced as fresh searing pain shot through his burned arm.

One of the guards, the taller one with a split lip, grinned at him. "Inside, heretic. Your judgement awaits."

Thanquil thought of a reply but decided instead to keep silent. No sense in making matters any worse, not that he was sure they could get any worse. Inside the council chambers all was still and silent. None of the Inquisitors had gathered yet, no doubt they would make him wait a while.

"Any chance I could get these chains off?" Thanquil asked his guard as they stopped him in the centre of the chamber.

"Sorry, Thanquil," the flat-nosed guard said with a shake of his head.

"Don't talk to him, Gull. He's a Darkheart!"

Thanquil chuckled. "Don't worry, it's not contagious."

The guard who had warned Gull looked about ready to backhand Thanquil, but the side door opened and the Inquisitors started to file in. Eleven of them where there should have been twelve.

Grand Inquisitor Vance strode in at the head of the column, his face as hard and stern as always. Even rock would yield before the Grand Inquisitor's stare. Then came Inquisitor Downe, the last woman on the council for now. Her face was flat and her eyes beady. Inquisitors Vert, Khanos, and Westrus entered, conversing with each other in quiet voices. None of the three even glanced towards Thanquil. Inquisitors Dale, Jeyne, Fel'en, and Aurelus took a different approach, each staring at him like it was going out of fashion. Last came Inquisitors Ellswin and Markus. They both glanced at Thanquil and dismissed his presence as if the whole reason they were there was not to pass judgement on him.

After all eleven Inquisitors had entered, another man stepped through the door. Arbiter Hironous Vance seemed to glide through the portal, closing the door afterwards. He stopped behind the twelfth chair, not sitting in it but standing, waiting. He looked like a younger, softer version of his father, with a round face where the Grand Inquisitor's was all hard angles. It might have seemed strange once for an Arbiter to be included in this gathering, but Thanquil had no doubt Arbiter Hironous Vance would soon be Inquisitor Hironous Vance.

There was a heavy silence once all the Inquisitors were seated. It was almost as if none of them wanted to be the first to speak so they just stared at Thanquil, judging him with silent eyes. The way the lanterns in the room were angled meant Thanquil could barely see his betters, but they could see him clear as day.

He rattled his chains a little. "Could I get these taken off? They've been chafing the burn a bit." Silence. "You can't be scared of me, not all eleven of you." Thanquil bit his tongue to stop himself from saying more. Every time in this room he had to find some way to mock those sat in judgement of him.

"Take them off, Arbiter Gull," boomed the Grand Inquisitor's voice.

A few moments later and he was free. Thanquil stretched out his shoulders and marvelled at the stiffness he felt. He looked down at his right hand to see blood showing through the bandage where the cuffs had been. The old Arbiter in charge of the infirmary was not going to be pleased... assuming Thanquil walked out of this chamber alive.

"Only six months since you were last in front of us, Thanquil Darkheart." The voice was heavy and brutish, Inquisitor Aurelus. The fact that he missed off the title of Arbiter was not a good sign.

"A lot has happened in those six months it would seem, Inquisitor," Thanquil responded.

"You killed Inquisitor Heron."

"She had it coming."

"Enough." The Grand Inquisitor didn't shout. His voice carried to all corners of the council chambers and could have silenced the ocean such was the command in it. "Arbiter Darkheart, you are here to account for your actions, which amount to heresy. You will tell us all that has happened and you will be judged accordingly. Be warned, Arbiter, if you lie it will mean your death."

Thanquil nodded and launched into recounting everything that had happened. He started his tale in Chade, leaving out all mention of the Emperor or his orders. He told them of his interrogation of the woman in the gaol and that his tests to pertain what she was had been inconclusive. He told them of his freeing of Jezzet Vel'urn and thus binding her to his service. He told them about how the woman in gaol had escaped before the Chade council allowed him to pass judgement and how he went to Lord Xho's mansion in the hopes of obtaining more information from the council members only to find two of them dead. He told them of his running into the Black Thorn and how Thorn had given him a lead of the escaped woman being connected to H'ost.

He told them of his journey through the Wilds and how he had enlisted the Black Thorn's help with a promise of pardon. He left out all mention of Thorn's crew, deeming that it could only serve to confuse matters. Thanquil told the Inquisitors of his arrival in Hostown, his meeting with H'ost, and everything the man had confessed. His involvement with an Arbiter named Kessick, the fact that he was working for a female Inquisitor, that they were putting demons from the void into the bodies of those with the potential. He also told the Inquisitors of H'ost's summoning of the shades and how they had set to the destruction of Hostown. Then Thanquil told them of his judging of H'ost and his execution. He left out the bit about killing the blooded lord with a spoon.

He told the Inquisitors of his return to Sarth, how he kept Jezzet in his service with the promise of gold. He left out the extent of their relationship. She was less likely to be hunted down for being paid to work for a heretic than if they knew she was sleeping with one.

Thanquil told them how he had followed Kessick and determined the Inquisitor was Selice Heron and that Arbiter Kosh had also been in league with her. He told them about how he had planned to ambush all three of them at once, of how he sent the Black Thorn after Kessick, Jezzet after Kosh, and how he himself had gone after Inquisitor Heron. Then he told them of what the Inquisitor had said to him, how she had claimed the Inquisition was stagnant and her intent was to destroy it from the inside.

Finally, when the council of Inquisitors asked him if he had any proof, he told them what little he knew of Inquisitor Selice Heron's contract with the demons of the void. The council members looked less than pleased to hear that the contract was hidden away where no one could ever get to it.

By the end of his telling Thanquil had lost count of how many lies he'd told. Most hadn't been blatant untruths but more lies of omission told to protect the others involved, but all were enough to see him killed should the council have spotted them. He waited on fraying nerves while the Inquisitors chewed over his story in their heads, some conversing with their fellows. His burnt arm hurt and itched at the same time and

Thanquil fought the urge to scratch at it.

The cold scrutiny seemed to stretch on forever and after a while it was too much for Thanquil to bear.

"Could you tell me, what happened to Kosh and Kessick? What happened to those I sent after them?" he asked the Inquisitors and was ignored save for a scathing glare from the Grand Inquisitor himself.

More silence followed complete with more itching and a slight shaking of his legs that convinced Thanquil he was far from recovered.

"It is... convenient that this contract you speak of is unavailable for scrutiny," Inquisitor Jeyne said in a voice like silk dipped in honey.

"I'd call it inconvenient myself," Thanquil responded.

"But there is no proof, one way or the other."

"Seeing as how you're likely to err on the side of judging me a heretic... Inconvenient. Ask me if I'm telling the truth. Use your compulsion, Inquisitor."

The Grand Inquisitor leaned forward, piercing Thanquil with eyes as blue as the sea and twice as deep. "I think we all know there are ways around the compulsion, Arbiter Darkheart."

Thanquil found it hard to meet the Grand Inquisitor's gaze but he held it all the same. "I brought down and survived the Judgement of the Righteous..."

"You stole a rune from the God-Emperor's personal collection," Inquisitor Khanos said in a dangerous tone. "And, by your own account, Inquisitor Heron also survived the Judgement. Not conclusive proof either way."

Thanquil opened his mouth to say more but realised he was out of ideas. He had no way to prove his innocence and they had no way to prove his guilt. On those grounds they would judge him and they would judge him harshly.

"You say this contract is held by the demons in the void," Arbiter Vance said from behind the twelfth chair.

"Quiet, Arbiter Vance. You are here to observe only," Inquisitor Vert's voice rang with the accent of the Five Kingdoms.

"Let the Arbiter finish, Inquisitor Vert." This from Inquisitor Downe.

The Heresy Within

All eyes turned to the Grand Inquisitor. The man gave his son only the barest of nods and so Arbiter Vance continued.

"According to you, Inquisitor Heron ordered the demons not to release the contract to anyone save herself and so the creatures cannot obey us without disobeying her. But there may be one who can overturn that order. The demons may be sworn to obey the Inquisition, but more than us, they are sworn to obey Volmar." A murmur of voices echoed through the chambers, Arbiter Vance spoke over them all. "The God-Emperor can command the demons to release the contract. Assuming there is one, that is."

It was so perfect Thanquil almost laughed. The Inquisition had been the ones to find Emperor Francis, had been the ones to decree that he was Volmar reborn. If they chose not to go through with Arbiter Vance's suggestion here they may as well admit that the Emperor was not who they claimed him to be. Then, if the demons did obey the God-Emperor's order it was proof he was Volmar, if they refused, it was proof he was not. Thanquil had asked the Emperor whether he was Volmar reborn and the man had avoided the question, but now... now Thanquil would find out for certain just before he died.

Grand Inquisitor Vance looked over to the two Arbiters standing guard by the entrance and spoke, his voice echoing around the room. "Bring the Emperor here at once."

It said something about Grand Inquisitor Vance's authority that he could order the immediate presence of the Emperor of Sarth and the man would obey. Thanquil found himself standing under the scrutiny of the Inquisitors for just less than an hour before Emperor Francis strode through the doors in a white, silken suit, looking like a titan as he towered over everyone else around him. The man was close to eight feet tall and was as wide as a bear yet as handsome and resplendent as the sun. Thanquil felt short and drab and ugly in comparison as the Emperor finished his entrance just a few strides away. Two servants attended the Emperor, one Thanquil recognised, though the thin dusting of hair on his top lip had since bloomed into a small blonde ferret.

"Inquisitors," the God-Emperor said with a slight bow of his head, "Arbiter Vance. How may I be of service in this judgement?" The man seemed to radiate power, Thanquil felt stronger just by being close to him.

It was the Grand Inquisitor who answered. "Arbiter Darkheart stands accused of heresy and of the murder of an Inquisitor. He claims there is proof that Inquisitor Heron was the heretic, that he was protecting the Inquisition. That proof, however, is secreted away in the void, hidden by the demons that Volmar bound to our service. If this is true, only you can order the release of the contract, Emperor Francis."

The God-Emperor nodded along to the Grand Inquisitor's words and then smiled. "That may not be necessary, Inquisitors."

Thanquil felt his heart lurch to a stop, he had lied to protect the Emperor. Even should the man reveal that Thanquil had been acting on his orders it would still condemn him.

The God-Emperor waved forwards his servant with the bushy top lip who laid the bundle he was carrying on the cold stone floor.

"I present to you all the sword of Inquisitor Heron. I had it taken from her estate on the night of her... death. Inquisitor Vance, I believe you may be the only one who can safely inspect the sword."

The Grand Inquisitor's eyes narrowed to two small slits in his face ashe stood and descended from the dais. He looked down at the bundle of cloth on the floor and then up towards the Emperor.

"I assure you, Inquisitor Vance. You alone can handle the sword unharmed."

The Grand Inquisitor knelt and unwrapped the cloth to reveal a sword. It was Inquisitor Heron's for sure. Some of Thanquil's wounds began to ache at the mere sight of the serrated monstrosity.

Slowly, Grand Inquisitor Vance reached out a hand and touched the hilt of the sword. His eyes went wide and his jaw clenched shut. Then he took his hand away and wrapped the blade back in the cloth.

"It is Myorzo, the demon blade," he said.

The council chambers erupted into formless noise, each Inquisitor trying to be heard over the others, each demanding answers from the Grand Inquisitor and from the God-Emperor.

The story of the demon blade was well-known. It dated from before the time of the Inquisition, from the time when Volmar had first walked

The Heresy Within

in the world. As the tale went, Volmar had a brother, Arn. Arn was the first to seek to bind the demons of the void. He summoned a shade to attempt to study it, to learn its weaknesses. But the creature he summoned was too powerful to contain. So the younger brother went to the older and Volmar, being the benevolent hero he was in all the stories of old, agreed to help.

Volmar forged a blade of the blackest metal and enchanted it with old, powerful charms that were since lost to the world. The God and the demon from the void fought for one-hundred days and one-hundred nights before Volmar pierced the creature's heart with the blade. The demon's essence was sucked into the blade and its body faded back into the void. Volmar named the sword Myorzo, the demon blade, and hid it somewhere it was said it could never be found.

Some historians claimed that Volmar never had a brother, that it was the God himself who made the mistake of summoning a creature too powerful to control. To Thanquil's knowledge such historians were usually tried for heresy soon after. Either way, it looked like Volmar's hiding place for the demon blade had not been as secure as he might have wished.

The Grand Inquisitor looked a grim picture standing tall and silent in the centre of a maelstrom of noise. Some Inquisitors shouted, others looked almost panicked. The Grand Inquisitor himself was locked in a staring contest with the God-Emperor of Sarth. Only one man in the world could win such a contest against a living God and the Grand Inquisitor proved it was him. Emperor Francis was the first to look away.

"Enough!" Grand Inquisitor Vance didn't shout to be heard over the cacophony, he didn't need to. As if the other Inquisitors had sensed his demand, they all fell silent.

"Guards. Take Arbiter Darkheart back to his cell. Have his wounds looked at, it appears he is bleeding."

Thanquil looked down at his hand. The bandage was beginning to look more red than white. The guards moved forward with cuffs and chains in hand.

"He won't be needing those anymore." This came from the God-Emperor. The guards looked to the Grand Inquisitor and the orders were confirmed with only the barest of nods.

    The silence held while Thanquil was escorted from the chambers. Once on the outside he strained his ears to hear what was said, but the door boomed shut and blocked out all other noise. The guards led him back to his cell in silence.

THE BLADEMASTER

Jezzet woke still huddled under the cloak that was little more than a large sheet of wool, still aching from sleeping sat upright in the cold, still surrounded by cold stone and cold, iron bars. The gaols in Sarth were little better than those in Chade, they supplied a bed for the prisoners but Jez didn't trust it.

Too easy to get comfortable on a bed. Less likely to wake when they come for me.

In the two weeks she had been a prisoner here others had come and gone. Some were little more than drunkards sleeping off a belly full and a bar fight, others were true criminals on their way to the gallows, all of them were men and all of them leered at her with hungry eyes. One had even tried to reach between the bars and steal her cloak to get a better look. She had broken his wrist with a practised twist.

Of course after that I had to put up with his crying and spitting insults for two days.

The guards brought her food twice a day though it wasn't up to much, sloppy, cold porridge in the mornings and hard, stale bread in the evenings with a jug of water a day. Poor food was better than no food though. They could just have let her starve to death. She'd had no visitors, no word of the outside world, no word of Thanquil or of Thorn. They had taken her sword from her too and with no clothing to speak of she had nowhere to hide a knife.

A Blademaster without a blade... can still break a man's wrist.

At first she'd thought about trying to escape. If she could pick the lock she could make a break for it. But security in Sarth was not near as lax as in Chade. There were guards outside the gaol cells at all times. Even if she did make it out, without clothing she would draw attention to herself and without a sword she couldn't fight her way free. Instead of thinking of escape, she filled her days with imagining why she was still languishing in a cell, why they hadn't executed her yet.

It must be because you killed an Arbiter, Jez. The guards are waiting for the Inquisition to deal with you... just the bloody witch hunters seem to be taking their sweet time about it.

Almost, she wished she had fought her way free back when she had killed Kosh. Ten men they had been, armed with spears. She could have taken them. She had known it then. They had known it then. Jezzet had been on the verge of attacking when what she thought was better judgement had won out. She surrendered her sword and allowed them to take her prisoner. That was when she had gained her cloak. The guards decided it was better than marching a naked woman through the streets of Sarth. Still, they hadn't bothered to bring her any real clothing, so naked she remained.

Truth was Jezzet Vel'urn was starting to wish she hadn't come to Sarth at all. In the Wilds she was free from the pressure of Constance hunting her and yet she chose to follow the Arbiter to Sarth on his foolish crusade to save the Inquisition.

She heard the key in the door and the guard Captain's voice, a fair man that one but not a nice man. Jezzet had no wish to see the new prisoner so she huddled deeper into her corner, pulled the cloak around her, and closed her eyes, pretending to sleep. Her right hand itched towards where her sword should be.

A Blademaster without a blade... Truth was the lack of sword made her feel far more naked than the lack of clothing.

"In there," said the guard Captain in his thick, brusque voice.

"You can go. I'll fetch you when I'm done." Jezzet knew that voice.

She heard the Captain grumble and move away. Then she opened her eyes to find Arbiter Thanquil Darkheart leaning on the bars to her cell with a faint smile on his face.

"This seems a familiar sight," the Arbiter teased.

Jezzet found herself grinning. "Does it?" She stood up and let her cloak fall to the floor then approached the bars.

"You look..." Thanquil started to say.

"Step inside. You can do more than just look."

Thanquil gripped hold of the bars with his left hand and his smile faded. "Would that I could." Jezzet noticed his right arm was bandaged and hung in a sling. His coat hung loose across his shoulders. A new coat, she noticed, it didn't have all the stains and tears of his old coat.

"Are you alright?" she asked him.

"Me... oh... the arm. I'm fine. Just the usual really, set myself on fire, blew myself up." Jez couldn't tell if he was joking or not. "What about... you're naked."

"Just noticed that, did you?"

"Why..."

Because I fucked your friend the heretic before killing him.

Jezzet shrugged. If Thanquil was here he had heard the conditions of her capture from the guards, she would let him draw his own conclusions.

"The guards... they didn't..."

"Rape me?" Jezzet laughed. "Two of them tried. After I broke the ugly one's nose the Captain came in to see what all the noise was. He had both of them whipped for the attempt and even apologised to me. Mark of a civilised society, I reckon, guards apologising to the prisoners."

"Rape is treated severely here in Sarth."

"Aye, so I hear. He didn't think giving me some clothing might help the matter though," Jezzet said with a grin. The Arbiter hadn't stopped staring at her body since he walked in.

"Mhmm. Oh, sorry." He shrugged out his coat and passed it through the bars with his left hand.

"Thank you," Jezzet said as she slipped her arms through the coat and pulled it close. It was warm and more comfortable than she'd have guessed and only a little bit on the large side. "Did you deal with the Inquisitor?"

Thanquil nodded. "Inquisitor Heron is dead and I'm only a little worse for wear. The Inquisition kept me in a cell for two weeks but the evidence they found against her was... overwhelming. They were forced to let me go."

"Just like that?"

Thanquil smiled. "Oh no, they couldn't let me go without punishment. What I did was right but apparently the way I did it was wrong. Though no one seems to be able to agree on how I should have done it."

"Punishment?" Jezzet was almost afraid to ask.

"The council have decreed that I shall never be able to attain the rank of Inquisitor," the Arbiter laughed.

"Did you want to be one? An Inquisitor?"

He shook his head. "My name precluded me from joining that select group long ago. They would never allow an Inquisitor Darkheart."

"Oh." Jezzet didn't understand. "What about Thorn?"

Thanquil shrugged. "No sign of the Black Thorn, or of Arbiter Kessick, was found. I assume he went through with his promise to leave after killing the Arbiter."

Jezzet nodded. The Black Thorn would never have stuck around in Sarth. He was no doubt half way back to the Wilds by now. "So... where are you going from here?" she asked.

"The Dragon Empire. I've always wanted to see a dragon and it seems the Emperor of Sarth still has further need of me. My ship sets sail tomorrow morning. *The Screaming Gale*. You should see the size of the cabin they've given me, the bed could easily sleep two people. Passage is expensive though, ten gold coins per person."

Wouldn't mind seeing a dragon myself. Nor sleeping in a bed for two.

"So... how about you get me out of here?" she asked with a smile.

Thanquil winced and the silence seemed to stretch on for hours. He couldn't meet her eyes. His gaze was locked on the bars.

"You are here to get me out?" she asked without the smile.

The Arbiter shook his head. "I can't. You were seen committing murder on the streets of Sarth. Your case is a matter for the guard. The Inquisition has no authority."

"The man I murdered was an Arbiter!"

"No. He wasn't. The Inquisition has claimed no knowledge of the man you murdered because doing so would... undermine their authority and their image."

Just like that, Jez. Do a good deed, take the fall. She wasn't surprised, nor was she angry. A part of her had expected it if she was honest.

"I'm sorry, Jez."

She nodded and turned away from him. Last thing she wanted him to see was the disappointment on her face. "So why are you here, Arbiter?"

"Because I owe you a debt. I couldn't get you the full amount, but fifty gold colds will have to do. The purse is in my coat, left inside pocket, you'll find it."

Little good gold will do me in gaol. I'll be damned if I'm giving the coat back until he asks.

She heard him sigh. "Funny thing about being an Arbiter," he said, "when you put on that coat, you become invisible. No one wants to look at you. No one wants to question you. It's like magic... in a way."

Jezzet waited. Waited for him to say more, waited for him to ask for the coat back, waited for him to... do something. After a few minutes of silence she turned to find herself alone. The Arbiter had snuck out sometime during the silence.

Well? What the fuck did you expect, Jez? She sighed and leaned back against the bars and stumbled as the door to the cell swung open. For a long moment Jezzet Vel'urn stood there, frozen in shock and unsure of what to do.

She fumbled at the buttons to the coat, to make sure the thing stayed closed.

Forty gold bits and only a few hours to spend them, Jez. First things first. A Blademaster without a blade...

Books by Rob J. Hayes

The Ties that Bind
The Heresy Within
The Colour of Vengeance
The Price of Faith

Best Laid Plans
Where Loyalties Lie
The Fifth Empire of Man

It Takes a Thief...
It Takes a Thief to Catch a Sunrise
It Takes a Thief to Start a Fire

Printed in Great Britain
by Amazon